Beautiful OBLIVION

ALSO BY JAMIE McGUIRE

Beautiful Disaster
Walking Disaster
Red Hill
A Beautiful Wedding

Beautiful OBLIVION

JAMIE McGUIRE

SIMON & SCHUSTER

London · New York · Sydney · Toronto · New Delhi

A CBS COMPANY

First published in Great Britain by Simon & Schuster UK Ltd, 2014
A CBS COMPANY

Copyright © Jamie McGuire 2014

5 7 9 10 8 6

Simon & Schuster UK Ltd
1st Floor
222 Gray's Inn Road
London WC1X 8HB

www.simonandschuster.co.uk

Simon & Schuster Australia, Sydney
Simon & Schuster India, New Delhi

A CIP catalogue record for this book is available from the British Library

Paperback ISBN: 978-1-47113-352-7
EBOOK ISBN: 978-1-47113-353-4

Printed and bound by CPI Group (UK) Ltd, Croydon, CR0 4YY

*For Kim Easton and Liis McKinstry. Thank you
for all that you do, and for everything that you are,*

*And for Jessica Landers,
you are a reason to smile and a generous spirit.*

I won't break his heart to fix you.
—Emily Kinney, "Times Square"

Beautiful OBLIVION

CHAPTER ONE

His words hung there, in the darkness between our voices. I sometimes found comfort in that space, but in three months, I'd only found unrest. That space became more like a convenient place to hide. Not for me, for him. My fingers ached, so I allowed them to relax, not realizing how hard I'd been gripping my cell phone.

My roommate, Raegan, was sitting next to my open suitcase on the bed, her legs crisscrossed. Whatever look was on my face prompted her to take my hand. *T.J.?* she mouthed.

I nodded.

"Will you please say something?" T.J. asked.

"What do you want me to say? I'm packed. I took vacation time. Hank has already given Jorie my shifts."

"I feel like a huge asshole. I wish I didn't have to go, but I warned you. When I have an ongoing project, I can be called out at any time. If you need help with rent or anything . . ."

"I don't want your money," I said, rubbing my eyes.

"I thought this would be a good weekend. I swear to God I did."

"I thought I'd be getting on a plane tomorrow morning, and instead you're calling me to say I can't come. Again."

"I know this seems like a dick move. I swear to you I told them I had important plans. But when things come up, Cami . . . I have to do my job."

I wiped a tear from my cheek, but I refused to let him hear me cry. I kept the trembling from my voice. "Are you coming home for Thanksgiving, then?"

He sighed. "I want to. But I don't know if I can. It depends on if this is wrapped up. I do miss you. A lot. I don't like this, either."

"Will your schedule ever get better?" I asked. It took him longer than it should to answer.

"What if I said probably not?"

I lifted my eyebrows. I expected that answer but didn't expect him to be so . . . truthful.

"I'm sorry," he said. I imagined him cringing. "I just pulled into the airport. I have to go."

"Yeah, okay. Talk to you later." I forced my voice to stay level. I didn't want to sound upset. I didn't want him to think I was weak or emotional. He was strong, and self-reliant, and did what had to be done without complaint. I tried to be that for him. Whining about something out of his control wouldn't help anything.

He sighed again. "I know you don't believe me, but I do love you."

"I believe you," I said, and I meant it.

I pressed the red button on the screen and let my phone fall to the bed.

Raegan was already in damage control mode. "He was called into work?"

I nodded.

"Okay, well, maybe you guys will just have to be more spontaneous. Maybe you can just show up, and if he's called out while you're there, you wait on him. When he gets back, you pick up where you left off."

"Maybe."

She squeezed my hand. "Or maybe he's a tool who should stop choosing his job over you?"

I shook my head. "He's worked really hard for this position."

"You don't even know what position it is."

"I told you. He's utilizing his degree. He specializes in statistical analysis and data reconfiguration, whatever that means."

She shot me a dubious look. "Yeah, you also told me to keep it all a secret. Which makes me think he's not being completely honest with you."

I stood up and dumped out my suitcase, letting all the contents spill onto my comforter. Usually I only made my bed when I was packing, so I could now see the comforter's light-blue fabric with a few navy-blue octopus tentacles reaching across it. T.J. hated it, but it made me feel like I was being hugged while I slept. My room was made up of strange, random things, but then, so was I.

Raegan rummaged through the pile of clothes, and held up a black top with the shoulders and front strategically ripped. "We both have the night off. We should go out. Get drinks served to us for once."

I grabbed the shirt from her hands and inspected it while I mulled over Raegan's suggestion. "You're right. We should. Are we taking your car, or the Smurf?"

Raegan shrugged. "I'm almost on empty and we don't get paid until tomorrow."

"Looks like it's the Smurf, then."

After a crash session in the bathroom, Raegan and I jumped up into my light-blue, modified CJ Jeep. It wasn't in the best of shape, but at one time someone had had enough vision and love to mold it into a Jeep/truck hybrid. The spoiled college dropout who owned the Smurf between that owner and me didn't love it as much. The seat cushions were exposed in some places where the black leather seats were torn, the carpet had cigarette holes and stains, and the hard top needed to be replaced, but that neglect meant that I could pay for it in full, and a payment-free vehicle was the best kind to own.

I buckled my seat belt, and stabbed the key into the ignition.

"Should I pray?" Raegan asked.

I turned the key, and the Smurf made a sickly whirring noise. The engine sputtered, and then purred, and we both clapped. My parents raised four children on a factory worker's salary. I never asked them to help me buy a car, instead I got a job at the local ice cream shop when I was fifteen, and saved $557.11. The Smurf wasn't the vehicle I dreamed about when I was little, but 550 bucks bought me an independence, and that was priceless.

Twenty minutes later, Raegan and I were on the opposite side of town, strutting across the gravel lot of the Red Door, slowly and in unison, as if we were being filmed while walking to a bad-ass soundtrack.

Kody was standing at the entrance, his huge arms probably the same size as my head. He eyed us as we approached. "IDs."

"Fuck off!" Raegan snarled. "We work here. You know how old we are."

He shrugged. "Still have to see IDs."

I frowned at Raegan, and she rolled her eyes, digging into her back pocket. "If you don't know how old I am at this point, we have issues."

"C'mon, Raegan. Quit busting my balls and let me see the damn thing."

"The last time I let you see something you didn't call me for three days."

He cringed. "You're never going to get over that, are you?"

She tossed her ID at Kody and he slapped it against his chest. He glanced at it, and then handed it back, looking at me expectantly. I handed him my driver's license.

"Thought you were leaving town?" he asked, glancing down before returning the thin plastic card to me.

"Long story," I said, stuffing my license into my back pocket. My jeans were so tight I was amazed I could fit anything besides my ass back there.

Kody opened the oversize red door, and Raegan smiled sweetly. "Thanks, baby."

"Love you. Be good."

"I'm always good," she said, winking.

"See you when I get off work?"

"Yep." She pulled me through the door.

"You are the weirdest couple," I said over the bass. It was buzzing in my chest, and I was fairly certain every beat made my bones shake.

"Yep," Raegan said again.

The dance floor was already packed with sweaty, drunk college kids. The fall semester was in full swing. Raegan walked over to the bar and stood at the end. Jorie winked at her.

"Want me to clear you out some seats?" she asked.

Raegan shook her head. "You're just offering because you want my tips from last night!"

Jorie laughed. Her long, platinum blond hair fell in loose waves past her shoulders, with a few black peekaboo strands. She wore a black minidress and combat boots, and was pushing buttons on the cash register to ring someone up while she talked to us. We had all learned to multitask and move like every tip was a hundred-dollar bill. If you could bartend fast enough, you stood a chance of working the east bar, and the tips made there could pay a month's worth of bills in a weekend.

That was where I'd been tending bar for a year, placed just three months after I was hired at the Red Door. Raegan worked right beside me, and together we kept that machine greased like a stripper in a plastic pool full of baby oil. Jorie and the other bartender, Blia, worked the south bar at the entrance. It was basically a kiosk, and they loved it when Raegan or I were out of town.

"So? What are you drinking?" Jorie asked.

Raegan looked at me, and then back at Jorie. "Whiskey sours."

I made a face. "Minus the sour, please."

Once Jorie passed us our drinks, Raegan and I found an empty table and sat, shocked at our luck. Weekends were always packed, and an open table at ten thirty wasn't common.

I held a brand-new pack of cigarettes in my hand and hit the end of it against my palm to pack them, then tore off the plastic, flipping the top. Even though the Red was so smoky that just sitting there made me feel like I was smoking an entire pack of cigarettes, it was nice to sit at a table and relax. When I was working, I usually had time for one drag and the rest burned away, unsmoked.

Raegan watched me light it. "I want one."

"No, you don't."

"Yes, I do!"

"You haven't smoked in two months, Raegan. You'll blame me tomorrow for ruining your streak."

She gestured at the room. "I'm smoking! Right now!"

I narrowed my eyes at her. Raegan was exotically beautiful, with long, chestnut-brown hair, bronze skin, and honey-brown eyes. Her nose was perfectly small, not too round or too pointy, and her skin made her look like she came fresh off of a Neutrogena commercial. We met in elementary school, and I was instantly drawn to her brutal honesty. Raegan could be incredibly intimidating, even for Kody, who, at six foot four, was over a foot taller than she was. Her personality was charming to those she loved, and repellent to those she didn't.

I was the opposite of exotic. My tousled brown bob and heavy bangs were easy to maintain, but not a lot of men found it sexy. Not a lot of men found me sexy in general. I was the girl next door, your brother's best friend. Growing up with three brothers and our cousin Colin, I could have been a tomboy if my subtle but still present curves hadn't ousted me from the boys-only clubhouse at fourteen.

"Don't be that girl," I said. "If you want one, go buy your own."

She crossed her arms, pouting. "That's why I quit. They're fucking expensive."

I stared at the burning paper and tobacco nestled between my fingers. "That is a fact my broke ass continues to make note of."

The song switched from something everyone wanted to dance

to, to a song no one wanted to dance to, and dozens of people began making their way off the dance floor. Two girls walked up to our table and traded glances.

"That's our table," the blonde said.

Raegan barely acknowledged them.

"Excuse me, bitch, she's talking to you," the brunette said, setting her beer on the table.

"Raegan," I warned.

Raegan looked at me with a blank face, and then up at the girl with the same expression. "It *was* your table. Now it's ours."

"We were here first," the blonde hissed.

"And now you're not," Raegan said. She picked up the unwelcome beer bottle and tossed it across the floor. It spilled out onto the dark, tightly stitched carpet. "Fetch."

The brunette watched her beer slide across the floor, and then took a step toward Raegan, but her friend grabbed both of her arms. Raegan offered an unimpressed laugh, and then turned her gaze toward the dance floor. The brunette finally followed her friend to the bar.

I took a drag from my cigarette. "I thought we were going to have a good time tonight."

"That was fun, right?"

I shook my head, stifling a smile. Raegan was a great friend, but I wouldn't cross her. Growing up with so many boys in the house, I'd had enough fighting to last a lifetime. They didn't baby me. If I didn't fight back, they'd just fight dirtier until I did. And I always did.

Raegan didn't have an excuse. She was just a scrappy bitch. "Oh, look. Megan's here," she said, pointing to the blue-eyed, crow-headed beauty on the dance floor. I shook my head. She was out there with Travis Maddox, basically getting screwed in front of everyone on the dance floor.

"Oh, those Maddox boys," Raegan said.

"Yeah," I said, downing my whiskey. "This was a bad idea. I'm not feeling clubby tonight."

"Oh, stop." Raegan gulped her whiskey sour and then stood. "The whine bags are still eyeing this table. I'm going to get us another round. You know the beginning of the night starts off slow."

She took my glass and hers and left me for the bar.

I turned, seeing the girls staring at me, clearly hoping I would step away from the table. I wasn't about to stand up. Raegan would get the table back if they tried to take it, and that would only cause trouble.

When I turned around, a boy was sitting in Raegan's chair. At first I thought Travis had somehow made his way over, but when I realized my mistake, I smiled. Trenton Maddox was leaning toward me, his tattooed arms crossed, his elbows resting on the table across from me. He rubbed the five o'clock shadow that peppered his square jaw with his fingers, his shoulder muscles bulging through his T-shirt. He had as much stubble on his face as he did on the top of his head, except for the absence of hair from one small scar near his left temple.

"You look familiar."

I raised an eyebrow. "Really? You walk all the way over here and sit down, and that's the best you've got?"

He made a show of running his eyes over every part of me. "You don't have any tattoos, that I can see. I'm guessing we haven't met at the shop."

"The shop?"

"The ink shop I work at."

"You're tattooing now?"

He smiled, a deep dimple appearing in the center of his left cheek. "I knew we've met before."

"We haven't." I turned to watch the women on the dance floor, laughing and smiling and watching Travis and Megan vertically dry fucking. But the second the song was over, he left and walked straight over to the blonde who claimed ownership over my table. Even though she'd seen Travis running his hands all over Megan's sweaty skin two seconds earlier, she was grinning like an idiot, hoping she was next.

Trenton laughed once. "That's my baby brother."

"I wouldn't admit it," I said, shaking my head.

"Did we go to school together?" he asked.

"I don't remember."

"Do you remember if you went to Eakins at any time between kindergarten through twelfth grade?"

"I did."

Trenton's left dimple sunk in when he grinned. "Then we know each other."

"Not necessarily."

Trenton laughed again. "You want a drink?"

"I have one coming."

"You wanna dance?"

"Nope."

A group of girls passed by, and Trenton's eyes focused on one. "Is that Shannon from home ec? Damn," he said, turning a one-eighty in his seat.

"Indeed it is. You should go reminisce."

Trenton shook his head. "We reminisced in high school."

"I remember. Pretty sure she still hates you."

Trenton shook his head, smiled, and then, before taking another swig, said, "They always do."

"It's a small town. You shouldn't have burned all of your bridges."

He lowered his chin, his famous charm turning up a notch. "There's a few I haven't lit a fire under. Yet."

I rolled my eyes, and he chuckled.

Raegan returned, curving her long fingers around four standard rocks glasses and two shot glasses. "My whiskey sours, your whiskey straights, and a buttery nipple each."

"What is with all the sweet stuff tonight, Ray?" I said, wrinkling my nose.

Trenton picked up one of the shot glasses and touched it to his lips, tilting his head back. He slammed it on the table and winked. "Don't worry, babe. I'll take care of it." He stood up and walked away.

I didn't realize my mouth was hanging open until my eyes met Raegan's and it snapped shut.

"Did he just drink your shot? Did that really just happen?"

"Who does that?" I said, turning to see where he went. He'd already disappeared into the crowd.

"A Maddox boy."

I shot the double whiskey and took another drag of my cigarette. Everyone knew Trenton Maddox was bad news, but that never seemed to stop women from trying to tame him. Watching him since grade school, I promised myself that I would never be a notch on his headboard—if the rumors were true and he had notches, but I didn't plan to find out.

"You're going to let him get away with that?" Raegan asked.

I blew out the smoke from the side of my mouth, annoyed. I wasn't in the frame of mind to have fun, or deal with obnoxious flirting, or complain that Trenton Maddox had just drunk the shot glass of sugar that I didn't want. But before I could answer my friend, I had to choke back the whiskey I'd just drunk.

"Oh, no."

"What?" Raegan said, flipping around in her chair. She immediately righted herself in the chair, cringing.

All three of my brothers and our cousin Colin were walking toward our table.

Colin, the oldest and the only one with a legit ID, spoke first. "What the hell, Camille? I thought you were out of town tonight."

"My plans changed," I snapped.

Chase spoke second, as I expected he would. He was the oldest of my brothers, and liked to pretend he was older than me, too. "Dad's not going to be happy that you missed family lunch if you were in town."

"He can't be unhappy if he doesn't know," I said, narrowing my eyes.

He recoiled. "Why are you being so pissy? Are you on the rag or something?"

"Really?" Raegan said, lowering her chin and raising her eyebrows. "We're in public. Grow up."

"So he canceled on you?" Clark asked. Unlike the others, Clark looked genuinely concerned.

Before I could answer, the youngest of the three spoke up. "Wait, that worthless piece of shit canceled on you?" Coby said. The boys were all only eleven months apart, making Coby just eighteen. My coworkers knew my brothers had all scored fake

IDs and thought they were doing me a favor by looking the other way, but most of the time I wished they wouldn't. Coby in particular still acted like a twelve-year-old boy not quite sure what to do with his testosterone. He was bowing up behind the others, letting them hold him back from a fight that didn't exist.

"What are you doing, Coby?" I asked. "He's not even here!"

"You're damn right he's not," Coby said. He relaxed, cracking his neck. "Canceling on my big sister. I'll bust his fuckin' face." I thought about Coby and T.J. getting into a brawl, and it made my heart race. T.J. was intimidating when he was younger, and lethal as an adult. No one fucked with him, and Coby knew it.

A disgusted noise came from my throat, and I rolled my eyes. "Just . . . find another table."

All four boys pulled chairs around Raegan and me. Colin had light-brown hair, but my brothers were all redheads. Colin and Chase had blue eyes, Clark and Coby had green. Some redheaded men aren't all that great-looking, but my brothers were tall, chiseled, and outgoing. Clark was the only one with freckles, and they still somehow looked good on him. I was the outcast, the only child with mousy brown hair and big, round, light-blue eyes. More than once the boys tried to convince me that I'd been adopted. If I wasn't the female version of my father, I might have believed them.

I touched my forehead to the table and groaned. "I can't believe it, but this day just got worse."

"Aw, c'mon, Camille. You know you love us," Clark said, nudging me with his shoulder. When I didn't answer, he leaned in to whisper in my ear. "You sure you're all right?"

I kept my head down, but nodded. Clark patted my back a couple of times, and then the table grew quiet.

I lifted my head. Everyone was staring behind me, so I turned around. Trenton Maddox was standing there, holding two shot glasses and another glass of something that looked decidedly less sweet.

"This table turned into a party fast," Trenton said with a surprised but charming smile.

Chase narrowed his eyes at Trenton. "Is that him?" he asked, nodding.

"What?" Trenton asked.

Coby's knee began to bounce, and he leaned forward in his chair. "That's him. He fuckin' canceled on her, and then he showed up here."

"Wait. Coby, no," I said, holding up my hands.

Coby stood up. "You jackin' with our sister?"

"Sister?" Trenton said, his eyes bouncing between me and the volatile gingers sitting on each side of me.

"Oh, God," I said, closing my eyes. "Colin, tell Coby to stop. It's not him."

"Who's not me?" Trenton said. "We got a problem here?"

Travis appeared at his brother's side. He wore the same amused expression as Trenton, both flashing their matching left-sided dimples. They could have been their mother's second set of twins. Only subtle differences set them apart, including the fact that Travis was maybe an inch or two taller than Trenton.

Travis crossed his arms across his chest, making his already large biceps bulge. The only thing that kept me from exploding from my chair was that his shoulders relaxed. He wasn't ready to fight. Yet.

"Evening," Travis said.

The Maddoxes could sense trouble. At least it seemed that

way, because whenever there was a fight, they had either started it, or finished it. Usually both.

"Coby, sit down," I commanded through my teeth.

"No, I'm not sittin' down. This dickhead insulted my sister, I'm not fuckin' sittin' down."

Raegan leaned over to Chase. "That's Trent and Travis Maddox."

"Maddox?" Clark asked.

"Yeah. You still got something to say?" Travis said.

Coby shook his head slowly and smiled. "I can talk all night long, motherfu—"

I stood. "Coby! Sit your ass down!" I said, pointing to his chair. He sat. "I said it wasn't him, and I meant it! Now everybody *calm* the *fuck* down! I've had a *bad* day, I'm here to drink, and relax, and have a good *goddamn* time! Now if that's a problem for you, back the fuck off my table!" I closed my eyes and screamed the last part, looking completely insane. People around us were staring.

Breathing hard, I glanced at Trenton, who handed me a drink.

One corner of his mouth turned up. "I think I'll stay."

CHAPTER TWO

MY PHONE CHIRPED FOR THE THIRD TIME. I PICKED IT UP from my nightstand to take a look. It was a text from Trenton.

Get up, lazy. Yeah, I'm talking to u.

"Turn off your phone, asshole! Some of us have hangovers!" Raegan yelled from her bedroom.

I clicked it over to silent and put it back on the table to charge. Damn it. What was I thinking, giving him my phone number?

Kody lumbered down the hall and peeked in, his eyes still half shut. "What time is it?"

"Not even eight."

"Who's blowing up your phone?"

"None of your business," I said, turning over onto my side. Kody chuckled, and then he began banging around pots and pans in the kitchen, probably getting ready to feed his ginormousness.

"I hate everyone!" Raegan yelled again.

I sat up, letting my legs dangle off the side of the bed. I had the entire weekend off, something that hadn't happened since the last weekend I took off to see T.J.—and he canceled. Back then, I had cleaned the apartment until my fingers were raw, and then washed, dried, and folded all of my laundry—and Raegan's.

I wasn't going to mope around the apartment this time, though. I looked over at the pictures of my brothers and me on my wall, next to a picture of my parents, and a few of the drawings I'd attempted in high school. The black frames were a stark contrast to the white walls throughout the apartment. I'd been working on making it look more lived-in—buying one set of curtains with every paycheck. Raegan's parents got her a gift card to Pottery Barn for Christmas, so we now had a nice dinnerware set and a rustic, mahogany-stained coffee table. But the apartment still mostly looked like we'd just moved in, even though I'd lived there going on three years, and Raegan more than one. It wasn't the nicest property in town, but at least the neighborhood had more young families and single professionals than loud, obnoxious college kids, and it was far enough away from the campus that we didn't have to deal with a lot of game day traffic.

It wasn't much, but it was home.

My phone buzzed. I rolled my eyes, thinking it was Trenton, and leaned over to check the display. It was T.J.

Miss you. We should be snuggling in my bed instead of what I'm doing right now.

Cami can't talk right now. She's hungover. Leave a message at the beep. BEEP.

You went out last night?

You expected me to stay home and cry myself to sleep?

Good. I don't feel so bad, now.

No, keep feeling bad. It's really okay.

I want to hear your voice, but I can't call right
now. I'll try to call tonight.

k.

K? Seems like a waste of a text.

Work seems like a waste of a weekend.

Touché.

I guess we'll talk later.

Don't worry, the groveling will be sufficient.

I should hope so.

T.J. was difficult to stay mad at, but he was impossible to get
close to. Granted, we'd only been dating for six months. The
first three were amazing, and then T.J. was assigned to head
this critical assignment. He warned me what it might be like,

when we decided to try to make the distance work. It was the first time he'd been put in charge of an entire project, and he was both a perfectionist and an overachiever. But the assignment was the biggest he'd ever worked on, and T.J. wanted to make sure he didn't miss anything. It—whatever *it* was—was important. As in, if it ended well, he would get a huge promotion. He mentioned one late night that maybe he could get a bigger place, and we could discuss me possibly moving out there the next year.

I'd rather be anywhere else but here. Living in a smallish college town when you're not exactly in college isn't that great. There was nothing wrong with the college. Eastern State University was quaint, and beautiful. I'd wanted to go there for as long as I could remember, but after just one year in the dorms, I had to move into an apartment of my own. Even if it provided a safe haven away from the ridiculousness of dorm life, independence came with its own difficulties. I was down to only a few classes a semester, and instead of graduating this year, I was only a sophomore.

The many sacrifices I had made to maintain the independence I needed was exactly why I couldn't resent T.J. for making sacrifices for his—even if I was the sacrifice.

The bed dipped behind me, and the covers flipped up. A small, icy hand touched my skin, and I jumped.

"Damn it, Ray! Get your cold, nasty hands off me."

She laughed, and hugged me tighter. "It's already cooled off in the mornings! Kody is scrambling his dozen or so eggs, and my bed is like ice now!"

"God, he eats like a horse."

"He's the size of a horse. *Everywhere.*"

"Ew. Ew, ew, ew," I said, covering my ears. "I did not need that visual this early in the morning. Or ever."

"So who is blowing up your phone? Trent?"

I turned over to see her expression. "Trent?"

"Oh, do not play coy with me, Camille Renee! I saw the look on your face when he handed you that drink."

"There was no face."

"There was definitely a face!"

I scooted back toward the edge of the bed, pushing Raegan until she realized what I was doing and squealed as she fell to the floor with a thud.

"You are a mean, awful human being!"

"I'm mean?" I said, leaning over the edge of the bed. "I didn't toss a girl's beer just because she wanted her table back!"

Raegan sat with her legs crisscrossed, and sighed. "You're right. I was being a huge bitch. Next time I promise to put a cap on it before I toss it."

I fell back against my pillow and stared up at the ceiling. "You're hopeless."

"Breakfast!" Kody called from the kitchen.

We both scrambled from the room, giggling as we fought to be the first one out the door.

Raegan sat on the stool behind the breakfast bar for about half a second before I kicked it over. She landed on her feet, but her mouth hung open.

"You are just asking for it today!"

I took the first bite of cinnamon and raisin bagel with apple butter, and hummed as the calorific goodness melted in my mouth. Kody had spent enough nights here that he knew I despised eggs, but since he made me an alternative breakfast, I forgave the putrid egg smell that filled up our apartment every time he stayed the night.

"So," Kody said as he chewed, "Trent Maddox."

I shook my head. "No. Don't even start."

"Looks like you already did," Kody said with a wry smile.

"You're both acting like I was all over him. We talked."

"He bought you four drinks. And you let him," Raegan said.

"And he walked you to the car," Kody said.

"And you traded phone numbers," Raegan said.

"I have a boyfriend," I said, a bit snotty and maybe a little valley girl. Getting ganged up on did weird things to me.

"Who you haven't seen in almost three months, and who's canceled on you twice," Raegan said.

"So, he's selfish because he's dedicated to his job and wants to move up the ladder?" I asked, not really wanting to hear the answer. "We all knew this was coming. T.J. was honest from the beginning about how demanding his job could be. Why am I the only one not surprised?"

Kody and Raegan traded glances, and then continued eating their disgusting chicken fetuses.

"What are you guys doing today?" I asked.

"I'm going to lunch at my parents' house," Raegan said. "And so is Kody."

I paused midbite, and pulled the bagel out of my mouth. "Really? That's kind of a big deal," I said with a smile.

Kody smirked. "She's already warned me about her dad. I'm not nervous."

"You're not?" I asked, in disbelief.

He shook his head, but seemed less confident. "Why?"

"He's a retired Navy SEAL, and Raegan's not just his daughter.

She's his only child. This is a man who has strived for perfection and pushed himself beyond his limits his entire life. You think you're going to walk in the door, threatening to take more of Raegan's time and attention from him, and he's just going to welcome you to the family?"

Kody was speechless. Raegan narrowed her eyes at me. "Thanks, friend." She patted Kody's hand. "He doesn't like anyone at first."

"Except me," I said, raising my hand.

"Except Cami. But she doesn't count. She isn't a threat to his daughter's virginity."

Kody made a face. "Wasn't that Jason Brazil like four years ago?"

"Yes. But Daddy doesn't know that," Raegan said, a little annoyed that Kody said The Name We Shall Not Speak.

Jason Brazil wasn't a bad guy, we just pretended that he was. We all went to high school together, but Jason was a year younger. They decided to *seal the deal* before she went to college, hoping it would solidify their relationship. I thought she would tire of having a boyfriend who was still in high school, but Raegan was dedicated, and they spent most of their time together. Not long after Jason began his own freshman year at ESU, the wonders of college, joining a fraternity, and being Eastern State football's star true freshman kept him busy, and the change spawned nightly arguments. He respectfully broke it off, and never once spoke a bad word about her. But he took Raegan's virginity and then didn't keep his end of the bargain: to spend the rest of his life with her. And for that, he was forever the enemy of this house.

Kody finished his eggs, and then began the dishes.

"You cooked. I'll do those," I said, pushing him away from the dishwasher.

"What are you doing today?" Raegan asked.

"Studying. Writing that paper that is due Monday. I may or may not shower. Definitely not stopping by Mom and Dad's to explain why I didn't leave town as planned."

"Understandable," Raegan said. She knew the real reason. I had already told my parents I was going to see T.J., and they would want to know why he'd canceled again. They already didn't approve of him, and I had no interest in perpetuating the dysfunctional cycle of hostility that was created when more than one of us were in the same room. Dad would be in a hostile mood like he always was, and someone would say too much, like we always have, and Dad would yell. Mom would beg him to stop. And some way, somehow, it would always end up being my fault.

You're stupid for trusting him, Camille. He's secretive, my father had said. *I don't trust him. He watches everything with those judgmental eyes.*

But that was one of the reasons I fell in love with him. He made me feel so safe. Like no matter where we went or what happened, he would protect me.

"Does T.J. know you went out last night?"

"Yes."

"Does he know about Trent?"

"He didn't ask."

"He never asks about your nights out. If Trent was no big deal, you'd think you'd mention it," Raegan said with a smirk.

"Shut up. Go to your parents' house and let your dad torture Kody."

Kody's eyebrows pulled together, and Raegan shook her

head, patting his massive shoulder as they walked to her bedroom. "She's kidding."

When Raegan and Kody left a couple of hours later, I opened my books and laptop, and began to write my paper on the effects of growing up with a personal computer. "Who comes up with this shit?" I groaned.

When the paper was written and printed, I began to study for the psych test I had on Friday. It was the better part of a week away, but experience had taught me that if I waited until the last minute, something would inevitably come up. It wasn't as if I could study at work, and this test would be particularly difficult.

My cell phone pinged. It was Trenton again.

This is new. I've never had a girl give me her
number n then ignore me.

I laughed, and picked up my phone with both hands, punching in the letters.

I'm not ignoring you. I'm studying.

Need a break?

Not until I'm done.

Okay, and then can we eat? I'm starving.

Did we make plans to eat?

You don't eat?

. . . yes?

K, then. You plan to eat. I plan to eat. Let's
eat.

I have to study.

K . . . THEN can we eat?

U don't have to wait on me. Go ahead.

I know I don't have to. I want to.

But I can't. So go ahead.

k.

I put my phone on silent, and slid it under my pillow. His
persistence was as admirable as it was annoying. I knew who
Trenton was, of course. We were in the same graduating class
at Eakins High. I had watched him grow from a dirty, snot-
nosed kid who ate red pencils and glue, into the tall, tattooed,
excessively charming man he was now. From the second he got
his driver's license, he had made his way through high school
classmates and Eastern State coeds, and I swore I'd never be
one of them. Not that he'd ever tried. Until now. I didn't want
to be flattered, but it was hard not to be after being one of the

few females Trenton and Travis Maddox had never attempted to sleep with. I guess this proved that I couldn't be completely unfortunate-looking. T.J. was magazine-quality beautiful, and now Trenton was texting. I wasn't sure what was different about me between high school and college that had caught Trenton's attention, but I knew what was different for him.

Less than two years before, Trenton's life changed. He was riding in the passenger seat of Mackenzie Davis's Jeep Liberty on their way out to a spring break bonfire party. The Jeep was barely recognizable when it was hauled back into town on a flat-bed trailer the next day, just like Trenton when he returned to Eastern. Swallowed by the guilt of Mackenzie's death, Trenton couldn't concentrate in class, and by mid-April, he'd decided to move back in with his father and drop all of his classes. Travis had mentioned bits and pieces about his brother on slow nights at the Red, but I hadn't heard much more about Trenton.

After another half hour of studying and chewing at my barely there fingernails, my stomach began to growl. I ambled into the kitchen and opened the refrigerator. *Ranch dressing. Cilantro. Why in the hell is the black pepper in the fridge? Eggs . . . ew. Fat-free yogurt. Even worse.* I opened the freezer. *Score. Frozen burritos.*

Just before I pressed the buttons on the microwave, a knock sounded on the door. "Raegan! Stop forgetting your damn keys!" My bare feet padded around the breakfast bar and across the beige carpet. After twisting the bolt lock, I yanked on the heavy metal door, and I instantly crossed my arms over my breasts. I was only in a white tank top and boxer shorts, no bra. Trenton Maddox stood in the doorway, holding two white paper sacks.

"Lunch," he said with a smile.

For half a second, my mouth mirrored his, but then it

quickly disappeared. "How did you know where I live?"

"I asked around," he said, walking past me. He sat the sacks on the breakfast bar, and began pulling out containers of food. "From Golden Chick. Their mashed potatoes and gravy remind me of my mom's. I'm not really sure why. I don't remember her cooking."

Dianne Maddox's death had rocked our town. She was involved in the PTA, the Junior Welfare League, and coached Taylor's and Tyler's soccer team for three years before she was diagnosed with cancer. It caught me off guard that he mentioned her so casually, even though I suppose it shouldn't have.

"Do you always surprise attack a girl's apartment with food?"

"No, but it was time."

"Time for what?"

He looked at me, blank faced. "For lunch." He walked into the kitchen and began opening cabinets.

"What are you doing now?"

"Plates?" he asked.

I pointed to the correct cabinet, and he pulled out two, sat them on the bar, and then began spooning out potatoes, gravy, corn, and dividing up the chicken. And then he left.

I stood next to the bar, in my small, quiet apartment, with the smells of chicken and gravy wafting through the air. This had never happened to me before, and I wasn't sure how to react.

Suddenly the door blew open, and Trenton walked back in, kicking the door shut behind him. He was holding two large styrofoam cups with straws sticking out the top.

"I hope you like Cherry Coke, baby doll, or we can't be friends." He placed the drinks beside each plate, and then sat down. He looked up at me. "Well? Are you going to sit down or what?"

I sat.

Trenton shoveled the first piece of food into his mouth, and, after some hesitation, I did the same. It was like a little ball of paradise on my tongue, and once I started, the food on my plate just sort of disappeared.

Trenton held up a *Spaceballs* DVD. "I know you said you were studying, so if you can't, you can't, but I borrowed this from Thomas the last time he was in town, and I still haven't watched it."

"*Spaceballs?*" I asked, pushing up one of my eyebrows. I'd seen it with T.J. a million times. It was kind of our thing. I wasn't watching it with Trenton.

"Is that a yes?"

"No. It was really nice of you to bring over lunch, but I have to study."

He shrugged. "I can help."

"I have a boyfriend."

Trenton wasn't fazed. "Then he's not much of one. I've never seen him around."

"He doesn't live here. He's . . . he goes to school in California."

"He never comes home to visit?"

"Not yet. He's busy."

"Is he from here?"

"None of your business."

"Who is it?"

"Also none of your business."

"Fine," he said, picking up our trash and tossing it into the garbage can in the kitchen. He grabbed my plate and then his, and rinsed them off in the sink. "You have an imaginary boyfriend. I understand."

I opened my mouth to argue, but he motioned to the dishwasher. "These dirty?"

I nodded.

"Are you working tonight?" he asked, loading the dishwasher, and then looking for soap. When he found it, he poured some in the small container and then shut the door, pressing the start button. The room was filled with a low, soothing purring sound.

"No, I have the weekend off."

"Awesome, me too. I'll swing by later to get you."

"What? No, I—"

"See you at seven!" The door closed, and once again the apartment was quiet.

What just happened? I rushed into my room and grabbed my cell phone.

Not going anywhere w u. I told u, I have a bf.

Mmk.

My mouth fell open. He really wasn't going to take no for an answer. What was I going to do? Let him stand at my door, knocking until he gave up? That was rude. But so was he! I said no!

There was no reason to get riled up. Raegan would be home, likely with Kody, and she could tell him I went out. With someone else. That would explain why my car was still in its parking spot.

I was pretty damn smart. Smart enough to have kept my distance from Trenton all these years. I'd seen him flirt, seduce, and evade since we were kids. There was absolutely no trick Trenton Maddox could play that I wouldn't be ready for.

CHAPTER THREE

At seven o'clock, I was bent at the waist, blow-drying my wet hair. The steam that filled our tiny shared bathroom had fogged the mirror, so there was no point in trying to see my reflection. The thin, tattered towel twisted around my chest barely covered everything. We needed new towels. We needed new everything.

Raegan didn't get home until after six, so I had to hurry through explaining my plan to her so she would know exactly how to turn Trenton away. At 7:05, I put on my favorite Eastern State hoodie and matching gray sweats. At 7:10, Raegan fell onto the couch with her bowl of popcorn, sinking into the blue cushions, wearing her navy yoga pants and floral tank top.

"I think you talked him out of it."

"Good," I said, sitting on a barely cushioned arm of the couch.

"You say good, but there is a tiny bit of disappointment on your face."

"You're a dirty liar," I said, grabbing a handful of popcorn, and shoving it all into my mouth.

I was just beginning to relax as the obnoxious voice of *Family Guy* prattled on when the doorbell rang. Raegan scrambled to the door, dropping popcorn everywhere, and I scurried to my bedroom. Raegan turned the bolt lock and the knob, and then I heard her muffled voice. After a short pause, another voice that was much deeper hummed through the apartment. Trenton's.

After a short conversation, Raegan called my name. I stiffened, not sure what to do. Was she trying to prove to him that I wasn't there? My bedroom door swung open. Instinctively, I jumped back before the wood smacked me in the face.

Raegan stood before me, with a frown on her face. "He fights dirty."

I shook my head, not sure if I should speak.

She jerked her head to the side, gesturing to the front door. "Go see for yourself."

I walked around her and then across the hall to see Trenton standing in the living room, holding a miniature, fluffy pink coat, and standing next to a little girl. She was breathtaking. Her enormous green eyes were like telescopes, disappearing behind her long, dark lashes every time she blinked. Long, platinum hair cascaded down her back and shoulders. She was pinching and pulling at the threads of her mint-green sweater but didn't take her curious eyes off of me.

Trenton nodded to the tiny, perfect person next to him. "This is Olive. Her parents bought the house next door to my dad's two years ago. She's my buddy."

Olive turned to fasten herself casually to Trenton's leg. She didn't seem scared or intimidated, just comfortable enough to latch onto him.

"Hi, Olive," I said. "How old are you?" Wasn't that a normal question to ask a kid? I wasn't sure.

"I'm fife," she said with confidence. Her gritty, sweet voice was probably the most adorable sound I'd ever heard. She held up her hand, her tiny but plump fingers spreading out as far as they could, her palm facing out. When she was sure I understood, the hand went back to Trenton's jeans. "Twent said he would take me to Chicken Joe's, but we can't go until yow weddy." She blinked, but didn't smile. She was serious, and she was seriously holding me accountable for every second longer she had to wait.

I glared at him. "Oh, did he?"

Trenton simply shrugged and smiled. "Are you ready?"

I looked down at my sweats. "Clearly not, but I'm guessing I shouldn't keep Olive waiting."

"No. You shouldn't," Trenton said. He didn't even pretend to feel ashamed. Bastard.

Trying not to growl, swear, or do anything else that might scare Olive, I retreated to my bedroom. I replaced my hoodie with a rust-colored thermal Henley, and the sweatpants with a pair of well-worn jeans. While I slipped on my boots, Raegan opened the door to my room, and closed it behind her.

"Olive wants me to ask you to please hurry," she said, trying not to smile.

"Shut your face," I said, standing up. I dusted some makeup on, combed my lashes with the mascara wand, dabbed my lips with clear gloss, and walked out to the living room, where Trenton and Olive still stood. "All ready," I said with a smile. For Olive. Definitely no smiles for Trenton.

Olive looked up to Trenton. "Can we go to Chicken Joe's now?"

"Let's put on your coat, first."

Olive complied, and then wiped her nose with the back of her hand. "Now?"

"Yes, ma'am," he said, opening the door.

Olive's smile spanned the width of her face when the door

opened, and Trenton's expression brightened, clearly pleased that he'd made her happy.

I passed him without speaking, and as I walked out to the parking lot, Olive's little fingers found their way to my hand. Her skin was just as warm and soft as it looked.

Trenton unlocked the passenger door of his dilapidated Dodge Intrepid. The red paint was faded in some spots, and gone in others.

Trenton pulled the seat forward, helping Olive into the back. He strapped her into her pink car seat.

I leaned my head in and took a whiff. "You don't smoke in your car?"

"I do, but I clean out my car the night before I have Olive, and I don't smoke in it until after I drop her off for the day. It doesn't smell." He returned the passenger seat to its original position, and held out his hand, gesturing for me to get in.

"I am so going to get you back for this," I whispered as I passed him to sit down.

He smiled. "I look forward to it." Trenton shut the door, and then jogged around the front of the car and hopped into the driver's seat. He pulled the seat belt across his chest and clicked it into the latch, and then looked at me expectantly.

"Click it or ticket," Olive said from the backseat.

"Oh," I said, turning to grab the seat belt and repeating what Trenton had just completed. When the buckle clicked, Trenton started the car.

We rode in near silence across town to Chicken Joe's, except for the occasional requests for updates from Olive. At almost every stoplight, she wanted to know how many blocks were between us and our destination. Trenton answered her patiently, and when we were one block away, they both did a little celebration, dancing with their hands.

When Trenton pulled into a parking spot at Chicken Joe's, he turned off the engine, got out, jogged to my side, and then opened the door. He helped me climb out with one hand, and then pushed the seat forward, unbuckled Olive, and set her on the ground.

"Did you bwing coins?" she asked.

Trenton laughed once, feigning insult. "Is it even legal to go to Chicken Joe's without quarters?"

"I don't think so," Olive said, shaking her head.

Trenton held out his hand, and Olive took it, and then she held out her hand to me. I covered her hand with mine and followed them inside.

Chicken Joe's had been a fixture in Eakins since before I was born. My parents took us once or twice as kids, but I hadn't been back since the 1990s. Grease and spices still hung heavily in the air, and saturated everything else, including a thin film on the green tile floor.

Olive and I followed Trenton to a booth on the opposite side of the restaurant. Kids were running everywhere and practically climbing the walls. Multicolored lights from the oversize juke box and arcade games seemed to intensify the screaming and laughter.

Trenton dug into his jeans pockets and pulled out two fistfuls of quarters. Olive took an excited breath, grabbed as many as she could in her chubby fist, and ran away.

"You don't even feel bad about exploiting that poor little girl, do you?" I asked, crossing my arms on top of the table.

Trenton shrugged. "I get to have dinner with you. She gets to play. Her parents get a date night. It's a win/win . . . win."

"Negative. I am clearly not in the winning category, since I was coerced here."

"It's not my fault that I was one step ahead of you."

"Exploiting a child is not a good first date. That's not exactly a memory you want to share later."

"Who said this was a date? I mean . . . if you want to call it a date, that's cool, but I thought you had a boyfriend."

I nearly choked on my own spit, but that was still preferable to blushing. "Forgive me for thinking coercion was something you didn't do for just anyone."

"I don't. This is definitely a special case."

"You're a special case," I grumbled, searching the dozens of small faces for Olive. She was trying to stretch out her short arms across the pinball machine, and then resorted to leaning from side to side.

"I assume you still have the boyfriend," Trenton said.

"Not that it's any of your business, but yes."

"Then it's definitely not a date. Because if it was, you would be . . . well, I won't say it."

I narrowed my eyes at him. "I will reach across this table and slap you."

He chuckled. "No, you won't. You want the entire next generation of Eakins, Illinois, to think you're an ogre?"

"I don't care."

"Yes, you do."

The waitress waddled over to us, leaning back, away from her burgeoning belly. She looked about seven months pregnant, her green polo shirt barely stretching over her bump. She sat down a small drink with a lid and a straw, and then a bigger red cup full of something brown and fizzy. "Hi, Trent."

"Hi, Cindy. You should be at home with your feet up."

She smiled. "You say that every time. What would your friend like?"

I looked up at Cindy. "Just a water, please."

"You got it." She looked at Trenton. "Will Olive want the usual?"

He nodded. "But I think Cami's going to need a menu."

"Be right back," she said.

Trenton leaned in. "You should try the three-piece platter with sweet potato fries and slaw. Because . . . damn."

A man behind me yelled, "Christopher! I said get your ass over here and sit down!"

Trenton leaned over to look around me, and frowned. A little boy about eight years old ran over, closer to me than to his father, waiting.

"Sit down!" the father growled. The boy did as he was told, and turned to watch the other kids playing.

Trenton tried to ignore the scene behind me and leaned against the table. "You still like working at the Red?"

I nodded. "As jobs go, it's not bad. Hank is cool."

"Why didn't you work this weekend?"

"I took some time off."

"Sit still!" the father behind me snarled.

After a pause, Trenton continued, "I was just going to tell you that if you weren't happy at the bar, there is a receptionist spot open at the shop."

"What shop?"

"My shop. Well, the shop I work at."

"Skin Deep is hiring? I thought Cal just had whoever wasn't busy answer the phone?"

"He said Thirty-Fourth Street Ink has a hot chick at the desk, so he thinks we need one, too."

"A hot chick," I deadpanned, unimpressed.

"His words, not mine," Trenton said, scanning the crowd for Olive. He didn't look long. He knew where she would be.

"She likes pinball, huh?"

"Loves it," he said, smiling at her like a proud father.

"Damn it, Chris! What the hell is wrong with you?" the father behind me yelled, standing up at the same time. I turned, seeing the father's toppled glass, and a very nervous little boy staring at his father's wet lap. "Why do I even bother bringing you to places like this?" he yelled.

"I was thinking the same thing," Trenton said.

The father turned around, two deep horizontal lines in the center of his forehead.

"I mean, you don't really act like you want your kid running around, playing, or having fun in general. Why would you bring him here if you just want him to sit still?"

"No one asked you, asshole," the man said, turning around.

"No, but if you keep talking to your son like that, I'm going to ask you to step outside."

The man faced us again, began to speak, but something in Trenton's eyes made the man think better of it. "He's hyper."

Trenton shrugged. "Hey, man, I get it. You're here by yourself. It's probably been a long day."

The lines above the man's eyes softened. "It has."

"So let him burn off some energy. He'll be worn-out when he gets home. Kinda silly to bring him to an arcade and then get yourself all worked up when he wants to play."

Shame darkened the man's face, he nodded a few times, and

then he turned around, nodding once to his son. "Sorry, buddy. Go play."

The little boy's eyes lit up, and he jumped from the booth, blending into the continuously moving crowd of happy children. After a few awkward moments of silence, Trenton started a conversation with the man, and they began chitchatting about where they worked, Christopher, and Olive. Eventually we learned that the man's name was Randall, and he was a newly single father. Chris's mother was an addict and living with a boyfriend in the next town over, and Chris was having trouble adjusting. Randall admitted that he was, too. When it was time for them to leave, Randall held out his hand, and Trenton shook it. Christopher watched both men, grinned, and then took his dad's hand. They left, both of them with smiles on their faces.

When Olive's quarters were depleted, she sat at the table, the golden chicken strips before her. Trenton squirted some hand sanitizer onto her hands, she rubbed them together, and then devoured everything on her plate. Trenton and I ordered the adult version of her meal, and we all finished at about the same time.

"Pie?" Olive said, wiping her mouth with the back of her hand.

"I don't know," Trenton said. "Your mom got pretty mad at me last time."

I liked the way he talked to her. He wasn't condescending. He talked to her the same as he did to me, and she seemed to appreciate it.

"What do you think, Cami? Do you like pecan?"

Olive watched me with pleading eyes.

"I do."

Olive's sapphire eyes brightened. "Can we shayo?"

I shrugged. "I could handle a third of a pie. Want to share too, Trent?"

Trenton made eye contact with Cindy, and held up his index finger. She nodded, knowing exactly what he meant. Olive clapped her hands together as Cindy brought over the plate in one hand, and holding three forks in the other. The slice was nearly a third of the pie, with a heaping mound of white, whipped topping.

"Enjoy," Cindy said, sounding tired but pleasant.

We dug in, all humming when the first bite of sugary goodness found its way to our mouths. Within a couple of minutes, the plate was empty. Cindy brought the bill, and I tried to pay for half, but Trenton wouldn't even entertain the idea.

"If you pay, it's a date," I said.

"Do you ever pay for Raegan's lunch?"

"Yes, but—"

"Is that a date?"

"No, but—"

"Shh," he said, lifting Olive into his arms. "This is the part where you say thank you." He put two bills on the table, and then shoved his wallet into his back pocket.

"Thank you," Olive said, resting her head on Trenton's shoulder.

"You're welcome, Ew." He leaned over and grabbed his keys from the table.

"Ew?" I asked.

Olive eyed me with sleepy twin pools. I didn't push the subject.

The ride back to my apartment was quiet, but mostly because Olive had fallen asleep in her car seat. Her little cheek was smooshed against the cushion beside her face. She looked so peaceful, so happily lost wherever she had drifted off to.

"Her parents just let the neighbor covered in tattoos babysit their five-year-old?"

"No. This is new. We just started Chicken Joe's this year on my days off. I watched Olive for Shane and Liza a couple times for about half an hour or so in the beginning and we somehow graduated to Chicken Joe's."

"Weird."

"I've been her Twent for a long time."

"And she's your Ew?"

"Yep."

"What's up with that?"

"Her initials. Olive Ollivier. O.O. When you put them together, it makes an 'ew' sound."

I nodded. "Makes sense. She's going to hate you for that in six years."

Trenton glanced at the rearview mirror, and then back at the road. "Nah."

The headlights lit the front door of my apartment, and Trenton finally looked ashamed. "I'd walk you to the door, but I don't want to leave Olive in the car."

I waved him away. "I can get to the door by myself."

"Maybe we can kidnap you again."

"I work Saturdays. This was just a freak accident."

"We could change it to Chicken Joe's Sundays."

"I work Sundays."

"Me, too. But not until one, and you don't go in until later, too, right? We could do lunch. An early lunch."

I pulled my mouth to the side. "It's just not a good idea, Trent. But thank you."

"Chicken Joe's is *always* a good idea."

I chuckled and looked down. "Thanks for dinner."

"You owe me," Trenton said, watching me get out.

I leaned down. "You kidnapped me, remember?"

"And I'd do it again," he said as I shut the door.

I walked to the building, and Trenton waited until I stepped inside before he began to back away.

Raegan was sitting up on her knees on the couch cushions, gripping the back with her fingers. "So?"

I looked around the apartment and tossed my purse onto the love seat. "So . . . that was maybe the best nondate date I've ever had."

"Really? Even better than when you met T.J.?"

I frowned. "I don't know. That was a pretty good night. But tonight was . . . different."

"Good different?"

"It was kind of perfect."

Raegan raised an eyebrow and lowered her chin. "This could get messy. You should just tell him."

"Don't be stupid. You know I can't," I said, walking toward my bedroom.

My phone buzzed once, and then again. I fell onto my bed and looked at the display. It was T.J.

"Hello?" I said, holding the phone to my ear.

"Sorry it took me so long to call . . . we just got in . . . everything okay?" T.J. asked.

"Yes. Why?"

"I thought I heard something in your voice when you answered."

"You're hearing things," I said, trying not to think about how adorable Trenton looked with a sleepy Olive draped over his shoulder.

CHAPTER FOUR

THE BETTER PART OF SUNDAY MORNING WAS SPENT IN BED. Around ten thirty, my mother texted me, asking if I was coming to Sunday lunch. I informed her that because of the trip cancellation, Hank had taken the opportunity to call an employee meeting. It was mostly the truth. The employees hung out at the Red every Sunday afternoon, and then we'd all go home to freshen up for the Sunday night shift.

Mom didn't hesitate to send back a message meant to make me feel guilty.

"I'm riding with Kody!" Raegan yelled from her bedroom.

"K!" I yelled back from my bed. The phone call with T.J. hadn't ended until the wee hours of the morning. We discussed vague parts of his project that he could reveal, and then we talked about Trenton and Olive. T.J. didn't seem even the slightest bit jealous, which sort of pissed me off. And then I felt guilty when I realized I was trying to make him jealous, so I spent the rest of the conversation being super sweet to him.

After a long pep talk with myself, I threw off my covers and shuffled to the bathroom. Raegan had already been in there. The mirror was still fogged, and the walls were still sweaty from the steam.

I turned on the shower, grabbed two towels while the hot water kicked on, and then pulled off my worn Bulldog Football T-shirt and tossed it to the floor. The fabric was so thin it was see-through in some places. It was T.J.'s shirt, heather gray with royal-blue writing. I wore it the night before T.J. left to go back to California—the first night we slept together—and he didn't ask for it when he left. That shirt represented a time when everything was perfect between us, so it held a special significance for me.

By noon I had dressed, jumped in the Smurf with minimal makeup and wet hair, driven to the closest fast-food restaurant to grab a couple of items off the value menu, scrounged up $2.70 in coins to pay for lunch, and then made my way to the Red Door. The entrance area was empty, but music was playing through the speakers. Classic rock. That meant Hank was already there.

When I sat down at the east bar, Hank came around from the other side and smiled. He was wearing a black button-up shirt with black slacks and a black belt. Typical for him during work hours, but he was usually dressed down on Sundays.

I straddled a barstool, and rested my chin on my fist. "Hey, Hank. You look nice."

"Well, hello, good-lookin'," Hank said with a wink. "I'm not going home before open tonight. Paperwork and all that fun shit. Did you enjoy your weekend off?"

"I did, under the circumstances."

"Jorie said Trenton Maddox was hanging around your table Friday night. I must have missed it."

"I'm surprised. Usually you're watching the Maddoxes like a hawk."

Hank made a face. "I have to. They're either starting a fight or finishing one."

"Yeah, they almost finished one with Coby, the jackass. Even when I told him who they were, he still didn't back down."

"Sounds about right."

"I already need a drink!" Jorie called from the other side of the room. She was walking in with Blia. They both took a stool on each side of me and put their purses on the bar.

"Rough night?" Hank said, amused.

Jorie lifted an eyebrow. If it was possible to flirtatiously chomp on a piece of gum, she was doing it. "You tell me."

"I'd say you had a pretty good night," he said with a smirk.

"Ew," I said, my entire face compressing. Hank's dark, curly hair, light-blue eyes, five o'clock shadow, and tan skin made him attractive to nearly every female between the ages of fifteen and eighty, but Hank was twelve years older than us, and I'd witnessed so many of his shenanigans that he was more like a cute but ornery uncle to me. The only thing I wanted to visualize him doing was paperwork and counting money at the end of the night. "No one needs to hear that."

Hank was responsible for the end of at least a dozen marriages in our little town, and he was notorious for paying attention to barely legal young women just long enough to dip his stick. But when Jorie began working at the Red last year, he was obsessed. Jorie, an army brat with nine cities under her belt and unimpressed by most things, was definitely not falling for Hank's charms. It wasn't until there was a major turnaround in his behavior and reputation that she gave him the time of day. They'd had a couple of setbacks, but they were good for each other.

Jorie elbowed me and gave Hank a playful glare.

Tuffy walked in, looking tired and depressed as usual. He was a bouncer at the Red until he was fired. Hank had a soft spot for him, though, and rehired him six months later as a DJ. After his third divorce and third bout with depression, he missed work too many times and got fired again. Now, on his fourth wife and fourth chance at the Red, he was reduced to working the entrance and checking IDs at half pay.

Just a few seconds later, Rafe Montez followed behind Tuffy. He took over for Tuffy as DJ, and frankly was far better. He was quiet and kept to himself, and even though he'd worked at the Red for nearly a year, I didn't know much about him other than that he never missed a night of work.

"Holy shit the bed, Cami! Debra Tillman told my mom that you were at Chicken Joe's with Trenton Maddox!" Blia said.

Jorie's bleached curls flipped from one shoulder to the other when she looked over at me. "Seriously?"

"I was coerced. He showed up at my apartment with a little girl. He told her she could go to Chicken Joe's as soon as I got ready."

"That's kind of sweet." Blia brushed her long black hair off her shoulder and smiled, making her beautiful almond-shaped eyes turn into thin slits. She was barely five foot two and always wore sky-high shoes to make up for being vertically challenged. Today she wore inches-thick wedges with white skinny jeans and a floral top that scrunched at her midriff and fell off one shoulder. With her beauty-queen smile and flawless saffron skin, I always thought she was destined to be famous rather than waste her time behind the front beer kiosk, but she didn't seem interested.

Jorie frowned. "Does T.J. know?"

"Yes."

"Isn't that . . . awkward?" Jorie asked.

I shrugged. "T.J. didn't seem fazed."

Hank looked past me and smiled, and I turned around to see Raegan and Kody walk in. Raegan was walking quickly, searching in her purse for something, and Kody was a few steps behind, trying to keep up.

Raegan sat down on a stool, and Kody stood next to her. "I can't find my damn keys. I've looked for them everywhere!"

I leaned forward. "Seriously?" Our apartment keys were on that key ring.

"I'll find them," Raegan assured me. She lost her keys at least twice a month, so I wasn't going to stress over it too much, but I always wondered if the next time would be the time that we would have to pay to change the locks.

"I'm going to glue those damn things to your hand, Ray," I said.

Kody gave Raegan's shoulder a gentle, reassuring squeeze. "She had them last night. They're either in my truck or in the apartment. We'll look again later."

The side door shut, and we all watched the door at the end of the hall to see the last of us, Chase Gruber, stroll in through the employee entrance in his typical attire. The six-foot-six college junior wore shorts year-round. In the winter he wore an ESU Bulldogs hoodie over the random T-shirt, but his short, curly hair was always covered by either a helmet or his favorite red baseball cap. His laces were untied, and he looked like he just rolled out of bed.

Blia's face lit up. "Radtastic, it's Gruber!"

Gruber didn't crack a smile or remove his sunglasses.

"Rough day, Booby?" Kody said with a smirk.

All of the football guys called each other by their last names. To be honest, I wasn't convinced they knew each other's first names. Gruber was quickly nicknamed Gruby during practice, and sometime after Gruber started at the Red, Kody began calling him Booby. It was funny last year, but the name had lost its shine, for Gruber and for everyone else but Kody.

Gruber sat on the empty stool next to Blia with his elbows on the bar and his fingers intertwined. "Fuck off, Kody. Coach ran our asses off today because we lost last night."

"Then don't lose," Tuffy said.

Kody chuckled.

"Eat my dick, quitter."

Kody laughed once and shook his head. It was true. Kody did quit the football team before the season started, but that was because he blew out his knee at the end of the last game of his sophomore year. He suffered multiple ligament tears, one was shredded, and his kneecap was dislocated. I didn't even know the kneecap could be dislocated, but the orthopedic surgeon said he would never play again. Raegan said he didn't talk about it, but he seemed to be dealing with it well. As a true freshman, Kody had helped our little university win the national championship. Without him, the team was struggling.

The door shut again, and we all froze. It was too early for patrons, and unless someone followed Gruber, only employees knew to come in through the side entrance. We all sucked in a collective gasp when T.J. appeared. He was holding up a set of shiny keys.

"I went by the apartment. These were lying on the stairs."

I jumped up from my stool and walked quickly over to him. T.J. took me into his arms and gave me a tight squeeze.

"What are you doing here?" I whispered.

"I felt horrible."

"That's sweet, but what are you really doing here?"

T.J. sighed. "The job."

"Here?" I said, pulling away from him to see his face. He was being truthful, but I knew he wouldn't tell me more.

T.J. smiled, and then kissed the corner of my mouth. He tossed the keys to Kody, who effortlessly caught them.

Raegan laughed once. "On the stairs? Did they fall out of my hand or something?" she asked in disbelief.

Kody shrugged. "No telling, woman."

T.J. leaned in to whisper into my ear. "I can't stay. My plane leaves in an hour."

I couldn't hide my disappointment, but nodded. There was no point in protesting. "Did you do what you needed to do?"

"I think so." T.J. took my hand, and nodded to the rest of the crew. "She'll be right back."

Everyone waved, and T.J. led me out the side door to the parking lot. A rented, shiny black Audi was parked just outside. He'd left it running.

"Wow, you weren't joking. You're really leaving right now."

He sighed. "I debated whether it would be worse to only see you for a second, or to not see you at all."

"I'm glad you came."

T.J. slid his hand between my hair and my neck, and pulled me into him, kissing me with the lips that made me fall in love with him. His tongue found its way into my mouth. It was warm and soft and forceful at the same time. My thighs involuntarily tensed. T.J.'s hand slid down my arm, and then to my hip, to my thigh, where he squeezed just enough to show his desperation.

"Me, too," he said, a bit breathless when he finally pulled away. "You don't know how much I wish I could stay."

I wanted him to, but I wouldn't ask. That just made it harder on both of us, and might make me look pathetic.

T.J. got into his car and drove away, and I walked back into the Red, feeling emotionally drained. Raegan's bottom lip was pushed out a bit, and Hank was frowning so severely that a deep line had formed between his brows.

"If you ask me," Hank said, crossing his arms over his chest, "that little bastard rushed home to piss on you real quick."

My face screwed into disgust. "Ick."

Gruber nodded. "If Trent's coming around, then that's exactly what that was."

I shook my head as I sat on the stool. "T.J.'s not threatened by Trent. He's barely mentioned him."

"So he knows," Gruber said.

"Well, yeah. I'm not trying to hide it."

"You think he's here to talk to Trent?" Kody asked.

I shook my head again, picking at a hangnail. "No. He's not big on announcing our relationship, so he definitely wouldn't approach Trent about me."

Hank grumbled and walked away, coming right back. "I don't like that, either. He should be shouting to the world that he loves you, not hiding you like a dirty secret!"

"It's hard to explain, Hank. T.J. is a very . . . private person. He's a complicated individual," I said.

Blia rested her cheek on her hand. "Holy shit balls, Cami. Your whole situation is complicated."

"You're telling me," I said, lifting my buzzing cell phone. It was T.J., saying that he missed me already. I returned the sentiment, and set my phone on the bar.

◆   ◆   ◆

For the first time in months, I didn't have to return to the bar after the Sunday employee meeting, which wasn't completely horrible, since it was thundering outside, and rain was pelting the windows. I had already caught up on my studying, all of my homework was complete, and the laundry was folded and put away. It felt weird having nothing to do.

Raegan was working the east bar with Jorie, and Kody was manning the entrance, so I was home alone and bored out of my mind. I watched a rather fascinating zombie show on television, and then pushed the power button on the remote, sitting in complete silence.

Thoughts about T.J. began to creep into my mind. I wondered whether continuing with something that seemed so futile was worth dragging my heart through the mud, and what it meant that he'd come all the way here to only see me for three minutes.

My cell phone buzzed. It was Trenton.

Hey.

Hey.

Open your door, loser. It's raining.

What?

He knocked on the door, and I jumped, turning around on the couch. I scampered over to the door and leaned in closer. "Who is it?"

"I told you who it was. Open the freakin' door!"

I unlocked the chain and bolt lock to see Trenton standing in the doorway, his jacket soaked, and the rain pouring off his scalp and down his face.

"Can I come in?" he said, shivering.

"Jesus, Trent!" I said, yanking him inside.

I jogged to the bathroom to get a freshly folded towel, and returned within a few seconds, tossing it to Trenton. He peeled off his jacket, and then his T-shirt, and then patted his face and head with the towel.

Trenton looked down at his jeans. They were soaked, too.

"Kody might have some sweatpants in Ray's room, hold on," I said, walking quickly down the hall to my roommate's room.

I returned with a T-shirt and sweatpants. "The bathroom is right there," I said, nodding toward the hallway.

"I'm good," he said, unbuckling his belt, unbuttoning and unzipping his jeans, and then kicking off his boots before letting the denim fall to the floor. He stepped out of them, and then looked at me with his most charming smile. "Think Kody will mind if I go commando under his sweats?"

"Yes, and so will I," I said.

Trenton feigned disappointment, and then slipped on the sweats. His chest and abs tightened and rolled under his skin, and I tried not to watch while he pulled the T-shirt over his head.

"Thanks," he said. "I went by the Red and had a few drinks after work. Raegan said you'd be here alone and bored to death, so I thought I'd stop by."

"It wasn't because the rain gave you an excuse to get naked?"

"No. Disappointed?"

"Not at all."

Trenton wasn't fazed. Instead, he jumped over the back of my couch and bounced on the cushions. "Let's watch a movie!" He reached for the remote.

"I was kind of enjoying my first night alone."

Trenton turned to me. "You want me to leave?"

I thought about it for a minute. I should have said yes, but that would have been a lie. I walked around the couch and sat as close to the arm as I could. "Where's Olive?"

"With her parents, I bet."

"I like her. She's cute."

"She's fucking adorable. I'm going to have to kill at least one teenage boy one of these days."

"Oh, she's going to be sorry she ever befriended a Maddox," I said, chuckling.

Trenton pressed the power button, and punched in three numbers. The channel switched, and an NFL football game appeared. "Is this okay?"

I shrugged. "I love the Forty-Niners, but they suck balls this year." I looked over to Trenton when I realized he was staring at me. "What?"

"I was just thinking now was as good a time as any to acknowledge that you're perfect and it wouldn't suck if you fell madly in love with me anytime soon."

"I have a boyfriend," I reminded him.

He waved me away. "Speed bump."

"I don't know," I said. "He's a pretty hot speed bump."

Trent scoffed. "You've seen me nearly naked, baby doll. Your long-distance boy doesn't look anything like this."

I watched as he flexed his arm. It wasn't as big as Kody's but was still impressive. "You're right. He doesn't have that many tattoos. Or any."

Trenton rolled his eyes. "You have a pretty boy for a boy-friend? Disappointing!"

"He's not a pretty boy. He's a badass. Just in a different way than you."

A wide smile spread across Trenton's face. "You think I'm a badass?"

I purposefully kept myself from smiling, but it was hard. His expression was contagious. "Everyone knows about the Maddox brothers."

"Especially," Trenton said, standing up on the cushions and put-ting one foot on one side of me, the other he wedged between me and the arm of the couch, "this Maddox brother!" He began bounc-ing and, at the same time, flexing his muscles in different poses.

I playfully smacked his calves, giggling. "Knock it off!" I said, bouncing.

Trenton leaned down and grabbed my hands, forcing me to smack myself in the face a few times. It didn't hurt but, being the big sister of three brothers, this, of course, meant war.

I fought back, and then Trenton grabbed my T-shirt, rolling onto the floor and bringing me with him, and then he began to tickle.

"No! Stop it!" I squealed, laughing. I placed my thumbs under his armpits and dug in, and Trenton instantly jumped back. The same maneuver worked with T.J.

T.J. Oh, God. I was rolling around on the floor with Trenton. This was not okay . . . not even kind of okay.

"Okay!" I said, holding up my hands. "You win."

Trenton froze. I was flat on my back, and he was on his knees, straddling me. "I win?"

"Yeah. And you have to get off of me. This is not appropriate."

Trenton laughed, stood, and pulled me up by the hand. "We're not doing anything wrong."

"Yeah, it's kind of wrong. If I was your girlfriend, would you think this is okay?"

"Hell yeah. I'd expect this shit to be a nightly event."

"No. I mean with someone else."

Trenton's face fell. "Definitely not."

"Mmk, then. Let's watch the Forty-Niners get their asses kicked, and then you can tell Raegan you did your duty."

"My duty? Raegan didn't tell me to come over here. She just said you were alone and bored."

"Isn't that the same thing?"

"No way, Cami, I'm taking full credit for this one. I don't need anyone convincing me to hang out with you."

I smiled, and then turned up the volume.

"So, Cal said that for sure he's going to need someone at the desk."

"Oh, yeah?" I said, still watching the television. "Are you going to apply?"

Trenton laughed once. "He said, and I quote, 'Someone hot, Trent. Someone with nice tits.'"

"Every girl's dream job. Answering phones and handing out waivers while being ordered around by a sexist asshole."

"He's not an asshole. Sexist, yes, but not an asshole."

"No, thank you."

Just then my phone buzzed. I dug into the space between the arm and the couch cushion to get it. It was Coby.

So . . . bad news.

What?

I got a final notice for my car payment.

Pay your bill, doofus.

I'm a little behind. I was wondering if you could spot me some cash.

My blood ran cold. The last time Coby got behind on his bills, it was because he was sinking his entire paycheck into steroids. Coby was the shortest of my brothers, but he was the thickest, both in body mass and in brains. He was hot tempered, but the way he was behaving at the Red Friday night should have been a red flag.

Are you using again?

Really, Cami? Goddamn . . .

Really. Are you using?

No.

Lie to me again, and you can explain to Dad where your car went when it gets repo'd.

It took him several minutes to respond.

Yeah.

My hands began to shake, but I managed to keep typing.

You enroll in a program, show me the proof.
I'll pay the bill. Deal?

That could be next week.

Take it or leave it.

Fuck you, Cami. You're such a self-righteous
bitch sometimes.

Maybe, but I'm not the one who's going to
be without a car in a few weeks.

Fine. Deal.

I took a deep breath and let the phone fall to my lap. If I'm going to help out Coby, I need a second job.

Trenton watched me with concern in his eyes. "You okay?"

I was quiet for a long time, and then slowly met Trenton's eyes. "Cal's really looking for a receptionist?"

"Yeah."

"I'll give him a call tomorrow."

CHAPTER FIVE

JESUS CHRIST, CALVIN," TRENTON SAID. HE WAS LOOKING AT the large Chinese mural on the wall, trying not to notice that Calvin couldn't manage to stare anywhere else but at my breasts. Trenton's red ball cap was on backward, and his boots were untied. On anyone else the look would have appeared sloppy and screamed douche bag, but somehow the look made Trenton even more appealing. It felt wrong to notice anything about him, but I couldn't help it.

I didn't have the most voluptuous chest in the world, but my slight frame made my small D cups seem bigger than they were. I hated to admit it, but they helped score extra tips at the Red, and now they could help me get a second job. It was a vicious cycle of not wanting to be objectified, and using the gifts God gave me to my advantage.

"When did you say you could start?" Calvin said absently, straightening a picture of a brunette beauty on the wall behind the counter. Her tattoos covered nearly every part of her, and ink and a smile were the only things she wore as she lay across the bodies of other naked, apparently sleepy women. Most of the walls were covered in either art or photographs of tatted-up models draped over muscle cars or sprawled in a way that best displayed their skin art. The counter was a mess of papers, pens, receipts, and paper clips, but the rest of the place seemed to be clean, even if it did look like Calvin had bought the décor at an auction held by a failed Chinese restaurant.

"Right now. I can work Mondays and Tuesdays, noon until close, but Wednesday through Friday I can only work until seven. Saturday I have to be off by five. I can't work Sundays."

"Why not?" Calvin asked.

"I have to study and do homework sometime, and then I have an employee meeting at the Red, before working the bar."

Calvin looked over at Trenton for approval. Trenton nodded.

"Okay, I'll let Trent and Hazel train you on the phone, computer, and paperwork. It's fairly simple. Mostly customer service and cleanup," he said, walking out from behind the desk. "You got any tats?"

"No," I said. "Is that a requirement?"

"No, but I bet you'll get one within the first month," he said, walking down the hall.

"I doubt it," I said, walking past him to stand behind the counter.

Trenton came over to me and rested his elbows on the desk. "Welcome to Skin Deep."

"That's my line," I teased. The phone rang, and I picked it up. "Skin Deep Tattoo," I said.

"Yeah . . . uh . . . what time do you guys close tonight?" Whoever he was, he sounded drunk off his ass, and it was only three in the afternoon.

I looked at the door. "We close at eleven, but you'd better sober up first. They won't ink you if you're intoxicated."

Trenton made a face. I wasn't sure if that was a rule or not, but it should be. I was used to dealing with drunks, and I would probably see my fair share of them here, too. In a weird way, I felt more at ease with drunks. My dad had popped the top of a Busch beer can every morning for breakfast since before I was born. The slurring, the stumbling, the inappropriate comments, the giggling, and even the anger was what I was used to. Working in a cubicle around a bunch of uptight weenies discussing memos would be more unsettling to me than listening to a fully grown man crying into his beer over his ex-girlfriend.

"So, if it's a personal call, and it's for one of us, you can either transfer it to the back like this," Trenton said, pushing hold, the transfer button, and then one of five numbered buttons at the top. "One hundred is Cal's office. One-oh-one is my room. One-oh-two is Hazel's room. One-oh-three is Bishop's room . . . you'll meet him later . . . and if you hang up, that's okay, they'll call back. The list is taped under the phone base," he said, pushing the base to the side.

"Fantastic," I said.

"I'm Hazel," a tiny woman said from the other side of the room. She walked over to me and held out her hand. The dark bronze skin of her arms was covered from wrist to shoulder by dozens of pieces of colorful artwork. Her ears glistened with hardware that spanned the entire rim of her cartilage, and a rhinestone glistened in the place of a beauty mark. She was naturally a dark brunette, but her faux hawk was a brassy blond. "I'm the body piercer," she said, her thick lips forming around the words with elegance and the tiniest hint of an accent. For such a tiny thing, her grip was tight; her bright turquoise nails were so long, I wondered how she did anything, especially the complicated task of piercing small areas of the body.

"Cami. As of two minutes ago, I'm the receptionist."

"Cool," she said with a smile. "If anyone asks for me, always get their name and take a message. If it's a girl by the name of Alisha, tell her to choke on a dick."

She walked away, and I looked at Trenton, eyebrows raised high. "Okay, then."

"They broke up a few months ago. She's still angry."

"I caught that."

"So, here are the forms," Trenton said, pulling out the long, bottom drawer of a metal filing cabinet. We went over those between phone calls and customers, and when Trenton was busy, Hazel came up to help. Calvin stayed back in his office for the most part, and it didn't occur to me to mind.

After Trenton finished a client, he saw her out, and then poked his head inside one of the double glass doors. "You're probably getting hungry. Want me to grab you something from next door?"

Next door was Pei Wei's, and the delicious, salty, and savory smells of their food wafted in every time someone opened the doors, but I was working two jobs to help Coby get caught up on his bills. Eating out wasn't a luxury I could afford.

"No, thanks," I said, feeling my stomach growl. "It's almost closing time. I'll just grab a sandwich at home."

"You're not starving?" Trenton asked.

"Nope," I said.

He nodded. "Well, I'm going. Tell Cal I'll be right back."

"No problem," I said, feeling my shoulders sag a bit when the door closed.

Hazel was in her room with a customer, so I went back there and watched her impale the septum of some guy's nose. He didn't even flinch.

I recoiled.

Hazel noticed my expression and smiled. "I call these The Bull. They're pretty popular because you can just tuck the ring right up into the nostrils and hide it, like so."

I winced. "That's . . . fantastic. Trent went next door for dinner. He'll be back."

"He better bring me something," she said. "I'm fucking famished."

"How do you fit food in that body?" the client said. "If I eat rice, I gain ten pounds, and all you Chinese chicks are tiny. I don't get it."

"I'm Filipina, you fucktard," she said, flicking his ear, hard. He yelped.

I pressed my lips together, and walked back to the vestibule. A few minutes later, Trenton walked in, two large plastic bags in his hands. He set them on the counter and began pulling out different dishes.

Hazel walked up with her customer. "I already went over the care instructions, so he's good to go," she said. She took one look at the thin boxes on the counter and her eyes brightened. "I love you, Trent. I seriously, motherfucking love you."

"You're making me blush," he said with a smile. I had seen the scary sides of Trenton more than once, in middle school, high school, and more recently, at the Red. Now he had the most content look on his face, just happy that he'd made Hazel happy. "And this is for you," Trenton said, pulling out a box.

"But . . ."

"I know. You said you weren't hungry. Just eat so you don't hurt my feelings."

I didn't argue. I peeled the cellophane off a set of plastic utensils and dug in, not caring if I looked like a wild animal.

Calvin strolled up from the back, clearly led by his nose. "Dinner?"

"For us. Go get your own," Trenton said, waving Calvin off with his plastic fork.

"Goddamn," Calvin said. "I almost wish I had a vagina so I could get fed around here." Trenton ignored him. "Did Bishop ever come in?"

"Nope," Hazel said, her mouth full of food.

Calvin shook his head and pushed out the double doors, likely on his way to Pei Wei's.

The phone rang, and I answered, still chewing. "Skin Deep Tattoo . . ."

"Is uh . . . is Hazel busy?" a voice said, low pitched but feminine, like mine.

"She's with a client. Can I take your name?"

"No. Actually . . . uh . . . yeah. Tell her it's Alisha."

"Alisha?" I said, looking at Hazel. She began silently mouthing every cuss word in existence, and flipping off the phone with fingers from both hands.

"Yeah?" she said, sounding hopeful.

"*The* Alisha?"

She chuckled. "Yeah, I guess so. Is she coming to the phone?"

"No, but she left a message for you. Eat a dick, Alisha."

Trenton and Hazel froze, and the other end of the line was silent for a few seconds.

"Excuse me?"

"Eat. A. Dick," I said, and then hung up the phone.

After a few moments of shock, Hazel and Trenton burst into a duet of laughter. After a full minute of trying to stop laughing and making that tired sigh sound in between giggles, they both began wiping their eyes. Hazel's thick mascara was running down her cheeks.

Hazel leaned in to pull a tissue out of the box sitting on the counter next to the computer. She dabbed under her eyes, and then patted me on the shoulder. "We're going to get along just fine." She pointed back with her thumb as she retreated to her room. "Land that one, Trent. She's right up your alley."

"She has a boyfriend," Trenton called to her, staring into my eyes and grinning.

We just stood there for a few moments, exchanging small smiles, and then I righted my posture, looking for a clock. "I've got to go. Need to read a chapter before bed."

"I'd offer you help, but school wasn't really my thing."

I slipped my red hobo over my shoulder. "That's only because while you were there, partying and girls were your thing. It might be different now. You should look into taking a class."

"Nah," he said, pulling his cap off his head and turning it forward. He adjusted it a few times as he mulled over my suggestion, as if he had never considered it until that moment.

Just then, three college kids stumbled in, loud, obnoxious, and giggling. Even if they weren't drunk, it was easy for us locals to spot the transplants. Two guys, probably freshmen, approached the counter, and the girl, wearing a pink sundress and thigh-high boots, followed behind. Trenton immediately caught her eye, and she began smoothing out her hair.

"Jeremy lost a bet," one of the kids said. "He's going to need a Justin Bieber tat."

Jeremy let his head fall to the counter. "I can't believe you're making me do this."

"We're closed," I said.

"We have money," the kid said, opening his wallet. "I'm prepared to give everyone in here a tip that will blow your mind."

"We're closed," I said. "Sorry."

"She doesn't want your money, Clay," the girl said with a smirk.

"She wants my money," Clay said, leaning in. "You work at the Red, don't you?"

I just stared at him.

"Working more than one job . . ." Clay said, thinking.

Jeremy cringed. "Come on, Clay. Let's just go."

"I have a proposition for you to earn some extra cash. You'd make in one night what you probably make in a month here."

"Tempting . . . but no," I said, but before I could finish the sentence, Trenton had Clay's collar in both fists.

"Does she look like a whore to you?" Trenton seethed. I'd seen that look in his eyes before—right before he beat the shit out of someone.

"Whoa!" I said, rushing around the counter. Clay's eyes were wide. Jeremy put his arm on Trenton. Trenton looked down at Jeremy's hand. "Do you want to die tonight?"

Jeremy shook his head quickly.

"Then don't fuckin' touch me, bro."

Hazel jogged to the vestibule, but she didn't seem afraid. She just wanted to see the show.

Trenton kicked open the door and then shoved Clay out backward. Clay landed on his backside, and then scrambled up. The girl with them walked slowly outside, watching Trenton, twirling a small piece of her long, golden locks.

"Don't be too impressed, Kylie. He's that psycho that got that girl killed a couple of years ago."

Trenton rushed the door, but I stood between him and the

glass. Trenton immediately stopped, breathing hard, and Clay retreated quickly to his shiny black truck.

As the kids backed out of the parking lot, I kept a hand on Trenton's chest. He was still breathing hard, and shaking from anger. He could have stared a hole through the truck as it drove away.

Hazel turned on her heels and returned to her room without saying a word.

"I didn't kill her," Trenton said quietly.

"I know," I said. I patted him a couple of times, and then dug my keys out of my purse. "You okay?"

"Yeah," he said. His eyes lost focus, and I could see that he wasn't. I knew exactly what it was like to get lost in a bad memory, and even over a year later, just one mention of the accident had sent Trenton down the rabbit hole.

"I've got a bottle of Crown at my apartment and some lunch meat. Let's drink until we throw up ham sandwiches."

One corner of Trenton's mouth turned up. "That sounds pretty awesome."

"Doesn't it? Let's go. See you tomorrow, Hazel!" I called.

Trenton followed me to my apartment, and I went straight to the liquor cabinet. "Crown and Coke or just Crown?" I called from the kitchen.

"Just Crown," he said from behind me. I jumped, and then laughed. "Jesus, you scared me."

Trenton managed a small smile. "Sorry."

I flipped the bottle in the air with my left hand and caught it with my right, and then poured double shots into two tumblers.

Trenton's smile got a little wider. "It's pretty cool having a personal bartender."

"I'm surprised I can still do it. I've had too many days off. By the time I get back to work on Wednesday, I'll probably forget everything." I handed him his shot glass and clinked my glass to his. "To Crown."

"To fucking up," he said, his smile fading.

"To surviving," I said, pressing the glass against my lips and throwing my head back.

Trenton did the same. I took his empty glass, and poured us another. "Do we want teeth numb drunk, or porcelain praying drunk?"

"I'll know when I get there."

I handed him the glass, picked up the bottle, and led Trenton to the love seat. I held up my glass. "To second jobs."

"To spending more time with awesome people."

"To brothers who make life impossible."

"I'll drink to that shit," Trenton said, throwing back his shot. "I love my brothers. I'd do anything for them, but sometimes I feel like the only one who gives a shit about Dad, you know?"

"Sometimes I feel like the only one that doesn't give a shit about mine."

Trenton looked up from his empty glass.

"He's old school. Don't talk back. Don't have an opinion unless it's his. Don't cry when he beats the shit out of my mom."

Trenton's eyes tightened.

"He doesn't do it anymore. But he used to. Fucked with us kids, you know? That she stayed. That she could still love him."

"Goddamn. That's awful."

"Your parents loved each other?" I asked.

The smallest hint of a smile touched Trenton's lips. "Like crazy."

My expression mirrored his. "I love that."

"So . . . now?"

"Everyone acts like nothing happened. He's better now, so whoever doesn't pretend that she didn't have to spend extra time in the mornings covering bruises is the bad guy. So . . . I'm the bad guy."

"No, you're not. If someone hurt my mom . . . even if it was my dad . . . I'd never forgive him. Has he apologized?"

"Never," I said without hesitation. "But he should. To her. To us. To all of us."

He held out his empty glass this time. I poured a single, and we held them out again.

"To loyalty," he said.

"To running away," I said.

"I'll drink to that shit," he said, and we both knocked back the drinks.

I pulled my knees up to my chest, and rested my cheek on my knee, looking over at Trenton. His eyes were shadowed by the brim of his red baseball cap. He had brothers who were identical twins, but the youngest four could have been quadruplets.

Trenton reached for my shirt and pulled me into his chest. He folded me into his arms and squeezed. I noticed on the inside of his left forearm was thick script that spelled DIANNE, and a few inches down, in much smaller, cursive font that read MACKENZIE.

"Is that . . ."

Trenton turned over his arm to get a better look. "Yeah." We sat in silence for a moment, and then he continued. "The rumors aren't true, ya know."

I sat up and waved him away. "No, I know."

"I just couldn't go back there, with everyone looking at me like I'd killed her."

I shook my head. "No one thinks that."

"Mackenzie's parents do."

"They need to blame someone, Trent. Someone else."

Trenton's phone buzzed. He lifted it, took one look at the screen, and smiled.

"Hot date?"

"Shepley. Travis has a fight tonight. At Jefferson."

"Good," I said. "Every time they schedule one on a night the Red is open, it's empty."

"Really?"

"I guess you wouldn't know that, since you go to all of them."

"Not all of them. I'm not going tonight."

I raised an eyebrow.

"I have better things to do than watch Travis beat somebody's ass. Again. Besides, he doesn't have any moves I haven't seen."

"Right. You've taught him everything he knows, I'm sure."

"One third of everything he knows. That little shit. We beat his ass so many times growing up, he picked up on everything to keep from getting pummeled. Now he could beat all of us . . . at the same time. No wonder no one can beat him."

"I've seen you and Travis fight. You won."

"When?"

"Over a year ago. Right after . . . he told you to quit drinking before you drank yourself to death and you beat him pretty bad for it."

"Yeah," he said, rubbing the back of his neck. "I'm not proud of that. My dad still hasn't let me live that down, even though Travis forgave me the second it was over. I love that little bastard."

"You sure you don't want to go to Jefferson?"

He shook his head, and then smiled. "So . . . I still have *Space-balls.*"

I laughed. "What is your obsession with *Spaceballs?*"

He shrugged. "I don't know. We watched it a lot as kids. It was something we did as brothers. It just makes me feel good, ya know?"

"You just keep it in your car?" I asked, skeptically.

"No, it's at home. Maybe you can come over. Watch it with me sometime?"

I righted my posture, creating more space between us. "I'm thinking that's a horrible idea."

"Why?" he asked with his charming smile. "Don't trust yourself alone with me?"

"I'm alone with you right now. Not even worried about it."

Trenton leaned in, just a couple of inches from my face. "Is that why you just leaned away? Because you're not worried about being close to me?"

His warm, brown eyes fell to my lips, and his breath was the only thing I could hear until the front door swung open.

"I told you not to mention the Dallas Cowboys. Daddy hates the Dallas Cowboys."

"They're America's football team. It's un-American to hate the Cowboys."

Raegan turned on her heels, and Kody leaned back. "But you didn't have to say that to him! Jesus!" Raegan turned to look at Trenton and me on the couch. I was leaning back, and Trenton was leaning in close.

"Oh," she said with a smile. "Did we interrupt?"

"Nope," I said, pushing Trenton away. "Not at all."

"Sure looks like it—" Kody began, but Raegan turned her wrath on him again.

"Just . . . stop talking!" she yelled, and then retreated to her room, Kody following quickly behind.

"Great. They'll probably be fighting all night," I said.

"Just . . . go home!" Raegan said, slamming her bedroom door. Kody rounded the corner, looking distraught.

"Look at the bright side," I said. "If she didn't like you, she wouldn't be so upset."

"Her dad fights dirty," Kody said. "I didn't say shit until he'd been talking about Brazil for an hour. Then I tried to change the subject, and couldn't resist."

Trenton laughed, and then looked at Kody. "Can you give me a ride home? We've had a little bit to drink."

Kody jingled his keys. "Yeah, man. I'm heading over here in the morning to grovel if you want to pick up your car."

"Sweet," Trenton said. He stood up, ruffled my hair with his fingers, and then grabbed his keys. "See you at work tomorrow."

"Good night," I said, smoothing my hair.

"You get anywhere with her, man?" Kody said, purposefully louder than necessary.

Trenton chuckled. "Third base."

"You know what I hate?" I asked. "You."

Trenton rushed me and turned, lying on top of me, letting his entire weight push me down. "No way. Who else can you drink Crown straight from the bottle with?"

"Myself," I said, grunting against his weight. I elbowed him in the ribs, and he pulled himself up by the back of the couch, awkward and dramatic.

"Exactly. See you tomorrow, Cami."

When the door shut, I tried not to smile, but failed.

CHAPTER SIX

THE BOTTLE CRASHED TO THE FLOOR, AND BOTH HANK and Raegan stared down at the broken shards and splattered liquid.

"Coors Light!"

"Vegas Bomb!"

"Fuck!" I said, bending down to pick it up.

"I got it," Gruber said, hurrying behind the bar to clean up my mess.

Week two of my new job, and it was already beginning to wear on me. Going straight from class to Skin Deep wasn't difficult Mondays or Tuesdays, but Wednesday through Sunday kicked my ass. Trying to keep up with studying and papers after a shift that lasted until after 2:00 AM, and then waking up for a 9:00 AM class was grueling.

"You all right?" Hank said into my ear. "That's the first time you've dropped a bottle since you learned to flip 'em."

"I'm fine," I said, wiping my wet hands on the towel that was tucked into my back pocket.

"I said Coors Light!"

"Wait a goddamn minute!" Raegan yelled at the impatient jerk standing among forty other impatient jerks at my station.

"I still don't understand why you're doing this for Coby," she said, a residual frown still on her face.

"It's just easier."

"I'm pretty sure it's called enabling. Why would he straighten up, Cami? He has you to bail him out after a two-minute guilt trip."

"He's a stupid kid, Ray. He's allowed to screw up," I said, stepping over Gruber to get to the Blue Curaçao.

"He's your younger brother. He shouldn't be a bigger fuckup than you."

"Everything isn't always the way it's supposed to be."

"Blue Moon!"

"Blind Pig!"

"You got Zombie Dust on tap?"

I shook my head. "Only in October."

"What kind of bar is this? That's one of the top ten beers ever made! You should have it year-round!"

I rolled my eyes. Thursday night was coin beer night, and always packed. The dance floor was shoulder to shoulder, and the bar was three rows deep of drink calling and doubled as a prime spot for what Hank affectionately called the Meat Market, and it wasn't even eleven o'clock, when the rush would start.

"West corner!" Hank called.

"Got it!" Kody said, pushing through the crowd to get to a writhing mob.

The patrons were always more violent for two or three days after a fight. They'd watch Travis Maddox maul some guy without mercy, and then everyone at that fight walked away thinking they were equally invincible.

Raegan smiled, pausing for a few seconds to watch Kody work. "Damn, he's hot."

"Work, bitch," I said, shaking the hell out of a New Orleans Fizz until my arms burned.

Raegan groaned, lined up five shot glasses, pulled the stack of napkins to the lower shelf, and then tipped a bottle of Chartreuse upside down. She overpoured the shot glasses, and then ran a thin line across a clean section of the bar. She flipped a lighter, and fire erupted.

The group closest to the bar leaned back, away from the flames crawling across the wooden plank in front of them, and then cheered.

"Back the fuck up!" Raegan yelled as the fire burned itself out after thirty seconds.

"Nice!" Trenton said, standing in front of me with his arms crossed.

"Stay away from the west corner," I said, nodding to the red sea of swinging idiots parted by Kody and Gruber.

Trenton turned, and then shook his head. "Don't tell me what to do."

"Then get the hell away from my bar," I said with a smirk.

"Feisty," Trenton said, shrugging a few times.

"Bud Light!"

"Margarita, please!"

"Hey, sexy," a familiar voice said.

"Hey, Baker," I said with a smile. He'd been slipping twenties into my tip jar for over a year.

Trenton frowned. "You're missing your shirt," he said.

I looked down at my leather vest. Yes, my tits were out to

play, but I worked at a bar, not a day care. "Are you saying you don't approve of my attire?" Trenton began to speak, but I put my finger against his lips. "Aw, that's cute. You thought I was really asking."

Trenton kissed my finger, and I pulled back my hand.

Raegan slid a shot to Trenton, and winked at him. He winked back, lifted his glass to her, and then walked across the dance floor to the pool tables, not ten feet from the fight Kody and Gruber were still struggling with. Trenton watched for a few more seconds, shot the complimentary whiskey from Raegan, and then walked to the middle of the mob. Like a drop of oil in a bowl of water, the squabbling group backed away.

Trenton said a few words, and Kody and Gruber escorted two of the guys toward the exit.

"I should offer him a job," Hank said, watching the scene from behind me.

"He wouldn't take it," I said, mixing another drink. Unlike his little brother, I could tell that Trenton would rather not fight. He just wasn't afraid to, and like the other Maddox boys, it was ingrained in him as a default option for solving a problem.

Every few minutes for almost an hour, I found myself scanning the room for that buzzed brown hair and white T-shirt. The short sleeves fit snug around his biceps and broad chest, and I inwardly cringed for noticing. Trenton had always stood out to me, but I'd never tried to get to know him well enough to figure out why. He'd obviously stood out to a lot of females, and the thought of waiting in line didn't appeal to me, but I still noticed. It was hard not to.

Trenton leaned over to take the winning shot at one of the pool tables, his white hat turned backward. Clearly one of his favorites, the dingy white still made his leftover tan from summer look even darker.

"Holy cow balls! There's already been two fights at the entrance!" Blia said, her eyes wide. "Need a break?"

I nodded, taking payment for the last cocktail I'd made.

"Don't be long. This place is five seconds away from blowing up."

I winked. "I'm just going to pee, smoke, and I'll be right back."

"Don't ever quit us," Blia said, already starting a drink order. "I've decided that I'm not ready for the east bar, yet."

"Don't worry. Hank would have to fire me first."

Hank threw a wadded-up napkin at my face. "You don't have to worry about that, killer."

I playfully punched his arm, and then made a beeline for the employees' bathroom. Once inside the stall, I shimmied my panties down to my knees and sat, the bass of the music outside keeping a muffled but steady beat. The thin walls vibrated, and I envisioned my bones doing the same.

After checking my phone, I set it on top of the gray plastic toilet paper container. Still nothing from T.J., but I was the last person to text. I wasn't going to be the kind of girl who begged for attention.

"You 'bout done?" Trenton said from the other side of the stall.

My entire body tensed. "What the hell are you doing in here? This is the girls' bathroom, Stalker Texas Ranger."

"Did you just insinuate I'm comparable to Chuck Norris? Because I'll take that."

"Get out!"

"Calm down. I can't see you."

I flushed the toilet, and then pushed open the stall door so hard it slammed against the sink counter. After washing my hands, and pulling out a couple of paper towels, I made sure to glare at Trenton.

"Glad to see employees really do what the sign says. I've always wondered."

I left him alone in the bathroom, and headed out the employee entrance door.

The moment I stepped outside the chill cooled the bare parts of my skin. Cars were still pulling in and parking haphazardly on the grass on the far side of the lot. Car doors were slamming, and friends and couples were walking to the entrance, slowed by a long line of college students waiting for others to leave so they could get in.

Trenton stood next to me, pulled out a cigarette and lit it, and then lit mine. "You should really quit," he said. "Nasty habit. Not attractive for a girl."

I craned my neck at him.

"What? I'm not trying to be pretty. I'm not a girl."

"I don't like you."

"Yeah, you do."

"I'm not trying to be pretty, either."

"You're failing."

I peeked over at him, trying my hardest not to feel flattered. A warm feeling pooled in my chest, and then began to spread, making it all the way down to my fingers and toes. He had the best worst effect on me. As if everything I was—and wasn't—was desirable. I didn't even have to try. Trenton's unrepentant appreciation for everything he knew about me was addictive. I found myself wanting more, but I wasn't sure if it was the way he made me feel that I liked so much, or the familiar feeling. This was like my first three months with T.J. The warmth I'd felt a second before faded, and I began to shiver.

"I'd offer you my jacket, but I didn't bring one," Trenton said. "I have these, though." He held his arms a bit away from his body, palms up.

I shrugged. "I'm fine. How was the last few hours of work tonight?"

He crossed his arms across his chest. "You're doing too good of a job. Hazel was bitching that you weren't there, and then Calvin started in, too."

"Did you at least take up for me?"

"What did you want me to say? *Shut the fuck up, Hazel! She's a terrible worker and I don't want her here!*"

"A real friend would have."

Trenton shook his head. "You make no fucking sense. But I think I like it."

"Thanks, I think." I pinched the cherry off my cigarette and stepped on it. "Back to work."

"Always," Trenton said, following me back inside.

Blia returned to the front kiosk, and then Jorie came up to relieve Raegan. Trenton was working on his fourth bottle of beer by the time Raegan returned, and he seemed more irritated after every drink I made.

"You okay?" I asked over the music.

He nodded but didn't stop staring at his intertwined fingers resting on the bar. I noticed for the first time that his T-shirt featured two pale bluebirds, above the words DO YOU SWALLOW? His many tattoos complemented the shirt and distressed jeans, but the pink, white, and purple plastic bracelet didn't.

I touched the plastic with my index finger. "Olive?"

He turned his wrist a bit. "Yep." Even the mention of his best friend didn't cheer him up.

"What's up, Trenton? You're acting weird."

"He's here."

"Who's here?" I said, squinting while I shook another cocktail.

"The preppy douche bag I tossed out of Skin Deep."

I glanced around, and there he was, just a few feet down from Trenton's left, flanked by Jeremy and Kylie. She was in another short dress, only this one was gold and a lot tighter. "Just ignore him. We're having a good time tonight."

"*We* are? I'm sitting here by myself," he snapped.

Clay smiled at me, but I looked down, hoping not to encourage any snide comments from him that would set Trenton off. No such luck.

"Look, Jeremy! It's the bitchy secretary!" Clay said. He was drunker than he was in the tattoo parlor.

I looked for Kody, but didn't see him. He was likely at the entrance, where the fights had been breaking out. Gruber was on the west wall, where scuffles were also known to occur. Tuffy was on break, so Hank was probably at the entrance checking IDs and taking money.

Clay still hadn't seen Trenton, but Kylie had. She had one arm around Clay's back, and one hand on his stomach, the tip of her ring finger tucked into the waist of his jeans. Even though she was draped against Clay, she kept her eyes on Trenton, waiting for him to notice her.

"I'll take a bottle of Bud, Bitchy! And you're not getting a tip, because you kicked me out the other night."

"Want me to do it again?" I asked.

"I can take you into a dark alley and bend you over," he said, weaving.

Trenton tensed, and I put my hand on his. "He's plastered. Give me a sec and I'll have Kody escort him out."

Trenton didn't look up at me, he just nodded, his knuckles white.

"I'm not in the mood for your shit tonight. Go order from the kiosk."

"Beer me, bitch!" Clay said, just before he noticed whose hands I was holding.

Trenton left his seat, barreling through a few people.

"Trent, no! Goddammit!" I jumped over the bar, but not before Trenton got a couple of punches in. Clay was already on the ground, bleeding. I fell on my knees and covered my head, covering Clay with my body at the same time.

Jorie screamed over the music. "Cami, no!"

When nothing happened, I looked up, seeing Trenton standing over us, his fist shaking and high in the air. Kylie was standing next to Trenton, looking down on us. She was simply spectating, not the least bit concerned about Clay.

Kody and Raegan were standing next to me when I stood up, and Kody helped Clay to his feet. Jorie pointed to Clay, and Kody took him by the arm.

"All right. Let's go," Kody said.

Clay yanked his arm from Kody's grasp and wiped the blood from his mouth with his sleeve.

"You want to go again, sunshine?" Trenton asked.

"Fuck you," Clay said, spitting blood on the floor. "Let's go, Kylie."

Trenton pulled Kylie against his side and pointed at her. "Is this your girl?"

"What about it?" Clay asked.

Trenton grabbed Kylie and leaned her back, planting an open kiss on her mouth. She kissed him back, and for a few seconds they were both more than enthusiastic. Trenton slid his hand down her side and then cupped her ass with one hand, keeping her neck in the crook of his other arm.

My stomach dropped, and just like everyone else, I froze until Trenton stood her upright and gently pushed her toward Clay.

Clay made a face, but he didn't react. Kylie was more than pleased, and turned to give Trenton one last flirtatious glance while Clay dragged her by the hand toward the entrance. Kody followed them out, but not before making a *what the fuck* face to Raegan, and then to me.

It wasn't until then that I realized every muscle in my body was tense.

I approached Trenton and pointed at his chest. "You pull that shit again, and I'll have you thrown out of here."

One side of Trenton's mouth turned up. "The punching, or the kissing?"

"Is your ass jealous of the amount of shit that comes out of your mouth?" I said, walking around the bar.

"I've already heard that one!" Trenton called back. He grabbed his beer off the bar, and then strolled over to the pool tables like nothing happened.

"Not to piss all over your parade, sister, but you look angry," Raegan said.

I began washing mugs like I hated them, because in that moment, I hated everything. "I couldn't stand him in high school, and I can't stand him now."

"You've been hanging out with him a lot for someone you can't stand."

"I thought he'd changed, but apparently not."

"Apparently not," Raegan deadpanned, popping the top on three beer bottles, one after another.

"Shut up, shut up, shut up," I chanted, trying to drown out her words. I didn't want him, anyway. What did it matter to me if he was a man whore who stuck his tongue down someone's throat just to piss off her boyfriend?

The fast pace behind the bar continued, but fortunately the fights died down just before last call. It was always a huge pain in the ass trying to get out of there when the whole place broke out into a brawl at closing time. The lights came on, and the crowd dispersed. For once, Kody and Gruber didn't have to go into asshole mode to get the stragglers out. Instead, they politely encouraged people to leave, and Raegan and I closed down the bar. Lita and Ronna walked in with brooms and other cleaning supplies. By 3:00 a.m., the bartenders were all ready to leave, and per policy, Kody and Gruber walked us to our cars. Walking Raegan out every night and filling those short moments with subtle charm was exactly how Kody had finally convinced her to let him take her on a date. Gruber walked me to the Smurf, both of us pulling our coats tighter to ward off the cold. When Trenton's car, and then Trenton standing next to it, came into view, Gruber and I paused at the same time.

"Need me to stay?" Gruber asked quietly as we continued walking.

"What are you going to do?" Trenton hissed. "Nothin'."

I wrinkled my nose, disgusted. "Don't be a dick. You don't get to be an ass to guys who are mean *and* nice to me."

"What about those of us who are both?" he said, his eyebrows moving in.

I nodded to Gruber. "I'm good."

Gruber nodded, and walked back into the Red.

"You're drunk," I said unlocking the driver's-side door of the Jeep. "Did you call a cab?"

"Nope."

"One of your brothers?"

"Nope."

"So you're walking home?" I said, pulling on the shiny red bottle cap opener key ring sticking out of his jeans pocket. His keys came along with it.

"Nope," he said, smiling.

"I'm not driving you home."

"Nope. I don't let girls drive me, anymore."

I opened my car door, and then sighed, pulling out my cell phone. "I'll call you a cab."

"Kody is going to give me a lift."

"If he keeps taking you home, you're going to have to make it Facebook official."

Trenton laughed, but then his smile faded. "I don't know why I did that. With her. Habit, I guess."

"Weren't you the one talking about nasty habits earlier?"

"I'm a piece of shit. I'm sorry."

I shrugged. "Do what you want."

He looked wounded. "You don't care."

After a short pause, I shook my head. I couldn't bring myself to lie out loud.

"Are you in love with him? Your guy?"

"C'mon, Trent. What is this?"

Trenton's face compressed. "You and me . . . we're just friends, aren't we?"

"Sometimes I'm not sure if we're that."

Trenton nodded, and then looked down. "All right. Just checking." He walked away, and I huffed in frustration.

"Yes," I called out to him.

He turned, watching me expectantly.

"We're friends."

A small smile touched his lips, and then it spread into a full-blown grin. "I know." He shoved his hands into his pockets as he strolled across the parking lot like he owned the world.

Once he hopped inside Kody's truck, my stomach sank. I was in trouble. Big, disastrous, Maddox trouble.

CHAPTER SEVEN

STILL NO WORD ON THANKSGIVING?" I HATED ASKING, BUT he wouldn't mention it if I didn't, and at that moment I was nearly desperate to know. I was beginning to forget what it felt like to be near him, and I was getting confused about things I shouldn't be confused about.

T.J. didn't make a sound for several seconds. He didn't even breathe. "I miss you."

"So that's a no."

"I won't know until the day before. Maybe the day of. If something comes up . . ."

"I understand. You warned me. Stop acting like I'm going to throw a tantrum every time you can't give me a straight answer."

He sighed. "I'm sorry. It's not that. I'm just worried the next time you ask, and I answer . . . you're going to say something I don't want to hear."

I smiled against the phone, wishing I could hug him. "It's nice to know you don't want to hear it."

"I don't. It's hard to explain . . . wanting this promotion and wanting to be with you just as much."

"I get it. It's not easy, but it's going to be okay. We won't always have to miss each other. We just have to get over the tough part in the beginning, right?"

"Right." His reply was immediate and without hesitation, but I could hear the uncertainty in his voice.

"I love you," I said.

"You know I do," he said. "Have a good night, love."

Knowing he couldn't hear, I nodded, but it was all I could manage. We hung up without discussing Coby, or my second job, or that I'd been spending so much time with Trenton. My weekend tips had helped my brother pay most of one payment, but I worried it would just be a matter of time before he dropped out of his program.

I slipped a long-sleeved lacy black top over my head and fought with a pair of my favorite ripped jeans. Then I dabbed on some lip gloss before running out the door before I was late for my Friday night shift at the Red.

As soon as I walked into the employees' entrance, I knew something was off. Everyone was dragging ass, and the bar was quiet. Too quiet. Normally I would treasure that first hour before everyone poured in through the doors. Friday was ladies' night, so the rush began even earlier, but the bar was dead.

Thirty minutes in, Raegan was grumbling under her breath as she wiped down the bar for the third time. "Is there an underground fight thing tonight?"

I shook my head. "The Circle? It's never held this early."

"Oh, look. Something to do," Raegan said, pulling down the Jim Beam.

Travis Maddox was trudging to his usual barstool, looking pitiful. Raegan put a double in front of him, and he sucked it down in one gulp, letting the glass crash to the wood.

"Uh-oh," I said, taking the bottle Raegan handed me. "There's only two things that could be that bad. Is everyone in the family okay?" I asked, bristling in anticipation of his answer.

"Yep. Everyone except me."

"I don't believe it," I said, stunned. "Who is she?"

Travis's shoulders fell. "She's a freshman. And don't ask me what it is about her. I don't know, yet. But, when I was bagging this other chick today, I felt like I was doing something wrong, and then this girl's face popped into my head."

"The freshman's?"

"Yeah! What the fuck, Cami? This has never happened to me before!"

Raegan and I traded glances. "Well," I said. "It's not the end of the world. You like her. So what?"

"I don't like girls like this. That's what."

"Like *this*?" I said, surprised.

He took another shot, and then held his hands over his head, moving them around in circles. "She's all in my head."

"You're such a pussy for a guy that doesn't lose!" Raegan said, teasing.

"Tell me what to do, Cami. You know about girls. You're kind of one."

"Okay, first of all," I said, leaning toward him, "suck my dick."

"See? Girls don't say that."

"The cool ones do," Raegan said.

I continued, "Second of all, you're Travis fucking Maddox. You can have any girl you want."

"Almost," Raegan said from the sink, five feet away.

Travis's nose wrinkled. "You were Brazil's girl. I've never even tried."

Raegan narrowed her eyes at the youngest Maddox brother. "Did you just say that to me?"

"Well," he said. "It's the truth."

"Still would have never happened."

"We'll never know," he said, raising his third shot before letting it wash down his throat.

"Easy, Mad Dog," I said.

Travis cringed. "You know I fucking hate that."

"I know," I said lifting the bottle. "But it gets your attention. Here's your plan. Number one, stop being a little bitch. Number two, remember who the hell you are, and work your magic. She's no different from any other—"

"Oh, she's different," Travis said.

I sighed and looked at Raegan. "He's got it bad."

"Shut up and help me," Travis said, frustrated.

"There are three tricks to landing a hard-to-get: patience, having other options, and being aloof. You are not the BFF. You're sex on a stick, flirting just out of reach. In other words, Travis Maddox."

"I knew it. You've always wanted me," he said, smug.

I stood up. "Uh . . . no. Not at all. Not even in high school."

"Liar," he said, standing. "I never tried with you, either. My brother has always been in love with you."

I froze. What the hell was that supposed to mean? Did he know something?

Travis continued, "Aloof. Other options. Patience. Got it."

I nodded. "If you guys end up married, you owe me a hundred bucks."

"Married?" Travis said, his face screwing into disgust. "What the fuck, Cami? I'm nineteen! Nobody gets married at nineteen."

I looked around, checking to see if anyone heard him admit to being underage. "Say that a little louder."

He snorted. "Me getting married at all is unlikely? Anytime soon? Never gonna happen."

"Travis Maddox doesn't walk into a bar upset over a girl, either. You never know."

"Shame on you for wishing that on me," he said, winking. "I better see you at my next fight, Camille! Be a good friend, would ya?"

"You know I have to work."

"I'll make sure we schedule a late one."

"I still won't come! It's barbaric!"

"Come with Trent!"

Travis turned to walk away, and I stood, stunned. Was he talking about Trenton before? So, Trenton was talking about me. Who else had he told? As Travis walked out through the thick, red door, a large group walked in, and then the crowd continued to trickle in after that. I was grateful that I didn't have time to worry about whether or not there were rumors circulating, or if those rumors would get back to T.J.

◆   ◆   ◆

Late the next morning, I walked into Skin Deep, already in a bad mood. T.J. hadn't called or texted me back, which only fueled my paranoia about possible fallout from Trenton's big mouth.

"Cami's here!" Hazel said with a smile. She pushed black, thick-rimmed glasses up her nose.

I forced a smile. Hazel pouted her red-stained lips. "Why so sad? Did the Alpha Gamma party put you out of business last night?"

"Was that it? You went?"

She winked. "Gotta love sorority chicks. So what's up with you?"

"Just tired," I said, flipping the OPEN sign.

"Heads up. Calvin is going to ask you to start working Sundays."

"Are you serious?" I said, a little whinier than I'd intended. Today was not a good day to ask me to up my hours. By the time I rounded the counter, Trenton walked in.

"Chamomile!" he said. He was holding a bowl full of plastic fruit.

"Oh, please don't. It wasn't funny in middle school, and it's definitely not funny now."

Trenton shrugged. "I liked it."

"You didn't even know who I was in middle school."

He frowned. "Says who?"

I made a show of looking around. "You didn't speak to me until I grew tits."

Hazel cackled. "Work has been so much more entertaining since she was hired!"

"Doesn't mean I didn't know who you were," Trenton said, unamused.

Hazel pointed to the bowl in Trenton's arms. "What's with the fruit?"

"For my room. It's decoration."

"It's hideous," she said.

"It was my mom's," he said, unfazed. "I decided I needed something of hers at work. Puts me in a good mood." He walked down the hall and disappeared into his room.

"So," Hazel said, leaning her elbows on the counter. Her

thin, penciled eyebrow shot up. "The sexual tension around here is getting ridiculous."

I raised an eyebrow. "I didn't know you liked Calvin."

Hazel wrinkled her nose. "No one likes Calvin."

"I heard that!" Calvin called from down the hall.

"Good!" Hazel yelled back. "So, you're really not interested in Trent?"

"Nope," I said.

"Not even a little bit."

"I have a boyfriend, and he makes me very happy," I said, licking my thumb and counting forms.

"Damn," Hazel said. "I kinda liked you two together."

"Sorry to disappoint you," I said, straightening the stack in my hands before returning them to their bin.

The door chimed, and a group of four girls walked in: all blond, all tan, and all showcasing their double-D-cup breasts in tight shirts that were in various shades of pink.

I began to welcome them, but Hazel pointed to the door. The girls stopped in their tracks.

"C'mon, Hazel. We told him we'd stop by," one of them whined.

"Out," she said, still pointing with one finger, then looking down to turn a page of *Cosmopolitan* magazine with the other. When she didn't hear the chime again, she looked up. "Are you fucking deaf? I said out!"

The girls frowned, and pouted for a few seconds before filing out the way they came in.

"What was that about?" I asked.

She shook her head and sighed. "Trent groupies. Bishop has them, too. Women who hang out at the shop, hoping to score free tattoos, or . . . I don't know . . . that the guys score." She rolled her eyes. "Quite frankly they annoy me, but up until recently they were allowed in."

"What changed?"

Hazel shrugged. "Bishop stopped coming in as much, and Trenton told me to send them away not long after you started here. See? You're not a total disappointment." She elbowed me.

"I suppose I haven't really been worth the paycheck. I can't even mix the MadaCide right. Disinfectant is kind of important around here."

"Shut the fuck up!" she said with a wry smile. "No one else could have talked Calvin into getting rid of the cheap Asian décor and restructuring the files. You've been here less than a month and we're already more organized, and customers don't wonder if they'll get a free fortune cookie with their tattoo."

"Thanks. It's nice to feel appreciated."

"I appreciate you," Trenton said, walking into the lobby. "I appreciate that you're finally going to watch *Spaceballs* with me tonight. I'm bringing it over."

"No," I said, shaking my head.

"Why not?"

"I'm working."

"And then what?"

"Going to bed."

"Bullshit."

"You're right. I have plans."

He sneered. "With who?"

"I don't know yet, but definitely not you."

Hazel giggled. "Ouch."

Trenton put his entire palm on Hazel's tiny face and playfully pushed her away, keeping his hand on her as he spoke. "That's not nice. I thought you said we're friends."

"We are," I said.

Hazel finally struggled away from Trenton, and began slapping the shit out of his arm. Barely noticing, and only holding up one hand to fend her off, he continued, "Friends watch *Spaceballs* together."

"We're not that good of friends," I said, concentrating on lining up the paper clips just right in their new organizer.

The door chimed, and two customers walked in: a couple. They were neck-deep in tattoos already.

"Hi," I said with a smile. "How can I help you?"

"Rachel!" Hazel said, tackle-hugging the girl. She had an eyebrow piercing, a diamond for a beauty mark, and nose and lip rings. Her rocket-fire-red pixie cut almost glowed, it was so intense. Even with a head full of holes and arms covered in skulls and fairies, she was breathtaking. I sat back and watched them chat. Her boyfriend was tall and skinny, and just as glad to see Hazel. I couldn't imagine either of them wanted more piercings or tattoos. Unless they wanted face tattoos, they had run out of blank skin to ink.

Hazel escorted them back to her room, and laughter and chatting ensued.

"It's going to be a slow day." Trenton sighed.

"You don't know that. It just started."

"I can always call it, though," he said.

"Who are they?" I asked, nodding toward the hall.

"Rachel is Hazel's sister."

I raised an eyebrow, dubious. "Maybe this is ignorant, but Rachel isn't Asian. Not even a little bit."

"They're both adopted. They were foster kids. There's like a dozen of them or more. They're spread all over the country now, and they all love each other like crazy. It's awesome."

I smiled at the thought.

"So you really won't watch *Spaceballs* with me tonight?"

"Really."

"Why not?" he said, crossing his arms and shifting his weight.

I smirked. "Getting ready for a fight?"

"Answer the question, Camlin. What do you have against *Spaceballs*? I need to know before we go any further."

"Further than what?"

"You're stalling."

I sighed. "Between work and the Red, and . . . we're seeing a lot of each other."

He watched me for a moment, a hundred thoughts scrolling behind his warm russet eyes. He walked the few steps to stand next to me, putting the heel of his hand on the counter beside my hip, his chest touching my left arm. He leaned down, his mouth almost touching my hair. "And that's a bad thing?"

"Yes. No. I don't know," I said, my face compressing. He was confusing me, and way too close for me to think straight. I turned to tell him to back away, but when I looked up, I paused. He was right there. Inches away. Looking down at me with a look in his eyes I couldn't decipher.

He looked down at my bare shoulder. "That's a perfect spot for me to ink."

I laughed once. "No."

"Come on. You've seen my work."

"I have," I said, nodding emphatically. "It's amazing."

"Then what?"

I looked back up at him, trying to interpret his expression. "I don't trust you. I'd probably end up with MAY THE SCHWARTZ BE WITH YOU."

Trenton beamed. "Is that a *Spaceballs* reference? I'm impressed!"

"See? I've already seen it. A lot."

"You can never see *Spaceballs* too much."

Hazel, Rachel, and Rachel's boyfriend returned to the lobby. Hazel gave Rachel a big hug, and then they said tearful goodbyes.

"Christmas is right around the corner," Trenton said.

When Rachel left, Hazel was smiling, but a little sad. "Damn it. I love her."

"You love all of them," Trenton said. "If you get them on a monthly cycle, you could see one of them every day."

Hazel elbowed Trenton, and he elbowed her back. They fought like brother and sister.

"So," Hazel said, chomping on a piece of gum. "I heard you guys talking. I can't believe you're scared to get a tattoo."

I shook my head. "Not at all."

Calvin walked to the vestibule. "Has Bishop been in?" he asked.

Hazel shook her head. "No, Cal. You've already asked me that today. We were just discussing Cami's first tattoo."

Calvin's scanned me from head to toe. "That's bad for business, a receptionist that doesn't have any tats. You can make it up to me by picking up some hours on Sunday."

"Only if you let me start working on papers and homework when we're not busy."

He shrugged. "Deal."

My shoulders fell. I didn't expect him to agree.

"Let me pierce your nose," Hazel said, her eyes bright.

"One of these days," I said.

"Baby doll, don't let them talk you into anything you don't want to do. There's no shame in being scared of needles," Trenton said.

"I'm not scared," I said, exasperated.

"Then let me ink you," he said.

"You're a bartender for Christ's sake," Hazel said. "You should have at least one tat."

I glared at each of them. "Is this peer pressure? Because that's lame."

"How am I pressuring you? I just said not to let anyone talk you into anything," Trenton said.

"And then you told me to let you give me a tat."

He shrugged. "I admit it would be kickass to know I inked you first. It's kind of like taking your virginity."

"Well, that would require going back in time, and that's not going to happen," I said with a smirk.

"Exactly. This is the next best thing. *Trust me*," he said, his voice low and smooth.

Hazel cackled. "Oh, God. I'm ashamed to admit that line totally worked on me."

"Yeah?" I said, suddenly feeling very uncomfortable. "From Trent?"

She burst out laughing again. "I wish!" She closed her eyes and cringed. "Bobby Prince. Smooth talker. Tiny penis." She spoke the last sentence in falsetto, and held up her index finger and thumb, not even an inch apart.

We all shook with laughter. Hazel was dabbing the wet skin

beneath her eyes. Once we regained our composure, I caught Trenton staring at me. Something in the way he was looking at me made me forget all about being responsible, and reason. For once, I just wanted to be young, and not think too hard or too much. "Okay, Trent. Pop my cherry."

"Seriously?" he asked, standing up straight.

"Are we doing this or what?" I asked.

"What do you want?" He walked over to the computer and popped a pen in his mouth, holding it lengthwise in his teeth.

I thought for a moment, and then smiled. "Baby Doll. Across my fingers."

"You're shittin' me," Trenton said around the pen, stunned.

"No good?" I asked.

He chuckled and took the pen out of his mouth. "No, I like it . . . a lot . . . but that's a helluva tattoo for a virgin." He popped the pen back in, freeing up his hand to move the mouse.

I smirked. "If I'm going to lose it, I want to be broken in right."

The pen fell from Trenton's mouth to the floor, and he bent down to pick it up. "Uh . . . any, uh . . . any special font?" he said, glancing back at me once before drawing it up on the computer.

"I want it to look a little girly so I don't look like I came straight from prison."

"Color? Or black and white?"

"Black outline. I don't know about color. Blue, maybe?"

"Like Smurf blue?" he teased. When I didn't answer, he continued. "How about a gradient look. Blue at the bottom and then as I get higher on the letters it slowly fades out?"

"Radtastic," I said, nudging him with my shoulder.

Once I decided on font and color, Trenton printed out the transfers, and I followed him back to his room.

I sat on the chair, and Trenton got his equipment ready.

"This is going to be badass," Hazel said, sitting in a chair not far from me.

Trenton slipped on some latex gloves. "I'm just going to use a single needle. It's still going to hurt like a bitch, though. Going to be right on the bone. You don't have any fat on your fingers."

"Or anywhere else," Hazel said.

I winked at her.

Trenton laughed once as he cleaned each of my fingers with a green soap, wiped that off, and then put alcohol on a cotton square and rubbed each of the fingers he planned to tattoo. "It might not take the first time. You might have to get it done again." He used one finger to wipe a tiny bit of Vaseline where he cleaned with alcohol.

"Really?" I said with a frown.

Hazel nodded. "Yeah. Feet do that, too."

Trenton situated the transfers. "What do you think? Do they look straight? Is that how you want them?"

"Just make sure it's spelled right. I don't want to be one of those jackasses with a misspelled tattoo."

Trenton chuckled. "It's spelled right. I'd be a complete jerk-off if I couldn't spell two four-letter words correctly."

"You said it, not me," I teased.

Hazel shook her head. "Don't insult him before he permanently draws on your skin, girl!"

"He'll make it beautiful, won't you?" I asked.

Trenton turned on the machine, and then looked at me with a soft expression. "You're already beautiful."

I could feel my cheeks flush. When Trenton was sure the transfers were dry and he touched the needle to my skin, it was more of a nice distraction than excruciating pain. Trenton drew, then wiped, and repeated the process, concentrating hard. I knew he would make sure it was perfect. Even though the pain wasn't as bad at first, as the minutes ticked by, the annoying burning I felt on my fingers each time he began to mark my skin made it very tempting to pull away.

"Done!" he said, barely fifteen minutes later. He cleaned off the smeared ink, revealing the letters on my fingers. The blue was so vivid. It was gorgeous. I faced the mirror, made fists, and held them together.

"Lookin' good, baby doll," Trenton said with a wide grin.

It was perfect.

"Damn, that's badass," Hazel said. "I want finger tats, now!"

Trenton handed me a few packages of Aquaphor. "Keep this on it. Good shit. Especially for color."

"Thank you," I said.

For just a moment, he stared at me as if he really had just taken my virginity. Butterflies swarmed in my stomach, and my chest felt warm. I took a few steps backward, and turned toward the vestibule. The phone rang, but Hazel answered for me.

Trenton leaned his elbows on the counter, smiling at me with the most ridiculous simper.

"Stop it," I said, trying not to smile back.

"I didn't say anything," he said, still grinning like an idiot.

My cell phone buzzed, and then buzzed again. "Hey, Chase," I said, already knowing why he was calling.

"Mom's cooking tonight. See you at five."

"I have to work. She knows I work weekends."

"Which is why it's family dinner instead of family lunch."

I sighed. "I don't get off until seven."

"From where? You're not working at the Red?"

"Yes . . ." I said, silently cussing myself for slipping. "I'm still bartending. I got a second job."

"A second job? Why?" he asked, his voice full of disdain. Chase was a pacemaker rep and thought he was hot shit. He made good money, but he liked to pretend he was a doctor when, in fact, he just fetched coffee to suck up to the staff.

"I'm . . . helping out a friend."

Chase was quiet for a long time, and then finally spoke. "Coby's using again, isn't he?"

I closed my eyes tight, not knowing what to say.

"Get your ass to Mom's at five, or I'm coming to get you."

"Fine," I said, hanging up and tossing my phone on the counter. I put my hands on my hips and stared at the computer monitor.

"Everything okay?" Trenton asked.

"I just started a huge family fight. My mom's heart is going to be broken, and it's all somehow going to be my fault. Cal?" I yelled. "I'm going to have to leave at four thirty."

"You don't get off until seven!" he yelled from his office.

"It's for family! She's leaving at four thirty!" Hazel yelled back.

"Whatever, then!" Calvin said, not sounding all that upset.

"Cal!" Trenton yelled. "I'm going with her!"

Calvin didn't answer, instead his door slammed, and he walked into the lobby. "What the fuck is going on?"

"Family dinner," I said.

Calvin watched me with suspicious eyes for a moment, and then looked to Trenton. "Have you seen Bishop today?"

Trenton turned his head. "Nope. Have not."

Calvin turned to me. "You really need backup to go home for dinner?" Calvin said, dubious.

"No."

"Yeah, she does," Trenton said. "Even though she won't admit it."

I couldn't keep the pleading tone from my voice. "You don't know what they're like. And tonight is going to be . . . you don't want to go, trust me."

"You need at least one person at that table on your side, and that's going to be me."

How could I argue with that? Even though I didn't want Trenton to see the insanity that was my family, it would be comforting when they inevitably decided that Coby's relapse and their ignorance of it was somehow my fault. And then there would be the moment when Coby found out I'd ratted him out.

"Just don't . . . punch anyone."

"Deal," he said, hugging me to his side.

CHAPTER EIGHT

Trenton pulled into the drive, and turned off the ignition. The last time we were in his Intrepid, Olive was in the back, and I was irritated about being coerced into a trip to Chicken Joe's. Now an evening with Trenton and Olive in a noisy restaurant sounded like heaven.

"You ready for this?" Trenton asked with a reassuring wink.

"Are you?"

"I'm ready for anything."

"I believe it," I said, pulling on the door handle. The door squealed as it opened, and then it took me a couple of tries and a push with my hip to get it to close all the way.

"Sorry," Trenton said, shoving his hands in his jeans pockets. He held out his elbow, and I took it. All of my brothers and my parents were standing at the open door, watching us walk up the drive.

"I'm the one who will be apologizing later."

"Why's that?"

"Who the fuck is this jackass?" Dad said.

I sighed. "This is Trent Maddox. Trent, this is my dad, Felix."

"It's Mr. Camlin," Dad sneered.

Trenton held out his hand, and Dad took it, staring him

down. Trenton wasn't the least bit intimidated, but I was still inwardly cringing.

"This is my mom, Susan."

"Nice to meet you," Trenton said, lightly shaking her hand.

Mom offered a small smile, and then pulled me into her chest, kissing my cheek. "It's about time you visit your mama."

"Sorry," I said, even though we both knew I wasn't.

We all walked into the dining room, except for Mom, who disappeared into the kitchen. She returned with an extra setting for Trenton, and then went back into the kitchen. This time, she came to the table with a steaming bowl of mashed potatoes that she set on a hot pad, next to all the other food.

"All right, all right," Dad said. "Sit down so we can get to eat already."

Trenton's eye twitched.

"It all looks great, Mom, thanks," Clark said.

Mom smiled, and leaned toward the table, "You're welcome, so—"

"What's with all the goddamn formalities? I'm starvin' here!" Dad growled.

We all passed the various dishes around the table and filled our plates. I picked at my food, waiting for the first shot that would start the war. Mom was on edge, which meant she knew something was up.

"What the hell is all that on your fingers?" Dad asked me.

"Uh . . ." I held up my hands for a moment, trying to think of a lie.

"We were messing around with a Sharpie," Trenton said.

"Is that what all that black shit is all over?" Dad asked.

"Ink. Yes," I said, rolling my food around on my plate. My

mother was an exceptional cook, but Dad always had a way of robbing me of my appetite.

"Pass the salt," Dad said, snapping at Coby when he took too long. "Damn it, Susan. You never put in enough salt. How many times have I told you?"

"You can add the salt, Dad," Clark said. "This way it's not too salty for the rest of us."

"Too salty? This is my goddamn house. She's my wife! She cooks for me! She cooks the way I like it, not the way you like it!"

"Don't rile yourself up, honey," Mom said.

Dad slammed the side of his fist on the table. "I'm not riled up! I'm just not going to stand for someone to come into my house and tell me how my wife should prepare my food!"

"Shut up, Clark," Chase growled.

Clark shoveled another bite into his mouth and chewed. He had been the peacekeeper for years, and still wasn't ready to give up. Out of all of my brothers, he was the easiest to be around, and to love. He delivered Coke products to convenience stores around town, and always ran behind schedule because the female employees would chat his ear off. He had a kindness in his eyes that couldn't be missed. He got that from our mother.

Dad nodded, and then eyed Trenton. "Does Cami know you from school, or work?"

"Both," Trenton said.

"Trent grew up in Eakins," I said.

"Born and raised," Trenton said.

Dad thought for a moment, and then narrowed his eyes. "Maddox . . . you're Jim's boy, aren't ya?"

"Yes," Trenton answered.

"Oh, I just loved your mother. She was a wonderful woman," Mom said.

"Thank you," Trenton said with a smile.

"For fuck's sake, Susan, you didn't even know her," Dad chided. "Why does everyone who dies have to turn into a god-damn saint?"

"She was pretty close," Trenton said.

Dad looked up, unappreciative of Trenton's tone. "And how would you know? Weren't you a toddler when she died?"

"Dad!" I yelled.

"Did you just raise your voice to me in my house? I oughta come across this table and slap your sass mouth!"

"Felix, please," Mom begged.

"I remember her," Trenton said. He was showing an exorbi-tant amount of control, but I could hear the strain in his voice. "Mrs. Camlin's memory is accurate."

"So you work with her at the Red?" Chase asked, unmistak-able superiority in his voice.

I'm not sure what expression was on my face, but Chase lifted his chin, defiant.

Trenton didn't answer. Chase was corralling us into a trap, and I knew exactly why.

"Which job, then?" Chase asked.

"Stop it," I said through my teeth.

"What do you mean which job?" Dad asked. "She only has one job, at the bar, you know that." When no one agreed, he looked to Trenton. "You work at the Red?"

"No."

"So you're a patron."

"Yes."

Dad nodded. I sighed in relief, grateful Trenton wasn't giving any more information than necessary.

"Didn't you say you were working a second job?" Chase asked.

I pressed my palms flat against the table. "Why? Why are you doing this?"

Coby caught on to what was happening, and stood up. "I just remembered. I have a . . . I have to make a phone call."

"Sit down!" Dad yelled. "You don't just stand up at the dinner table! What the hell's wrong with you?"

"Is this true?" Mom asked in her quiet voice.

"I took a part-time gig at Skin Deep Tattoo. It's not a big deal," I said.

"What? You can't pay your bills? You said that bartending job makes you a month's worth in one weekend!" Dad said.

"It does."

"So you're spending more than you're making? What did I tell you about being responsible? Damn it, Camille! How many times have I told you not to get the credit cards?" He wiped his mouth and threw his napkin on the table. "I didn't whip your ass enough as a child! If I had, you might listen to me once in a goddamn while!"

Trenton was staring at his plate, breathing faster, and leaning a bit forward. I reached over to touch his knee.

"I don't have credit cards," I said.

"Then why in God's name would you get a second job when you're still in school? That doesn't make any sense, and I know you're not stupid! No daughter of mine is stupid! So what is the reasoning?" he asked, yelling as if I were across the street.

Mom looked over at Coby, then, who was still standing, and the rest of my family did, too. When recognition lit my father's eyes, he stood up, pounding the table as he did. "You're on that shit again, aren't you?" he said, holding a shaking fist in the air.

"What?" Coby said, his voice raised an octave. "No, Dad, what the fuck?"

"You're on that shit again, and your sister is paying your bills? Are you out of your fucking mind?" Dad said. His face was red, and there was a line so deep between his eyebrows, the skin around it was white. "What did I tell you? What did I say would happen if you got near that shit again? Did you think I was joking?"

"Why would I think that?" Coby said, his voice shaking. "You don't have a sense of humor!"

Dad ran around the table and attacked Coby, and my mother and brothers tried to intervene. There was yelling, red faces, pointing, but Trenton and I just watched from our seats. Judgment and shock were absent from Trenton's face, but I was sunk back against my chair, completely humiliated. No amount of warning could have prepared him for the weekly Camlin circus.

"He's not using again," I said.

Everyone turned to me.

"What did you say?" Dad said with labored breath.

"I'm paying Coby back. He was short bailing me out a while back."

Coby's eyebrows pulled together. "Camille . . ."

Dad took a step toward me. "You couldn't say anything until now? Let your brother take the blame for your irresponsibility?" He took another step. Trenton turned his entire torso toward my dad, shielding me.

"I think you need to sit down, sir," Trenton said.

Dad's face morphed from anger to rage, and Coby and Clark

held onto him. "Did you just tell me to sit down in my own fucking house?" he said, screaming the last bit.

Finally Mom yelled, her voice breaking. "Enough! We're not a bunch of wild animals! We have a guest! Sit down!"

"See what you've done?" Dad said to me. "You've upset your mother!"

"Felix, sit!" Mom yelled, pointing at Dad's wooden chair.

He sat.

"I'm so sorry," Mom said to Trenton. Her voice was shaking as she nervously situated herself in her seat. She dabbed her eyes with her cloth napkin, and then put it gently in her lap. "This is very embarrassing for me. I can just imagine how Camille must feel."

"My family is pretty rowdy, too, Mrs. Camlin," Trenton said.

Under the table, his fingers began to ease up from where they had dug into my knee. I hadn't even noticed until that moment, but my fingers found their way to his, and I squeezed his hand tight. He squeezed back. His understanding made a wave of emotion crash over me, and I had to choke back tears. That feeling vanished quickly when Dad's fork scraped against his plate.

"When were you going to tell us that you were mooching off your brother, Camille?"

I looked up at him, suddenly angry. I knew the blame was coming, but having Trenton beside me made me feel a surge in confidence I'd never felt around my father. "When I thought you would behave like a mature adult about it."

Dad's mouth fell open, and so did Mom's.

"Camille!" Mom said.

Dad put his knuckles on the table and stood.

"Save your voice," I said. "We're leaving." I stood, and Trenton stood with me. We walked to the front door.

"Camille Renee! Get your ass back to this table!" Dad said.

I pulled opened the door. It had chips and dents in the bottom of the wood where my father had kicked the door open or closed during his many tantrums. I paused before pushing the lever on the screen door but didn't look back.

"Camille! I'm warning you!" Dad said.

I pushed open the door and tried not to sprint to the Intrepid. Trenton opened the passenger door, I got in, and then he walked around. He was rushing to get the keys into the ignition.

"Thank you," I said, once he pulled away.

"For what? I didn't do a damn thing," Trenton said, clearly unhappy about it.

"For keeping your promise. And for getting me the hell out of there before Dad came out to get me."

"I had to hurry. I knew if he made it out there and yelled at or threatened you one more time, I wouldn't be able to keep my promise."

"That was a waste of an afternoon off," I said, staring out the window.

"Why did Chase push the issue? What was the point in starting all that shit?"

I sighed. "Chase has ongoing resentment toward Coby. My parents have always treated Coby like he could do no wrong. Chase loves to rub Coby's addiction in everyone's face."

"So why did you bother going if you knew that he knew?"

I looked out the window. "Because someone needed to take the blame for it."

It was quiet for a few moments, and then Trenton grumbled, "Coby sounds like a good candidate."

"I know it sounds crazy, but I just need one of us to think they're good parents. If we all hated the way we were raised, it makes it more real, you know?"

Trenton reached over for my hand. "It's not crazy. I used to make Thomas tell me everything he remembered about Mom. I just have a few vague precious memories of her. Knowing his memories were more than just dreamlike, fuzzy moments made her more real to me."

I pulled my hand from his and touched my fingers to my lips. "I'm so embarrassed but so grateful that you were there. I never would have spoken to my dad that way if you weren't."

"If you ever need me, I'm just a phone call away." He snapped his fingers a few times, and then began singing—horribly—a very loud and heartfelt chorus from "I'll Be There" by the Jackson 5.

"That's a little high for you," I said, stifling laughter.

He kept singing.

I covered my face, and then the giggling began. Trenton sang louder, and I covered my ears, shaking my head and feigning disapproval.

"'Just look ova ya shoulders!'" he squawked.

"Both of them?" I asked, still giggling.

"I guess." He shrugged. "Mikey really does say that."

Trenton pulled into the parking lot of my apartment, and pulled into the spot next to my Jeep.

"You going out tonight?" I asked.

He turned to me, an apologetic frown on his face. "No. I need to start saving more money. I'm going to get a place of my own soon."

"Won't your dad miss your help with the rent?"

"I could move out now, but I'm saving up to help him, too. His pension ain't that great."

"You're going to keep paying rent to your dad after you move out?"

Trenton picked at his steering wheel. "Yeah. He's done a lot for us."

Trenton was nothing like I thought he was. "Thanks again. I owe you one."

One side of Trenton's mouth turned up. "Can I make you dinner?"

"In order to pay you back, I would need to make *you* dinner."

"You're paying me back by letting me cook at your place."

I thought for a minute. "Okay. Only if you bring me a list of groceries, and you let me buy."

"Deal."

I climbed out of the car and shut the door. The headlights painted my silhouette across the front of my apartment as I twisted the key in the dead bolt and then twisted the knob. I waved once to Trenton as he backed away, but then he pulled back into the parking spot, hopped out, and jogged to my door.

"What are you doing?"

"Isn't that . . ." He nodded toward a car driving fast in our direction.

"It's Coby," I said, swallowing hard. "You'd better go."

"I'm not going anywhere."

Coby's electric-blue Camaro jerked to a stop behind both my

Jeep and Trenton's Intrepid, and he hopped out, slamming the car door. I wasn't sure if I should insist he come inside so the neighbors wouldn't hear, or keep it outside to prevent my apartment from being trashed.

Trenton steadied himself, preparing to stop whatever Coby might do. Coby stomped toward me, his face severe, his eyes red and puffy, and then he crashed into me, wrapped his arms around me so tight I could barely breathe.

"I'm so sorry, Cami," he said between sobs. "I'm such a piece of shit!"

Trenton watched us, looking as surprised as I felt. After a short pause, I hugged Coby back, patting him with one hand. "It's okay, Coby. It's okay. We'll figure it out."

"I got rid of everything. I swear. I won't touch it again. I'll pay you back."

"Okay. It's okay," I said. We were rocking back and forth, and probably looked a little silly.

"Dad's still on a rampage. I couldn't listen to it anymore."

We both pulled away. "Come in for a little bit. I have to get ready for work soon, but you can hang out here until I leave."

Coby nodded.

Trenton shoved his hands in his pockets. "You need me to stay?"

I shook my head. "No, he's just upset. But thank you for sticking around to be sure."

Trenton nodded, glanced behind me, and then, as if it were the most natural thing in the world, leaned over to kiss my cheek, and then turned to walk away.

I stood in the doorway for a moment. The part of my skin where his lips touched still tingled.

"What happened to the guy from California?" Coby sniffed.

"He's still in California," I said, closing the door and leaning against it.

"Then what's the story with Trent Maddox?"

"He's just a friend."

Coby raised an eyebrow. "You've never brought a guy to the house. And I don't kiss my friends. Just sayin'."

"He kissed me on the cheek," I said, sitting next to him on the couch. "I think we have more important things to talk about, don't you?"

"Maybe," Coby said, deflated.

"Did you find a program?"

"I'm just going to quit cold turkey."

"That didn't work out so well last time, did it?"

Coby frowned. "I have bills to pay, Cami. If bill collectors start calling the house, Dad'll find out."

I patted his knee. "Let me worry about that. You worry about getting clean."

Coby's eyes lost focus. "Why are you so good to me, Cami? I'm such a loser." His face compressed, and he began to cry again.

"Because I know you're not."

Depression was one of the side effects of anabolic steroids, so it was important for Coby to get help with quitting. I sat with him on the love seat until he was calm, and then I got ready for work. He flipped on the television and sat quietly, probably glad to be away from the constant war that waged inside my parents' home. If Dad wasn't yelling at Mom, he was yelling at one of the boys, or they were yelling at each other. Just one more reason why I couldn't wait to get out of there. Living with that was enough to get depressed. Coby wasn't quite ready to move out on his own, so unlike the rest of us, he was stuck there.

After changing clothes and freshening up my makeup, I grabbed my purse and keys, and reached for the doorknob.

"You're just going to stay here?" I asked.

"Yeah," Coby said. "If that's okay."

"Don't do anything that will make me tell you no the next time you want to come over."

"I'm not staying long. Just maybe until Dad goes to sleep."

"Okay. Call me tomorrow."

"Cami?"

"Yeah?" I said, jerking to a stop, and poking my head back in.

"I love you."

I smiled. "Love you, too. It's going to be all right. I promise."

He nodded, and I jogged out to the Smurf, praying that it would start. Thank God it did.

My drive to work was spent worrying about Coby, and T.J., and Trent, and still trying to psych myself up for a busy Saturday night.

Raegan was already behind the east bar, prepping and wiping things down.

"Hey, lovey!" Raegan said. Her bright smile immediately fell when her eyes met mine. "Uh-oh. You went to your parents' today, didn't you?"

"How did you guess?"

"What happened?"

"Trent went with me, so it wasn't as bad as it could have been. Chase found out I had a second job."

"That shit head told your parents why, didn't he?"

"Pretty much."

Raegan sighed. "Always causing trouble."

"Have you been with Kody all day?"

Raegan's cheeks flushed. "No. We're sort of . . . on a break."

"On a what?"

"Ssh! On a break. Until I get some things figured out."

"Then where were you all day?"

"I stopped by Sig Tau. Just for a few hours before work."

"Sig Tau?" It took my brain a little bit to catch up. I watched her for a moment, and then shook my head. "He called you, didn't he?"

Raegan grimaced. "I'm not talking about this here. It's already awkward enough. Kody's here, so let's just sit on it until we get home."

I shook my head again. "You are so stupid. Brazil saw you happy with Kody, so he made the call. Now you're screwing up something good, and Brazil isn't going to change."

Kody walked up, looking wounded. "Uh, you guys need anything?"

Raegan shook her head, and so did I. Kody realized I knew something. His shoulders sagged, and he simply nodded and walked away.

"Damn it, Cami! I said not here!" Raegan hissed.

"Sorry," I said, counting my drawer. Saying anything else would have just made her angrier, so I kept my thoughts to myself.

The rush happened earlier than usual, and I was grateful for the distraction. Kody kept busy at the entrance, so I barely saw him until just before close. He was standing at the west wall, in a dark corner, watching Raegan. The DJ was playing their song, so it was particularly infuriating to see Brazil standing at the end of the bar, leaning across and smiling at Raegan, who was also leaning and smiling.

I couldn't believe she was being so cold to Kody. I walked

a pitcher of beer over to her, pretended to trip, and the entire pitcher went across the bar and all over Brazil. He jumped back, and held up his arms. It was too late: his brown plaid shirt and jeans were soaked.

"Cami!" Raegan squealed.

I leaned into her face. "Do you hear what song is playing? Kody is working the door, so you know he knows Brazil is here. No need to be a heartless bitch, Ray."

"I'm a heartless bitch? Let's not even talk about what you're doing."

My mouth fell open. Her knee-jerk reaction wasn't a surprise, but her bringing up Trenton was. "I'm not doing anything! We're just friends!"

"Yeah, let's label it something benign so you can sleep at night. Everyone else sees what you're doing, Cami. We're just not self-righteous enough to scold you for it."

Raegan popped the top on a beer, and exchanged it for money. She walked over to the register and furiously tapped in numbers like she was mad at them.

I might have felt bad if I hadn't looked across the room and seen that for just a moment, Kody didn't look quite so miserable.

Raegan walked up to stand beside me, her eyes on Kody across the room. "I didn't realize what song was playing."

"Did you realize Brazil was within kissing distance of your face in front of everyone not twenty-four hours after you dumped Kody?"

"You're right. I'll tell him to stay away." She reached up to the horn and pulled it, signaling last call. Kody shoved his hands in his pockets and walked toward the entrance.

"I guess Kody's walking me to my car tonight," I said.

"That would be better," Raegan said.

We cleaned our station and set up for the next night. Within an hour after close, we grabbed our coats. Raegan slung her purse over her shoulder and nodded at Gruber. "Walk me?" she asked.

Gruber hesitated, and Kody appeared at her side. "I can walk you."

"Kody . . ." Raegan began.

Kody shrugged, laughing once. "I can't walk you to the car? It's part of my job, Ray."

"Gruber can walk me, can't you, Gruby?"

"I . . . uh . . ." Gruber stuttered.

"C'mon, Ray. Let me walk you. Please?"

Raegan's shoulders fell, and she sighed. "See you at home, Cami."

I waved to her, and made sure to stay several feet back.

Gruber and I could hear Kody pleading with Raegan at her car all the way across the parking lot, and it broke my heart. Gruber stood with me at my car until Raegan got into hers. She followed me home, and when we pulled into the parking lot, I looked over, to see Raegan sobbing into her hands.

I opened her door. "Come on. We'll watch scary movies and eat ice cream."

Raegan looked up at me, her eyes red and puffy. "Have you ever loved two people at the same time?" she asked.

After a long pause, I held out my hand. "If I ever try, slap me, okay?"

CHAPTER NINE

At the height of the Red's Friday night crowd, Travis Maddox headed for his usual stool at my station, strutting across the bar like he always did: sexy, confident, and in command of the room. Shepley was with him, so was Shepley's girlfriend, America, and another girl—the one who I assumed he had been talking about the weekend before: the Freshman. I let the guy sitting in his usual seat know he was coming. He and his friend scattered without protest.

Travis straddled his stool. He ordered a beer, drank half of it in a few swallows, and then turned to watch the dance floor. The Freshman was out there, dancing with America.

Three girls were standing behind Travis, hovering like groupies, waiting for him to turn around.

America and her friend returned, smiling and sweaty. The Freshman was a knockout, I'd give Travis that. She had that something special that one might expect from the girl who finally caught Travis Maddox's attention, but I couldn't pinpoint it. There was a certain confidence in her eyes. She knew something that no one else knew.

"It's going to be like this all night, Mare. Just ignore them," Shepley said.

America snarled, and glanced over at the three women who were staring at Travis and whispering among themselves. I wasn't sure why America was so angry. They weren't looking at Shepley.

"It looks like Vegas threw up on a flock on vultures," America said.

Travis looked over his shoulder to see who America was talking about, and then turned back, chugging his beer. He lit a cigarette and puffed out a cloud of smoke. He looked at me and held up two fingers.

This should be interesting. I pulled two Bud Lights out of the cooler, popped the tops, and sat them in front of Travis.

One of the vultures picked one up, but Travis took it away from her. "Uh . . . not yours," he said, handing it to the Freshman.

The corners on the Freshman's mouth turned up just a tiny bit right before she chugged the beer for a few seconds.

"Can you make a—" Marty, Raegan's regular, began. Raegan was on the other side of the bar, having an intense conversation with Kody.

"Yes," I said, cutting him off. "Don't worry, Marty. I'll get you taken care of." As I was pouring Marty's particularly tricky Warninks Crème Egg Shooter, Travis and the Freshman were having a good time on the dance floor, making quite a scene. By the time Marty had finished his shot, Travis had already pissed her off, and she was storming away from him, toward the bar.

She offered me a half smile, and held up one finger. I pulled her a beer, popped the cap, and set it in front of her. She had sucked down more than half when Travis made it back to the bar. No wonder he was so unhappy about his feelings. The two of them were exhausting me, and I didn't even know her name yet.

Megan, Travis's tried-and-true Plan B, appeared next to him. "Well, if it isn't Travis Maddox."

Megan didn't cause a lot of drama, but she wasn't my favorite. In addition to Travis, she had a few other guys that she liked to chase around. But never when they wanted her, and never when they were single. She liked the challenge of taking a man away from his girlfriend, and women like that are the enemy of couples everywhere.

"What's going on?" Raegan said softly.

Just then, Travis pulled Megan by the hand out to the dance floor, and they proceeded to dry fuck each other in front of God and everyone else.

"Oh, Travis," I said, disappointed. "What the hell are you doing?"

Travis wasn't gone five minutes before Ethan Coats swooped in and appropriated Travis's stool. He leaned in, immediately turning on the charm. The Freshman appreciated the attention. I wouldn't have blamed her, if the attention weren't coming from Ethan.

"Oh, that's not good. Get that slime away from her!" Raegan hissed.

We all knew what Ethan had done, and what he was capable of. We tried to police him while he was at the bar, but not all girls would heed our warnings.

I saw Travis walking back to the east bar, his eyes targeting Ethan.

"I don't think I'll have to," I said.

Travis nearly stood in between them, and after a short exchange, Ethan was walking away with his tail tucked between his legs and Travis and the Freshman were on their way out, both seemingly on the verge of war.

Raegan smirked. "I think Travis Maddox has met his match."

"I think you're right," I said.

A full hour from last call, and I was already ahead in tips for the night. Raegan was in a good mood, despite Kody walking by every so often and stopping just long enough for her to tell him she couldn't talk.

I looked over to see Trenton take his cover charge change from Tuffy, and I gave him a nod and a smile. With the Maddox swagger no one could miss, he strolled over to the east bar and sat directly in front of me.

"Whiskey?" I asked.

"Water."

"Water?" I asked, in disbelief.

"I told you. I'm trying to save money."

"Water it is," I said.

Trenton took a sip, and then sat the glass down, looking around. "I saw Travis yelling at some chick in the parking lot."

"Oh? How did that turn out?"

"She yelled back. I don't know who she is, but I kind of like her."

"Me, too."

Trenton stared at the ice floating in his glass. "It's kind of weird. Watching him try to settle down."

"You think that's what he's doing?"

"He's talked to you about her, hasn't he?"

I nodded.

"There you go."

I watched him for a while. Something was off with him, but I couldn't figure out what it was. "Anything you want to talk about?"

He pondered that for a moment. "Nah. There's no point." He took another sip of water. He glanced behind him and noticed someone standing at the pool tables. "I'm going to head over."

"Okay," I said. I shouldn't have been disappointed that he didn't seem all that interested in talking to me. Just a few weeks before, he'd come to the Red for drinks, to hang out with his brothers, or to find a piece of ass. But as he crossed the dance floor and picked up a pool stick, his arms flexing as he polished the tip with the cue, a weird feeling came over me.

"What's up with him?" Raegan asked.

"I don't know. Glad it's not just me that noticed."

"What's up with you? You had a look on your face when he walked away. Did he say something?"

"No," I said, shaking my head. "You wouldn't believe me if I told you."

"I'm your best friend. I probably already know."

"It's hard to explain . . . I . . . just got this bizarre, sad feeling. Like Trent and I aren't friends anymore."

"Maybe it's because you know that he finally believes you're just friends."

"Maybe. I mean no," I said, backpedaling.

"I knew it, bitch. I don't even know why you try." She stood behind me and wrapped her arms around my waist, resting her chin on my shoulder.

We both watched as a couple of girls who had just arrived walked over to the west wall and hovered around Trenton's pool table. The pair were obviously familiar with bleach in a box, but as much as I hated to admit it, they were both stunningly beautiful. Within twenty minutes, a third girl joined them. It wasn't long before she had Trenton's full attention, and he had her backed against the pool table. She was twirling one strand of her long, brown hair around her finger, laughing as if Trenton were the funniest person she'd ever met. Her cackling could be heard over the music.

"Christ on a cracker, I'm ready to go home," Raegan said, turning to touch her temple to my shoulder.

"Me, too," I said, watching Trenton lean closer to the girl's face.

Even across the room, I could see she had supermodel lips and bedroom eyes. He was looking down at her, smiling. It was kind of revolting how close they were. I'd never seen her before, so she had probably come over from Southwestern State. It was likely that Trenton had never met her either, and less than half an hour later, they were inches apart.

Trenton put his hands on the pool table, and her ass was nestled tightly in between them. She leaned up to his ear and whispered.

Five minutes before last call, a rowdy crowd walked in and came to the east bar calling drinks, even though most of them had already had more than a few. As I began to get back into busy mode, I caught a glimpse of Trenton leading the girl outside by the hand. I instantly felt sick to my stomach.

"You okay?" Raegan called to me, popping the top off several beers at the same time.

"Fine," I said. I wasn't sure if she could hear me, but it didn't matter. She knew the truth.

CHAPTER TEN

A KNOCK AT THE DOOR STARTLED ME AWAKE. ANOTHER SET of knocks made me fully awake. Then the pounding began. I crawled out of bed, cringing when the bright, early morning sun struck my face the second I walked into the hall.

I stumbled across the living room and opened the door.

"What in the hell are you doing here?" I asked.

"She slept in hew clowes," Olive said in her sweet, tiny voice.

I looked down, shielding the sun from my eyes with my hands. "Oh, hi, Olive. Sorry, I didn't see you down there," I said, unable to stop frowning, even for her.

"It's okay," she said. "Twent says I'm showt."

"We brought you breakfast," Trenton said, holding up a white sack.

"I don't eat breakfast."

"Yes, you do. Raisin cinnamon bagels with butter. Kody told me."

The two lines that were already formed between my eyebrows grew deeper. I glared at Trenton, and then looked down to Olive. My expression softened, and I sighed. "I love her," I said to no one in particular. "Olive, you know I love you, but I'm going back to bed." I looked at Trenton, and narrowed my eyes. "It's not going to work this time. Take her home."

"I can't. Her parents are out all day."

"Then take her to your home."

"My dad's got a cold. You don't want her to get a cold, do you?"

"You know what I hate?" I asked.

Trenton had desperation in his eyes. "Me. I know. I just . . . I'm a selfish, insecure idiot."

"Yes."

"But I'm a sorry selfish, insecure idiot with a little girl outside in the cold."

It was my turn to sigh. I waved for Olive to come in. She happily complied, sitting on the couch. She immediately found the remote and flipped on the television, turning to Saturday morning cartoons.

Trenton took a step and I held out my hand. "Not you."

"What?"

"You don't get to come in."

"But . . . I'm watching Olive."

"You can watch her from the window."

Trenton crossed his arms across his chest. "You think I won't?"

"No, I know you will." I grabbed the white sack from his hand, and then slammed the door in his face, locking the door. I tossed Olive the sack. "You like bagels, kiddo?"

"Yep!" she said, opening the sack. "Aw you weally going to make Twent stand outside?"

"Yes, I am," I said, walking back to my room, and falling into my bed.

✦   ✦   ✦

"Cami!" Raegan said, shaking me. I looked at the clock. It had been almost two hours since Trenton had knocked on my door. "That little girl is watching cartoons in our living room!" she whispered, clearly uneasy.

"I know."

"How did she get there?"

"Trent brought her."

"Where's Trent?"

"Outside, I think," I said, yawning.

Raegan stomped out to the living room, and then back to my room. "He's sitting on the ground outside our window, playing Flappy Bird on his cell phone."

I nodded.

"It's thirty-three degrees outside."

"Good," I said, sitting up. "I wish it were sleeting."

Raegan's face screwed into disgust. "He waved at me like it was the most normal thing in the world. What the hell is going on?"

"He brought Olive over. His dad has a cold, so he couldn't bring her home, and her parents are somewhere else all day."

"So he couldn't watch her at her house?"

I thought about that for a moment, and then crawled out of bed for the second time that day. I walked over to the couch. "Why didn't Trent watch you at your house?" I asked.

"I wanted to come see you," she said matter-of-factly.

"Oh," I said. "Trenton didn't want to see me?"

"Yes, but he said you wouldn't like it."

"Oh?"

"Yeah, so then I said, pweety, pweety pwease? And he said okay."

I smiled at her, and then walked over to the front door, opening it. Trenton turned around, and looked up at me. My smile vanished. "Come in."

Trenton stood up and walked inside, but that's as far as he got. "You're mad at me."

I narrowed my eyes at him.

"Why?" he asked.

I didn't answer.

"Is it because I went home with that girl last night?"

I still didn't answer.

"I didn't bag her."

"You want a cookie?" I asked. "Because that is prize worthy."

"What is your deal? You tell me five times a day that we're friends, and now you're jealous of some girl I flirted with for two seconds."

"I am *not* jealous!"

"Then what are you?"

"As your friend, I can't be concerned about your STD status?"

"What's an ust edie?" Olive asked from the love seat.

I closed my eyes tight. "Oh, God. I'm sorry, Olive. Forget you heard that."

Trenton took a step toward me. "Her parents let me babysit her. You think they're worried about foul language?"

I raised an eyebrow.

He lowered his chin, looking straight into my eyes. "Tell me the truth. Are you angry at me because you thought I took that girl home, or is it something else? Because you're mad at me for something."

I crossed my arms and looked away.

"What are we doing, Cami?" he asked. "What is this?"

"We're friends! I've told you that already!"

"Bullshit!"

Olive's finger hovered over the top of the love seat. "You have to put a nickow in my jawr."

"Sorry," Trenton said, his eyebrows pushed together.

"So you didn't . . . go home with her?" I asked.

"Where was I going to take her? My dad's?"

"I don't know, a hotel room?"

"I'm not buying drinks to save money, you think I'm going to spend a hundred bucks on a hotel room for some random chick I just met?"

"You've done less intelligent things."

"Like what?"

"Like eat glue!"

Trenton tucked his chin and looked away, clearly disgusted, and maybe a little bit embarrassed. "I never ate glue."

I crossed my arms. "Yes, you did. In Mrs. Brandt's class."

Raegan shrugged. "You did."

"You weren't in my class, Ray!" Trenton said.

"You also ate red pencils fairly regularly, according to Cami!" Raegan said, trying to stifle a laugh.

"Whatever!" Trenton yelled. "Where's my bagel?"

The white sack hovered above the love seat, the wrinkled, rolled top held by Olive's tiny fingers. Trenton sat beside his friend, fought with the sack, and then pulled out his breakfast, unwrapping it.

Raegan looked at me and held three fingers over her mouth. Her body jerked with a silent laugh like a tiny hiccup, and then she retreated to her room.

"I never ate glue," Trenton grumbled.

"Maybe you blocked it out. I would block it out if I ate glue . . ."

"I didn't eat glue," he snapped.

"Okay," I said, my eyes widening for a moment. "God."

"You want . . . you want half of my bagel?" Trenton asked.

"Yes, please," I said.

He handed it to me, and we ate together, quietly, while Olive watched cartoons between us. Her little feet just barely hung off the edge of the seat cushion, and she bounced them up and down once in a while.

After two cartoons, I drifted off and woke up when my head fell forward.

"Hey," Trenton said, patting my knee. "Why don't you go take a nap? We can go."

"No," I said, shaking my head. "I don't want you to go."

Trenton stared at me for a minute, and then motioned for Olive to trade places with him. She hopped up, more than happy to comply. Trenton sat next to me, leaning over a bit, and then nodded, gesturing to his shoulder. "It's comfy. Or so I hear."

I made a face, but instead of arguing, I wrapped my arms around his, and rested my head snugly between his shoulder and his neck. Trenton rested his cheek against my hair, and at the same time we took a deep breath and relaxed against each other.

I don't remember anything after that, until my eyes blinked open. Olive was asleep, her head on Trenton's lap. His arm was lying protectively over her, the other wrapped in my arms. His hand was resting on my thigh, and his chest rose and fell in a peaceful rhythm.

Raegan and Brazil were sitting on the sofa, watching the muted television. When Raegan realized I was awake, she smiled.

"Hey," she whispered.

"What time is it?" I said softly.

"Noon."

"Really?" I said, sitting up.

Trenton roused, and immediately checked Olive. "Whoa. How long have we been out?"

"A little over three hours," I said, wiping under my eyes.

"I didn't even know I was tired," Trenton said.

Brazil smiled. "I didn't know you were dating the bartender. Kyle and Brad will be disappointed."

I frowned at him. I didn't even know who Kyle and Brad were.

"They can cheer up. We're just friends," Trenton said.

"Really?" Brazil said, watching us both for signs of a joke.

"I told you," Raegan said, standing up. Her tank top came away from her teeny-tiny pink-and-white-striped boxers as she stretched. "Brazil has a game at four thirty. You guys up for some Bulldog Football?"

"I'm watching Olive," Trenton said. "We were going to ask Cami to come with us to Chicken Joe's."

"Olive might like football," Brazil said.

"Jason . . ." Trenton said, shaking his head. "Chicken Joe's outdoes a football game by like . . . a thousand cool points."

"How do you know unless you take her to one?"

"I have. She still hasn't let me live it down."

"Is she your baby cousin or something?" Brazil asked. "Why is she with you all the time?"

Trenton shrugged. "She had an older brother. He would have

been fourteen today. She worshipped him. He was hit by a car on his bike a few months before they moved next door. Olive sat next to him while he took his last breath. I'm just trying to fill the shoes."

"That's rough, man, but . . . and I mean no offense . . . but, you're a Maddox."

"Yeah? So?" Trenton said.

"I know you're a good guy, but you're a tatted-up, whiskey-drinking, foul-mouthed hothead. Her parents just let her get in the car with you?"

"It was just a natural progression, I guess."

"But . . . why is she your responsibility?" Brazil said. "I don't get it."

Trenton looked down at Olive, who was still sound asleep. He brushed a wispy ash-blond strand from her eyes, and then shrugged. "Why not?"

I smiled at his simple show of affection. "Chicken Joe's it is. But I'll have to cut out early to get ready for work."

"Deal," Trenton said with a smile, as if it were the easiest thing in the world.

"Well, I have errands to run," Raegan said.

"I've got to grab some carbs and head to the field house," Brazil said. When he stood, he patted Raegan's backside, leaned over to kiss her, and then grabbed his wallet, phone, and keys before slamming the door behind him.

Olive's eyes popped open.

"Yay!" Trenton said. "She's awake! Now we can EAT HER!" He leaned over and pretended to bite her belly while tickling her.

She giggled hysterically. "Nooooo. I have to peeeee!"

"Whoa!" Trenton said, holding up his hands.

"This way," I said, leading Olive by the hand to the bathroom in the hall. Her bare feet padded against the tile floor. "TP, soap, hand towel," I said, pointing to the various items.

"Got it," she said. She looked so tiny standing in the middle of the bathroom. She raised her eyebrows. "Are you going to stay?"

"Oh! No. I'm sorry," I said, backing out and closing the door.

I turned and walked over to Trenton, who was standing in the walk space between the breakfast bar and the love seat.

"She's pretty great," he said, smiling.

"You're pretty great," I said.

"Yeah?" he asked.

"Yeah." We stared a quiet moment, just watching each other and smiling, and then a familiar feeling came over me, a tingling in my gut, and a warmth on my lips. I focused on his mouth, and he took a step toward me.

"Trent . . ."

He shook his head, leaned in, and closed his eyes. I did the same, waiting to feel his lips on mine.

The toilet flushed, and we both pulled away. The air between us was suddenly thick and tense. As the anticipation of what we were about to do melted away, an overwhelming awkwardness replaced it.

Olive stood in the hallway, staring at us. She itched her elbow, and then her nose. "Lunch?"

I offered an apologetic half smile. "I need to make a grocery run."

"Good plan," Trenton said, clapping his hands and then rubbing them together. "Supermarket?"

Olive grinned from one ear to the other. "Can I sit in the basket that's also a cawr?"

Trenton looked to me, while helping Olive with her coat.

"Sure!" I said, realizing now why Trenton was so dedicated to making her happy. Making her smile was addictive.

Olive did a little dance, and then Trenton began to dance. He looked absolutely ridiculous, so I joined in, too.

We danced all the way out to the parking lot, with no music at all. Trent pointed to his Intrepid, but I stopped at my Jeep.

"You always drive. I'll drive this time. I have more trunk space for groceries, anyway."

"You don't have a trunk," Trenton said.

"I have a trunk equivalent."

"I have Olive's car seat."

"It's fairly easy to switch out, isn't it?"

Trenton shook his head. "I . . . have a thing. About riding with girls."

"Is that because of Mackenzie, or is that a sexist remark?"

"Since the accident."

I nodded. "Okay, then. But you're going to let me reimburse you for gas."

"You can pitch in for dinner," he said.

"Rock on," I said, then I bent my elbow and held my fist in the air, lifting my index finger and pinky.

Olive looked at her own hand and tried to do the same. "Wok on!" she said, once she mastered it.

We drove to the store, and while we walked down the aisles, I felt very domestic, and it was a little exciting. Not that I wanted kids of my own or anything—yet—but doing something so mundane with Trenton was oddly exhilarating. But the feeling didn't last long. T.J. and I had never done anything like this, and now this simple grocery trip made me feel shame. Even though it made no sense whatsoever, a flash of resentment burned through my veins. I couldn't be happy with T.J., and now he was robbing me of happiness when he wasn't around, too. Of course it wasn't his fault, but it was easier to blame him than to acknowledge my own shortcomings.

Nothing made sense anymore: why we were still together, why I was spending so much time with Trenton, or why I stayed in a barely-there relationship when I had someone who liked me— and who I liked—two feet away, just waiting for a green light.

Most people would just give up, but they didn't have T.J. He had come into the Red one night, asked for my number an hour later, and in a few days we went on our first date. I didn't even have to think about it. Being with him just made sense. T.J. pretty much spent the next week and a half at my apartment, and then for the next three months, he flew home every other weekend. After that, his project began, and I'd only seen him a handful of times. I stopped in the aisle, pretending to look over the soups, but I was really frozen, wondering why I was so committed to T.J., when I wasn't even sure if we were in a real relationship at this point.

T.J. hadn't texted me in three days. Before, I reasoned that he was busy with work. But suddenly, realizing what it was like to spend so much time with someone—and loving it—the sporadic texts, phone calls, and the hope of seeing each other one day wasn't enough. Not even close.

"Chunky vegetable beef with brown gravy?" Trenton asked, holding up a large can. "This is good shit."

I smiled and gripped the push bar of the grocery cart. "Throw it in. It's going to come in handy soon when the nights get even colder."

"You can borrow me anytime. I'm perfect for sweater weather."

"Be careful. I might hold you to that."

"Don't threaten me with a good time." He stopped in the middle of the aisle. "Wait. Really?"

I shrugged. "You were pretty comfortable today."

"Comfortable? I'm fucking cashmere."

I burst out laughing, and shook my head. We pushed the basket that doubled as a kid-size car while Olive pretended to steer and crash into things.

"I bet your California boyfriend isn't as comfortable as I am," Trenton said as we turned down the deli aisle.

"It's cold!" Olive said, pretending to shiver. Trenton shed his coat and draped it over her. I reached out for a package of deli meat and tossed it into the basket.

"I don't know," I said. "I don't really remember how soft he is."

"What is that like? Being with someone you never see?"

"Military wives do it all the time. I don't really see a point in complaining."

"But you're not his wife."

"Not sure how I could be if we don't see each other more often."

"Exactly. So, what keeps you going?"

I shrugged. "I can't put my finger on it. There's just something about him."

"Does he love you?"

Trenton's direct and very personal question made the muscles in my neck tense. It felt like an attack on our relationship, but I knew those feelings of defensiveness were so strong because Trenton was asking questions that I had asked myself many times. "He does."

"But he loves California more? He's in school, right?"

I cringed. I didn't like talking specifics about T.J. T.J. didn't like me talking specifics, either. "It's not school that keeps him there. It's his job." Trenton shoved his hands into his pockets. He was wearing a brown leather cuff around his wrist, a brown leather braided bracelet, and the bracelet Olive had made for him. "Do you ever take Olive's bracelet off?" I asked.

"I promised her I wouldn't. Don't change the subject."

"Why do you want to talk about T.J.?"

"Because I'm curious. I want to know what makes you stay in a relationship like that."

"Like what?"

"Where you're not a priority. I don't get the sense that this guy is an idiot, so I'm trying to figure it out."

I bit my lip. Trenton was being endearing and making me feel sick about T.J. all at the same time. "It's kind of like you and Olive. It might not make sense to people standing on the outside, and it sounds weird even when he tries to explain, but he has responsibilities that are important."

"So are you."

I leaned into his side, and he put his arm around me, squeezing me even tighter.

CHAPTER ELEVEN

After ham and cheese sandwiches, a movie, and a short trip to Chicken Joe's, Trenton and Olive were on their way to her house, and I was on my way to the Red. I could see my breath as I walked to the employees' side entrance, and kept my coat on until more bodies filtered in and warmed the bar.

"Holy flippindip!" Blia said, rubbing her hands together as she passed by. "It's colder than a frog's ass in January!"

"And it's only October," I grumbled.

The Saturday night crowd never came in, and three hours after we reported for work, it was still dead. Raegan propped her chin with her fist, and clicked the nails of the other hand on the bar. Two guys were playing pool over by the west wall. One of them was wearing a Legend of Zelda T-shirt, and the other guy's clothes were so wrinkled, he looked like he'd dressed straight from the dirty laundry hamper. They weren't the sort to attend an underground fight, so it wasn't hard to guess what had stolen our business.

Raegan's regular, Marty, was sitting alone at her end of the bar. He and the pimply faced boys at the pool tables, they were our only patrons, and it was ten o'clock.

"Goddamn it. Goddamn those fights. Why can't they have them during the week when it won't cut into our tips?" Raegan said.

"They'll come after, and then the whole bar will be one big fight, and you'll wish they had all stayed away," I said, sweeping the floor for the third time.

Kody walked by, glancing at Raegan from the corner of his eye. He depended on being busy to get through a whole night of Raegan being across the room. He had been moping around for two weeks, and taking his frustration out on the drunken idiots who dared fight on his side of the bar. The Wednesday before, Gruber had had to pull Kody out of the heap. Hank had already spoken to him once, and I was afraid if he didn't snap out of it soon, he was going to get fired.

Raegan glanced over at him, just for a moment, when she was sure he wasn't looking.

"Have you talked to him?" I asked.

Raegan shrugged. "I try not to. He makes me feel like an asshole when I'm *not* talking to him, so I'm not eager to start a conversation."

"He's upset. He loves you."

Raegan's face fell. "I know."

"How are things with Brazil?"

Her face lit up. "He's busy with football and Sig Tau, but there's a Valentine's date party. He asked me yesterday."

I raised an eyebrow. "Oh. So it's like . . . this is serious."

Raegan pulled her mouth to the side, looked at Kody, and then looked down. "Brazil was my first love, Cami."

I reached out and touched her shoulder. "I do not envy you. What a shitty situation."

"Speaking of first loves . . . I think you're his," she said, nodding toward the entrance.

Trenton strolled in, a big smile on his face. I couldn't help but match his expression. From the corner of my eye, I could see Raegan watching us, but I didn't care.

"Hey," he said, leaning forward against the bar.

"I thought you would be at the fight."

"Unlike boyfriends in California, I have my priorities straight."

"Very funny," I said, but my stomach fluttered.

"What are you doing later?" he asked.

"Sleeping."

"It's really cold outside. I thought maybe you'd need the extra layer."

I tried not to smile like an idiot, but I couldn't help it. He was having that effect on me lately.

"Where the hell did Ray sneak off to?" Hank said.

I shrugged. "It's fight night, Hank. We're dead. I can handle it."

"Who fucking cares where she is?" Kody said. His arms were crossed as he leaned his back against the bar. He was watching the near empty room with a frown on his face.

"Did you get that job?" Hank asked.

"No," Kody said, shifting.

Hank put his hands on each side of his mouth in an attempt to amplify what he was about to yell, and then took a breath. "Hey, Gruby! Send Blia over here to cover for Raegan while she's outside, would ya?"

Gruber nodded and walked toward the kiosk. I cringed, wishing Hank hadn't reminded Kody and everyone else that Raegan was likely outside, talking to Brazil.

Kody's entire face crumpled.

I felt bad for him. He hated the job he once loved, and none of us could blame him. Hank had even given him a good reference for the hardware store where Kody had applied.

"I'm sorry," I said. "I know it's hard for you."

Kody turned to look at me, a wounded expression on his face. "You don't know shit, Cami. If you did, you would have talked some sense into her."

"Hey," Trenton said, turning around. "What the fuck, dude? Don't talk to her like that."

I motioned for Trenton to stand down, and I crossed my arms, ready for the full force of Kody's frustration to blow my way. "Ray does what she wants, Kody. You of all people know that."

His jaws danced under his skin, and he looked down. "I just . . . I don't get it. We were good. We didn't fight. Not really. Stupid shit about her dad sometimes, but most of the time we had fun. I loved spending time with her, but I gave her space when she needed it. She loved me. I mean . . . she said she did."

"She did," I said. It was hard watching him talk. He was leaning against the bar like it was hard to stand.

I reached across to put my hand on his shoulder. "You're just going to have to accept that it doesn't have anything to do with you."

He shrugged away from me. "He's just using her. That's the worst part. I love her more than my life and he doesn't give a shit about her."

"You don't know that," I said.

"Yeah, I do. You don't think the guys at Sig Tau talk, Cami? You don't think they're discussing your drama, too? They're worse than the Cap Sig girls, sitting around gossiping about who's fucking who. And then it trickles down to me and I have to hear about all of it."

"*My* drama?" I glanced around. "I don't have drama."

Kody pointed at Trenton. "You're racing toward it at ninety miles an hour. You shouldn't mess with that, Cami. They've been through enough."

Kody walked away, and I stood, stunned for a few moments.

Trenton made a face. "What the fuck is that supposed to mean?"

"Nothing," I said. I kept my face smooth, pretending that my heart wasn't trying to beat through my chest. T.J. and I weren't exactly a secret, but we didn't broadcast our relationship. I was the only one from our little town that knew the nature of his job, and it was important to him that we kept it that way. A little bit of knowledge led to questions, and avoiding questions meant keeping secrets. It really hadn't been that big a deal because we'd never given anyone a reason to talk about us. Until now.

"What's he talkin' about, Cami?" Trenton asked.

I rolled my eyes and shrugged. "Who fucking knows? He's just mad."

Kody turned around and touched his chest. "You don't know what I'm talking about? You're not any better than her, and you know it!" He walked away again.

Trenton was completely confused, but instead of sticking around to explain, I pushed up on the hinged piece of the bar, let it slam down behind me, and followed Kody across the room. "Hey. Hey!" I yelled a second time, jogging to catch up to him.

Kody stopped, but he didn't turn around.

I tugged on his shirt, forcing him to face me. "I'm not Raegan, so stop taking your anger out on me! I have tried to talk to her. I was rooting for you, damn it! But now you're being a whiny, pouty, intolerable asshole!"

Kody's eyes softened, and he began to say something.

I held up my hand, not interested in what was likely going to be an apology. I pointed at his broad chest. "You don't know *dick* about my personal life, so don't *ever* talk to me like you do. Do we understand each other?"

Kody nodded, and I left him standing in the middle of the room to return to my post.

"Fuckity squared," Blia said, her eyes wide. "Remind me to never piss you off. Even the bouncer is scared of you."

"Camille!" a voice said from the other side of the bar.

"Oh, hell," I said under my breath. Out of habit, I tried to make myself small, tried not to be noticed, but it was too late. Clark and Colin were waiting patiently for me on Blia's end of the bar. I walked over to them and faked a smile. "Sam Adams?"

"Yes, please," Clark said. He was the least offensive of my brothers, and most of the time I wished we were closer. But on the average day, being around one meant being around all of them, and that wasn't an environment I wanted to tolerate anymore.

"Uncle Felix is still pissed at you," Colin said.

"Christ, Colin. I'm at work."

"I just thought you should know," he said, a smug look on his face.

"He's always pissed at me," I said, pulling two bottles out of the cooler and popping the tops. I slid them across the bar.

Clark's face fell. "No, but Mom's had to stop him from taking off for your apartment every time he and Coby get into it."

"Jesus, he's still on Coby's ass?" I asked.

"It's been pretty . . . unstable at their house lately."

"Don't tell me," I said, shaking my head. "I can't listen to it."

"He's not," Colin said, frowning. "My dad said Felix swore he'd never do that again."

"Not that it would matter if he did," I grumbled. "She'd still stay."

"Hey, that's their business," Colin said.

I glared at him. "That was my childhood. She's my mother. It's my business."

Clark took a swig of his beer. "He's mad because you missed family lunch again today."

"I wasn't invited," I said.

"You're always invited. Mom was disappointed, too."

"I'm sorry, but I can't deal with him. I have other things I'd rather do."

Clark's brows pulled together. "That's harsh. We're still your family. We'd all still take a bullet for you, Camille."

"What about Mom?" I asked. "Would you take a bullet for her?"

"Damn it, Cami. Can you just let it go?" Colin asked.

I raised an eyebrow. "No, and Chase, Clark, and Coby shouldn't, either. I have to work," I said, returning to my side of the bar.

A large hand wrapped around my arm. Trenton stood when he saw Clark grab me, but I shook my head and turned.

Clark sighed. "We've never been the type of family to gush about our feelings, but we're still family. You're still family. I know he's a lot to take sometimes, but we still have to keep it together. We have to try."

"You're not in his crosshairs, Clark. You don't know what it's like."

Clark's jaw worked under the skin. "I know you're the oldest, Cami. But you've been gone for three years. If you think I don't know what it's like to take the brunt of his anger, you're wrong."

"Then why pretend? We're hanging on by a thread. I'm not even sure what's keeping us together anymore."

"It doesn't matter. It's all we've got," Clark said.

I watched him for a while, and then pulled them both another beer. "Here. These are on me."

"Thanks, sis," Clark said.

"You okay?" Trenton asked when I walked back to my station.

I nodded. "They said Dad's still pissed about Coby. I guess Dad and Coby have been fighting a lot. Dad's been threatening to come over and set me straight."

"Set you straight how, exactly?"

I shrugged. "When my brothers fall out of line, it somehow always falls back on me."

"How does that play out? When he comes over pissed off?"

"He's never come to my apartment before. But, I suppose if he's mad enough, one of these days he will."

Trenton didn't respond, but he shifted in his chair, seeming very unsettled.

Blia came over and showed me the display on her cell phone. "Just got a text from Laney. She said the fight is over and most of them are headed this way."

"Woo!" Raegan said as she walked behind the bar. She pulled out her empty tip jar—a hurricane glass—and set it on top of the bar. Marty immediately pulled out a twenty and dropped it in.

Raegan winked at him and smiled.

Trenton patted the bar a few times. "I'd better head out. Don't want to be here when the dumb fucks from the fight get here and I end up almost killing someone. Again."

I winked at him. "Mr. Responsible."

"Text me later. I wanna hang out tomorrow," he said, walking away.

"Again?" Raegan asked, her eyebrows floating near her hairline.

"Shut up," I said, not wanting to even hear her opinion.

The postfight crowd trickled in at first, and then the Red was standing room only. The DJ was playing upbeat music, but it didn't matter: the men were drunk and they all thought they were as invincible as Travis Maddox.

Within half an hour, Kody, Gruber, and Hank were all breaking up fights. At one point, most of the bar was in one massive clash, and Hank was throwing dozens out at a time. Police cruisers were parked outside, helping with the masses, and arresting some of the rowdier guys for public intoxication before they could get into their vehicles.

Before long, the bar was a ghost town again. The club music returned to classic rock and Top Forty, and Raegan was counting her tips, grumbling, and once in a while shouting a single curse word.

"Between you helping your brother and these shitty tips, we'll be lucky to make bills this month. I need to start saving for a party dress sometime."

"So bet on Travis," I said. "That's an easy fifty."

"I have to have money to bet on Travis, first," she snapped.

Someone sat down, hard, onto one of the barstools in front of me. "Whiskey," he said. "And keep 'em coming."

"Were your ears burning, Trav?" I asked, handing him a beer. "Doesn't seem like a whiskey night to me."

"You wouldn't be the only females talking shit about me." He tilted back his head and let the amber liquid slide down his throat, nearly in one gulp. The glass bottle crashed to the bar, and I popped the second top, setting the bottle before Travis.

"Someone's talking shit on you? Not very smart of them," I said, watching Travis light a cigarette.

"The pigeon," he said, crossing his arms over the top of the bar. He leaned, hunched over, looking lost. I watched him for a moment, unsure if he was talking code or already drunk.

"Did you get hit harder than usual tonight?" I asked, genuinely concerned.

Another large group walked in, probably stragglers from the fight. They were happier and seemed to all get along, at least. Travis and I had to pause our conversation. For the next twenty minutes or so, I was too busy to chat, but when the last of the postfight crowd pushed through the red door to head home, I sat a glass of Jim Beam in front of Travis, and then topped it off. He still looked depressed. Maybe even more than before.

"Okay, Trav. Let's hear it."

"Hear what?" he asked, leaning away.

I shook my head. "The girl." That was the only explanation for Travis Maddox having that look on his face. I'd never seen it before, so that could only mean one thing.

"What girl?"

I rolled my eyes. "What girl. Seriously? Who do you think you're talking to?"

"All right, all right," he said, looking around. He leaned in. "It's Pigeon."

"*Pigeon?* You're joking."

Travis managed a small laugh. "Abby. She's a pigeon. A demonic pigeon that fucks with my head so bad I can't think straight. Nothing makes sense anymore, Cam. Every rule I've ever made's getting broken one by one. I'm a pussy. No . . . worse. I'm Shep."

I laughed. "Be nice."

"You're right. Shepley's a good guy."

I poured him another drink, and he slammed it back.

"Be nice to yourself, too," I said as I wiped off the counter. "Falling for someone isn't a sin, Trav. Jesus."

Travis's eyes bounced from side to side. "I'm confused. You talking to me, or Jesus?"

"I'm serious," I said. "So you have feelings for her, so what?"

"She hates me."

"Nah."

"No, I heard her tonight. By accident. She thinks I'm a scumbag."

"She said that?"

"Pretty much."

"Well, you kinda are."

Travis frowned. He wasn't expecting that. "Thanks a lot."

I poured him another drink. He tossed it down his throat before I could pull another beer from the cooler. I set the beer on the bar, and then held out my hands, palms up. "Based on your past behavior, do you disagree? My point is . . . maybe for her, you could be a better man."

I poured him another shot. He immediately tilted back his head, opened his throat, and let it all wash down.

"You're right. I've been a scumbag. Could I change? I don't fuckin' know. Probably not enough to deserve her."

Travis's eyes were already glassing over, so I set the bottle of Jim Beam back in its home, and then turned to my friend. He lit another cigarette. "Toss me another beer."

"Trav, I think you've had enough already," I said. He was too drunk to realize that he already had one.

"Cami, just fucking do it."

I grabbed the glass bottle not six inches away, and placed it directly in his line of sight.

"Oh," he said.

"Yeah. Like I said. You've had plenty to drink in the short time you've been here."

"There's not enough liquor in the world that could make me forget what she said tonight." His words were slurring. Shit.

"What exactly did she say?" I asked.

"She said I wasn't good enough. I mean . . . in a roundabout way, but that's what she fucking meant. She thinks I'm a piece of shit, and I . . . I think I'm falling for her. I don't know. I can't think straight anymore. But when I got her home after the fight, and I knew she was there for a month"—he rubbed the back of his neck—"I think that's the happiest I've ever been, Cami."

My brows pulled together. I'd never seen him so distraught. "She's staying with you for a month?"

"We made a bet tonight. If I didn't get hit, she had to move in for a month."

"That was your idea?" I asked. Damn. He was already in love with this girl and didn't even know it.

"Yeah. I thought I was a fucking genius up until an hour ago." He tilted the glass. "Another."

"Nope. Drink your damn beer," I said, pushing it toward him.

"I know I don't deserve her. She's"—his eyes lost focus—

"incredible. There's something in her eyes that's familiar. Something I can relate to, ya know?"

I nodded. I knew exactly what he meant. I felt that way about a pair of eyes that looked a lot like his.

"So maybe you should talk to her about it," I said. "Don't have one of those stupid misunderstandings."

"She's got a date tomorrow night. With Parker Hayes."

My nose wrinkled. "Parker Hayes? Haven't you warned her about him?"

"She wouldn't believe me. She'd just think I was saying that because I'm jealous."

He was swaying in his chair. I was going to have to call him a cab.

"Aren't you? Jealous?"

"Yeah, but he's also a shit stick."

"True."

Travis tilted his beer bottle and took a big swig. His eyelids were heavy. He wasn't pacing himself at all.

"Trav . . ."

"Not tonight, Cami. I just want to get drunk."

I nodded. "Looks like you've accomplished that. Want me to call a cab?"

He shook his head slightly.

"Fine, but find a ride home." He tried to take another swig of his beer, but I held onto the neck of the bottle until he made eye contact. "I mean it."

"I heard you."

I let go, and then watched him finish off the bottle.

"Trent was talking about you the other day," he said.

"Oh yeah?"

"I'm going to get her a puppy," Travis said. At least he was too drunk to stay on the subject of Trenton. "Think Trent will keep him for me?"

"How am I supposed to know?"

"Aren't you guys attached at the hip these days?"

"Not really."

Travis's face compressed. "This is awful," he said, his words melding together. "Who fucking wants to feel like this? Who would purposefully do this to themselves?"

"Shepley," I said with a smile.

He raised both eyebrows. "You ain't fuckin' kiddin'." After a short pause, his face fell. "What do I do, Cami? Tell me what to do, because I don't fuckin' know."

I shook my head. "You're sure she doesn't want you?"

Travis looked up at me with sad eyes. "That's what she said."

I shrugged. "Then you try to forget about her."

Travis looked down at his empty bottle. The two girls from State who Trenton had left behind the night before began buying Travis drinks, and before long, he could barely stay on his stool. For the next hour and a half, he'd fully committed to finding the bottom of every bottle he could get his hands on.

The Southern State sisters took a stool on each side of Travis. I walked away, tending to my regulars for a while. I wouldn't be surprised if they thought he was Trenton. The youngest four Maddox boys looked so much alike, and Travis was wearing a white T-shirt that looked a lot like what Trenton had been wearing.

From the corner of my eye, I saw one of the girls drape her leg over Travis's thigh. The other turned his face, and then they were sucking face in a way that made me feel like a pervert for watching.

"Uh, Travis?" I said.

He stood up and threw a one-hundred-dollar bill on the bar. He held his finger up to his lips, and then winked. "This is me. Forgetting."

The girls walked on each side of him, and he leaned on them, barely able to walk.

"Travis! They better be your ride home!" I yelled.

He didn't acknowledge me.

Raegan laughed. "Oh, Travis," she said. "He's certainly entertaining."

I crossed my arms across my stomach. "I hope they get a hotel room."

"Why?" Raegan asked.

"Because the girl he's in love with is at his apartment. And if those State girls go home with him, he is going to wake up in the morning and hate himself."

"He'll figure a way out of it. He always does."

"Yeah, but this time it's different. He was pretty desperate. If he loses that girl, I don't know what he'll do."

"He'll get drunk, and then get laid. That's what all the Maddox boys do." I craned my neck at her, and she offered an apologetic smile. "I warned you a long time ago not to get mixed up with them. You have yet to listen to any of my advice."

"You should talk," I said, reaching up and pulling the horn for last call.

CHAPTER TWELVE

I CAN'T BELIEVE YOU LET HIM TALK YOU INTO KEEPING THE dog," I said, shaking my head.

Trenton stretched out on my couch, covering his eyes with his arm. "It's just for a couple more days. Travis is throwing Abby a surprise party on Sunday, and he's going to give it to her then. The puppy's actually kind of cute. I'm going to miss him."

"Did you name him?"

"No," Trenton said, making a face. "Okay, I kind of named him. But Abby's going to name him, so it's not permanent. I explained that to him."

I chuckled. "Are you going to tell me?"

"No, because it's not his name."

"Tell me anyway."

Trenton smiled, his arm still covering his eyes. "Crook."

"Crook?"

"He steals my dad's socks and hides them. He's a little criminal."

"I like it," I said. "Raegan's birthday is coming up, too. I need to get her something. She's so hard to shop for."

"Get her one of those GPS stickers for her keys."

"That's not a bad idea. When is your birthday?"

Trenton smiled. "July fourth."

"Bullshit."

"I'm not bullshitting you."

"Is your real name Yankee Doodle?"

"I haven't heard that one before," he deadpanned.

"Aren't you going to ask when mine is?"

"I already know."

"No, you don't."

He didn't hesitate. "May sixth."

My eyebrows shot up.

"Chamomile. I've known since, like, the fourth grade."

"*How* do you remember that?"

"Your grandparents sent you balloons every year on the same day until you graduated."

My eyes wandered as my mind did. "One balloon for every year. I had to stuff eighteen balloons into the Smurf my senior year. I miss them." I snapped out of it. "Wait a minute . . . you *are* bullshitting me. Isn't Travis's birthday April Fool's Day?"

"April first, yeah."

"And yours is on Independence Day?"

"Yeah, and Thomas's is on St. Patrick's Day, and the twins were born January first."

"You are such a liar! Taylor and Tyler's birthday is in March! They came in to celebrate at the Red last year!"

"No, Thomas's birthday is in March. They came to help him celebrate and just said it was their birthday to get free shots."

I glared at him.

He chuckled. "I swear!"

"Maddox boys can't be trusted."

"I resent that."

I looked at my watch. "It's almost time for work. We better get going."

Trenton sat up, and then rested his elbows on his knees. "I can't keep coming to see you at the Red every night and then working all day. It's exhausting."

"No one said you have to."

"No one pulls this schedule if they don't have to. Only if they really want to. And I really want to."

I couldn't stop the grin that touched my lips. "You should try working all night at the Red and then working all day."

"Quit your bitchin', ya big baby," he teased.

I held my fists together. "That's Baby Doll to you."

Someone knocked on the door. I frowned, looked at Trenton, and then walked over to the entry way, and looked through the peephole. It was a man about my age, with big eyes, flawlessly coifed hair, and a face so perfect he looked like he had walked straight out of a Banana Republic catalog. He wore a mint-green Oxford button-down, jeans, and loafers. I recognized him but wasn't sure from where, so I kept the chain on the door when I opened it.

"Hi," he said, chuckling nervously.

"Can I help you?"

He leaned over and touched his hand to his chest. "I'm Parker. My friend Amber Jennings lives next door. I saw you coming home last night as I was heading home, and I thought maybe you'd like to—"

The chain clinked when it fell, and Trenton opened the door the rest of the way.

"Oh," Parker said. "Maybe not."

"Maybe not," Trenton said. "Get the fuck outta here, Parker."

"You two have a good day."

Trenton nodded once, and I shut the door.

"I knew he looked familiar. People look different outside of the Red."

Trenton sneered. "I've hated that shit stain since high school."

"You barely knew him in high school."

"He was a country club brat. His parents own that Italian restaurant downtown."

"So?"

"So, I don't want him sniffing around here," he said. "Guys like him think the rules don't apply to them."

"What rules?"

"Rules of respect."

"Is that what that was about?" I said, gesturing to the door.

"What are you talking about?"

"That whole unnecessary scene you just made."

Trenton shifted his weight, agitated. "He was getting ready to ask you out!"

"So?"

Trenton frowned. "He's a bottom feeder!"

"So?"

"So I didn't want him to!"

"I'm perfectly capable of turning someone down. You just wanted to intimidate him so he wouldn't come around again."

"He was watching you walk to the apartment this morning. I find that a little predatory. Excuse the fuck out of me for wanting him to think you have a guy around."

I crossed my arms. "Oh, is that what you were doing?"

"Yes. It was."

"Had nothing to do with you wanting to eliminate the competition?"

He wrinkled his nose, insulted. "That is assuming I would ever have competition. Which I don't. Definitely not from Parker fucking Hayes."

I narrowed my eyes at him. "You're right, because we're just friends."

"Christ, Cami, I know. You don't have to keep rubbing it in my face."

My eyes widened. "Wow. Rubbing it in your face? Okay."

Trenton laughed, frustrated. "How can you not know? Everyone else in the entire fucking world knows but you!"

"I know. I'm just trying to keep things simple."

Trenton took a step toward me. "This isn't simple. Not even close."

"It *is* simple. Black and white. Cut and dry."

Trenton grabbed me by the shoulders and planted a kiss on my mouth. Sheer shock made my lips hard and unforgiving, but then they melted against his, along with the rest of my body. I relaxed, but my breathing picked up, and my heart beat so loud I was sure Trenton could hear it. His tongue slipped between my lips, and his hands slid down my arms to my hips, his fingers digging into my skin. He pulled my hips against his as he kissed me, and then sucked my bottom lip when he pulled away.

"Now it's complicated." He grabbed his keys and shut the door behind him.

I reached for the knob and leaned on my hand, trying not to fall over. I had never in my life been kissed like that, and something told me that wasn't even the best Trenton Maddox could do. The way his tongue moved against mine would have caused the vertigo I was feeling even if I had expected him to kiss me. The way the muscles in his forearms moved when his hands pulled at me was like he couldn't get close enough, but they were controlled, in the way only two experienced hands could be. My pulse was racing, throbbing throughout my entire body every time my heart crashed against my chest. I was speechless, and breathless, and defenseless.

Standing alone in my apartment felt strange, when thirty seconds before I had experienced the best kiss of my life. My thighs tensed just thinking about it.

Still breathing hard, I glanced at the clock in the kitchen. Trenton had come over early to hang out before work, and now he was on his way to Skin Deep. I should have been in the Smurf, heading over there, too, but I wasn't sure if I could.

Not only would it be awkward, but I had just cheated on T.J. Why would any guy, especially Trenton, want a cheater? All this time we'd been spending together, and then the fact that I didn't land a solid punch to his nose the second his mouth was on mine made me guilty. He was right. He'd just made this so complicated that we could never pretend we were just friends again. Not after that kiss, not after that touch, and definitely not after the way he made me feel.

I pulled my cell phone from my back pocket and speed-dialed.

"Skin Deep," Hazel answered.

"Hey, it's Cami. I'm not going to make it today."

"Are you sick?"

"No . . . it's . . . complicated. Really, *really* complicated."

"I get it. No problem, but that sucks for me. Sundays are boring, and now it's going to suck even worse."

"Sorry, Hazel."

"No worries. I'll tell Cal."

"Thanks," I said. "Hopefully he won't fire me for calling in so soon after starting the job."

Hazel blew air through her lips. "Truthfully, we're not busy enough on Sundays for a receptionist. He's not going to say anything."

"Okay. Later," I said.

I put on my shoes, grabbed my purse, and drove the Smurf to the Red. Hank's black Jaguar XKR sat alone in the parking lot. I parked next to it, allowing plenty of room between vehicles, and pulled my coat tightly around me as I walked across the parking lot.

Queen was playing over the speakers when I walked in, and Hank was lying on the east bar, looking up at the ceiling.

"What are you doing, crazy?" I asked.

"Relaxing before Jorie gets here. I'm going to ask her to move in with me today."

My eyebrows shot up. "Seriously? Congratulations, Hank, that's awesome."

He sat up and sighed. "Only if she says yes."

"What is your ex going to say about it?"

"I talked to Vickie on Friday. She's okay with it. Jorie gets along great with the boys."

"Wow," I said, taking in a deep breath. I sat on the stool next to him. "That's a big deal."

"What if she says no?" he said. There was a worry in his voice that I'd never heard before.

"Then you'll figure it out."

"What if she says no and then dumps me?"

I nodded slowly. "That would be bad."

He hopped off the bar. "I need a drink."

"Me, too."

Hank poured whiskey into two glasses, and then slid one closer to me. I took a drink and frowned. "Whoa. What is this?"

"Magic," he said, taking a drink, too. "I love her, Cami. I don't know what I'd do if she said no."

"She loves you, too," I said. "Focus on that."

Hank's eyebrows pulled in. "Why are *you* drinking?"

"I cheated on T.J."

"When?"

"Half an hour ago."

Hank's eyes widened for just a moment. "With who?"

I paused, hesitant to say it aloud. "Trent."

His eyes got wide again, and he mumbled something in Italian.

"Yeah, what you said." I took another drink, finishing off the glass. My cell phone rang, and I turned it over. It was Trenton.

"Hello?"

"Hazel said you're not coming in. You okay?"

"Uh . . ."

"Are you sick?"

"No."

"Then why aren't you coming to work?"

"I have a bad case of awkward as fuck."

"Because I kissed you?" he asked, incensed. I could hear Hazel in the background.

"You kissed her?" Hazel squealed. "You bad ass motherfu—"

"You made it complicated! You can't complain now!" I said.

"What the fuck does it matter if I kissed you?"

"Because! I have! A boyfriend!" I yelled into the phone.

"Will he even notice? You haven't spoken to him in a week!"

"That's none of your business!"

"Yes, it is! You're my business!"

"Fuck off!"

"You fuck off!" he yelled back. We were both quiet for a while, and then Trenton finally spoke. "I'm coming over after I get off work."

"No," I said, rubbing my temple. "You messed everything up, Trent. It's . . . it's too weird, now."

"That's stupid. Everything is the same," he said. "The only difference is that now you know I'm a damn good kisser."

I couldn't help but smile.

"I won't surprise attack your face. I just want to see you," he said.

The truth was, I had gotten used to him being around, but if we kept spending so much time together, I needed to end things with T.J. . . . but I wasn't sure I wanted to do that.

"No," I said, and disconnected the call.

My phone rang again.

"Hello?"

"Did you just hang up on me?" Trenton asked, annoyed.

"Yes."

"Why?"

"Because I was finished talking."

"You can't say good-bye?"

"Good-bye . . ."

"Wait!"

"That's why I hung up. I knew you wouldn't let me say good-bye."

"You're really going to cut me out of your life because of one fucking kiss?"

"Was that all it was?" I asked.

Trenton fell quiet.

"That's what I thought." I hit End again.

He didn't call back.

Hank stood across from me, and we both drank our troubles away. We finished one bottle, and he opened another. We were giggling and being stupid by the time Jorie walked in the door. Hank tried to pretend he was sober but failed miserably.

"Hello, my love," he said.

"Hi," Jorie said, smiling. She hugged him, and he wrapped his arms around her, squeezing her long, pearly waves against her back. She studied both of us, but it didn't take her long to come to a conclusion. "You guys have been here a while. Got into the stash, huh?"

Hank grinned as he weaved back and forth. "Baby, I wanted to—"

"Hank," I said, shaking my head quickly before Jorie could see me. Jorie turned, and I smiled at her.

"What are you two up to?" she asked.

"A bottle and a half," Hank said, chuckling at his own joke.

Jorie took the rest of the bottle away from us and placed it back in the lower cabinet, locking it and putting the key in her pocket. She was wearing black shorts that looked like mini tuxedo pants, and a pretty champagne-colored, see-through blouse that revealed her black lacy bra. Her black heels were sky-high, but she still wasn't as tall as Hank.

"I'm going to put a pot of coffee on. We don't want the employees thinking it's a good idea to come to the Sunday employee meeting hammered."

Hank kissed her cheek. "Always thinking. What would I do without you?"

"Drink the rest of the bottle," she teased. She picked up the empty pot and filled it with water. "Oh, damn. I forgot we're out of filters."

"No, they came in this morning," Hank said, slurring. "They're still in the back room."

"I'll go grab them," she said.

"I'll go with you," Hank said, cupping her backside as they walked together.

I swiped the screen on my phone, contemplating the phone call I was about to make. Before I punched in the numbers, I opened my message screen instead. It was such a cowardly thing to do, but I did it, anyway.

You got a minute?

Can't talk long. Miss you like crazy. What's up?

We need to talk.

I was afraid you'd say that.

Call me as soon as you can.

I'd planned on it.

He was always so sweet. Was I really going to break things off with him because he'd been busy? He had warned me about this, and I agreed to try. I promised it wouldn't be an issue. Then again, we'd barely spoken, with no hopes of the situation improving. And then there was the little matter of Trenton. It didn't really matter if I broke things off with T.J. Going from T.J. to Trenton would still feel wrong, even if I waited six months. Even if I waited six years. I had been running around with Trenton behind T.J.'s back. Anything that came out of that was tainted.

Kody wasn't within miles of being right about me. I wasn't doing the same thing as Raegan. It was much worse. At least she had the decency to break up with Kody before she started seeing Brazil again. She didn't string along two men at the same time. She was honest with both of them, and I had tried to lecture *her*.

I covered my eyes with my hand, so ashamed that I couldn't even face an empty room. Even if spending time with Trenton was fun or comforting in the moment, I knew what it meant to Trenton, and how I would feel if T.J. were doing the same thing. Seeing them both—whether it involved sex or not—was dishonest. T.J. and Trenton both deserved better than that.

I kissed him.

I hit Send, and instantly my hands began to shake. Several minutes went by before T.J. sent a reply.

Who?

Trenton.

You kissed him, or he kissed you?

Does it matter?

Yes.

He kissed me.

Figures.

Now what?

You tell me.

I've been spending a lot of time with him.

What does that mean?

Idk. It is what it is.

Do you still want to be with me?

The question is, do you still want to be with me?

Again, I had to wait several minutes for him to respond. When my cell phone pinged, I had to force myself to look at the words on the screen. Even if I deserved it, I didn't want him to throw me away like the trash that I was.

I'm booking you a flight to California.

CHAPTER THIRTEEN

My flight was at seven thirty. I left the employee meeting early to pack, and then tried not to let thoughts of Trenton sneak into my mind as I drove the Smurf to the airport. I glanced down at my left hand, which sat atop the steering wheel. Together, my fingers read DOLL. T.J. was not going to approve, and I hoped to God he didn't ask why I'd chosen those words.

Parking, catching a shuttle, and getting checked in seemed to take forever. I hated being in a rush, but T.J. had booked me on the last flight out, and no matter what, I was going to get on that plane. I needed to know that I wasn't just falling out of love with T.J. because of the distance.

I stood in the long line at security and heard my name being called from across the room. I turned to see Trenton running full speed toward me. A TSA agent took a step, but when Trenton slowed down next to me, he relaxed.

"What the hell are you doing?" he asked, his chest heaving. He put his hands on his hips. He was wearing red basketball shorts, a white T-shirt, and a worn, red Sig Tau ball cap. My stomach fluttered at the sight of him, more because I felt caught than flattered.

"What the hell are *you* doing?" I said, glancing around at all the people staring at us.

"You said I'd see you tomorrow, and now you're getting on a fucking plane?" A woman several people ahead of me covered her young daughter's ears. "Sorry," Trenton said.

The line moved forward, and I moved with it. Trenton moved with me. "It was kind of last-minute."

"You're going to California, aren't you?" he asked, looking wounded.

I didn't answer.

We took a few more steps. "Because I kissed you?" he asked, this time louder.

"He booked the ticket, Trent. Was I supposed to say no?"

"Yes, you say no! He hasn't bothered to see you in over three months, and all of a sudden he's booking you a ticket? C'mon!" he said, letting his hand fall to his thigh.

"Trent," I said quietly, "go home. This is embarrassing." The line moved forward again, and I took a few steps.

Trenton sidestepped until he was next to me. "Don't get on that plane." He said the words without emotion, but his eyes were begging me.

I laughed once, trying to somehow make light of the situation. "I'll be back in a few days. You act like you're never going to see me again."

"It'll be different when you get back. You know it will."

"Please stop," I begged, glancing around. The line moved again.

Trenton held out his hands. "Just . . . give it a few days."

"Give what a few days?"

He took off his hat and rubbed the top of his head while he thought. The desperate expression on his face forced me to swallow back a sob. I wanted to hug him, to tell him it was okay, but how could I comfort him, when I was the reason he was hurting?

Trenton returned his hat to his head, pulling it down low over his eyes in frustration. He sighed. "Jesus Christ, Cami, *please*. I can't do it. I can't be here, thinking about you there, with him."

The line moved forward again. I was next.

"Please?" he asked. He laughed once, nervous. "I'm in love with you."

"Next," the TSA agent said, motioning for me to approach his podium.

After a long pause, I cringed at the words I was about to say. "If you knew what I know . . . you wouldn't be."

He shook his head. "I don't wanna know. I just want you."

"We're just friends, Trent."

Trent's face and shoulders fell.

"Next!" the agent said again. He had been watching us talking, and wasn't in a patient mood.

"I have to go. I'll see you when I get back, okay?"

Trenton's eyes fell to the ground, and he nodded. "Yeah." He started to walk away but turned around. "We haven't been just friends for a while. And you know it." He turned his back to me, and I handed my ticket and ID to the agent.

"You okay?" the agent asked, scribbling on my ticket.

"No," I said. My breath caught, and I looked up as my eyes filled with tears. "I'm a huge asshole."

The agent nodded, and motioned for me to move on. "Next," he called to the person behind me.

+   +   +

I didn't want to move, just in case it was a dream. As a child, when I visited the homes of my friends, I began to realize that other dads weren't like mine, and that a lot of other families were happier than mine. From that moment, I dreamed about moving out on my own, if for nothing else more than to just have a little peace. But even adulthood seemed more like a source of constant disappointment than adventure, so just to be sure this moment of happiness wasn't some dirty trick, I stayed still.

This immaculate and minimalist town house was exactly where I wanted to be: wearing nothing but a satisfied smile, tangled in white Egyptian cotton sheets, in the middle of T.J.'s king-size bed. He was lying next to me, breathing soft and deep through his nose. He would have to wake up in a few minutes to get ready for work, and I would get a great view of his tight backside as he crawled out of bed. That, of course, wasn't the problem. The next eight hours left alone with my own thoughts would take this staycation from nirvana to nerve-wracking.

A plethora of doubts had crowded my mind during the flight, making me wonder if this time was the last time. Months of built-up nervousness continued right up to the moment I saw him in baggage claim, but then I saw his smile. The same smile that made lying there with him feel like the right kind of wrong.

Maybe I'd serve breakfast in bed to celebrate our first twelve hours together in months? Maybe not. That was me trying too hard again, and I was done being that girl. I would never be that girl again. Raegan had said it perfectly while I furiously packed the evening before:

What happened to you, Cam? Confidence used to radiate off

you. Now you're like a whipped puppy. If T.J. isn't it, you can't control it, anyway, so you might as well stop worrying about it.

I didn't know what happened between me being that amazingly confident girl and now. Actually, yes, I did. T.J. walked into my life, and I'd spent the last six months trying to deserve him. Well, half of that time anyway. The other half I spent doing the opposite.

T.J. turned his head and kissed my temple. "Morning. Want me to run to the corner and get breakfast?" he said.

"That sounds amazing, actually," I said, kissing his bare chest.

T.J. gently pulled his arm out from underneath me and sat up, stretching for a few moments before standing up and giving me the view I'd been fantasizing about for over three months.

He slipped on the jeans that were folded over the chair, and pulled a T-shirt from the closet. "Everything bagel and cream cheese?"

"And orange juice. Please."

He slipped his sneakers on and grabbed his keys. "Yes, ma'am. Be right back," he called out before closing the front door behind him.

Obviously, I didn't feel undeserving of him because T.J. was an asshole. It was the reverse. When someone this amazing walks into your bar and asks for your number before he's had a single drink, you work your tail off to keep him. Somewhere along the way, I'd forgotten that I'd managed to snag him in the first place. And then I'd forgotten about him altogether.

But the moment T.J. wrapped his arms around me in baggage claim, I immediately compared the way he held me with the way Trenton had. When T.J. put his lips on mine, his mouth was just as amazing as I remembered, but it didn't feel like he needed me the way Trenton did. I was glaringly aware that I was making unfair and unnecessary comparisons, and tried not to the moment it happened, but I failed—every time, on every level. Whether it was fair or not, Trenton was what I knew, and T.J. had become unfamiliar.

Ten minutes later, T.J. jogged back in, placed the bagel on my lap, and the orange juice on the nightstand. He kissed me quickly.

"They called you?"

"Yeah, early meeting. I'm not sure what's going on, so I'm not sure when I'm coming home."

I shrugged. "It's okay. I'll see you when I see you."

He kissed me again, quickly undressed, put on a pressed white shirt and a dark gray suit, and slipped on his shoes before jogging out the door with a tie in his hand.

The door slammed.

"Bye," I said, sitting alone.

I lay back down, looking up at the ceiling and picking my nails. His town house was quiet. No roommate, no pet. Not even a goldfish. I thought about the fact that Trenton would probably be sitting next to me on the love seat at home, watching anything with me while I prattled on about work, or school, or both. How nice it was just to have someone that wanted to be around me, in any capacity. Instead, I was staring up at a white ceiling, noticing how nicely it stood out against the clay beige walls.

Beige was so T.J. He was safe. He was stable. But anything could look good from a few thousand miles away. We never fought, but you don't have anything to fight about if you're never around one another. T.J. knew what kind of bagel I liked, but did he know that I hate commercials, or what radio station I listen to, or that the first thing I do when I get home from work is take off my bra? Did he know that my dad is a grade-A asshole, or my brothers were both endearing and intolerable? Did he know that I never make my bed? Because Trenton did. He knew all of that, and he wanted me anyway.

I reached over and checked my phone. An email from Single in Your Area Now, but that was it. Trenton hated me, and that was about right, because he asked me to choose, and I didn't choose him. Now I was lying naked in another man's bed, thinking about Trenton.

I covered my face, and cussed the hot tears as they ran down my temples and into my ears. I wanted to be here. But I wanted to be there. Raegan had asked me if I'd ever been in love with two men. I didn't know at the time that I already was. Two men who couldn't be more different, and yet were so alike. Both lovable, and insufferable, but for completely different reasons.

Dragging the sheet along with me, I climbed from the bed and walked around T.J.'s tidy town house. It looked staged, as if no one really lived there. I suppose for the most part, no one did. A few silver square frames sat atop a narrow table that stood against the living room wall. They contained black-and-white photos of T.J. as a child, with his siblings, his parents, and one of him and me on the pier during my first visit.

The television was black, the remote control sat perfectly straight on an end table. I wondered if he even had cable. He'd rarely have enough downtime to watch it. *Men's Health* magazine and *Rolling Stone* sat on top of the glass coffee table, spread apart like a hand of cards. I picked one up and flipped through it, suddenly feeling restless and bored. Why had I come? To prove to myself that I loved T.J.? Or that I didn't?

The couch barely gave when I sat down. It was light gray, tweed, with brown leather piping. The fabric felt itchy against my back. The space had a completely different feel to it compared to the last time I was there. The musky yet clean smell wasn't as appealing. The view from the large windows, with a glimpse of the bay, wasn't as magical; T.J.'s brand of perfection wasn't as mesmerizing anymore. Just a few weeks with Trenton had changed all of that. Suddenly it was okay to want messy, and flaws, and uncertainty, so much of what Trenton embodied . . . everything I saw in myself that I thought I didn't like. Because even if we were struggling, we had goals. It didn't matter that we weren't there yet. What mattered is that we both experienced setbacks, and full-blown failures, but we got up, brushed ourselves off, and kept going—and were making the best of it. Trenton didn't just make all of those things acceptable; he made getting there fun. Instead of feeling ashamed of where we weren't, we could be proud of where we were going, and what we would overcome to get there.

I stood and walked over to the long windows, looking down at the street below. Trenton had found out what I was up to, raced to the airport, and begged me to stay. If I was the one on the other side of the security ropes, would I forgive him? Thinking about him feeling rejected and alone on his drive home made tears sting my eyes. As I stood in the perfect place owned by the perfect man, I wrapped his sheets tighter around me and let the tears fall, wishing for the struggling tattoo artist I'd left behind.

I had spent my childhood craving my first day of freedom. Almost every day for the better part of eighteen years, wishes were spent on tomorrow. But for the first time in my life, I wished that I could go back in time.

CHAPTER FOURTEEN

I SAID I WAS SORRY," T.J. SAID, STARING AT ME FROM UNDER his brow.

"I'm not upset."

"You're a little upset."

"No. I'm really not," I said, rolling a piece of my Marinated Steak Salad around on my plate.

"You don't like the salad?"

"No, I do," I said, acutely aware of my facial expressions and every movement I made. It was exhausting trying to prove I wasn't pouting. T.J. didn't get home until after eight thirty, and he didn't text or call the entire time. Not even when he was on his way home.

"Want to try some of my fish?" He was within two bites of finishing his Alaskan Sea Bass, but pushed his plate forward. I shook my head. Everything smelled wonderful, but I just didn't feel like eating, and it had nothing to do with T.J.

We were at a corner table, against the far wall of T.J.'s favorite neighborhood restaurant, Brooklyn Girl. The gray walls and simple but modern décor looked a lot like his apartment. Clean, everything in its place, and yet inviting.

T.J. sighed and sat back against his chair. "This isn't going how I wanted at all." He leaned forward, putting his elbows on the table. "I work fifty hours a week, Camille. I just don't have time for . . ."

"Me," I said finishing the cringeworthy sentence for him.

"Anything. I barely see my family. I talk to you more than I do them."

"Thanksgiving?"

"It's looking more likely as this assignment moves forward."

I offered a small smile. "I don't mind that you were late. I know you work long hours. I knew I wouldn't see you much when I got here."

"But you came," he said, reaching across the table for my hand.

I sat back, putting my hands in my lap. "But I can't drop everything every time you decide you want to see me."

His shoulders fell, but he was still smiling. For whatever reason, he was amused. "I know. And that's fair."

I leaned forward again to poke at my salad with the fork. "He came to the airport."

"Trenton?"

I nodded.

T.J. was quiet for a long time, and then he finally spoke. "What's going on with you two?"

I squirmed in my seat. "I told you. We've been spending a lot of time together."

"What kind of time together?"

I frowned. "We watch TV. We sit around and talk. We go out to eat. We work together."

"Work together?"

"At Skin Deep."

"You quit the Red? Why didn't you tell me?"

"I didn't quit. Coby had some trouble paying bills. I took a second job until he got back on his feet."

"I'm sorry. About Coby."

I nodded, not really wanting to get too far into that subject.

"Did Trenton do that?" he asked, lowering his chin and looking at my fingers.

I nodded.

He took in a deep breath, just as he was taking in the reality of the situation. "So you mean you spend a *lot* of time together."

I winced. "Yes."

"Has he spent the night?"

I shook my head. "No. But we . . . he . . ."

T.J. nodded. "Kissed you. You mentioned that. Is he seeing anyone?"

"Just me, mostly."

T.J. raised an eyebrow. "Has he been to the Red?"

"Yes. But no more than usual. Maybe even less."

"Still taking girls home?" he said, half joking.

"No."

"*No?*" he asked, surprised.

"Not at all. Not since . . ."

"He started pursuing you." I shook my head again. T.J. looked down. "Wow." He laughed once in disbelief. "Trenton's in love." He looked up at me. "With you."

"You act surprised. You loved me once, you know."

"I still do."

I closed my eyes tight. "How? How could you possibly feel that way after everything I've just told you?"

He kept his voice low. "I know I'm not good for you right now, Camille. I can't be there for you like you need me to be, and probably can't for a long time. It's hard to blame you when I know that our relationship is based on sporadic phone calls and texts."

"But you told me that when we met. You said it would be this way, and I told you that it was okay. That I was willing to make it work."

"Is that what you're doing? Sticking to your word?" T.J. searched my eyes for a moment, and then sighed. He drank the last bit of his white wine, and then set the empty glass down on the side of his plate.

"Do you love him?"

I froze for a moment, feeling like a cornered animal. He'd been giving me the third degree since the server set our dinner on the table, and I was becoming emotionally exhausted. Seeing him for the first time, and then being alone with my thoughts all day . . . it was too much. I was a runner without anywhere to go. My flight didn't leave until the next morning. Finally, I covered my face with my hands. Once I closed my eyes, the tears were pushed over my lower lids and down my cheeks.

T.J. sighed. "I'm going to say that's a yes."

"You know how you know you love someone? You get that feeling that doesn't go away. I still feel that for you."

"I feel the same way. But I always knew this would be too hard on you."

"People do it all the time."

"Yes, but they talk more than eight or nine times a month."

"So you knew it was over? Why bring me out here, then? To tell me it was okay that I couldn't make it work?"

"I thought maybe if you were here, with me, we could both get a sense of what was really going on with you—if it was just too hard because we hadn't seen each other in a while, or if you really had feelings for Trenton."

I began to cry into my napkin again. I suspected people were surely staring, but I didn't dare look up to check. "This is so humiliating," I said, trying not to sob.

"It's okay, honey. It's just us."

I lowered my hands just enough to look around. He was right. We were the last two customers in the restaurant. I was so preoccupied, I hadn't even noticed.

"Can I get anything else for you, sir?" the server said. I didn't have to see her face to know she was curious about what was going on at our table.

"Bring us the bottle," T.J. said.

"Of the white?"

"Of the white," T.J. said in his confident, smooth voice.

"Y-yes, sir," she said. I could hear her shoes tap the floor as she walked away.

"Aren't they closing soon?"

"Not for twenty minutes. We can kill a bottle by then, right?"

"Not a problem," I said, faking amusement. At the moment, all I felt was sad, guilty, and ashamed.

His small, contrived smile faded. "You're leaving tomorrow. We don't need to make any decisions tonight. Or even tomorrow. Let's just enjoy our time together." He reached across the table, and intertwined his fingers in mine.

After a moment's pause, I pulled away. "I think we both already know what's happened."

With sadness in his eyes, T.J. nodded.

✦　✦　✦

My eyes popped open when the airplane wheels touched down, and I looked around, seeing everyone around me pulling out their cell phones and texting friends, family, or colleagues about their arrival. I didn't bother turning my phone back on. Raegan would be at her parents', and my family didn't even know I'd been gone.

T.J. and I went to bed as soon as we got back to the town house the night before, knowing we both had to be up before sunrise to get me to the airport on time. He held me in his arms all night like he didn't want to let me go, but the next morning at the airport, he hugged and kissed me good-bye like he meant it. It was forced, and sad, and distant.

I pushed the Smurf's gearshift into Park, and stepped out onto the asphalt. Part of me hoped Trenton would be sitting on the cement in front of my door, but he wasn't.

San Diego had been nearly balmy, and now I was back where my breath was visible. The air actually hurt my face. How does air hurt your face?

I unlocked the door, pushed through it, let it slam behind me, and then trudged to my bedroom, falling face-first into my wonderfully messy bed.

Raegan padded down the hall in her bare feet. "How was it?" she asked from the doorway.

"I don't know."

The floor creaked under her as she walked to my bed and sat next to me. "Are you still together?"

"No."

"Oh. Well . . . that's good, right? I mean, even though T.J. hadn't spoken to you until Trent kissed you, and suddenly he bought you a ticket to California . . ."

"Not tonight, Ray."

"Trenton came by the Red tonight. He looked pretty awful."

"Yeah? Did he leave with anyone?" I peeked out from the pillow.

Raegan hesitated. "Right before last call. He was sloppy drunk."

I nodded, and then buried my face in the pillow.

"Just . . . tell him," Raegan pleaded. "Tell him about T.J."

"I can't," I said. "And you can't, either. You promised."

"I still don't understand what all the secrecy is about."

"You don't have to," I said, looking up at her, straight into her eyes. "You just have to keep the secret."

Raegan nodded. "I will."

It seemed like I'd barely closed my eyes when Raegan was shaking me awake.

I groaned.

"You're going to be late for work, Cami! Get your ass up!"

I didn't budge.

"You just took off two days, last-minute. Cal is going to fire your ass! Get up!" She clasped her hands around my ankle and dragged me until I fell off the bed, hard.

"Ow! Damn it, Ray!"

She leaned down. "It's eleven thirty! Get up!"

I looked at the clock and then jumped up, racing around my bedroom and swearing repeatedly. Barely brushing my teeth, I resorted to a bun and glasses. The Smurf didn't want to wake up, either, and she whirred like a dying cat before finally starting up.

The clock on the wall at Skin Deep said 12:07 when I walked

through the door. Hazel was already on the phone, and Calvin stood next to her, frowning.

"What the hell are you wearing?" he asked.

I looked down at my plum skinny jeans and black-and-white horizontal-striped long-sleeved shirt. "Clothes."

"I hired you to be the hot piece of ass at the counter, and you look like my cousin Annette. What is this look?" he asked Hazel.

"Hipster," she said briefly before returning to her conversation.

"Yeah. Like my hipster cousin Annette. Next time you come in, I want to see cleavage and sex hair!" he said, holding up one finger, and then two.

"What the hell is sex hair?" I asked.

Calvin shrugged. "You know. Messy, but sexy. Like you just had sex."

Hazel slammed the phone down. "Everything that comes out of your mouth is offensive. Hot piece of ass? Cleavage? You're a walking sexual harassment lawsuit!"

Calvin wasn't fazed.

"Is it the shoes?" I asked, looking down at my favorite black combat boots.

"The scarf!" he said, pointing all four fingers at me. "What is the point in having a nice rack if you're going to cover it up?"

Hazel smiled. "It's a cute scarf. I need a black one like yours."

Calvin frowned. "It's not cute! I don't want cute! I hired a sexy, edgy bartender, and I got a hipster in a bun with no tattoos! I can handle you taking off and coming in whenever the fuck you feel like it, but it's just wrong walking around here with a clean palette for skin. It looks bad if our own employees don't trust us enough to ink them!"

"Are you about finished?" Hazel deadpanned. She looked at me. "He started his period this morning."

"Fuck you, Hazel!" Calvin snapped, stomping down the hall to his office.

"Fuck you back!" she yelled.

Calvin poked his head around the corner. "Has Bishop been in?"

"Godammit, Cal, no! For the third time today, he hasn't been in!" Calvin nodded, and then disappeared again. Hazel frowned for half a second before turning to me with a smile.

"I think I'll show him my fingers today. Might take the edge off."

"No way," she said. "Let him stew." She was quiet for a minute, clearly working up to something, and then she elbowed me. "So. California."

"Yeah," I said, cocking my head while I pulled my purse over it. I tossed my bag on the counter and then logged onto the computer. "About that . . ."

The door chimed, and Trenton walked in, wearing a puffy navy-blue coat and a dirty white ball cap that was pulled low, shadowing his eyes. "Morning, ladies," he said, walking past us.

"Morning, sunshine," Hazel said, watching him pass.

He disappeared into his room, and Hazel shot me a look. "You mind-fucked him so hard."

I sighed. "I didn't mean to."

"It's good for him. No man should get every woman he wants. Keeps their douchebaggery to a tolerable level."

"I'm just going to . . ." I said, pointing down the hall. Hazel nodded.

Trenton was busy setting up his equipment when I walked into the room. Crossing my arms and leaning against the doorjamb while he ignored me was acceptable for the first few minutes, but then I began to feel stupid.

"Are you ever going to speak to me again?" I asked.

He kept his eyes on his equipment, and laughed once. "Sure, baby doll. I'll talk to you. What's up?"

"Calvin says I need more ink."

"Do you want more ink?"

"Only if you do it."

He still didn't look at me. "I don't know, Cami, I've got a pretty full day."

I watched him for a moment while he busied himself with organizing white packages full of various sanitized tools. "Just sometime. Doesn't have to be today."

"Yeah, sure. No problem," he said, picking through a drawer.

After another minute of Trenton pretending I wasn't there, I walked back to the vestibule. He had been truthful. He had one customer after another, but even when he had a little time in between, he only came to the counter once, and that was to chat with a potential new client. The rest of the day he stayed in his room, or talked to Calvin in his office. Hazel didn't seem concerned with his behavior, but she never seemed to be unsettled by anything.

Trenton didn't come into the Red that night, and the next day was another six hours of Operation Ignore Cami, as was the next day, and every day after that for three weeks. I spent a lot more time on papers and studying. Raegan was spending more time with Brazil, so I was grateful when Coby popped over for a visit one Monday evening.

Identical bowls of steaming chicken noodle soup sat on the breakfast bar between us.

"You look better," I said.

"I feel better. You were right, a program made it easier."

"How are things at home?" I asked.

Coby shrugged. "The same."

I picked at the noodles swimming around in my bowl. "He's never going to change, you know."

"I know. Just trying to get my shit together so I can get my own place."

"Good idea," I said, taking a bite.

"Let's take these to the couch and watch a movie," Coby said.

I nodded, and Coby set my bowl next to him on the cushion while I looked through DVD cases. My breath caught when I came across *Spaceballs*. Trenton had left it here the last time we'd watched it.

"What?" Coby asked.

"Trent left a movie over here."

"Where's he been? I figured he'd be over here."

"He doesn't really . . . come over here anymore."

"You guys broke up?"

"We were just friends, Coby."

"No one thinks that but you."

I looked up at him, and then trudged to the love seat, picking up my bowl and then sitting next to my brother. "He doesn't want me."

"He did."

"Not anymore. I fucked up."

"How?"

"I don't really want to talk about it. It's a long, boring story."

"Anything to do with the Maddoxes is never boring." He spooned the soup into his mouth, and then waited. He was like a different person when he was clean. He cared about things. He listened.

"We'd been spending pretty much every day together."

"I know that part."

I sighed. "He kissed me. It freaked me out. Then he told me he loved me."

"Both horrible, very bad things," he said, nodding.

"Don't patronize me."

"Sorry."

"They are very bad things. T.J. booked me a flight to California after I told him about the kiss."

"Makes complete sense from a man's perspective."

"Trent begged me not to go. He told me he loved me at the airport, and I walked away." My eyes filled with tears as my mind replayed the scene, and I remembered the look on Trenton's face. "While I was out there, T.J. and I figured out that we loved each other, but there was just no way to make it work."

"So, you broke up?"

"Kind of. Not really."

"C'mon, Camille. You're adults. If it was implied . . ."

"It doesn't matter," I said, rolling a diced carrot around in the broth. "Trent barely speaks to me. He hates me."

"Have you told him what happened in California?"

"No. What am I supposed to say. 'T.J. doesn't want me, so you can have me, now'?"

"Is that what it is?"

"No. I mean, kind of, but Trenton's not the next best thing. I don't want him to feel that way. And even if he somehow forgave me, there's always the fact that it would be completely wrong to go from one to the other."

"They're big boys, Cami. They'll work it out."

We finished our food in silence, and then Coby took my bowl and rinsed it in the sink. "I've gotta head out. I just wanted to bring you this." He pulled a check from his wallet.

"Thanks," I said. My eyes widened when I saw the amount. "You didn't have to pay it back all at once."

"I got a second job. It's not putting me behind."

I hugged him. "I love you. I'm so proud of you, and I'm so glad that you're going to be okay."

"We're all going to be okay. You'll see," he said with a small grin.

◆   ◆   ◆

The following Saturday, Trenton walked into Skin Deep an hour late, red faced and rushed. His dad's truck had broken down and he'd tried to get it up and running. Trenton wasn't forthcoming with the information. Like finding out everything else about Trenton since California, I had to ask Hazel.

By the end of the first week of November, T.J. had only called once to say that he was in town for work but he wouldn't be able to say hi, and Trenton and I had barely spoken. He had come to the Red a handful of times, getting his drinks from Raegan, Blia, or Jorie, and every night, just before last call, he could be seen walking out with a different girl.

I tried not to behave differently at Skin Deep. Technically,

I didn't need the second job, but I liked working there and the extra money, and I enjoyed seeing Trenton too much to quit, even if he was ignoring me.

It was easy to fool Calvin, but Hazel knew all. She would spend time with Trenton in his room, and then wink at me when she came out. I wasn't sure if she meant to be reassuring or she thought we shared some inside information that I wasn't privy to.

The door chimed, and in walked Travis and Shepley.

"Hi, boys." I smiled.

"Are you lending your beauty to every dive in town?" Travis asked, firing off his most charming smile.

"Someone's in a good mood," I said. "What can we do for you today?"

"Don't ask," Shepley said. He was most definitely not in a good mood.

"I'm getting a couple of tats. Where is that shit-stain brother of mine?"

Trenton poked his head out of his room. "Asshat!"

I checked Travis in, and once he signed the forms, the Maddoxes walked back to Trenton's room.

"You're fucking kidding me!" Trenton yelled, howling with laughter. "You're such a pussy!"

"Shut up, cocksucker, and just do it!"

Hazel walked into the hall and stood in Trenton's doorway. Soon she was laughing, too. The tattoo machine began to buzz, and over the next hour, Trenton's room was full of laughter and playful insults.

When they met back up at the counter, Travis had a bandage over his wrist. He was beaming. Shepley was not.

"This has fucked me so many ways," he grumbled.

Trenton slapped and then gripped Shepley's shoulders. "Oh, Shep. It's going to be okay. Travis will work his magic, and Abby will be fine with it."

"Abby? I'm talking about America!" he said. "What if she's pissed because I didn't brand myself with *her* name? What if Abby's not fine with it, she dumps Travis, and then it causes problems with Mare and me? I'm fucked!"

The brothers laughed, and Shepley mocked them, clearly not amused with their lack of concern.

Trenton smiled at his baby brother. "I'm happy for ya."

Travis couldn't contain the broad smile that lit his entire face. "Thanks, asshole." A shoulder-to-shoulder bro hug commenced, and then Travis and Shepley loaded into the Charger and left.

Trenton was smiling when he turned around, but the moment his eyes fell on me, it faded, and he walked back to his room.

I sat alone at the desk, listening to his and Hazel's whispering. I stood up and walked back to his room. He was just wiping off the chair. Hazel sat up straight, her eyes meeting Trenton's and then looking to me to signal that I was there.

"What are you guys whispering about?" I asked, trying to smile.

"Isn't my next client coming in soon?" Hazel asked.

I looked at the small metal clock on the wall. "Eleven minutes. Trent, you don't have an appointment anytime soon. Barring any walk-ins, it would be a good time to start the outline for that tat we talked about a while back."

He looked at me while he cleaned, and then shook his head. "I can't today, Cami."

"Why not?" I asked.

Hazel strolled out, letting us be alone.

Trenton reached over and dug into the candy bowl sitting on the counter closest to him. He unwrapped a small sucker and popped it in his mouth. "Jason said he might come in this afternoon around now if he got out of practice on time."

I frowned. "Just say you don't want to, Trent. Don't lie." I walked off, and sat on the stool behind the front desk in a huff. Not ten minutes later, a truck pulled into the parking lot, and Jason Brazil breezed through the door. "Is Trent busy?" he asked.

I hunched over and sank back into my seat. My entire face felt like it had caught fire as the adrenaline from pure humiliation burned through my veins.

"You okay?" Brazil asked.

"Yeah," I said. "He's back there."

Day after day Trenton ignored me, but I didn't dare confront him after that. It was particularly hurtful because his rapport with Hazel hadn't changed, and he was more than chatty with Raegan when he came to the Red. He was deliberately giving me the cold shoulder, and I hated it.

The second Saturday in November, Trenton strolled into the Red alone and sat at his new favorite stool in front of Raegan. She was busy with her regular, Marty, but Trenton sat there patiently, not once looking over to me for service. My heart sank. The past weeks of being around Trenton had taught me an appreciation for the misery Kody went through every Wednesday through Sunday night since he and Raegan had broken up. I looked over to Kody, seeing him glance in Raegan's direction with sad eyes. He did that dozens of times every night.

My regular, Baker, had a full, frosted mug, so I walked over to Raegan's side of the bar, popped the top off Trenton's favorite beer, and handed it to him.

He nodded once and then reached for it, but something came over me, and I yanked it away.

Trenton's eyes popped up to meet mine for less than a second, a combination of shock and confusion on his face.

"Okay, Maddox. It's been five weeks."

"Five weeks of what?" Trenton asked.

"Miller Lite!" a guy called from behind Trenton. I acknowledged him with a nod, and then lowered my chin at Trenton, crossing my arms and letting his beer bottle sit snugly in the crook of my arm.

"Five weeks of pretending," I said.

Trenton looked behind him on each side, and everywhere but at me. He shook his head a couple of times. "Don't know what you're talking about."

"Okay. So you hate me." The words felt like poison coming out of my mouth. "Want me to quit Skin Deep?"

"What?" he said, finally looking at me for the first time in weeks.

"I can do it if that's what you need."

"Why would you quit?" he asked.

"You answer my question, first."

"What question?"

"Do you hate me?"

"Cami, I could never hate you. Even if I wanted to. Trust me, I've tried."

"Then why won't you talk to me?"

His face screwed into disgust. He started to speak, and then changed his mind. He lit a cigarette and took a drag.

I pulled it from between his fingers and broke it in half.

"C'mon, Cami!"

"I'm sorry, okay? Can we at least talk about this?"

"No!" he said, getting more agitated by the second. "What's the fucking point?"

"Wow. Thanks."

"You walked away from me, Cami."

"I don't deserve for you to talk to me, I get it. I'll give Cal my notice tomorrow."

Trenton's face contorted. "That's fucking stupid."

"We're both miserable. I don't like it any more than you do, but what's stupid is being around each other when we don't have to be."

"Fine."

"Fine?" I wasn't sure what I expected him to say, but it wasn't that. I tried to choke back the lump that formed in my throat, but instead it just got bigger and tears began to form in my eyes.

He reached out for me. "Can I have my beer now?"

I laughed once, in disbelief. "You wanted a reaction when you kissed me and you got one."

"If I'd known you were going to get on a flight to California and fuck someone else a few hours later, I might have reconsidered."

"Do you really want to keep track of who's fucked who lately?" I sat his beer down and began to walk back to my station.

"I'm trying to handle this!"

I flipped around. "Well, you're sucking at it!"

Raegan was staring at us, along with everyone else within shouting distance.

"You saw Travis on Halloween! He's out of control over this

girl! She left the morning after he bagged her the first time without telling him good-bye, and he trashed his fucking apartment!
Trust me, I would love to bash something or someone, but I don't
have that luxury, Cami. I have to keep it together! I don't need
you judging me about what I do to keep my mind off of you!"

"Don't make excuses. Especially not stupid ones, it's just insulting."

"You . . . I . . . fucking shit lord, Camille! I thought that's what
you wanted!"

"*Why* would I want that? You're my *best friend*!" I felt a tear
fall down my cheek, and I quickly wiped it away.

"Because you're back with Califucktard!"

"*Back* with him? If you would just talk to me, we could clear
this up. We could—"

"Not that you've ever been with him," he grumbled, swip-
ing the bottle off the bar. He took a swig, muttering something
under his breath.

"What?" I snapped.

"I said if you like being a backup plan, that's fine with me!"

"Miller Lite, Cami!" the guy yelled again, this time less patient.

I glared at Trenton. "Backup plan? Are you fucking kidding
me right now? All you deal in is backup plans! How many of
those have you walked out of here with in the last month?"

Trenton's cheeks flushed. He stood up, kicking the stool
backward, sending it flying almost all the way to the dance floor.
"You're not a fucking backup plan, Cami! Why are you letting
someone treat you like one?"

"He's not treating me like anything! I haven't spoken to him
in weeks!"

"Oh, so now that he's ignoring you, I'm good enough to be your friend?"

"I'm sorry, I thought we were already friends!"

"Miller Lite! Will one of you do your damn job?" the guy yelled again.

Trenton turned around, and pointed in the guy's face. "You talk to her like that again, and I'm going to knock you the fuck out."

Beginning with a wry smile, the guy began to say something more, but Trenton didn't give him the chance. He lunged, grabbing the guy by the collar. They fell to the floor, and I lost sight of them. A crowd quickly formed a tight circle around the spot where they went down, and after a few seconds, Trenton's audience flinched, covered their mouths, and shouted "Oh!" in unison.

Within seconds, Kody and Gruber descended upon them. Suddenly Trenton was standing and looking as if he'd never been in a fight. He wasn't even breathing hard. He walked back to his beer and took a drink. His T-shirt was ripped a few inches at the collar, and his neck and cheek were spattered with blood.

Gruber wrestled Trenton's victim out the side entrance, and Kody stood next to Trenton, out of breath.

"Sorry, Trent. You know the rules. I gotta ask you to leave."

Trenton nodded once, took one last swig, and then walked away. Kody followed him out. I opened my mouth to call to him but wasn't sure what else to say.

Raegan stood beside me. "Whoa."

CHAPTER FIFTEEN

MY HANDS WERE SHAKING, AND WITHOUT ANY GOOD reason or excuse, I steered the Smurf into Jim Maddox's driveway. The roads were thick with sleet and ice, and I had no business driving, but every turn I took brought me closer to Trenton. I switched off the lights before they hit the front windows of the house, and then killed the engine, letting the Jeep cruise to a stop.

My phone chimed. It was Trenton, wondering if it was my Jeep in the drive . . . as if it could be anyone else's. When I confirmed his suspicion, the screen door opened, and Trenton walked down the steps. He was wearing fuzzy slippers and royal-blue basketball shorts, his arms crossed over his bare torso. Inch-thick, black tribal tattoos crawled over his shoulders and across his chest, and colorful, various tattoos overlapped one another as they traveled down both of his arms, cutting off abruptly at his wrists.

Trenton stopped next to my window, waiting for me to crank the window down. He readjusted his white ball cap and sat his hands on his hips, waiting for me to speak.

My eyes ran over the definition of his pec muscles, and then traveled down to appreciate all six of his beautifully protruding abdominals.

"Did I wake you?" I asked.

He shook his head. "Just got out of the tub."

I bit my lip, trying to think of something to say.

"What are you doing here, Cami?"

Looking forward, I shook my head and pressed my lips into a hard line. "I have no idea."

He crossed his arms over the edge of my door and leaned in. "Would you mind figuring it out? It's cold as fuck out here."

"Oh! God! I'm sorry," I said, turning on the Smurf. I turned up the heater. "Get in."

"Move over," Trenton said.

I crawled over the gearshift and console, and bounced when I hit the passenger seat. Trenton hopped in, shut the door, and rolled the window up until there was just a crack.

"You got cigarettes?" he asked. I handed him my pack and he pulled out two. He lit them both, and then handed one to me.

I took a drag and blew it out, watching him do the same. The tension was thicker than the smoke swirling between us. Tiny bits of ice began tapping at the windows and the metal frame of the Smurf, then the sky opened up and the sound of ice tapping against the car intensified.

"You're right. I did go home with girls," Trenton said, raising his voice over the noise of the sleet. "More than just the ones you saw at the Red."

"You don't have to tell me."

"I needed to get my mind off of you." When I didn't respond, he turned to me. "I would let a girl rescue me from that torture every night of the week, but even when I was with someone else, all I thought about was you."

"That's not really . . . a compliment," I said.

Trenton hit the steering wheel with the heel of his hand, and then blew out another puff of smoke. "I'm not trying to compliment you! I thought I was going to go out of my damn mind thinking about you being in California. I swore to myself that I wouldn't call you, and when you got back, I was going to accept your choice. But you drove to my house. You're here. I don't know what to do with that."

"I just didn't want to miss you anymore," I said, not knowing what else to say. "It's so selfish, I know. I shouldn't be here." I breathed out all the air from my lungs and sank back into the ratty passenger seat as far as I could. Being that truthful made me feel so vulnerable. It was the first time I'd even admitted it to myself.

"What the fuck does that mean?"

"I don't know!" I yelled. "Have you ever wanted something that you knew you shouldn't have? That it was wrong on every level, but you knew you needed it? I liked where we were, Trent! And then you . . . we can't get that back."

"C'mon, Cami. I couldn't keep going like that."

"I know that it wasn't fair to you. To no one else but me, really. But I still miss it, because it was preferable to the alternatives: to be with you under false pretenses, or to lose you altogether," I said, wiping my nose. I opened the door, put my cigarette out on the runner, and then tossed the butt on the floorboard. "I'm sorry. This was such a shitty thing to do. I'll go." I began to step out, but Trenton grabbed my arm.

"Cami, stop. You're not making any sense. You came here. Now you're leaving. If there wasn't . . . the thing, whatever it is . . . what would you do?"

I laughed once, but it sounded more like a cry. "I walked away from you in the airport. And then I spent the next two days wishing I'd stayed."

A spark of happiness lit his eyes. "Then let's—"

"But there is more to it than that, Trenton. I wish I could tell you so it's out there, but I can't."

"You don't have to tell me. If you need me to say that I'm okay with whatever I don't know, I'm okay with it. I don't give a single fuck," he said, shaking his head.

"You can't say that. You wouldn't if you knew . . ."

"I know there's something you want to tell me but can't. If it comes out later, no matter what it is, I made the choice to move forward without knowing. That's on me."

"For anything else, that would be enough."

Trenton flicked his cigarette out the window. "That makes zero fucking sense. None."

"I know. I'm sorry," I said, fighting back tears.

Trenton rubbed his face, beyond frustrated. "What do you want from me? I keep telling you I don't care about this secret. I'm telling you I want you. I don't know what else to say to convince you."

"You need to be the one to walk away. Tell me to fuck off, and end it. I'll quit Skin Deep, you find a different bar. I can't . . . you have to be the one."

He shook his head. "I *am* the one, Cami. I'm it for you. I know because you're it for me."

"You're not helping."

"Good!"

I watched him, begging him with my eyes. It was such a strange feeling, hoping for someone to break my heart. When I realized he was going to be just as stubborn as I was being weak, a switch inside of me flipped. "Okay, then. I'll do it. I have to. It's better than you hating me later. It's better than letting you do something I know is wrong."

"I'm so tired of this cryptic shit. You know what I think about right and wrong?" he asked, but before I could answer, he grabbed each side of my face and planted his lips on mine.

I immediately opened my mouth, letting his tongue slip inside. He grabbed at my skin, touching me everywhere, as if he couldn't get enough of me, and then he reached across me for the seat lever. The seat leaned backward slowly, and at the same time, Trenton climbed over the console in one smooth movement. Keeping his mouth on mine, he grabbed each of my knees and hiked them up to his ribs. I planted my feet on the dashboard, and lifted my hips up to meet his. He groaned into my mouth. His shorts didn't conceal his excitement, and he pressed the hardness against the exact spot where I already wished he was.

His hips moved and rolled against mine as he kissed and nipped my neck with his teeth. My panties were instantly soaked, and just as I slid my fingers between his shorts and his skin, his kisses slowed, and then stopped.

We were both breathing hard, staring into one another's eyes. Every window of the Jeep was fogged over.

"What?" I asked.

He shook his head, looked down, and then laughed once before raising his eyes to meet mine. "I'm going to hate myself later, but I'm not doing this in a car, and definitely not in fuzzy slippers."

"Take them off," I said, planting a dozen tiny kisses on his neck and shoulder.

He half hummed, half sighed. "I'd be just as bad as every other dick who doesn't treat you the way you deserve." He leaned away from my lips, giving me one more sweet peck. "I'm going to go warm up the Intrepid."

"Why?"

"I don't want you driving home in this shit, and the Intrepid has front-wheel drive. Handles better. I'll drop off your Jeep before you wake up in the morning." He pulled the door handle and jumped out, running into the house for a few minutes, and then reappearing, this time with sneakers, a hoodie, and keys in his hand. He started the Intrepid, and then ran back to the Smurf, hopping in and rubbing his hands. "Shit!"

"It's freezing," I said, nodding.

"That's not it." He looked at me. "I don't want you to leave."

I smiled, and he reached over, running his thumb along my lips. After a few moments, we reluctantly got out of the Smurf and climbed into his car.

As happy as I thought I was lying in T.J.'s bed a few weeks before, sitting next to Trenton in his dilapidated Intrepid while he drove me home was so much better. His hand was on my knee, and he wore the utmost satisfied smile all the way to my apartment.

"You sure you don't want to come in?" I asked when he parked.

"No," he said, but he clearly wasn't happy with his answer. He leaned over and kissed me with the softest lips, slow at first, and then we both began to tug at each other's clothes again. Trenton's shorts were standing at full attention, and his fingers tugged gently at my hair, but eventually he pulled away. "Damn it," he said, breathless. "I'm going to take you on a proper date first if it kills me."

I let my head fall back against the headrest, and I looked up, frustrated. "Nice. You can take a random girl home from the Red forty-five minutes after you meet her, and I get shut down."

"This isn't you getting shut down, baby. Not even close."

I looked over at him, and my brows pulled in. I wanted to pretend that everything would be okay, and I could forget what I knew, but I had to warn him one last time. "I don't know what this is. But I know if you knew the whole story, Trenton, you would walk away from me and never look back."

He leaned his head against his headrest, and then held his palm against my cheek. "I don't want the whole story. I just want you."

I shook my head, tears threatening to well in my eyes for the third time that day. "No. You deserve to know. Certain things in our lives are so fragile . . . and you and me, Trent? We could ruin it all."

He shook his head. "Listen to what I'm saying, Cami. If it keeps me from being with you, I know what it is."

I looked over at him, my heart slamming against my chest, louder than even the sleet hitting the windshield or the Intrepid's rumbling muffler.

"Oh, yeah? What is it?"

"It's in the way." He leaned over to me, and touched my cheek with his hand the same time that his lips touched mine.

"Just remember later that I'm sorry for whatever happens after this, and I'm sorry that when you walked away like I asked, I didn't let you go," I said.

"I'm not, and I never will be." The skin around his eyes tightened as he stared straight into mine. He truly believed in what he was saying, and it made me want to believe it, too.

I ran into my apartment, shut the door, and leaned against it until I heard the Intrepid pull away. It was irresponsible and self-ish, but part of me wanted to believe Trenton when he said that what he didn't know wouldn't matter.

✦   ✦   ✦

Just before the sun rose, and before my eyes opened, I felt something warm running along the length of my body. I moved just a centimeter toward whatever it was, just to make sure my mind wasn't playing tricks on me.

I blinked a few times, and then focused, seeing a shadowed figure lying next to me. The clock on my nightstand read 6:00 AM. The apartment was dark and quiet, the same as it always was at that time of the morning. But the second the memories from earlier that morning crept into my mind, everything felt different.

Oh, God. What had I done? A boundary had been crossed, and there was no going back or going forward without real consequences. I thought from the moment Trenton had sat at my table at the Red that I could handle whatever he threw my way, but he was like quicksand. The more I struggled, the deeper I sank.

I was right on the edge of the bed, and tried to inch over without success.

"Why are you in my bed, Ray?" I asked.

"Huh?" Trenton said, his voice deep and raspy.

A jolt ran through my body, and I squealed as I fell off the bed. Trenton scrambled to the edge, reaching for me, but it was too late. I was already on the floor.

"Oh! Shit! Are you all right?"

With my back pressed against the wall, I quickly brushed my hair from my face. When recognition sunk in, I hit the floor with both of my fists. "What the hell are you doing in my bed? How did you even get in here?"

Trenton winced. "I brought the Jeep back about an hour ago. Brazil happened to be dropping off Raegan, and she let me in."

"So you just . . . crawled into bed with me?" My voice was high-pitched and bordering on a screech.

"I said I wasn't going to come in, and then I did. And then I told myself I'd sleep on the floor, but then I didn't. I just . . . had to be next to you. I was just lying there awake at Dad's." He leaned over, and reached for me with one hand. His muscles danced under his smooth, inked arm. His hand grasped mine, and then he pulled me onto the bed next to him. "Hope that was okay."

"Does it matter at this point?"

Half of Trenton's mouth turned up. He was clearly amused at my early morning tantrum.

Raegan rushed down the hall and then whipped around the corner, her eyes wide. "Why are you yelling?"

"You let him in?"

"Yeah. Is that okay?" she said, breathless. Her hair was wild, and her mascara was smudged under her eyes.

"Why is everyone asking me after the fact? No! It's not okay!"

"Do you want me to go?" Trenton asked, still smiling.

I looked at him, at Raegan, and then back at him. "No! I just don't want you sneaking into my bed when I'm asleep!"

Raegan rolled her eyes and walked back down the hall, shutting her door.

Trenton hooked his arm around my middle and pulled me

against him, burying his face between my neck and the pillow. I lay still, looking up at the ceiling, caught between wanting desperately to tangle my arms and legs with his, and knowing that from that moment forward, if I did anything else but kick him out and never speak to him again, no one would be to blame but me.

CHAPTER SIXTEEN

WITH ONE EAR AGAINST THE PHONE, AND THE OTHER EAR being kissed and licked quietly by Trenton, I tried to schedule a three-thirty outline. Normally Trenton behaved a little more professionally at work, but it was Sunday, we were painfully slow, and Calvin had taken Hazel to lunch for her birthday. Trenton and I were totally alone.

"Yes. Got you down. Thank you, Jessica."

I hung up the phone, and Trenton grabbed my hips and lifted me up, planting my ass on the counter. He hooked my ankles at the small of his back, and then slid his fingers into my hair, combing it back just enough to provide a clear path to run his tongue up my neck until it reached its destination: my earlobe. He took the tender piece of skin into his mouth, applying the tiniest bit of pressure between his top teeth and tongue. It had become my very favorite thing . . . so far. He'd been torturing me that way all week, but refused to undress me—or touch me anywhere fun—until we went to dinner Monday night after work.

Trenton pulled me toward him and pressed his pelvis against me. "I have never looked forward to a Monday so much in my life."

I smiled, dubious. "I don't know why you have these strange rules. We could break them ten feet away in your room."

Trenton hummed. "Oh. We will."

I turned my wrist over to check my watch. "You don't have anyone for an hour and a half. Why don't you start outlining that shoulder tattoo we've talked about?"

Trenton thought for a moment. "The poppies?"

I hopped down from the counter, opened a drawer, and pulled out the drawing Trenton had created the week before. I held it up to his face. "They're pretty, and they're significant."

"You've said that. But you haven't told me why they're significant."

"*The Wizard of Oz.* They make you forget."

Trenton made a face.

"What? Is that dumb?" I said, immediately defensive.

"No. It's just that your Oz reference reminded me of Travis's girlfriend's new name for Crook."

"What is it?"

"Toto. Travis said she's from Kansas . . . that's why he got that breed in the first place, blah, blah, blah."

"I agree. Crook is better."

Trenton narrowed his eyes. "You really want the poppies?"

I nodded an emphatic yes.

"Red?" he asked.

I held up his artwork again. "Just like this."

He shrugged. "Okay, baby doll. Poppies it is." He took my hand, leading me back to his room.

I undressed while Trenton finished his prep, but he paused just long enough to watch me pull my shirt over my head, and then slip my left arm out of my black, lacy bra strap. He shook his head and smiled wryly, amused by the G-rated striptease I'd just given him.

By the time the tattoo machine had begun to buzz, I was completely relaxed against the chair. Trenton tattooing my skin was so extraordinarily intimate. There was something about being so close to him, the way he manipulated and stretched my skin while he worked, and the look of concentration on his face while he permanently marked my skin with one of his remarkable pieces of art. The pain was secondary to all of that.

Trenton was just finishing up the line work when Hazel and Calvin returned. Hazel had a sack in her hand when she walked into Trenton's room.

"I brought you both a slice of cheesecake," she said, noticing my shoulder. "Oh, that's going to be fucking amazing."

"Thanks," I said, beaming.

"It's been that slow, huh?" Calvin said. "I don't suppose you coulda picked up a broom?"

"Uh . . . she's not dressed, Cal," Trenton said, dismayed.

"She ain't got anything I haven't seen before," Calvin said.

"You haven't seen Cami before. Get the fuck out."

Calvin simply turned his back to us, crossing his arms. "She can't find something to organize when we're not busy? I'm paying her by the hour."

"Everything is organized, Cal," I said. "I did sweep. I even dusted."

Trenton frowned. "You bitch because she doesn't have tats, and now you're bitching because I'm tatting her. Make up your damn mind."

Calvin craned his neck at Trenton, snarled his lip, and then disappeared around the corner.

Hazel giggled, clearly not worried about the boys' confrontation.

After Trenton doctored my tattoo site, I slipped my arm

through my bra strap—carefully—and then pulled my shirt back over my head. "You're going to get fired if you keep pissing him off."

"Nah," Trenton said, cleaning up his workspace. "He's secretly in love with me."

"Calvin doesn't love anyone," Hazel said. "He's married to this shop."

Trenton narrowed his eyes. "What about Bishop? I'm pretty sure he loves Bishop."

Hazel rolled her eyes. "You'll need to let that go."

I left them both and walked to the counter, noticing a buzzing noise coming from the drawer where I kept my cell phone. I pulled it open slowly, and looked at the display. It was Clark.

"What's wrong?" Trenton asked, coming up behind me to kiss a small section of my shoulder that wasn't angry and red from the needle.

"It's Clark. I love him, I'm just not in the mood to be in a bad mood, ya know?"

Trenton's lips touched the outside edge of my ear. "You don't have to answer," he said softly.

Holding the phone in the palm of my hand, I declined the call, and then tapped out a text.

@ work. Can't talk. What's up?

Family lunch today. Don't forget.

Can't today. I'll try next week.

Bad idea. Dad's already pissed about you missing last week.

Exactly.

Ok. I'll let them know closer to time.

Thx.

Trenton's one appointment was the only customer we had all day. The sky was full of low-lying gray clouds; winter threatened to throw up on us at any moment. With at least an inch of sleet and ice already on the roads, not many people were braving the weather. The shop wasn't far from campus, so we usually saw a steady stream of vehicles passing in each direction, but with the crap weather, the traffic was nonexistent.

Trenton was drawing doodles on a piece of paper, and Hazel was lying in a straight line on the floor in front of the brown leather sofa that sat next to the entrance doors. I was typing out a paper for class. Calvin still hadn't come out of his office.

Hazel let out a dramatic sigh. "I'm leaving. I can't take this."

"No, you're not," Calvin yelled from the back.

A muffled scream emanated from Hazel's throat. When she finished, she was quiet for a moment, and then sat up quickly, her eyes bright. "Let me pierce your nose, Cami."

I frowned and shook my head. "Hell no."

"Oh, c'mon! We'll do a really tiny diamond. It'll be ladylike, but fierce."

"The thought of my nose being impaled makes my eyes water," I said.

"I'm so bored! Please?" she whined.

I looked over at Trenton, who was shading in his drawing of what looked like a troll. "Don't look at me. It's your nose."

"I'm not asking for your permission. I want your opinion," I said.

"I think it's hot," he said.

I cocked my head a bit, impatient. "Great, but does it hurt?"

"Yeah," Trenton said. "I've heard it hurts like a son of a bitch."

I thought for a moment, and then looked at Hazel. "I'm bored, too."

Her beaming smile spanned from one side of her face to the other. Her cheeks pushed up, making her eyes just two slits. "Really?"

"C'mon," I said, already walking back to her room. She scrambled to her feet and followed.

By the time I left Skin Deep for the day, I had extensive line work on my left shoulder, and a new nose piercing. Hazel was right. It was tiny; dainty, even. I would have never thought to get a nose ring, but I loved it.

"See you tomorrow, Hazel," I said, walking toward the door.

"Thank you for preserving my sanity, Cami!" Hazel said, waving. "Next time we're slow, we'll put gauges in your ears."

"Uh . . . no," I said, pushing the door.

I started the Smurf, and then Trenton jogged up to my door, signaling for me to roll down my window. When I did, he leaned in and kissed my lips.

"You weren't even going to say good-bye?" he asked.

"Sorry," I said. "I'm a little out of practice with this whole thing."

Trenton winked. "Me, too. But it won't take long."

I narrowed my eyes. "When was the last time you were in a relationship?"

The look on Trenton's face was one I couldn't quite read. "A few years. What?" he said. I had looked down and chuckled, and Trenton tucked his chin, forcing me to make eye contact.

"I didn't know you'd ever dated anyone."

"Contrary to popular belief, I am capable of being a one-woman man. Just has to be the right woman."

My mouth pulled to the side in a half-smile. "Why didn't I know about this? Seems like the whole campus would have been talking about it."

"Because it was new."

I thought for a moment, and then my eyes widened. "Was it Mackenzie?"

"For about forty-eight hours," Trenton said. His eyes lost focus, and then they snapped back to mine. He leaned in and gave me a soft peck on the mouth. "See you later?" he asked.

I nodded, rolled up my window, and then backed out of the parking lot, and pulled into the Red parking lot fifteen minutes later. The roads weren't getting better, and I wondered if the Red would be just as dead as Skin Deep.

Everyone's vehicles except Jorie's were parked side by side, leaving one space open between the employees' cars and Hank's. I ran into the side entrance and rubbed my hands together as I hurried to my stool at the east bar. Hank and Jorie were standing on the other side together, hugging and kissing more than usual.

"Cami!" Blia said, smiling.

Gruber and Kody were sitting together, and Raegan sat on the other side of me. Immediately I sensed that she was being quiet but didn't dare ask when Kody was nearby.

"I thought you weren't here, Jorie," I said. "I didn't see your car."

"I rode with Hank," she said with a mischievous smile. "Car-pooling is definitely a plus for shacking up."

My eyebrows shot up. "Yeah?" I said, standing up, opening my arms wide. "She said yes? You moved in together?"

"Yeah!" they both said in unison. They both leaned over the bar and hugged me.

"Yay! Congratulations!" I said, squeezing them. My head was between both of theirs, and even though I considered the employees of the Red my work family, they felt more like the real thing than my own family did lately.

Everyone else hugged and offered their congratulations. They must have been waiting for me to get there before they announced it so they could tell all of us at the same time.

Hank pulled out several bottles of wine—the good stuff from his personal stash—and began to pour glasses. We were all celebrating. Everyone but Raegan. I sat next to her after a while, and nudged her arm.

"What's up, Ray?" I asked quietly.

A small smile touched her lips. "Nice tat."

"Thanks," I said, turning to the side, showing my tiny nose ring. "Got this, too."

"Wow. Your dad's going to shit a wildcat."

"Spill it," I said.

She sighed. "I'm sorry. I don't want to ruin the party."

I made a face. "What's wrong?"

"It's happening again," she said, her shoulders sagging. "Brazil's getting busy. He's made it pretty clear that he'd rather be with his frat brothers and at football parties than with me. He had that Abby chick's birthday party at his apartment last month and didn't even invite me. I found out about it from Kendra Collins last night. I mean . . . really? We got into it bad today. He said almost all the things he said last time."

I raised an eyebrow. "That's shit, Ray."

She nodded and looked down at her hands in her lap, and then, for less than a second, glanced over at Kody. She laughed once, without humor. "Daddy loves Brazil. All I hear about at the house is"—her eyebrows pulled together and her voice deepened to emulate her father—"Jason Brazil would be accepted into the Naval Academy in a heartbeat. Jason Brazil would be a contender for the SEAL program . . . blah, blah, blah. Daddy thinks Jason would make a good soldier."

"I wouldn't let that cloud your judgment. Sounds like sending him off to the Naval Academy is a good way to get rid of him."

Raegan began to laugh, but then a tear fell down her cheek, and she leaned into my shoulder. I put my arm around her, and the celebration half a bar away instantly died down. Kody appeared on Raegan's other side.

"What's wrong?" he asked, genuine concern in his eyes.

"Nothing," she said, wiping her eyes quickly.

Kody looked wounded. "You can tell me, you know. I still care if you're hurting."

"I can't talk to you about it," she said, her face crumpling.

Kody put his thumb under Raegan's chin and lifted her eyes to meet his. "I just want you to be happy. That's all I care about."

Raegan looked up at his big green eyes, and then threw her arms around his chest. He pulled her against him, cupping the back of her hair with his huge hand. He kissed her temple, and just held her, not saying a word.

I stood up and joined everyone else while Kody and Raegan had their moment.

"Cheesus Crust, does this mean they're back together?" Blia asked.

I shook my head. "No. But they're friends again."

"Kody's such a good guy," Jorie said. "She'll figure it out eventually."

My cell phone buzzed. It was Trenton.

"Hello?" I answered.

"The fucking Intrepid won't start. I don't guess you could pick me up from work?"

"You're just now finishing up?" I asked, looking at my watch.

"Cal and I were talking."

"Yeah . . . I have to run home to change for work tonight, though . . ." The line got quiet. "Trenton?"

"Yeah? I mean, yes. Sorry, I'm just fucking pissed. It has one of those two-point-seven-liter engines so I knew it was gonna . . . you have no idea what I'm talking about, do you?"

I smiled, even though he couldn't see me. "No. But I'll be there in fifteen."

"Sweet. Thanks, baby. Take your time. The roads are getting worse."

I looked down at the phone gripped in my fingers after I hung up. I loved the way he spoke to me. The little nicknames. The texts. His grin with that amazing dimple in his left cheek.

Jorie winked at me. "Must have been a guy on the phone."

"Sorry, I have to go. I'll see you all tonight."

Everyone waved and said their good-byes to me, and I jogged out to the Smurf, nearly busting my ass when I tried to stop. The tall security lights were on, breaking up the darkness. Freezing rain stung where it touched my skin and made tiny tapping noises against the parked vehicles. No wonder Trenton said the roads were worse. I couldn't remember when we'd had this much wintery precipitation so early in the season.

The Smurf resisted for a few moments before starting up, but within minutes of Trenton's call, I was driving carefully back to Skin Deep. Trenton was waiting outside in his puffy blue coat, his arms crossed over his chest. He walked to my side and waited, watching me expectantly.

I cranked down the window halfway. "Get in!"

He shook his head. "C'mon, Cami. You know I'm weird about that."

"Quit it," I said.

"I have to drive," he said, shivering.

"You don't trust me by now?"

He shook his head again. "It doesn't have anything to do with trust. I just . . . I can't. It messes with my head."

"All right, all right," I said, sliding away from him, over the console, and into the passenger seat.

Trenton opened the door and hopped in, rubbing his hands together. "Shit on a stick, it's cold! Let's move to California!" As soon as the words left his mouth, he regretted them, staring at me with both shock and remorse in his eyes.

I wanted to tell him it was okay, but I was too busy handling the guilt and shame that washed over me in huge, suffocating waves. T.J. hadn't contacted me in weeks, but besides a respectful amount of time to wait between relationships, this was particularly insulting—to T.J. and to Trenton.

I pulled two cigarettes from my pack and put them both in my mouth, lighting them simultaneously. Trenton pulled one out of my mouth and took a drag. When he pulled into my parking spot in front of my apartment, he turned to me. "I didn't mean . . ."

"I know," I said. "It's really okay. Let's just forget about it."

Trenton nodded, clearly relieved that I wasn't going to make a big deal of it. He didn't want to acknowledge whatever I had left with T.J. any more than I did. Pretending to be oblivious was much more comfortable.

"Can I ask you for a favor, though?" Trenton nodded, waiting for my request. "Don't say anything to your brothers about us just yet. I know Thomas, Taylor, and Tyler aren't in town much, but I'm not really ready to have the talk with Travis the next time he comes in to the Red. He knows about T.J. It's just . . ."

"No, I get it. As far as Travis will know, everything is still the same. But he's going to know something's up."

I smiled. "If you tell him you're working on me, he won't be so surprised later."

Trenton chuckled and nodded.

We both ran to the door of my apartment, and I shoved the key in the lock. When it clicked, I pushed through, and Trenton shut it behind him. I turned up the temperature on the thermostat, and then started to walk toward my bedroom, but there was a knock on the door. I froze, and turned slowly on my heels. Trenton watched me for some sign of who it might be. I shrugged.

Before either of us could make it to the door, the person on the other side pounded violently with the side of their fist. I winced, my shoulders shooting up to my ears. When it was quiet again, I looked out the peephole.

"Fuck!" I whispered, looking around. "It's my dad."

"Camille! You open this goddamn door!" he yelled. He slurred his words together. He'd been drinking.

I turned the knob, but before I could pull, Dad was pushing through, charging straight at me. I trotted backward, stopping when my back slammed into the doorjamb leading to the hallway.

"I am sick of your shit, Camille! You think I don't know what you're up to? You think I don't see the disrespect?"

Trenton was immediately next to me, his arm between my dad and me, his hand on Dad's chest. "Mr. Camlin, you need to step away. Right now." His voice was calm, but firm.

Surprised to see someone else inside the apartment, Dad backed away for just a moment before leaning into Trenton's face. "Who the hell do you think you are? This is personal business, so you can get the fuck out!" he said, jerking his head toward the door.

I shook my head, pleading with my eyes for Trenton not to leave me alone. My father had spanked me when I was a child, and backhanded me a time or two, but my mother had always been there to distract him, and even redirect his anger. This was the first time I'd seen him physically violent since middle school, because Mom finally stood up for herself and told him that the next time he drank would be the last time—and he knew she meant it.

Trenton frowned and lowered his chin, with the same look in his eyes he had right before he attacked an enemy. "I don't want to fight you, sir, but if you don't leave, right now, I'm going to make you leave."

Dad lunged at Trenton, and they crashed into the end table next to the couch. The lamp crashed to the floor with them. My father's fist was flying, but Trenton dodged it, and moved to restrain him.

"No! Stop it! Dad! Stop it!" I screamed. My hands covered my mouth as they fought.

Dad pushed away from Trenton and stood up, stomping to-ward me. Trenton scrambled to his feet and grabbed him, pulling him back, but Dad continued to reach for me. The look in my father's eyes was monstrous, and for the first time I realized exactly what my mother had gone through. Being on the wrong end of that kind of rage was terrifying.

Trenton slung Dad to the ground and pointed down as he stood over him. "Stay! The fuck! Down!"

Dad was breathing hard, but he stumbled to his feet, obstinate. His body weaved when he spoke. "I'm going to fuckin' kill you. And then I'm going to teach her what happens when she disrespects me."

So quick I nearly missed it, Trenton reared back and sent his fist into my father's nose. Blood exploded as Dad stumbled back, and then fell forward, hitting the ground so hard he bounced. It was quiet and very still for several seconds. Dad didn't move, he just lay there, facedown.

"Oh, Jesus!" I said, rushing over to him. I was afraid he was dead, not because I'd miss him, but for the trouble Trenton would be in if he'd killed him. I tugged on my father's shoulder until he rolled over. Blood was streaming from a gash across the bridge of his nose. His head fell to the side. He was unconscious.

"Oh, thank God. He's alive," I said. I covered my mouth again, and looked to Trenton. "I'm so sorry. I am *so* sorry."

He sat back on his knees in a state of disbelief. "What the fuck just happened?"

I shook my head, and closed my eyes. When my brothers found out about this, it would be war.

CHAPTER SEVENTEEN

O<small>H MY GOD!" MOM SAID WHEN SHE OPENED THE DOOR.</small> "What did you do, Felix? What happened?"

Dad moaned.

She helped us carry him to the couch, and then covered her mouth. She ran to get a pillow and blanket, and then made him comfortable. She hugged me.

"He's been drinking," I said.

She pulled away from me, and tried to play off the news with a worried smile. "He doesn't drink anymore. You know that."

"Mom," I said. "Smell him. He's drunk."

She looked down at her husband, and touched her mouth with trembling fingers.

"He came to my apartment. He attacked me." She jerked her head to look at me with wide eyes. "If Trent hadn't been there, Mom . . . he was set on beating the hell out of me. Trent had to hold him back, and he still came at me."

Mom looked down at Dad again. "He was angry you didn't come for lunch. And then Chase started in. Oh, God. This family is falling apart." She reached down and yanked the pillow out from under Dad's head. His skull cracked against the arm. She hit him once with the pillow, and then again. "Goddamn you!" she yelled.

I held her arms, and then she dropped the pillow and began to cry.

"Mom? If the boys find out that Trent did this . . . I'm afraid they'll come after him."

"I can handle it, babe. Don't worry about me," Trenton said, reaching out for me.

I shrugged away from him. "Mom?"

She nodded. "I'll take care of it. I promise." I could tell by the look in her eyes that she meant what she said. She looked down at him again, nearly snarling.

"We'd better go," I said, motioning to Trenton.

"What the hell?" Coby said, stepping out from the dark hallway into the living room. He was wearing a pair of shorts and nothing else. His eyes were heavy and tired.

"Coby," I said, reaching out to him. "Listen to me. It wasn't Trent's fault."

"I heard," Coby said, frowning. "He really attacked you?"

I nodded. "He's drunk."

Coby looked up at Mom. "What are you going to do?"

"What?" she said. "What do you mean?"

"He attacked Camille. He's a grown fucking man, and he attacked your twenty-two-year-old daughter. What the fuck are you going to do about it?"

"Coby," I warned.

"Let me guess," he said. "You're going to threaten him to leave, and then stay. Like you always do."

"I don't know this time," Mom said. She looked down at him,

watched him for a while, and then hit him with the pillow again. "Stupid!" she said, her voice cracking.

"Coby, please don't say anything," I begged. "We don't need a Maddox-versus-Camlin situation on top of this."

Coby glared at Trenton, and then nodded at me. "I owe you one."

I sighed. "Thank you."

Trenton drove us to his dad's house, pulled into the drive, and left the Smurf running. "Christ, Cami. I still can't believe I hit your dad. I'm sorry."

"Don't apologize," I said, covering my eyes with my hand. The humiliation was almost too much to bear.

"We're having Thanksgiving at our house this year. I mean, we have it every year, but we're actually cooking. A real turkey. Dressing. Dessert. The works. You should come." I broke down, then, and Trenton pulled me into his arms.

I sniffed and wiped my eyes, opening the door. "I have to go to work." I got out, and Trenton did, too, leaving the driver's-side door open. He pulled me into his arms to ward off the cold.

"You should call in. Stay here with me and Dad. We'll watch old westerns. It'll be the most boring night of your life."

I shook my head. "I need to work. I need to be busy."

Trenton nodded. "Okay. I'll be there as quick as I can." He cupped each side of my face, kissing my forehead.

I pulled away from him. "You can't come tonight. Just in case my brothers find out what happened."

Trenton laughed once. "I'm not afraid of your brothers. Not even all three of them at the same time."

"Trent, they're my family. They can be assholes, but they're all I've got. I don't want them to get hurt any more than I want you to."

Trenton hugged me, this time squeezing me tight. "They're not all you've got. Not anymore."

I buried my face in his chest.

He kissed the top of my hair. "Besides, that's one thing you don't mess with."

"What?" I asked, pressing my cheek against his chest.

"Family."

I swallowed hard, and then rose up on the balls of my feet, pressing my lips against his. "I have to go." I hopped up into the driver's side of the Smurf and slammed the door.

Trenton waited for me to roll down the window before he responded. "Fine. I'll stay home tonight. But I'm callin' Kody so he can keep an eye on you."

"Please don't tell him what happened," I pleaded.

"I won't. I know he'll tell Raegan, and she'll tell Hank, and then your brothers will find out."

"Exactly," I said, appreciating that someone else saw how protective Hank was of me. "See you later."

"Is it all right if I come by after you get home?"

I thought about it for a moment. "Can you be there when I get home?"

"I was hoping you'd say that," he said with a grin. "I'll be in Dad's truck."

Trenton stood in the yard, watching me back out of the driveway. I drove to the Red, and was thankful that it was the busiest Sunday night we'd seen in a while. Freezing temperatures were a deterrent to tattoos, but clearly not to liquor, flirting, and dancing. The girls still wore sleeveless club tanks and dresses, and I shook my head at every woman who walked in shivering. I worked my ass off, slinging beers and mixing cocktails, which was a nice change from a long day at Skin Deep, and then went home. As promised, Trenton was sitting in Jim's bronze pickup next to my parking spot.

He walked me inside, and helped me clean up the mess we'd left when we carried my dad out to the Jeep. The pieces of the lamp jingled and clattered as we dumped them into the trash can. Trenton propped the end table back onto its broken legs.

"I'll fix that tomorrow."

I nodded, and then retreated to my room. Trenton waited in my bed while I washed my face and brushed my teeth. When I crawled under the covers next to him, he pulled me against his bare skin. He had undressed down to his boxers, and had only been in my bed for less than five minutes, but the sheets were already warm. I shivered against him, and he squeezed me tighter.

After a few minutes of silence, Trenton sighed. "I've been thinking about dinner tomorrow night. I think we should wait a little while. It just seems like . . . I don't know. I feel like we should wait."

I nodded. I didn't want our first date to be weighed down with thoughts of the earlier events of that day, either.

"Hey," he whispered, his voice low and tired. "Those drawings on the walls. Are they yours?"

"Yeah," I said.

"They're good. Why don't you draw me something?"

"I don't really do that anymore."

"You should start. You have my art on your walls," he said, nodding to a couple of framed drawings. One was a penciled sketch of my hands, one lying on top of the other, my fingers displaying my first tattoo, the other was a charcoal of an emaciated girl holding a skull that I had to have when he'd finished. "I'd like to have some of your originals."

"Maybe," I said, settling against the pillow.

Neither of us had much to say after that. Trenton's breathing evened out, and I fell asleep with my cheek against his chest, rising and falling in a slow rhythm.

◆   ◆   ◆

Every night for a week and a half, Jim's truck was a fixture in various parking spaces outside my apartment. Though I should have been worrying about my brothers coming over to pester me, or even fearing that my father would come back, I had never felt so safe. Once the Intrepid was fixed, Trenton began coming to the Red at close and walking me to my Jeep.

In the early morning hours of Thanksgiving, I was lying with my back to Trenton, and he was running his fingers softly up and down my arm.

I sniffed, and wiped a tear that was getting ready to fall from the tip of my nose. Dad was still living at the house. Those of us who knew about what had happened decided to keep it from the rest of the boys, and to keep the peace at least until after the holidays, I would celebrate elsewhere.

"I'm sorry you're upset. I wish there were something I could do," Trenton said.

"I'm just sad for my mom. This is the first Thanksgiving we won't see each other. She doesn't think it's fair that he gets to be there and I don't."

"Why doesn't she make him leave?" Trenton asked.

"She's thinking about it. But she didn't want to do that to the boys during the holidays. She's always tried to do what was best for all of us."

"This is not what's best for all of you. It's a no-win situation.

She should just kick his ass out and let you spend Thanksgiving with your family."

My lip trembled. "The boys will blame me, Trent. She knows what she's doing."

"They won't ask where you are?"

"I haven't been to family lunch in weeks. Mom figures Dad won't let them ask too many questions."

"Come to my house, Cami. Please? My brothers are all coming in."

"All of them?" I asked.

"Yeah. It's the first time we've all been together since Thomas moved away for that job."

I pulled a tissue from the box on my nightstand, and wiped my nose. "I already volunteered to work the bar. It's just Kody and me."

Trenton sighed, but he didn't push the issue any further.

When the sun rose, Trenton kissed me good-bye and left for home. I slept in for another hour and then forced myself to get up and around, finding Raegan cooking eggs in the kitchen. For half a second, I expected to see Kody, but it was just her, looking lost.

"Are you spending the night at your parents' tonight?" I asked.

"Yeah. Sorry you're stuck working."

"I volunteered."

"Why? Didn't your dad freak out?"

"It's Hank and Jorie's first Thanksgiving at their house, and yes, Felix did freak out."

"Aw, that's nice of you," she said, letting the scrambled chicken fetuses slide off the skillet onto her plate. "Want some?" she asked, already knowing the answer.

I made a face.

"So," she said, shoveling a forkful into her mouth. "Trenton has practically moved in."

"He's just . . . making sure I'm okay."

"What does that even mean?" she asked, looking at me with disgust.

"Felix might have come over last weekend after I got back from the employee meeting. And he might have tried to attack me."

Raegan's fork froze halfway between the plate and her mouth, and her expression morphed from confusion, to shock, to anger. "What?"

"Trenton was here. But I'm not really . . . speaking to Dad, or any of my family, really."

"What?" she said, getting angrier by the second. "Why didn't you tell me?" she shrieked.

"Because you overreact. Like this."

"How exactly am I supposed to react? Felix was in our apartment, attacking you—whatever the fucking fuck that means—and you decide not to tell me? I live here, too!"

I frowned. "You're right. God, Ray. I'm sorry. I didn't think about you coming home and him being here."

She put her palm flat on the counter. "Is Trent staying here tonight?"

I shook my head, and my brows pulled in. "No, he has family coming in."

"I'm not leaving you here alone."

"Ray . . ."

"Shut your face! You're coming to my parents' house with me."

"No way . . ."

"You are, and you're going to like it, as punishment for not telling me your psycho, wife-beating father barged into our apartment to attack you, and is still at large!"

"Mom has him under control. I don't know what she did, but he hasn't been back, and Colin, Chase, and Clark have no clue."

"Did Trent beat his ass?"

"I'm pretty sure he broke his nose," I said, cringing.

"Good!" she yelled. "Pack your shit! We're leaving in twenty minutes."

I complied, throwing together an overnight bag. We threw our luggage into Raegan's trunk, and just as she began backing out of the parking lot, my phone chirped. I lifted it and stared at the display.

"What?" Raegan said, her eyes dancing between me and the road. "Is it Trent?"

I shook my head. "T.J. He was hoping I could drop him off at the airport tomorrow."

Raegan frowned. "Can't his dad or somebody?"

"I can't," I said, tapping my answer into the phone. I dropped it into my lap. "So much could go wrong if I did."

Raegan patted my knee. "Good girl."

"I can't believe he's in town. He was so sure he wouldn't be able to come home for Thanksgiving."

My phone chirped again. I looked down.

"What does it say?" Raegan asked.

"'I know what you're thinking, but I didn't know until a couple of days ago that I would be home,'" I said, reading his text aloud.

Raegan's eyes narrowed as she watched me tap out a short response. "I'm confused."

"I don't know what Eakins has to do with his work, either, but it's probably the truth."

"What makes you say that?" she asked.

"Because he wouldn't be coming here otherwise."

When we got to Raegan's, her parents were surprised but happy to see me and welcomed me with open arms. I sat on the navy-blue kitchen counter, listening to Sarah tease Raegan about how hard it was to break her from her blankie, and listening to Raegan tell stories about Bo, her dad. Their home was decorated in red, white, and blue, American flags, and stars. Black-and-white pictures were framed on the walls, telling stories of Bo's naval career.

Raegan and her parents waved good-bye as I left for my shift. The Red Door's parking lot was more concrete than cars, and the small crowd didn't stay long. I was glad I was the only bartender. I barely had enough tips to make the night worth it.

Trenton texted me a half dozen times, still asking me to come over. They were playing dominoes and then watching a movie. I imagined what it would be like to be snuggled on their dad's couch with Trenton, and was a little jealous of Abby that she got to spend time with the Maddoxes. Part of me wanted to be there more than anything.

When I checked my messages just after close, I saw that Trenton had texted with news that Travis and Abby had called it quits. Just when I didn't think I could take one more disappointment, my phone rang, and Trenton's name appeared in the display.

"Hello?" I answered.

"I feel terrible," he said, quiet. He sounded terrible, too. "I don't think I can slip out of here tonight. Travis is in pretty bad shape."

I swallowed back the lump forming in my throat. "It's okay."

"No. It's a lot of things, but it's definitely not okay."

I tried to smile, hoping it would carry over into my voice. "You can make it up to me tomorrow."

"I'm so sorry, Cami. I don't know what to say."

"Say you'll see me tomorrow."

"I'll see you tomorrow. I promise."

After we locked up, Kody walked me to my car. Our breath glowed white under the security lights.

"Happy Thanksgiving, Cami," Kody said, hugging me.

I wrapped my arms around his large frame as best I could. "Happy Thanksgiving, buddy."

"Tell Raegan, too."

"I will."

Kody began texting the moment he walked away.

"I assume that's not Ray," I said.

"Nope," he called back. "It's Trenton. He wanted me to text him after I dropped you off at your Jeep."

I smiled as I hopped up into the driver's seat, wishing I was on my way to see him.

When I got back to Bo and Sarah's, the windows were glowing. They had all waited up for me. I hopped down out of the Jeep and slammed the door. I'd nearly made it to the front door when a car pulled up to the curb. I froze. It wasn't a car I recognized.

T.J. stepped out.

"Oh, God," I said, puffing out the breath I'd been holding. "You scared the shit out of me."

"Jumpy?"

I shrugged. "A little. How did you know where I was?"

"I'm pretty good at finding people."

I nodded once. "That you are."

T.J.'s eyes softened. "I can't stay long. I just wanted to . . . I don't really know why I'm here. I just needed to see you." When I didn't respond, he continued. "I've been thinking about us a lot. Some days I think we can make it work, but then I put those thoughts away when reality sets in."

I furrowed my brow. "What do you want from me, T.J.?"

"You want the honest truth?" he asked. I nodded, and he continued, "I'm a selfish bastard, and want you all to myself . . . even though I know I don't have time to spend with you. I don't want you with him. I don't want you with anyone. I'm trying to be an adult about this, but I'm sick of holding everything in, Cami. I'm sick of being the bigger person. Maybe if you moved to California? I don't know."

"We wouldn't see each other even then. Look at the last weekend I spent there. I'm not your priority." He didn't argue. He didn't respond at all. But I needed to hear him say it. "I'm not, am I?"

He lifted his chin, the softness in his eyes disappeared. "No, you're not. You never have been, and you know that. But that's not because I don't love you. It just is what it is."

I sighed. "Remember when I came to California, and I mentioned that feeling that doesn't go away? It just did."

T.J. nodded, his eyes floating around as he processed my words. He reached for me, kissed the corner of my mouth, and then walked back to his car, driving away. As the taillights disappeared when he turned the corner, I waited for a feeling of emptiness, or tears, or something to hurt. Nothing happened. It was possible that it just hadn't hit me, yet. Or maybe I hadn't been in love with him for a long time. Maybe I was falling in love with someone else.

Raegan opened the door before I knocked, and she handed me a bottle of beer.

"It's Black Friday!" Sarah said from the couch, smiling. Bo held up his beer, welcoming me inside.

"Less than five weeks to Christmas," I said, holding up the beer to greet Raegan and Bo. The thought of a Christmas alone made me feel sick to my stomach. Hank would close the Red, so I wouldn't even have the option of working. I wondered how Felix would explain that away to the boys. Maybe he wouldn't get the chance. Maybe Mom would kick him out, and the dust would settle enough by then that I could come home.

We sat in the living room chatting for a while, and then Raegan and I crawled into her pink, frilly bed. Posters of Zac Efron and Adam Levine still covered the walls. After we changed into sweats, we lay on our backs and propped our feet on the wall above her headboard, crossing our sock-covered feet at the ankle. Raegan clinked her beer bottle to mine.

"Happy Thanksgiving, roomie," she said, tucking her chin to take a drink.

"Back atcha," I said.

My cell phone pinged. It was Trenton, wondering if I'd made it home yet.

I tapped in the words "Staying w Raegan at her parents tonight."

He replied, "Good. Huge relief. I've been worrying about you all day."

I sent back a wink face, not sure what else to say, and then let the phone fall to the mattress next to my head.

"Trenton or T.J.?" Raegan asked.

"God, when you say it that way, it sounds awful."

"I happen to know the situation. Who was it?"

"Trenton."

"Are you worried about T.J. being in town at all?"

"This is so awkward. I keep waiting for him to text me that he's heard all the dirty details about Trent and me."

"It's a small town. It's bound to happen."

"I'm hoping whatever brought him here is keeping him too busy to talk to anyone."

Raegan touched her bottle to mine again. "To impossibilities."

"Thanks," I said, drinking the rest in a few swallows.

"It's not like there are that many dirty details anyway, right?"

I cringed. Trenton wasn't exactly a virgin or insecure, so admittedly I was more than surprised that not one of the nights he'd spent in my bed did he try to undress me.

"Maybe you should tell him you have glow-in-the-dark condoms in your nightstand from Audra's bachelorette party," she said, taking a swig. "That is always a good icebreaker."

I chuckled. "I also have regular."

"Oh, right. The Magnums. For T.J.'s tree trunk."

We both burst out laughing. I giggled until my sides hurt, and then my entire body relaxed. I let out one last sigh, and then flipped around and rested my head on the pillow. Raegan did the same, but instead of lying on her side, she was resting on her belly with her hands tucked beneath her chest.

She looked around the room. "I've missed talking about boys in here."

"What's it like?" I asked.

Raegan narrowed her eyes at me and smiled, curious. "What is what like?"

"Having that kind of childhood. I can't imagine wishing I could go back. Not even for one day."

Raegan's mouth pulled to the side. "It makes me sad to hear you say that."

"It shouldn't. I'm happy now."

"I know," she said. "You deserve it, you know. Stop thinking you don't."

I sighed. "I'm trying."

"T.J. should let you tell. It's not fair to put this burden on you. Especially now."

"Ray?"

"Yeah?"

"Good night."

CHAPTER EIGHTEEN

I N THE EARLY HOURS OF SATURDAY MORNING, TRENTON shot me a text that he was at my door, so I hopped up from the love seat and opened it.

"I have a doorbell, you know," I said.

He frowned, pulling his coat off and hanging it on the closest barstool. "What are we? In 1997?" He grabbed me and flipped us both over the back of the love seat, landing on his back with me on top of him.

"Smooth," I said, my eyes falling to his lips.

He leaned up and kissed me, and then looked up. "Where's Ray?"

"With Brazil. They're on a date. That's why she left early from work tonight."

"Weren't they just arguing yesterday?"

"Hence the date."

Trenton shook his head. "Am I nuts, or was she happier with Kody?"

"She feels like this is her second chance with Jason, so she's trying to iron out the kinks, I guess. She said she was staying at his apartment tonight."

He sat up, bringing me with him. "Did you get your paper written?"

"I did," I said, lifting my chin. "And my statistics homework finished."

"Oh!" Trenton said, wrapping his arms around me. "She's beautiful *and* smart!"

"Don't sound so surprised, jerk face!" I said, feigning insult.

Trenton flipped his red ball cap backward, and I giggled as he planted tiny kisses on my neck. When we realized—at the same time—that we were alone and would be all night, my laughter faded.

Trenton leaned in, staring at my lips for a moment, and then pressed his mouth against mine. The way he kissed me was different from before. It was slow, full of meaning. He even held me in a way that made it feel like it was the first time. I was suddenly nervous, and didn't know why.

His hips moved against mine in such a small movement, I wondered if I'd imagined it. He kissed me again, this time more firmly, and his breath faltered. "God, I want you so fucking bad."

I ran my fingers down his T-shirt, took the bottom hem in both of my fists, and then pulled. In one fluid movement, Trenton's shirt was off, and his warm, bare skin was against me. As his tongue found its way to mine, I ran my fingers down his smooth skin, this time settling on the small of his back.

Trenton anchored himself with his elbows, keeping his full weight from bearing down on me, but he still kept the bulge under the fly of his jeans pressed against the tender part just beneath my pelvic bone. His movements were restrained, but I could tell he wanted to get rid of the fabric between us just as much as I did. I wrapped my legs around him, interlocking my ankles behind his ass. He hummed, and then whispered against my mouth. "This isn't the way I wanted to do this." He kissed me again. "I wanted to take you to dinner first."

"Your girlfriend's a bartender who works on all the good date nights. We'll make an exception," I said.

Trenton immediately pulled away from me, searching my face. "Girlfriend?"

I covered my mouth with one hand, feeling my entire face catch fire.

"Girlfriend?" Trenton asked again, this time sounding more like a question and less like a *what the fuck* moment.

I closed my eyes, and my hand left my mouth to touch my forehead, and then my fingers slid back to grip my hair. "I don't know why I said that. It just came out."

Trenton's expression changed from confused to a surprised, appreciative smile. "I'm good with it if you are."

The corners of my mouth turned up. "That's sort of way better than dinner."

His eyes scanned my face. "Camille Camlin is mine. That's just crazy."

"Not really. It's been a long time coming."

He shook his head slowly. "You have no idea." He beamed. "My girl's fuckin' hot!" His mouth slammed into mine, and then he yanked my shirt over my head, exposing my red bra. He reached around my back, and with one hand pinched the clasps. They sprang loose. He slid the straps off my shoulders and down my arms, and then left a trail of warm kisses down my neck and chest. Gently but with purpose, Trenton cupped my breast, and then took it into his mouth, sucking and licking and kissing until I was so turned on, I squeezed his hips between my thighs.

I let my head fall back against the arm of the love seat as he continued to lick and kiss his way down my belly, and with both hands, he unbuttoned and unzipped my jeans, revealing my black and red lace panties. He shook his head and looked up at me. "If I'd known you were wearing stuff like this, I wouldn't have been able to wait so long."

"So get on with it." I smiled.

After a few frustrating attempts to maneuver on the love seat, Trenton sighed. "Fuck this," he said, sitting up, and bringing me with him. With my legs still wrapped around his midsection, he carried me toward the bedroom.

I could hear muffled voices right outside the door, and then it blew open, smacking against the wall.

Raegan's cheeks were streaked with mascara, and she had on the most beautiful pink cocktail dress I'd ever seen.

"You don't get it!" she yelled. "You can't bring me to a date party and then leave me alone all night so you can drink with your frat brothers at the keg!"

Brazil slammed the door shut. "You could have been over there with me, but you were hell-bent on pouting all damn night!"

Trenton froze, his back to Raegan and Brazil. I was glad, because his head was obscuring their view of my chest.

Raegan and Brazil stared at us for a few seconds, and then Raegan began to cry and ran to her room. Brazil followed her down the hall, but patted Trenton on his bare shoulder first.

Trenton sighed, lowering me to my feet. He reached over the love seat to get my shirt while I put on my bra. Raegan and Brazil were still yelling while we both put on our shirts. I didn't want this drama to be the backdrop to our first time together, and I could tell that Trenton didn't, either.

"Sorry," I said.

Trenton chuckled. "Baby, every second of what just happened was a good time. You have nothing to apologize for."

Raegan's bedroom door slammed, and as Raegan yelled, "Where are you going?" Brazil was stomping around the corner. She ran around him and stood between him and the door. "You're not leaving!"

"I'm not listening to you bitch at me all night!"

"If you would just listen! Why don't you hear what I'm trying to tell you? We can make this work if we just—"

"You don't want me to listen! You want me to obey! There were other people at that party besides you, Ray! When will you get it through your head that you don't fucking own me?"

"That's not what I want, I—"

"Move away from the door!" he yelled.

I frowned. "Brazil, don't yell at her like that. You guys have been drinking—"

Brazil flipped around, angrier than I'd ever seen him. "I don't need you telling me what to do either, Cami!"

Trenton took a step forward, and I put my hand on his shoulder. "I'm not telling you what to do," I said.

Brazil pointed all four fingers and a thumb at Raegan. "She's fucking yelling at me. That's okay, I guess? You women are all the fucking same! We're always the bad guys!"

"No one said you were the bad guy, Jason, just calm down," I said.

"I did! He's the fucking bad guy!" Raegan snapped.

"Ray—" I warned.

"Oh, I'm the bad guy?" Brazil said, touching his chest with both hands. "I'm not the one who's half naked with Trenton over here, when she was in your front yard kissing her ex last night!"

Raegan gasped, and I froze. Brazil seemed to be just as surprised that he had said it as the rest of us.

Trenton shifted nervously, and then he narrowed his eyes at Brazil. "That's not fuckin' funny, dude."

Brazil blanched. His anger had vanished, replaced with regret.

Trenton looked to me. "He's full of shit, right?"

"Christ, Cami, I'm sorry," Brazil said. "I feel like such a prick right now."

Raegan pushed him. "That's because you are a prick!" She moved to the side. "My bad! Get the fuck out!"

Trenton didn't take his eyes off of me. Raegan slammed the door, and then approached Trenton and me. Her anger was gone, but her bloodshot eyes and smeared mascara made her look like a psychotic prom queen.

"I heard you pull up, but you didn't come in. So I looked out the window, and saw . . . what I saw. I mentioned it to Brazil," she admitted, looking down at the floor. "I'm sorry."

Trenton laughed once, his face screwing into disgust. "Damn, Raegan. You're sorry I found out? That's just great."

Raegan tilted her head, determined to set things right. "Trent, what I saw was T.J. begging for Cami back. But she turned him down. So he . . . he kissed her good-bye. It wasn't even a *kiss* kiss," she said, shrugging as she shook her head. "It was kind of on her cheek."

"I got this, Ray. I don't need your help," I said.

She touched my shoulder. Her face was blotchy, and her mascara was smeared all around her eyes and down her cheeks. She looked pitiful. "I'm so sorry. I'm . . ."

I glared at her, and her shoulders fell. She nodded, and then walked to her room.

Trenton was looking at me from the corner of his eyes, clearly trying to rein in his temper.

"Did you hear her?" I asked.

He turned his hat forward, and pulled it low over his eyes. "Yeah." He was trembling.

"I wasn't kissing my ex in Raegan's yard. That's not what it was, so you can just get that image out of your head."

"Why didn't you tell me?" he asked, his voice strained.

I held my hands out to the side. "There was nothing to tell."

"Someone else had their motherfucking lips on you. That's pretty goddamn pertinent, Camille."

I cringed. "Don't call me Camille when you're pissed. You sound like Colin. Or my father."

Trenton's eyes lit with anger. "Don't compare me to them. That's not fair."

I crossed my arms.

"How did he know you were over there? Are you still talking to him?" he asked.

"I don't know how he knew. I asked the same thing. He wouldn't tell me."

He began to pace back and forth, from the front door to the beginning of the hallway. He would readjust his hat, rub the back of his neck, and stop for a moment to put his hands on his hips, his jaws working under the skin, and then he'd start all over again.

"Trenton, stop."

He held up one index finger. I wasn't sure if he was working himself up or trying to stay calm. He stopped, and then took a few steps toward me. "Where does he live?"

I rolled my eyes. "In California, Trent. What are you going to do? Get on a plane?"

"Maybe!" he screamed. His whole body tensed and shook when he yelled. The veins in his neck and forehead rose to the surface.

I didn't flinch, but Trenton stumbled back. The loss of his temper surprised him.

"Feel better?" I asked.

He bent over, grabbing his knees. He took a few breaths, and then nodded. "If he ever touches you again"—he stood up and looked straight into my eyes—"I'll kill him." He grabbed his keys, and then walked out the door, slamming it behind him.

I stood there for a moment in disbelief, and then I walked to my bedroom. Raegan was standing next to my door in the hallway, her eyes begging me for reprieve.

"Not now," I said, walking past her. I shut the door, and fell face-first into my bed.

The door creaked open, followed by silence. I peeked up from my pillow. Raegan was nervously hovering in the doorway, her bottom lip trembling, and she was wringing her hands at her chest. "Please?" she begged.

My mouth tugged to the side, and I lifted the blanket and gestured for her to come to bed with a nod. She rushed over, crawled under the covers, and then curled up into the fetal position next to me. I covered her with the blanket, and then held her while she cried herself to sleep.

✦   ✦   ✦

I woke to a gentle tapping on my door. Raegan walked in with a plate of pancakes slathered in peanut butter and maple syrup.

There was a toothpick poking out from the center of the stack with a white napkin flag taped to it that read, SORRY YOUR ROOMIE IS AN ASSHOLE.

Her eyes were heavy, and I could see that she was hurting more than I was over what she'd done. Forgiveness was not easy for someone like me. When it was granted, more often than not, I was just giving someone a second chance to hurt me. Most people weren't worth investing in. That wasn't my childhood talking, it was the hard truth. There were just a few people I trusted, and even fewer who I would trust again, but Raegan topped both lists.

I chuckled as I sat up, and then took the plate from her. "You didn't have to do this."

She held up a finger, left the room for a few seconds, and then returned with a small glass of orange juice. She set it on my nightstand, and then sat with her legs crisscrossed on the floor. Her face was clean, her hair brushed, and she had a fresh set of striped flannel pajamas on.

She waited until I put the first bite in my mouth, and then spoke. "I never thought in a million years that Jason would have said anything, but that's not an excuse. I shouldn't have told him. I know how those guys talk at the frat house, and I knew better than to give them something to gossip about. I'm so sorry. I'm going to follow you to Skin Deep today and explain."

"You've already explained, Ray. I think hashing it out at his job is a bad idea."

"Okay, so I'll wait for him after work."

"You'll be at work by then."

"Damn it! I need to fix this!"

"You can't fix it. I have royally fucked up. Now Trent is talking about going to California and killing T.J."

"Well, T.J. shouldn't have come to my parents' and kissed you. He knows you're with Trent. Whatever you think you're doing wrong, T.J. is right there with you."

I covered my face. "I don't want to hurt him . . . or anyone. I don't want to cause problems."

"You need to let them figure it out."

"That scenario terrifies me."

Raegan reached up and put her hand on mine. "Eat your pancakes. And then get up because Skin Deep opens in forty minutes."

I took a bite and grudgingly chewed, even though it was the best thing I'd eaten in a long time. I barely made a dent in the stack, and then hopped in the shower. I walked into the shop ten minutes late, but it didn't matter, because Hazel and Trenton were late, too. Calvin was there because the front door was un-locked, the computer was turned on, as well as the lights, but he didn't even bother to greet me.

Ten minutes later, Hazel came through the door, wearing layers of sweaters and wrapped in a thick, hot-pink scarf with black polka dots. She wore her black-rimmed glasses and black jeggings with boots. "I am *over* winter!" she said, plodding to her room.

Ten minutes after that, Trenton arrived. He wore his staple puffy blue coat, jeans, and boots, but he had added a slouchy gray beanie and didn't remove his sunglasses as he trekked to his room.

I lifted my eyebrows. "Good morning," I said to myself.

Ten minutes after that, the door opened again and chimed as a tall, lean man walked in. He wore large, black gauges in his ears, and tattoos covered every inch of skin I could see from his jawline down. He had long, stringy hair, blond and fried at the tips, and the rest was light brown. It was probably less than thirty degrees outside, and he was in a T-shirt and cargo shorts.

He stopped just inside the door and stared at me with his hazel-green, almond-shaped eyes. "Morning," he said. "No offense, but who the fuck are you?"

"None taken," I said. "I'm Cami. Who the fuck are you?"

"I'm Bishop."

"It's about time you showed up. Calvin's only been asking for you for two months."

He smiled. "Really?" He strolled over to the counter and leaned in on his elbows. "I'm kind of big shit around here. I don't know if you watch the tat shows or not, but I was featured in an episode last year and now I travel around a lot, doing gigs wherever. It's like vacationing for a living. It gets lonely, though . . ."

Trenton walked to the counter, grabbed a magazine, and began flipping through it, still wearing his sunglasses. "She's taken, shit dick. Go set up your room. Your machine has cobwebs on it."

"I've missed you, too," Bishop said, leaving us alone. He walked to what I assumed was his room at the opposite end of the hall.

Trenton flipped through a few more pages of the magazine, tossed it onto the counter, and then headed back to his room.

I followed him, crossed my arms, and leaned against the doorjamb. "Oh, hell no. You don't get to run Bishop off and then not even acknowledge me."

He looked up at me, sitting on his stool on the opposite side of the client chair, but I couldn't see his eyes because of his sunglasses.

"I figured you wouldn't want to talk to me," he said, sullen.

"Take off your glasses, Trenton. It's fucking annoying."

Trenton hesitated, and then pulled off his Ray-Ban knock-offs, revealing his bright red eyes.

I stood up straight. "Are you sick?"

"Kind of. Hungover. Drank my weight in Maker's Mark until four this morning."

"At least you chose a decent bourbon to get stupid with."

Trenton frowned. "So . . . let's have it."

"What?"

"The 'let's be friends' speech."

I crossed my arms again, feeling my face get hot. "I was sure you were tasting the douche water last night . . . now I know you're drinking it."

"Only my girlfriend could make a sick analogy like that and still sound hot."

"Oh, really? Your girlfriend? Because you kind of just asked me to break up with you!"

"I don't think people break up past high school, Cami . . ." he said, holding the heel of his hand to his temple.

"Do you have a headache?" I asked, grabbing an apple out of the bowl of plastic fruit on the counter by the door, and chucking it at his head.

He ducked. "C'mon, Cami! Damn!"

"News flash, Trenton Maddox!" I said, snatching a banana from the bowl. "You will not kill anyone for touching me, unless I don't want to be touched! And even then, I'll be the one committing murder! Got it?" I threw the banana at him, and he crossed his arms, making the fruit ricochet to the floor.

"C'mon, baby, I feel like shit," he groaned.

I picked up an orange. "You will not leave my apartment in a huff, or slam my goddamn door when you leave!" I pitched it straight at his head, and hit my target.

He nodded, blinked, and held out his hands, trying to protect his head. "All right! All right!"

I picked up a bunch of green plastic grapes. "And the first thing you say to me the day after being a royal shit bag will *not* be an invitation to dump you on your stupid, drunken ass!" I yelled the last three words, enunciating every syllable. I threw the grapes, and he caught them against his stomach. "You will apologize, and then you will be super fucking nice to me for the rest of the day, and buy me doughnuts!"

Trenton looked around the floor at all the fruit, and then he sighed, looking up at me. A tired smile spread across his face. "I fucking love you."

I stared at him for the longest time, surprised and flattered. "I'll be right back. I'm going to get you a cup of water and some aspirin."

"You love me, too!" he called after me, only half kidding.

I stopped, turned on my heels, and then strolled back into his room. I walked over to where he sat, straddled him, and then touched each side of his face. Looking into his russet eyes for the longest time, I smiled. "I love you, too."

He beamed, looking up into my eyes. "Are you fucking serious?"

I leaned down and kissed him, and he pushed off from the floor, sending us into a spin.

CHAPTER NINETEEN

As a sea of drunken and happy people passed through the Red Door, the party kicked into full swing. Raegan and I were buzzing behind the bar at full speed, in metallic dresses and high heels. Our tip jars were overflowing, and the live band was busting out a decent rendition of "Hungry Like the Wolf." A long line wrapped around the building as people waited to be let in as others left. We were at capacity, and it didn't look to be slowing down until close—typical for New Year's Eve.

"Yeah!" Raegan said, bouncing her head to the beat. "Love this song!"

I shook my head as I poured a cocktail into a glass.

Trenton, Travis, and Shepley made their way through the crowd to the bar, and I was instantly happy. "You made it!" I said. I pulled their favorite beers from the cooler, popped the tops, and set them on the bar.

"I said I would," Trenton said. He leaned across the bar and pecked my lips. I glanced over at Travis. "Did you happen to say anything?"

"Nope." He winked at me. A guy a row back from Trenton ordered a Jack and Coke, and I began to pour, trying not to stare as Trenton walked away. The holidays were always fun, and I loved working when it was crazy busy, but for the first time, I wished I was on the other side of the bar.

The boys found a table and sat. Shepley and Trenton seemed to be having a good time, but Travis was sipping his beer, trying to pretend he wasn't miserable, and failing.

"Jorie!" I called. "Keep that table loaded with beer and shots, please." I set up a tray, and she took it over.

"Yes, ma'am," she said, shaking her ass to the music as she walked.

A curvy redhead approached the Maddox table, and hugged Trenton. A strange, uncomfortable feeling came over me. I wasn't sure what it was, but I didn't like it. She spoke to him for a few moments, and then stood between the brothers. She had that look of hope in her eyes I'd seen many times when women spoke to Travis. Pretty soon the crowd obscured my view. I grabbed cash out of someone's hand and rang him up, handing him his change. The leftover dollars dropped into the tip jar, and I started on the next order. Between Raegan and me, this one night would pay our rent for the next three months.

The band stopped playing, and those standing at the bar looked around. The lead singer began to count down from ten, and everyone counted with him. Girls were pushing through the crowd, rushing to be next to their dates for the first kiss of the year.

"Five! Four! Three! Two! One! Happy New Year!"

Silver and gold ticker tape and balloons fell from the ceiling, right on cue. I looked up, proud of Hank. For a small-town bar, he always went all-out. I looked over at Trenton's table, seeing the redhead's lips on his. My stomach felt sick, and for half a second, I wanted to jump over the bar and pull her off of him.

Suddenly, Trenton's face appeared in front of me. He noticed me staring at his table and smiled.

"She had it bad for Travis before he even got here."

"They all do," I said, breathing a sigh of relief. Damn the Maddox boys and their identical DNA.

"Happy New Year, baby," Trenton said.

"Happy New Year," I said, sliding a beer down the bar to the person who had ordered it.

He jerked his head to the side, gesturing for me to come closer. I leaned across the bar, and he put his lips on mine, cupping his hand gently at the back of my head. His lips were warm and soft and amazing, and when he let me go, I felt a little light-headed.

"Now I'm fucked," Trenton said.

"Why's that?" I asked.

"Because the rest of my year will never live up to the first thirty seconds."

I pressed my lips together. "I love you."

Trenton looked back, noticing that Travis was back alone at their table. "Gotta go," he said, seeming disappointed. "I love you, too. I'm the breakup support team. I'll come back!"

Not a minute later, I saw Trenton waving frantically. Travis's face was red. He was upset, and they were leaving. I waved, and returned to the demanding crowd, glad to have something to keep my mind off of Trenton Maddox's lips.

When I got off work, Trenton was waiting at the employee entrance, and he walked me to the Smurf. He shoved his hands in his jean pockets while I unlocked the door, and when I hopped up into the driver's seat, Trenton frowned.

"What?"

"Why don't you let me drive you home?"

I looked past him to the Intrepid. "You want to leave your car here?"

"I want to drive you home."

"Okay. Care to explain why?"

He shook his head. "I don't know. I just have a bad feeling about you driving home. It's been bugging me every time I see you get into the car."

I watched him for a moment. "Have you ever thought about talking to someone? About what happened?"

"No," he said, dismissively.

"Seems like you've still got some anxiety going on. It might help."

"I don't need a shrink, baby. I just need to drive you home."

I shrugged, and then climbed over the console.

Trenton turned the ignition and put his hand on my thigh while he waited for the engine to warm. "Travis asked me about you tonight."

"Yeah?"

"I told him you were still with your California boyfriend. Damn near made me sick to say it."

I leaned over and kissed his lips, and he pulled me closer. "I'm sorry you had to lie to him. I know it's stupid, but it would start a conversation I'm not really ready to get into just yet. If we had just a little more time . . ."

"I don't like lying to my brothers, but I hated even saying you were with someone else. Made me really think about what it would be like to lose you. Made me really think about what Trav is going through." He shook his head. "I can't lose you, Cami."

I touched my lips with my fingers, and shook my head. He

was trusting me, and making himself so vulnerable, and I was keeping so much from him.

"Can you stay with me tonight?" I asked.

He lifted my hand to his mouth, turned it over, and kissed the thin skin of my wrist. "I'll stay here as long as you'll let me," he said, as if I should have already known.

He backed out of the parking spot, and then drove out of the lot, heading for my apartment. Trenton's frown from earlier had all but disappeared, and he looked lost in his thoughts as he drove with his hand in mine.

"When I get up enough money saved, I thought maybe you could help me find a place."

I smiled. "I can do that."

"Maybe you might like it enough to move in."

I stared at him for a moment, waiting for him to tell me he was joking, but he didn't, instead he pressed his brows together. "Shit plan?"

"No. Not necessarily. That's a ways down the road."

"Yeah. Especially since I lost a quarter of my savings to Travis's ex."

I giggled. "What? Are you serious? How did that happen?"

"Poker night. She's some poker phenom. Hustled us."

"Abby?"

He nodded. "Swear to God."

"That's kind of cool."

"I guess. If you like thieves."

"Well . . . her dog's name is Crook."

Trenton laughed and squeezed my knee as we pulled into my spot. He turned off the headlights, leaving the front of my apartment in the dark. With Trenton's fingers entwined with mine, we walked inside, and then I locked the chain on the door.

"Ray's not coming home?"

I shook my head. "She's staying with Brazil."

"I thought they broke up?"

"She did, too. But when she got a huge bouquet of flowers the next day, she decided they didn't."

I walked backward to my bedroom, pulling Trenton by both of his hands. He smiled at me as he walked, knowing by the look on my face what I had in mind.

I stood in the middle of my room and stepped out of my heels. Then I reached back, unzipped my dress, and let it fall to the floor around my ankles.

Trenton unbuttoned his white shirt, and then unbuckled his belt. I walked over to him, and unbuttoned his jeans and pulled down the zipper. We were looking into each other's eyes with that serious and sleepy stare that made my thighs ache. The look that meant something amazing was about to happen.

Trenton leaned in and barely touched his lips to mine, letting the full softness of them graze my mouth, and then down my jaw to my neck. Once he reached my collarbone, he returned his gaze to mine. I ran my hands down his chest, and then his stomach, kneeling as I grasped the waistline of his jeans and pulled down slowly. His black boxer briefs were directly in front of my face, and once Trenton stepped out of his jeans, I looked up at him, gripped the elastic, and pulled them down, too.

His dick was already fully erect, and I was glad I had the Magnums in the drawer of my nightstand, because we were definitely going to need them.

I kissed his stomach, and made a trail from his navel to the base of his shaft. The moment I put him inside my mouth, he tangled his fingers in my hair and groaned.

"Oh. My fucking. God."

My head bobbed back and forth, and I looked up at him. He was watching me, with that same amazing, serious look in his eyes. My fingers and palm slid nicely over his tender skin, and the deeper I took him into the back of my throat, the louder he groaned and the more he swore.

I moved my hand from his front to his backside, and gripped his tight ass with both hands, pushing him even deeper into my mouth. His fingers were knotted in my hair, and for ten minutes, he hummed and groaned and begged me to let him inside me.

When he seemed like he couldn't stand it anymore, I backed away, and lay back on the bed, my knees apart. Trenton followed, but instead of situating himself between my legs, he turned me onto my stomach, and pressed his chest against my back. His wet dick was nestled between my ass cheeks, and his lips were against my ear. He licked his index and middle finger, and then slipped his hand between the mattress and my stomach, reaching down until his warm, wet fingers were touching my pink, swollen skin.

I hummed as he caressed me, kissing the tender skin behind my earlobe. Once the sheets below me were soaked, I reached for the drawer. Trenton knew exactly what I wanted, and paused long enough to grab a square package, tear it with his teeth, and easily slide the latex over his rigid erection.

When the warmth of his chest and abs returned to my back, it nearly sent me over the edge. He reached beneath me, lifted my hips to prop up my backside a few inches, and guided himself inside me, slow, and controlled. We both groaned, and I arched my back and bucked my hips up to his, allowing him to go deeper.

As he began to rock against me, I gripped the sheets. When he reached down to touch me with his fingers again, I cried out. The feel of his hips and thighs against my bare ass was incredible, and I just wanted him deeper, closer, harder.

Trenton raked the strands of hair away from my face and out of my eyes. My entire body was overwhelmed by the most wonderful intensity. It enveloped me, and I cried out as it traveled like electricity throughout my body.

"Goddamn, keep making that sound," he said, breathless.

I wasn't even sure what sound I was making, I was so lost in the moment, lost in him. He rocked against me harder, each thrust sending shock waves from my pelvis to my toes. He bit my ear, firm and gentle, exactly how he was fucking me. His teeth set my ear free, and his fingers dug deep into my hips. He growled as he drove himself into me one last time, his body twitching as he moaned.

He collapsed beside me, breathless and smiling, his skin glistening with sweat. I know I had the same flushed, satisfied expression on my face.

Trenton gently brushed my damp hair from my face. "You're fucking amazing."

"Maybe. But I'm definitely in love with you."

Trenton laughed once. "It's crazy feeling this happy . . . are you as happy as I am?"

I smiled. "The happiest."

And that's when it all came crashing down.

CHAPTER TWENTY

"AND JUST SIGN HERE, AND HERE, AND YOU'RE GOOD TO GO,"
I said.

Landen Freeman made a few squiggles on each line, and then
leaned against the counter, onto his elbows. I'd seen him around
Eastern State's tiny campus when I was taking more classes, but
I hadn't seen him in over a year, and it wasn't surprising that he
didn't recognize me.

"What time does this place close?" He stared straight into my
eyes, flashing a sexy smile that I imagined he had been perfecting
in a mirror since puberty.

I pointed to the writing on the door with the pen, and then
purposefully busied myself with his paperwork. "Eleven."

"Mind if I stop by? I'd love to take you to the Red Door. Have
you been there?"

"Have you?" I asked, slightly amused.

"Once in a while. I'm loaded down with twenty hours a semester. Trying to finish and get the hell out of here as quick as
I can."

"I know the feeling," I said.

"So . . . what about that drink?"

"What drink?" I asked.

"The drink I want to buy you."

Trenton appeared beside me, picked up the papers, and began looking through them. "If you're wanting this freehanded, Calvin's your guy, and he's not working today."

Landen shrugged. "I'm cool with whoever. It doesn't have to be freehand."

"You want me to do it?" Trenton asked.

"Yeah, I mean, I've seen your work on the website. It's badass."

"I'll do it, but you're going to have to stop staring at my girl's tits."

I craned my neck at him. I hadn't caught Landen staring at my chest once.

"Uh . . ." Landen said, stammering.

"On second thought, you better call and make an appointment with Cal. I'm busy." Trenton tossed the waivers, and they rained down around us. He turned his hat to sit off center, and I watched, unimpressed, as Trenton strolled back to his station. He walked with an arrogant swagger—the way he did before beating someone down.

Landen looked at me, then down the hall, and then back at me.

"I'm . . . I'm so sorry," I said, handing him our card. "Here's the number for the shop. Calvin works on Wednesdays and Thursdays, by appointment only."

Landen took the card. "I didn't know," he said, smiling sheepishly. The door chimed when he left, and I turned on my heels, stomping down the hall into Trenton's room.

"What the hell was that?"

"He asked you out!"

"So?"

"So? I should have beat his ass!"

I sighed and closed my eyes. "Trent, I handled it. You can't run customers off every time they flirt with me. That's what Cal hired me for."

"He did *not* hire you to be flirted with. He hired—"

"A hot piece of ass to work the counter. A job you offered me, don't forget."

"He didn't even ask you if you were single, first! At least the douche nozzle could have started with that."

"I had it handled."

"I didn't hear you turn him down . . ."

My nose wrinkled. "I was dodging his question! I can't just shut him down while he's out here in the waiting area! It's called professionalism."

"Oh, is that what it's called?"

I narrowed my eyes at him.

"You could have told him you have a boyfriend."

"Is that what this is? That I'm not holding up my new label like a picket sign? What if I just tattoo TRENTON'S GIRL across my forehead?"

His face softened, and he chuckled. "I will gladly tat that somewhere else."

I growled in frustration and walked back to the front. Trenton jogged after me.

"It's not a horrible idea," he said, only half teasing.

"I am not tatting your name on me," I said, disgusted that he was even entertaining the idea. Trenton had already filled in the poppies the first week of Christmas break with a striking cherry red, and then two days before Christmas, he'd added some tribal art and black and bright green swirling clouds to the same arm. A week after New Year's, I had a gorgeous blooming red rose with yellow accents. I was on my way to an intricate, badass sleeve. We had begun to refer to our sessions as pain therapy. I would talk, and Trenton would draw and listen. I loved sharing that time with him, and knowing that I carried his beautiful pieces of art with me everywhere.

He sat on the counter, his palms planted flat against the Formica. "Maybe I'll hide it in one of your tattoos one of these days."

"Maybe I'll break your machine into a million pieces," I said.

"Whoa. Shit just got real," he said, hopping down to stand next to me. "I'm sorry you're angry that I ran the guy off. I'm not sorry for running him off, but I am sorry I made you mad. Think about it, though. I wasn't going to tat him up after he hit on my girl. Trust me. It was best for everyone."

"Stop making sense," I snapped.

Trenton wrapped his arms around me from behind, and then buried his face in my neck. "I'm almost not sorry for making you mad. You're fucking hot when you're angry."

I playfully elbowed him in the ribs, and the door chimed again. Colin and Chase walked toward the counter, and Chase crossed his arms over his chest.

"Tattoos?" I asked. They weren't amused.

Trenton's grip relaxed. "How can we help you, guys?"

Colin frowned. "We need to talk to Camille. Alone."

Trenton shook his head. "Not gonna happen."

Chase narrowed his eyes and leaned toward us. "She's our fucking family. We're not asking for your permission, Maddox."

Trenton raised an eyebrow. "You are, you just don't know it yet."

Colin's eye twitched. "Chase is here to talk to his sister. This is family business, Trent. You need to stay out of it. Camille, outside. Now."

"You can talk to me here, Colin. What do you need?"

He glared at me. "You really want to talk about this here?"

"What do you want to talk about?" I asked, trying to remain calm. I was sure if we went outside, Colin or Chase would lose his temper and a fight would break out. It was safer to stay put.

"You didn't show up for Thanksgiving. Dad said you had to work. Whatever. But then you don't show up at Christmas. Then your chair is empty again at lunch on New Year's Day. What the fuck is going on, Camille?" Chase asked, incensed.

"I have two jobs, and I'm taking classes. It's just the way things happened this year."

"Dad's birthday is next week," Chase said. "You better fucking be there."

"Or what?" Trenton said.

"The fuck did you just say to me, Maddox?" Chase snapped.

Trenton lifted his chin. "She better be there, or what? What are you going to do if she doesn't show?"

Chase leaned against the counter. "Come get her."

"No. You won't," Trenton said.

Colin leaned in, too, keeping his voice low when he spoke. "I'm only going to say this one more time. This is family business, Trent. You need to stay the fuck out of it."

Trenton's jaws worked under his skin. "Cami is my business. And her cocksucking brothers walking into her work trying to bully her is most definitely my business."

Colin and Chase glared at Trenton, both of them taking a step backward. Colin spoke first, like he always did. "Camille, come outside with us right now, or I'm going to tear this place apart while I kick your buddy's ass."

"I'm not her buddy. I'm her boyfriend, and I'll knock you the fuck out before you can scratch the paint."

Calvin appeared on the other side of me. I looked down and his hands were balled into fists. "Did you just say you were going to tear up my shop?"

"What are you going to do about it?" Chase spat on the floor.

"Chase, Jesus Christ!" I yelled. "What is wrong with you?" Trenton held me back, even though I wasn't trying all that hard to go anywhere.

Bishop and Hazel came out of their rooms, curious about the noise. Bishop stood on the other side of Calvin, and Hazel on the end.

Hazel crossed her arms. "I may not look like much, but when one of these big boys are holding you down and I'm clawing your eyes out, you'll understand why I'm standing here. But see . . . I don't want to claw your eyes out, because you're Cami's family. And we don't want to hurt her. Ever. Because she's part of our family, now. And you don't. Hurt. Family. So take a lesson from us, wipe those frowns off your punk ginger faces, and go home. When you cool off, Chase . . . give your sister a call. And talk to her nice. Unless you don't want to keep your eyes."

"Or your arms," Trenton added. "Because if you ever talk to her with anything less than a respectful tone again, I will rip those fuckers off and beat you with 'em. Do we understand each other?"

Colin and Chase watched our group with wary eyes, from Trenton to Hazel, and everyone in between. They were outnumbered, and I could see in Colin's eyes he wasn't going to take them all on.

Chase looked to me. "I'll call you later. We deserve an explanation for why our family's falling apart."

I nodded, and they both turned and pushed through the double doors.

When Colin's engine fired up, I looked down, embarrassed. "I'm so sorry, Calvin."

"The shop's good, kiddo. We're good." He walked back to his office, and Hazel walked over, sliding her arms between mine and pressing her cheek against my chest.

"We got you," she said simply. I kept my eyes on the floor, but when it was obvious Hazel wasn't letting go, I squeezed her tight.

Bishop watched us for a moment.

"Thank you," I said.

Bishop raised an eyebrow. "I wasn't going to fight. I was just out here to watch." He walked back to his room, and I chuckled.

Hazel let me go and took a step back. "All right. Show's over. Get back to work." She left for her room.

Trenton pulled me into his arms, and touched his lips to my hair. "They'll get it eventually."

I looked up at him, unsure of what he meant.

"I'm never going to let them intimidate you again."

I pressed my cheek against his chest again. "It's all they know, Trent. I can't really blame them."

"Why not? They blame you for everything. And they're not robots. They're adults, and they can make different choices. They choose to stick with what they know."

"Kind of like you and your brothers?" I didn't look up, and Trenton didn't respond right away.

Finally he took a breath. "We don't react to things because it's all we know. It's just the opposite. We have no fucking clue what we're doing."

"But you try," I said, nuzzling up against him. "You try to be good people. You work toward doing better, being better, more patient, and more understanding. But just because you can beat someone's ass . . . doesn't mean you should."

Trenton chuckled. "Yeah it does." I tried—and not very hard—to push him away. He held me tighter.

"I'm going to make you beef tips and rice tonight," I said.

Trenton made a face. "I love your cooking, baby doll, but I can't keep eating dinner at three AM."

I laughed. "Fine, I'll have it waiting for you. There's a spare key under the rock that sits in front of the pillar by my door. I'll leave it there."

"Can I take a rain check? I promised Olive I'd take her to Chicken Joe's."

I smiled, but I wasn't happy about missing out on Olive time.

"Wait. Did you just tell me where the spare key was?"

"Yeah?"

"So can I use it anytime?"

I shrugged. "Yeah."

A small smile tugged on one corner of Trenton's mouth, and then it spread across his face. "I'm going to bet on Travis's next fight. Try to get the money back I lost to Abby, and then some. I'm going to start looking for a place next week. I want you to come with me."

"Okay," I said, not sure why he had such a serious look on his face. I already knew he was working toward getting his own place.

Trenton's smile was beaming. "It's his end-of-the-year fight.

Big money. They'll probably get some has-been MMA fighter like they got last year."

"Who'd they get last year?"

"Kelly Heaton. He lost the championship four years ago. Travis beat the piss out of 'em." Trenton was clearly enjoying the memory. "I made fifteen hundred. If I can make at least that this year, we'll be set."

"You'll be set. I have a place."

"Yeah, well, maybe one of these days you'll decide to stay the night and you'll never go home."

"Don't count on it. I love having my space."

"You can have your space. You can have whatever you want."

I rose up on the balls of my feet, wrapped my arms around his neck, and kissed Trenton's soft lips. "I already have what I want."

He squeezed me tighter. "Come on. You know you want to."

"No, thank you. Not anytime soon."

Trenton's face fell for just a second, and then he winked and grabbed my keys. "I'm going to start the Jeep. Be right back."

He slipped on his coat and jogged outside.

Hazel came to the front and shook her head. "Trenton loves you, *kaibigan*. Like, the deep, forever kind. I've never seen him like this, doing this shit for girls." She was nearly cooing every word.

I turned to her. "What did you just call me?"

She smiled. "I called you 'friend,' bitch. In Tagalog. You have a problem with that?"

I laughed and pushed her, barely hard enough to budge her tiny frame. "No. I have a problem with the fact that I'm almost out of cigarettes, and I don't want to spend the money for another pack."

"Then fucking quit. It's gross, anyway."

"You don't smoke?" I asked. Everyone else at the shop did, so I just assumed she would, too.

Hazel made a face. "No. And I would never date you, based on that alone. It's disgusting. No one likes tonguing an ashtray."

I popped a cigarette in my mouth. Trenton ran in, shivering. "Heat's on high, baby!" He pulled the cigarette out of my mouth and kissed me, leaning me back a bit.

When he released me, I turned to Hazel. "Someone does."

Hazel stuck her tongue out at me. "Come in early tomorrow. I'm going to start your gauges."

"No. You're not."

"Yes, I am," she lilted, walking to her room.

"You want me to drive you to the Red? I don't want your shit head brothers showing up at your apartment. And it's nasty out."

"Brazil's there, and I can handle a little snow." There was a foot of dirty, melting mess on the ground, and the wind was brutal, but it was better than ice, and our little town was good about keeping most of the roads clear.

Trenton's cheeks and nose were bright red, and he was still shivering. "Brazil can't handle your brothers," he said, frowning.

I giggled, and grabbed my heavy black coat and purse. "Thank you for starting the Jeep. Stay in here where it's warm."

He handed me back my cigarette, but not before giving me one last kiss. "Valentine's is in a week."

"Yes. In exactly one week from today. So it's on a Saturday. Good for everyone else, bad for us."

"Ask off. You worked Thanksgiving."

"I'll think about it."

Trenton stood at the door while I backed out of the parking lot. I drove home without a problem. I shut the door behind me, tossed the keys onto the counter, and walked straight to the bathroom. Standing under a hot shower felt glorious, but the second I turned off the water, I could hear Brazil and Raegan bickering. By the time I brushed my teeth, wrapped myself in my white, fuzzy robe, and stepped out into the hallway, they had taken their argument to the front door.

Brazil saw me, and sighed. "I'm going, Ray. I told them I'd be there, and I'm going."

"But we had plans. It's not okay to cancel plans with me to go drinking with your frat brothers! Why don't you get that?"

Brazil pulled his hat down low over his eyes, zipped up his coat, and left.

Raegan walked straight into my room and sat on my bed. I sat on the floor in front of a full-size mirror, and unzipped my makeup bag.

"He's such a *dick*!" she said, pounding the mattress with her fists.

"He's not ready for a relationship. He wants the benefits of a girlfriend without the commitment."

She shook her head. "Then he'd just pull a Travis Maddox and fuck everything with a vag until he found the one, instead of trying so hard to make things work with me."

I raised an eyebrow. "He doesn't want you to be happy with anyone else."

Raegan's angry expression turned sad. "Kody called me today. He's worried about the roads and wants to pick me up for work. We had our stupid fights, but I miss him."

I painted my eyes and lips, and then plugged in my hair dryer and turned it on. "What are you waiting for, Ray?" I said loudly, above the noise.

She didn't answer, instead she just watched me blow my hair all over the place. When I was finished, she shrugged. "Brazil dumped me right about this time before last year's date party. I bought a dress, I told everyone he asked me. I'm going to that fucking party."

I glared into the mirror, staring at her reflection in disbelief. "Are you kidding me? You are putting up with this frat boy nonsense to go to a party?"

"I bought a dress!" she said. "You wouldn't understand."

"You're right. I wouldn't."

The doorbell rang, and Raegan and I stared at each other.

"Maybe it's Brazil," she said.

"Colin and Chase came by Skin Deep today. Almost got in a fight with Trenton . . . and everyone else."

"Shit, you think it's them?" she asked.

I stood up, crept over to the door, and looked through the peephole. I rolled my eyes and pulled off the chain, opening the door. Kody was standing there, bundled in a wool coat, scarf, gloves, and cap.

"What are you doing here?" Reagan asked, stepping out into the living room.

"It's getting worse, Ray. I don't think it's a good idea that you drive. Either of you."

She looked down. "I'm not ready for work, yet."

Kody fell onto the love seat. "I'll wait. I'll leave the truck running so it's warm when you get in."

Raegan stifled a smile, and then she rushed to her room and shut the door.

"I just got home less than twenty minutes ago. It's not that bad," I said with a smirk.

"Ssh," Kody said. "She doesn't need to know that."

"You're good," I said, walking back to my room.

CHAPTER TWENTY-ONE

SATURDAY NIGHT AFTER A GRUELING NIGHT AT THE RED, I dragged my ass into the apartment, and flipped on my bedroom light. Trenton was lying on top of my covers in a pair of navy-blue boxer briefs . . . and socks.

I peeled off my clothes, flipped off the light, and then crawled in bed next to him. He fought with the blankets as he tried to get beneath them with me, and then grabbed at me until I was close enough. He buried his head into my neck, and we lay there for the longest time, still and warm. I'd never come home to anyone before, but it wasn't a wretched feeling. Just the opposite: I was in a warm bed with the warm, incredibly-hard-to-resist body of the man who loved me more than anyone ever had. It could be worse. Way worse.

"How is Olive?"

"Hmmm?"

"Olive. Is she doing okay?"

"She misses you. I promised to bring her here to see you tomorrow."

I smiled. "How was Chicken Joe's?"

"Greasy. Loud. Awesome."

I squeezed his arm that was across my chest even tighter against me. "I see you found the key."

"No, I couldn't find it, so I crawled in through your bedroom window. Did you know it's been unlocked?"

I froze.

Trenton laughed, slow and breathy. I elbowed him.

The front door slammed, and Trenton and I both sat up.

"Quit! Don't fucking wave at him! Raegan!" Brazil yelled.

"He was being nice! He just didn't want me to drive in the snow!"

"There's no snow on the roads! They're just wet!"

"Yeah! Now!" she said. She stomped down the hall, and Brazil followed her, slamming her bedroom door.

I groaned. "Not tonight. I need sleep."

Brazil's muffled voice filtered through the wall. "Because you can't ride around with your ex-boyfriend, that's why!"

"Maybe if you had taken me to work . . ."

"Nuh-uh, don't pin this on me! If I had done the same thing . . ."

"Who says you didn't?"

"What does that mean? What do you mean, Raegan? Has someone said something to you?"

"No!"

"Then what?"

"Nothing! I don't know what you do when you're out! I'm not even sure I care anymore!"

It got really quiet then, and after several minutes, they continued speaking in lowered voices. Ten minutes later there were no voices at all, and just when I thought to go check on Raegan,

I heard her moaning and yelping, and her bed was knocking into the wall.

Ugh. "Seriously?" I said.

"Living together is sounding better all the time, isn't it?" Trenton said against my neck.

I settled in next to him. "It's been less than four months. Let's pace ourselves."

"Why?"

"Because that's a big deal. And I barely know you."

Trenton touched my knee, and then let his hand slide upward until his fingers were touching the cotton piece of my panties. "I know you fairly intimately."

"Really? You want to get it on with Buffy and Spike next door?"

"Huh?"

"They're fighting, and then they . . . never mind."

"Not in the mood, huh?" he asked.

Raegan's yelps were becoming shriller.

"Not . . . right now, no."

"See? We're practically married already."

"You got jokes!" I said as I dug my thumbs between his ribs. He tried fending me off, grunting and laughing as I tickled him. Eventually, he began emulating Raegan's high-pitched cries. I covered my mouth, giggling incessantly. Raegan grew quiet, and Trenton fist bumped me. Then we settled down again.

Half an hour later, Brazil and Raegan crept down the hall and then the front door opened and closed. A few seconds later, my bedroom door flew open and the light turned on. "Assholes!"

I covered my eyes until I heard Raegan gasp.

"Holy shit, Trenton, what happened to you?"

I turned to look at him. Three bloody scratches were on his cheekbone, and his lip was split. I jerked to a sitting position. "What happened to your face, Trent?"

"I haven't thought of a good lie to tell you yet."

"I thought you went to Chicken Joe's with Olive tonight? You went to that biker bar, didn't you?" I said, my voice thick with accusation.

Trenton chuckled. "No, I went to Chicken Joe's. So did Chase and Colin."

Raegan gasped, and so did I. My eyes filled with tears. "They fucking jumped you? When you were with Olive? Is she okay?"

"They tried. She's fine. We went outside. She didn't see much."

Raegan took a step. "What happened?"

"They won't try to jump me again, let's just put it that way."

I covered my face. "Goddammit! Damn it!" I picked up my phone and sent the same text to Colin and Chase. It only said one word.

ASSHOLES

Trenton's phone buzzed, and he picked it up, and then rolled his eyes. I'd sent the text to him, too.

"Hey. They came after me."

"Are they okay?" I asked.

"They're hurting. They'll hurt worse in the morning. But it's done."

My face compressed. "Trent! Damn it! This has got to stop!"

"I told you, baby, it's done. Coby was with them. He didn't

jump in. He tried to talk them out of it. I beat their asses. They agreed to back off."

My phone chirped. It was Chase.

Sorry. We worked it out. It's all good.

How does your face feel?

Not good.

Good.

Raegan's eyes widened a bit before she backed out and walked to her room.

I glared at Trenton.

"What did you want me to do? Let them beat my ass?"

My face smoothed. "No. I hate that it happened in front of Olive. I'm worried about her."

Trenton climbed out of bed, flipped off the light, and then crawled back in beside me. "You'll see her tomorrow. She's okay. I explained it to her, and then I explained it to her parents."

I cringed. "Were they mad?"

"A little. But not at me."

"Do you need an ice pack or anything?"

Trenton chuckled. "No, babe. I'm good. Go to sleep."

I relaxed against him, but it took me quite a while to fall asleep. My mind wouldn't stop racing, and I could tell from his breathing that Trenton wasn't asleep, either. Finally, my eyes got heavy, and I let myself drift off.

◆　◆　◆

When my eyes finally opened, the clock said 10:00, and Olive was standing next to my bed, staring at me. I held the covers against my chest, aware that I was nearly naked beneath them.

"Hey, Olive," I said, squinting. "Where's Trent?"

"He's bringing in the gwocewies."

"Groceries?" I said, sitting up. "What groceries?"

"We went shopping this mowning. He said you wuhr out of a few things, but he has six sacks."

I leaned over but only saw the open front door.

Brazil stepped into the hallway, his dark bronze skin covered only by a pair of green plaid boxers. He yawned, scratched his ass, and then turned around to see Olive. He crossed his hands over his groin that was just waking up as well.

"Whoa! What's she doing here?"

"She's here with Trent. You're back already?"

"Got here as Trent was leaving."

"Put your damn clothes on, you don't live here."

Olive shook her head, scolding him with her sparkling green eyes.

Brazil retreated to Raegan's room, and I nodded toward the door. "Beat it, kid. I've gotta get dressed, too." I winked at her, and she grinned before skipping into the living room.

I shut my bedroom door and dug into my drawers for socks and a bra, then slipped on a pair of jeans and a cream sweater. My hair still stunk like forty packs of cigarettes from working at the Red the night before, so I pulled it back into a tiny ponytail, sprayed some body spray on it, and called it good.

When I walked into the kitchen, Trenton was joking with Olive, putting away canned goods, among other things. All of the cabinets were open, and they were all full.

"Trenton Allen!" I gasped and covered my mouth. "Why did you do that? You're supposed to be saving money!"

"I spend a lot of time over here, eating a lot of your food, and I am three hundred bucks ahead, especially after Travis's year-end fight."

"But you don't know when it is or even if it's going to happen. Travis is all about Abby, now. What if he quits? What if the other guy backs out?"

Trenton smiled and pulled me into his arms. "You let me worry about it. I can buy a few groceries once in a while. I got some for my dad, too."

I hugged him, and then pulled the last cigarette out of my pack. "You didn't happen to pick up more cigarettes, did you?" I asked.

Trenton seemed disappointed. "No. Are you out? I can run back and pick up some."

Olive crossed her arms. "Smoking is bad fowr you."

I pulled the cigarette from my mouth and set it on the counter. "You're right. I'm sorry."

"Don't patwonize me. You should quit. Twent should quit, too."

Trenton watched Olive for a moment, and then looked to me. I shrugged. "It was getting expensive, anyway."

Trenton pulled his pack from his coat pocket and crushed them with one hand, and then I picked up my last one, and broke it in half. Trenton tossed his in the trash, and so did I.

Olive stood in the middle of my kitchen, happier than I'd ever seen her, and then her beautiful green eyes began to leak.

"Aw! Ew! Don't cry!" Trenton said, sweeping her up into his arms. She hugged him, and her little body began to shake.

She sat up, faced me, and wiped one of her wet eyes. "I'm just so bwessed!" she said, sniffling.

I hugged Trenton, sandwiching her in between us. Trenton's eyebrows shot up, both amused and touched by her reaction.

"Gosh, Ew, if I'd known it was that important to you, I would have thrown them away a long time ago."

She pressed her palms against his cheeks, making his lips pooch out. "Mommy says that she is more proud of quitting smoking than almost anything. Except me."

Trenton's eyes softened, and he hugged her to him.

Olive watched cartoons on the love seat until Trenton had to go home to get ready for work. I beat him to Skin Deep and decided to dust and vacuum because Calvin had already opened the shop, turning on all the lights and the computer, which is what I usually did when I arrived.

Hazel burst through the front door, nearly hidden behind her big orange coat and thick scarf. "I'm sorry! I'm so sorry!" she said, rushing to her room.

I followed her in, curious.

She sprayed the chair with MadaCide, and then disinfected everything else. She was rummaging through her drawers, setting out various packages, and then turned around to face me. "I'm going to wash my hands, glove up, and then I'll be ready!"

I frowned. "Ready for what? You don't have an appointment this morning."

A mischievous grin swept across her face. "Oh, but I do!"

She left for about five minutes and then returned, putting her gloves on. "Well?" she said, looking at me expectantly.

"Well what?"

"Sit down! Let's do this!"

"I'm not getting gauges, Hazel. I've told you that. Multiple times."

She jutted out her bottom lip. "But I'm gloved! I'm ready! Did you see the new leopard gauges we got in last week? They're fucking hot!"

"I don't want my ears sagging. That's gross."

"You don't have to size up. We can just start with a sixteen gauge. That's teeny! Just, like . . ." She curved her thumb and index finger to form a tiny hole in the center.

I shook my head. "No, sweets. I did the nose. I love it. I'm good."

"You love mine!" she said, becoming more deflated by the second.

"Yes. Yours. I don't want that for my ears."

Hazel ripped off her gloves and tossed them in the trash, and then she cursed, a lot, in Tagalog.

"Trent will be here any minute," I said. "Get a new tat. Blow off some steam."

"That works for you. I need to stab things. That's what brings me peace."

"Weird," I said, walking back to the front.

Trenton blew in, his keys dangling from his finger. He was clearly in a good mood. "Baby," he said, rushing to stand next to me. He gripped my arms. "The car's running. I need you to come with me for a second."

"Trent, the shop's open, I can't—"

"Cal!" Trenton yelled.

"Yeah?" Calvin called from the back.

"I'm taking Cami to see it! We'll be back in less than an hour!"

"Whatev!"

Trenton looked at me, eyes bright. "C'mon!" he said, pulling me by the hand.

I resisted. "Where are we going?"

"You'll see," he said, leading me to the Intrepid. He opened the door for me, and I sat inside. He ran around the back, and then slid into the driver's seat.

He drove fast to wherever we were headed, playing the radio a little louder than usual, as he tapped the steering wheel to the beat. We pulled up to Highland Ridge, one of the nicer apartment complexes in town, and parked in front of the office. A woman about my age was standing outside in a pants suit and heels.

"Good morning, Mr. Maddox. You must be Camille," she said, holding out her hand. "I'm Libby. I've been looking forward to today." I shook her hand, unsure about what was going on.

Trenton took my hand as we followed her to a building on the backside of the property. We climbed the stairs, and Libby pulled out a thick set of keys, using one to open the door.

"So, this is the two-bedroom." She held out one arm and twirled slowly in a half circle. She reminded me of one of those women on *The Price Is Right*. "Two bathrooms, seven hundred square feet, washer and dryer hookup, refrigerator, garbage disposal, dishwasher, fireplace, carpet throughout, and up to two pets allowed with pet deposit. Eight eighty a month, eight eighty deposit." She smiled. "That's without pets, and that includes water and trash. Trash pickup is on Tuesdays. Pool is open May through September, clubhouse year-round, fitness center twenty-four/seven, and of course designated, covered parking."

Trenton looked to me.

I shrugged. "It's amazing."

"Do you love it?"

"What's not to love? This blows my place out of the water."

Trenton smiled at Libby. "We'll take it."

"Uh . . . Trenton, can we . . . ?" I pulled him into a bedroom and shut the door.

"What, baby? This place isn't going to have vacancies for long."

"I thought you wouldn't have the money until after Travis's fight?"

Trenton laughed and wrapped his arms around me. "I was saving up for a year's worth of rent and bills, including my half of dad's. I can afford to move us in now."

"Wait, wait, wait . . . did you just say us?"

"What'd I say?" Trent asked, confused. "You just said you loved it and it was better than your place."

"But I didn't say I was going to move in, too! I said the opposite last night!"

Trenton stood there with his mouth open. It snapped shut, and he rubbed the back of his neck. "Okay, so . . . I have a key to your place, you have a key to mine. See how it goes. No pressure."

"I don't have to have a key to your apartment right now."

"Why not?"

"I just . . . I don't need one. I don't know, it feels weird. And why do you need a two-bedroom?"

Trenton shrugged. "You said you needed your space. That room is for whatever you want it to be."

I wanted to hug him and tell him yes and make him happy, but I didn't want to move in with my boyfriend. Not yet, and if I did, it would be a natural progression, not this ambushing bullshit. "No."

"No to what?"

"To everything. I'm not taking a key. I'm not moving in. I'm not getting gauges. Just . . . no!"

"Gauges . . . what?"

I stormed out, running past Libby, down the stairs, and back to the Intrepid. Trenton didn't make me stand in the cold long. He slid in next to me and started the car. As it warmed up, he sighed. "I picked a bad week to quit smoking."

"Tell me about it."

CHAPTER TWENTY-TWO

Busy with packing and moving, trenton wasn't around much for the next week. I helped him when I could, but things were awkward. Trenton was more than a little disappointed about me not moving in. He couldn't hide his feelings any better than I could, which wasn't always a good thing.

Saturday night, Raegan was sitting on our love seat, flipping channels in a show-stopping cocktail dress. The single shoulder strap looked like shimmering diamonds, and the rest was curve-hugging red satin. The sweetheart neckline made it that much sexier. Her silver heels were sky-high, and her hair was straight, shiny, and half up, half down.

"I wish Blia were here. This moment definitely calls for one of her customized phrases. You are flawless."

Her buff lip gloss glistened against her brilliant smile. "Thanks, Cami. What are your plans tonight?"

"Trenton was going to unpack for a little while after he left Skin Deep, but he said he'd be here by seven. Travis is having a rough time lately, so he's going to check on him and then come over."

"So you're taking the night off?"

I nodded.

"Brazil is picking me up at seven thirty."

"You don't look all that happy about it."

She shrugged.

I walked into my bedroom, and slid open my closet doors. The left one was hanging off the track, so I had to be careful. My clothes were carefully categorized by type and subtype, and then by color. Sweaters were hanging on the far left, various shirts, denim, and then dresses on the right. I didn't have very many—I was more focused on paying bills than padding my wardrobe, and Raegan let me borrow a lot of her stuff, anyway. Trenton was taking me to some fancy Italian restaurant in town, and then we were going to have a few drinks at the Red. It was supposed to be a laid-back evening. His card and present were sitting in a red gift sack on top of my dresser. It was fairly lame, but I knew he would appreciate the gesture.

I pulled out the only thing that was close to appropriate: a black crocheted dress with a white liner and three-quarter-length sleeves. With a modest scoop neckline, it was the one dress I owned that didn't accentuate my cleavage and wouldn't draw attention at a nice restaurant. I slipped on a pair of red heels and matching red necklace and earrings, and called it good.

There was a knock on the door just before seven, and I jogged across the floor. "Don't get up. It's probably Trent."

But it wasn't. It was Brazil. He looked at his watch. "Sorry I'm so early. I was just sitting around the house and . . ."

Raegan stood up, and Brazil was speechless for a moment. His mouth pulled to the side. "You look nice."

I frowned. Raegan looked like a million bucks, and I could tell Brazil was intentionally acting unimpressed. He wasn't being mean about it, but there was a hint of regret in his eyes.

Raegan didn't even complain about his nonreaction, she just mirrored his expression, and then picked up her purse from the breakfast bar.

"Better bring a coat, Ray," Brazil said. "It's chilly."

I opened the front closet and handed her black dress coat to her. She offered a small smile in thanks, and then they closed the door behind them.

I returned to my room and finished my hair. Seven came and went, and so did seven thirty. At eight, I picked up my phone and turned it over. Nothing. I tried calling, but it went straight to voicemail.

At fifteen 'til nine, I was sitting on the love seat, playing a stupid bird game on my cell phone. It didn't help my already building anger that Trenton hadn't called to explain his lateness.

Someone knocked on the door, and I leaped to my feet. I opened the door to find Trenton, or part of him, because he was hidden behind a vase full of several dozen dark red roses.

I gasped and covered my mouth. "Holy hell, are those for me?" I asked.

Trenton walked in and set the vase on the bar. He was in the same clothes he wore to work, and suddenly I felt overdressed.

When he turned, he wasn't smiling.

"What? Is Travis okay?" I asked.

"His bike was parked at Ugly Fixer Liquor's, so probably not."

I hugged him tight. "Thank you for the flowers." When I realized his hands were still at his sides, I pulled away.

Trenton was clearly working to keep his face smooth. "They were delivered to the shop late, after you left. They're not from me."

"Who are they from?" I asked.

He pointed to the vase. "There's a card."

I walked over and plucked the miniature red envelope from its plastic holder. When I pulled the card out, my lips moved but nothing came out as I quickly read the words.

> *I talked myself out of this several times this week, but*
> *I had to.*
>   *Love always,*
>   *T.*

I closed my eyes. "Damn it." I laid the card upside down and flat on the light-green Formica and held it there, glancing at Trenton. "I know what you're thinking."

"No, you don't."

"I am not talking to him. We haven't spoken in weeks."

"So it *was* T.J.," Trenton said, his face and neck turning three shades of red.

"Yes, but I don't even think he knows why he sent them. Let's just . . ." I reached for him, but he pulled away. "Let's just forget about them," I said, gesturing dismissively toward the roses, "and have a good time tonight." Trenton shoved his hands in his pockets, his lips pressed together in a hard line. "Please?" I begged.

"He sent them to fuck with your head. And mine."

"No," I said, "he wouldn't do that."

"Don't defend him! This is bullshit!" he said as he turned for the door, and then turned back to face me. "I've been sitting at work this whole time, staring at those fucking things. I wanted to calm down before I got here, but this is just . . . it's fucking disrespectful, is what it is! I bust my ass trying to prove to you that I'm better for you than he ever was. But he keeps pulling this shit, and showing up, and . . . I can't compete with some rich college boy from California. I'm barely getting by, with no degree, and up until a few days ago I still lived with my dad. But I am so fucking in love you, Cami," he said, reaching for me. "I have been since we were kids. The first time I saw you on the playground, I knew what beauty was. The first time you ignored me was my first broken heart. I thought I was playing this right, from the moment I sat down at your table at the Red. No one has ever wanted someone as much as I want you. For *years* I . . ." He was breathing hard, and he clenched his jaw. "When I heard about your dad, I wanted to rescue you," he said, chuckling, but not out of humor. "And that night at your apartment, I thought I'd finally gotten something right." He pointed to the ground. "That my purpose in life was to love you and keep you safe . . . but I didn't prepare for having to share you."

I didn't know if I could fix this. It was our first Valentine's Day, and he was furious. But I knew those flowers had nothing to do with Trenton and everything to do with T.J. being miserable. He loved me, but we just couldn't make it work. Trenton didn't understand because any attempt at an explanation would lead to questions—questions I couldn't answer. It was hard to be mad at either of them, and easy to be angry at myself for putting us all in this situation.

I walked into the kitchen, pulled out the trash can, picked up the vase, and let it fall straight to the bottom.

Trenton watched me with a grimace, and then his entire face softened. "You didn't have to do that!"

I rushed over to him and wrapped my arms around his middle, pressing my cheek against his shoulder. Even when I wore heels, he was taller than me. "I don't want those flowers." I looked up at him. "I do, however, want *you*. You're not the one I'm stuck with because I didn't get my first choice. If you think you're in love with two people, you pick the second one, right? Because if I really loved T.J., I couldn't have fallen in love with you."

Trenton looked down at me, his eyes heavy with sadness. "In theory," he said, laughing once.

"I wish you could see yourself through my eyes. Every woman who's met you wants a shot at you. How could you ever think you're the consolation prize?"

Trenton touched my jaw with his palm, and then he walked away from me. "Goddammit! I ruined our whole night! I'm such a fuckin' jerk, Cami! I was stressing because I wanted to get you flowers, but they're all so damn expensive . . . and then that ridiculously gigantic bouquet shows up. I'm a dick. I'm an unreasonable, selfish, insecure dick who is so scared of losing you. It's too hard to believe that you're already mine." His eyes were so sad, it broke my heart.

"Since we were kids? You never talked to me, though. I didn't think you knew who I was."

He laughed once. "You terrified me."

I raised an eyebrow. "A Maddox boy? Afraid?"

His face compressed. "We've already lost the first woman we ever loved. The thought of going through that again scares the shit out of us."

My eyes instantly filled with tears, and then spilled over. I gripped his shirt in my fists and pulled him against me, kissing him hard, and then I ran to my room, picked up the small sack and card, and returned to him. I held the sack in front of me.

"Happy Valentine's Day."

Trenton blanched. "I am the biggest dickhole in the history of dickholes."

"Why?"

"I was so worried about the flowers, I forgot your present at the shop."

"It's okay," I said, waving him off. "This is not a big deal."

He opened the card, read it, and looked up at me. "The card I got you is not this good."

"Stop. Open your present," I said, a little giddy.

He reached in, and pulled out something rolled in white tissue paper. He opened it up, and held out the T-shirt in front of him. Still holding it high, he poked his head around. "Your present isn't this awesome, either."

"It's not awesome. It's just a shirt."

He flipped it around, pointing at the *Star Wars* font. "'May the Schwartz Be with You'? This is the motherfucking pterodactyl of T-shirts!"

I blinked. "So . . . that's a good thing?"

Someone knocked on the door, and Trenton and I jumped. I wiped my eyes while Trenton peeked out the peephole. He turned to me, clearly confused.

"It's . . . it's Kody."

"Kody?" I asked, opening the door.

"Ray's been trying to call you," he said, upset. "She and Brazil got into it again. She needs a ride home. I was going to go get her, but she thinks it would go over better if you were there."

"Shit," I said, rushing to put on my coat.

"My truck's running," Kody said. "I'll drive."

I pointed at him. "Don't start any shit."

Kody held up his hands as I passed. We all piled into his truck and drove to the Sig Tau house.

Cars lined the street, and the house was decorated with red lights and strings adorned with beer cans and cutout hearts. Some people were milling about outside, but most were running from the street for the warmth of the house.

Trenton helped me down the four feet from Kody's lifted truck, and we met Kody on the driver's side. The bass from the music was thumping inside my chest, and it reminded me of the Red. Just as I began to take a step toward the house, Trenton held me back. He was staring at the space in front of Kody's truck.

"Fuck me," he said, his head jerking toward the house.

Travis's Harley was parked in the street, and an empty, half-pint bottle of whiskey was lying next to it, held up by the crisp, dead grass.

A girl screamed, "Put me down, damn it!"

It was Abby, and she was hanging over Travis's shoulder, beating the hell out of him with her fists, and kicking. He stomped over to a car and threw her into the backseat. After a short conversation with a guy in the driver's seat, Travis crawled into the back with Abby.

"Should we . . . ?" I began, but Trenton shook his head.

"They have been back and forth like this for weeks. I do not want to get caught up in that disaster."

The car pulled away, and we walked inside. The moment we stepped into the main room, people were staring and whispering to each other.

"Trent!" Shepley said, a wide smile on his face.

"I just saw Travis," Trenton said, pointing behind him.

Shepley chuckled. "Yeah. They're going to end up back to-gether tonight."

Trenton shook his head. "They're nuts."

Kody took a step. "We're looking for Brazil and Raegan. Have you seen them?"

Shepley glanced around and then shrugged. "Not for a while."

We searched downstairs, we searched the main floor, and then went upstairs. Kody didn't miss a single room, or even the closets. When we got to the balcony, we found Brazil.

"Jason," I said. He turned around. He nodded at Trenton, but gave Kody a once-over.

"This is a Sig Tau party, guys. Sorry, but you can't stay."

"I'm Sig Tau," Trenton said.

"No offense, man, but not anymore."

Kody turned his shoulder toward Brazil, clearly trying his hardest to keep from attacking him. "Where's Ray?"

Brazil shook his head and looked down. Then he looked up at me. "I tried to make it work. I really tried this time. I just can't do clingy."

Kody leaned in closer, and Trenton put his hand on his chest. "She's not clingy," he said through his teeth. "You should feel grateful for the time she wants to spend with you."

Brazil started to respond, but I held up my hand. "Jason, we're not here to judge you."

"Speak for yourself," Kody growled.

I jerked my head toward his large frame. "You're not helping. Shut up."

"Do you know where she is?" Trenton asked. "We're just here to take her home."

He shook his head. "I haven't seen her."

We left Brazil alone, taking the stairs to the main floor. We walked outside, and Trenton hooked his arm around me to ward off the cold.

"What now?" Kody asked.

"Try to call her," I said, shivering.

We walked back to the truck, and then froze when we saw Raegan sitting on the curb next to Kody's back tire.

"Ray?" Kody said.

She stood up and turned around, holding up her phone. "It died," she cried.

Kody scooped her up into his huge arms, and she hugged him, crying. He climbed up into his truck with her still in his arms, and then Trenton and I walked around. Oddly, Raegan didn't want to discuss her fight with Brazil. Instead, Travis was the topic of conversion.

"And then he said, 'and to the absolute fucking horror of losing your best friend, because you were stupid enough to fall in love with her,' or something like that." She put her palm on Kody's chest. "I died."

I looked to Trenton, but instead of the amused expression I expected, he was lost in thought.

"You okay?" I asked.

"That hit a little too close to home," he said.

I kissed his cheek. "Baby. Stop. We're good."

"We didn't even make dinner."

"Let's go to the store," Kody said. "Pick up some groceries. I'll cook."

"I'll help," Trenton said.

"Oh, I have groceries," I said. "I'm stocked for a while."

"Do you have pasta shells?" Kody asked.

"Yes," Raegan and I said in unison.

"Butter?" Kody asked. We nodded. "Flour? Southwest seasoning?" I looked to Trenton, who nodded. "Milk? Jack cheese?" I shook my head no.

Trenton spoke up. "You've got pepper jack, though."

Kody nodded once. "Just as good. Tomatoes? Green chiles? Bread crumbs?"

"No bread crumbs," Trenton said.

Kody jerked the wheel to the right, and we drove to his apartment. He was inside for less than a minute, and then we were on our way, with a box of bread crumbs.

"I'm starving," I said. "What are you making?"

"A gourmet Valentine's Day meal," Kody said, rather overdramatically. "Southwestern Mac and Cheese."

We all laughed, but my stomach growled. It sounded amazing.

Trenton whispered into my ear, "I'm sorry I didn't take you to dinner."

I hugged his arm. "This is much better than what we had planned."

He kissed my cheek and squeezed me against his side. "I agree."

CHAPTER TWENTY-THREE

Even for just a few classes, midterms were kicking my ass. Kody, Raegan, Gruber, Blia, and I were all studying at the Red before it got busy or when it was slow, and Trenton was helping me study at Skin Deep. Spring break was quickly approaching, and I was eager for the time off and the extra money I would make from working extra hours, but I had to get through exams first.

The first week of March was a blur, and the week of midterms was even worse, but even though it took me the entire allotted time, I finished my tests and felt good enough about them to enjoy break.

Sunday night after work, instead of driving to my apartment, I drove to Trenton's. If Kody wasn't spending the night at our apartment, Raegan was at his. After the first few days of *are we or aren't we?* they picked up where they'd left off, and I'd never seen Raegan so happy. Their honeymoon period was beginning to make me uncomfortable, though, even if I was getting to enjoy Kody's breakfasts again. As much as I loved seeing her smile, sleeping at Trenton's was a relief, for several reasons.

Monday morning, I rolled over, and slowly began to wake up. Trenton's entire body wrapped mine. Alternating between big spoon and little spoon as we turned from one side to the other had become a nightly ritual. I was more comfortable sleeping on my right side, and Trenton was more comfortable on his left, so we tossed and turned a lot.

I yawned, and out of habit, Trenton pulled me closer. His white walls were broken up by old bronze framed family pictures, portraits of his mother, and many snapshots of us: at the Red Door, at Skin Deep, and the ridiculous shot of us celebrating the completion of my sixth tattoo, an intricate peacock with deep yellows, blues, greens, reds, and purples, spanning from my hip to midrib. Trenton said it was the best he'd ever done, and he traced it tenderly at night before he fell asleep.

My body was becoming a walking piece of art, and that was just fine with me. Trenton had asked me a few times why I continued to work at the shop, even after Coby finished his program and was back on his feet, and I teased that it was for the free tattoos. But, truthfully, Trenton would have done them for free, anyway—a perk of being the artist's girlfriend.

Between appointments Trenton doodled and sketched at my desk, and when I fell in love with one, I would have him draw it on my skin. I had the originals framed and hung them in my bedroom, and Trenton had the re-creations in his bed.

I climbed out of bed and trudged to the bathroom. The sunlight hitting the bright white walls made my eyes squint. I stubbed my toe on the towel rack I'd helped him pick out, and then I opened the medicine cabinet to grab the toothbrush I kept there. It was all very domestic, and even though I thought I couldn't do this, I did . . . and I cherished every moment.

I sat on the bright orange couch and rubbed my eyes. At that time of the morning, if the blinds were open, the sun would hit the mosaic of broken glass and mirrors that hung above the couch just right and spray a million rainbows on the opposite wall. I loved to sit there with a cup of coffee and enjoy the view. I only drank coffee at Trenton's. Raegan and I didn't have a coffeemaker, and here I could make one cup at a time.

Trenton stumbled out of the bedroom and rubbed his face. "I'm fuckin' tired for some reason," he said, his voice deep and raspy. He sat next to me and then rested his head on my lap. We had buzzed his hair the night before, so it was particularly prickly when I ran my fingers over it.

"Don't forget," he said.

"I know. Travis's fight could be at any time, and you have to go the moment he calls to keep an eye on Abby."

"I hope that scumbag who attacked her last time shows his face. He'll wish it was Travis beating on him instead."

"If you beat him any worse than Travis did, you'll kill him. So let's hope he doesn't show."

"You can have my apartment while I'm in jail."

I rolled my eyes. "How about you just not go to jail? I'm kind of liking the way things are."

He looked up at me. "You are?"

"Immensely."

"I've got a key with your name on it."

"It's too early, baby, don't start," I groaned.

He sat up. "One of these days I'm going to quit asking, and you'll miss it."

"I doubt it."

"You doubt that I'll quit asking, or that you'll miss it?"

"Both."

He frowned. "That's not nice."

I looked at my watch. "We've got work in a couple of hours."

"No, we don't. I asked off."

"Okay, then. I have work in a couple of hours."

"I asked off for both of us."

My eyebrows pulled together. "Why?"

"Because I'm on call for Trav, and I thought maybe you'd like to come."

"You can't take my hours and not ask me, Trenton. And Cal shouldn't let you pull that shit, either."

"It's just one day. It's not like you need the second job, anyway."

"I like to work, and it doesn't matter if I need it or not, you crossed the line. That's my money, Trenton. Not cool," I said, standing up. His head fell to the cushions, and then he followed me to the bedroom.

"Okay, then. I'll call Cal and tell him you're coming in."

"No, I'll call Cal. Since when do you need to talk to my boss for me?" I said, pulling on my jeans and a shirt.

Trenton's shoulders sagged. "Don't leave, baby, c'mon. I was looking forward to spending the day with you. I'm sorry."

I slipped on my shoes and coat, and after tracking down my cell phone, keys, and purse, I headed for the front door.

Trenton pressed his palm against the door. "Don't leave mad."

"I'm not mad. I'm fucking furious. This is exactly why I don't want to move in with you, Trenton. You don't get to run my life."

"I'm not trying to run your life! I was trying to do something nice!"

"Okay, but do you understand why I think you crossed the line?"

"No, I think you're overreacting."

I sighed. "I'm leaving. Move your hand."

He didn't.

"Trenton, please move your hand. I want to go home."

He winced. "Home. This is your home. You've been here all week. You've loved it! I don't know why you're being so goddamn stubborn about it. You were thinking about moving to Califuckingfornia with the douche canoe in less time than we've been together!"

"T.J. lived in his apartment for *two years*! He was a little more stable!"

Trenton's mouth fell open, looking like I'd shot him. "Damn, babe. Don't hold back."

I cringed. "I shouldn't have said that. I'm sorry."

He took a step toward me, and I flinched. As bad as the comparison to T.J. wounded him, my tiny reflex hurt him even worse.

He spoke low and slow. "I would *never* hit you."

"I know. It was just out of habit . . . I . . ."

He walked away from me, went into the bedroom, and slammed the door. My shoulders jerked up to my ears, and I closed my eyes.

After a few quiet seconds, a loud noise came from behind his door, like he had pushed the dresser over, but I couldn't tell for sure. I didn't stick around to find out. I ran out the door and down the stairs and hopped into the Jeep.

◆   ◆   ◆

With the college kids on break, the shop was dead. As the hours dragged on with no customers, guilt consumed me. Trenton knew we would be bored out of our minds at work, so it made sense to take the day off. Still, I couldn't apologize for how I felt.

I'd worked hard to stand on my own, and there was nothing wrong with wanting to hold onto my independence for as long as I could.

I was sitting on the counter, my legs swinging back and forth. Hazel sat on the couch next to the front doors, filing her nails into claws.

"He made a good point," she said.

"Which one?" I asked, moping.

"You were going to move in with T.J. Why not Trent? He's as stable as anyone."

"Don't make me feel worse than I already do. I was just mad."

"He knows."

"Then why hasn't he called?"

"Maybe he feels guilty, too. Maybe he's mortified that you flinched."

"It was a reflex. I couldn't control it."

"He knows. Deep down, he knows. I think you just threw him for a loop. He's mentioned before that he feels it's his purpose to protect you, right?"

"That's what he said."

"But then he scares you."

"Not on purpose."

"Still. I can see why he'd take that hard. Calvin!" she yelled, making me jump.

"What?" he yelled back.

"Let's close this shit hole! No one's been in all day, and Cami's leaving for the Red, anyway."

Calvin walked to the front, all emotion absent from his face. "Did you just call the shop a shit hole?"

"Yes," she said. "Am I fired?"

"Has Bishop been in?" he asked.

Hazel nodded. "Yeah, but he got a text fifteen minutes ago. There's a fight tonight."

"What?" I said, standing up. "Is that where he went?"

Hazel nodded. "Yeah? So?"

"So Trent's going to be there tonight. He's betting big money, and he's supposed to watch Abby for Travis. I guess some guy attacked her last time."

"No shit?" Hazel said, her almond-shaped eyes wide.

"We can close, if you take back what you said about the shop, and if we can drink at the Red," Calvin said, looking to me, "for free."

I shook my head. "I'll buy your first round, but giving away drinks is grounds for termination, so that's a no."

"I take it back," Hazel said. "This is the prettiest, most wonderful shop ever, and I never want to leave. Except for right now."

Calvin nodded. "I'll meet you there."

Hazel clapped. "I have the best! Job! Ever!" She stood up and rushed back to her room to gather her things.

I closed out the register and the computer, and Calvin shut down the lights from the back.

I walked out to the Jeep, pausing when I noticed Trenton pulling up in the Intrepid. He parked quickly and jumped out. He pulled my keys out of my hand, opened the driver's side of the Jeep, started it, and then got out. "It's fight night. Keaton Hall. I gotta go, I'm already late, but I just wanted to see you." He kissed my cheek.

A weird panic came over me, like he was saying good-bye. I gripped his shirt, stopping him from walking away. "Are we okay?" I asked.

He looked relieved. "No, but we will be." He flashed a sad half-smile, his dimple sinking into his cheek.

"What does that mean?"

"It means I'm a fuckup, but I'm going to get it figured out. I swear. Just . . . don't give up on me, okay?"

I shook my head. "Stop."

"I have to go, baby." He kissed my forehead, and then jogged to his car.

"Call me when you're done. I have a weird feeling."

He winked at me. "Me, too. That means I'm going to win a shit ton of money tonight."

He backed out of the driveway, and I hopped into the Jeep. It was warm, and I hugged my steering wheel, overcome with affection for the man who always took such good care of me. Hazel honked the horn of her black Eagle Talon, and I followed her straight to the Red.

CHAPTER TWENTY-FOUR

Everyone is gone. it's a goddamn tragedy," Raegan said. "Those damn fights. Those *damn* fights!"

"So dramatic," I said, watching her angrily toss a quarter into her empty tip jar. "Do you remember last time you cursed the Circle? They all came in after, we worked our asses off, and they all got kicked out before they could even order a drink."

"I remember," Raegan said, smashing her cheek upward with the heel of her hand. She blew a strawberry, and her bangs blew upward.

"Don't look so sad, babe!" Kody called from across the room.

A girl ran in, making Kody jerk for half a second in reaction. She spoke quickly to one of five guys at the pool tables, pulled on his arm, and they both ran out at full speed.

Then I noticed people checking their text messages, and answering their phones, and then running out.

Raegan noticed, too. She stood up, her eyebrows pulling in. "That's . . . weird." She waved at Kody. "Fight outside?"

He leaned back, trying to make eye contact with Gruber at the entrance. "Something going on outside?" he yelled. His voice boomed, carrying across even the club music. Kody shook his head at Raegan. "Nothing."

Blia ran in, holding up her phone. "Holy fuck balls! It's all over Facebook!" she cried. "Keaton Hall is burning!"

"What?" I sat, every muscle in my body tensing.

"Turn that shit off!" Hank yelled to the DJ. The music was silenced, and Hank pulled out the remote, turning up the flat screen that usually broadcasted sports. He switched channels until the news came on.

The dark image was shaky, but finally it came into focus. Smoke was billowing from Keaton and terrified students were running across the lawn. The caption read *Amateur Video Taken by Cell Phone Outside Eastern State University's Keaton Hall.*

"No. No!" I yelled, grabbing for my keys. I pushed up the hinged section of the bar, taking two strides before Hank yanked me back.

"What are you doing?" Hank said.

"Trent is in there! He's at Travis's fight!" I pulled against his grip, but he wasn't letting me go.

Jorie appeared next to us, her eyes flickering. "You can't go in there, Cami. The place is on fire!"

I fought against Hank. "Let me go! Let me *go!*" I screamed.

Kody came over, but instead of helping me, he assisted Hank in holding me in place. Gruber rushed around the corner, but he stopped several feet away, watching with wide eyes.

"Shh," Raegan said, gently pulling me away from them. "Call him," she said, handing me her phone.

I took it, but my hands were shaking so much that I couldn't press the numbers. Raegan took the phone from me.

"What's his number?"

"Four-oh-two-one-four-four-eight," I said, trying not to freak out any more than I already was. My heart was trying to beat out of my chest, and I was gasping for air after my struggle with Hank and Kody.

We waited. No one moved. No one spoke. Raegan's eyes danced around until they finally settled on me. She shook her head.

I didn't wait to give them a chance to restrain me again. I sprinted for the entrance and burst through the double doors, to my Jeep. My hands still shaking, it took me a few tries before I got the key in the ignition, but once the engine started, I peeled out of the parking lot.

Campus was less than ten minutes away, and I rolled over several curbs to get past the traffic and to the parking lot closest to Keaton Hall. The scene was even more frightening in person. The water from the pumper trucks had already soaked the ground and had reached the asphalt. As I ran across the lawn, my boots sloshed on the saturated grass.

The red-and-blue lights from the emergency vehicles flashed on the surrounding buildings. What seemed like miles of hoses ran from the hydrants to various windows and doors of Keaton, where firefighters had run toward danger. People were screaming and crying, and calling out names. Dozens of bodies were lying in a line, covered with yellow, wool blankets. I walked along them, staring at the shoes, praying I didn't come across Trenton's yellow work boots. When I got to the end of the line, I recoiled. One pair of feet was missing a heel. The other foot was bare, displaying perfectly manicured toes. The big toe was painted with a black-and-white chevron, with a red heart. Whoever she was, she was alive when those toes were painted, and now she was lying lifeless on the cold, wet ground.

I covered my mouth, and then began searching the faces

around me. "Trent!" I screamed. "Trenton Maddox!" The more time that went by, the more bodies were dragged out, and fewer people were being saved. It looked like a war zone. So many of my regulars went to these fights—classmates, from college and high school. Since I'd arrived on the scene, I hadn't crossed paths with any of them. I didn't see Travis, or Abby, either, and I wondered if they were among the dead as well. Even if Trenton had made it out and his brother didn't, he would be devastated. After a time, it grew eerily quiet. The crying was reduced to whimpers, the only sound the buzzing of the hoses, and the occasional yelling among firefighters. I shivered, and realized for the first time that I wasn't wearing a coat.

My cell phone rang, and I nearly dropped it trying to get it to my ear. "Hello?" I cried.

"Cami?" Raegan said. "Stay put! Trent is on his way to you!"

"What? You talked to him?"

"Yes! He's okay! Stay put!"

I hung up, and held the phone to my chest, shaking uncontrollably, and looking around, waiting and hoping Raegan was right. Trenton appeared, a hundred yards away, running at full speed in my direction.

My legs gave out, and I fell to my knees, sobbing. Trenton fell in front of me, wrapping his arms around me. "I've got you! I'm here!"

I couldn't speak. I couldn't do anything but sob and claw at his shirt. Trenton ripped off his coat and draped it over my shoulders, and then his arms were around me again, rocking me until I calmed down.

"It's all right, baby," he said, his voice calm and soothing. His face was streaked with soot and sweat, and his shirt was filthy. He smelled like a campfire, but I still buried my face in his chest.

"Travis and Abby?" I finally managed.

"They're okay. Come on," he said, bracing himself to stand. "Let's get you home where it's warm."

Trenton drove the Jeep to my apartment. Hank had closed down the bar out of respect, so Raegan and Kody huddled together on the love seat, watching the news while Trenton and I took turns in the shower.

In a fresh pair of gray sweats and fuzzy socks, I snuggled up to Trenton in my bedroom. I hugged him tightly, pressing my temple against his side. My wet hair was soaking his *Spaceballs* T-shirt, but he didn't care. It was all too hard to process, so we just sat in silence, holding one another until I'd spontaneously break down again.

Kody knocked on my door, and then he came in, followed by Raegan. She looked everywhere but into my eyes. "Baker's mom was just interviewed. He didn't make it."

I was devastated, but I was all cried out. I just closed my eyes, and my lip quivered. Trenton held me close, and we both jumped when his cell phone rang.

He glanced at it. It rang again. "It's just a number."

"Local?" I asked. It rang a third time. He nodded. "Answer it."

He held the phone to his ear, hesitant. "Hello?" After a short pause, he lowered the phone to his lap. "Too late."

Kody and Raegan went to bed, but I just lay there in Trenton's lap. I didn't want to turn off the lights. I wanted to see him, with my own eyes, and know that he was alive and okay.

Trenton ran his fingers through my hair. "I left her," he said.

I sat up. "Who?"

"Abby. Travis couldn't get to us. He was going to go out the way everyone else came in, and Abby was going to take us through the back way. We got lost. We ran across a bunch of lost girls. They were following a guy, but he was just as lost as they were. I panicked." He shook his head, staring at the wall. "And I fucking left her." A tear fell down his cheek and he looked down.

"She got out," I said, touching his thigh.

"I promised Travis I would take care of her. When it came down to a life-or-death situation, I pussed out."

I grabbed his chin and turned him to face me. "You didn't puss out. You have strong instincts, and your mom is on the other side watching after you. What happened to that group you passed?"

"I broke a window and I lifted the guy up, and then lifted the girls so they could climb out."

"You saved their lives. No way could that guy have done it on his own. Your mom helped Travis find his way to Abby, and she helped you save more lives. That's not *pussing* out. That's stepping up."

Trenton's mouth turned up slightly, and he leaned toward me, kissing my lips. "I was so scared I was never going to see you again."

My lip began to quiver again, and I pressed my forehead against his, shaking my head. "I kept thinking about that bad feeling we both had earlier. And then when you left, how I felt like it was good-bye. I have never been that afraid in my life, and that's saying something. My dad can be pretty terrifying."

Trenton's phone chirped. He picked it up, reading a text message. "It's from Brad at Sig Tau. We've lost three so far."

My shoulders sagged.

Trenton frowned at his phone, pressed a button, and held the receiver to his ear. He looked at me. "I had a voicemail from that number. It never sent an alert."

"Maybe because you halfway answered it?"

"It's from that weird number."

A female voice said, *Ugh*, and nothing else. Trenton frowned, and then hit a button. I could hear it ringing several times, and then the same female voice answered.

"Hello?" she shrieked. "Trent?"

Trenton seemed confused and surprised at the same time. "Abby? Is everything okay?"

"Yeah, we're fine. How are you?"

"I've been sitting with Cami. She's pretty upset about the fire. She lost some of her regulars."

I lay down on his lap again, and all I could hear of Abby's voice was high-pitched chatter.

"Yeah," Trenton said. "It's like a war zone down there. What is that noise? Are you in an arcade?" he snapped at her.

I sat up.

"*What?*" he said, even more perturbed. Surely not. They wouldn't. "Okay, with what?" he asked. "Abby, stop playin'. Just fucking tell me." We were both exhausted, and whatever game she was playing, Trenton wasn't having it. I leaned in closer to the phone. Trenton held it away from his ear a bit, so I could hear.

"There were a lot of people at the fight last night. A lot of people died. Someone has got to go to prison for it."

I leaned back, and Trenton and I traded glances. She was right. Travis could be in serious trouble.

"You thinkin' it's gonna be Travis?" Trenton said, his voice low and serious. She had his total attention, now. "What are we gonna do?"

I leaned in to listen.

"I asked Travis to marry me."

"Uh . . ." Trenton said, he looked to me again. My eyebrows shot up halfway to my hairline. "Okay, how in the hell is that going to help him?"

"We're in Vegas . . ."

I leaned back to see Trenton's reaction. He was the one with elevated eyebrows, now, and several deep lines running across his forehead.

"Abby." He sighed. She spoke some more, her voice even higher, sounding more desperate. They were going to get married, hoping it was just crazy enough that the investigators would believe that Travis was in Vegas instead of at Keaton Hall. My heart broke for them. As upset as I was about the man I loved nearly losing his life, they had the same fears, in addition to the fear of dying themselves. And now they faced the possibility of losing each other again.

"I'm sorry," Trenton said. "He wouldn't want you to do this, either. He would want you to marry him because you want to. If he ever found out, it'd break his heart."

I leaned in.

"Don't be sorry, Trent. It's going to work. At least it will give him a chance. It's a chance, right? Better odds than he had."

"I guess," Trenton said, sounding defeated. Abby remained quiet. "Congratulations."

"Congratulations!" I said, desperate to feel something other than depressed.

Abby said something, and Trenton nodded. "Will do . . . and it's really fucking weird that our baby brother is the first to get married."

Abby laughed, but she sounded tired. "Get over it."

"Fuck off," Trenton said. "And, I love ya." He hung up, and tossed the phone to the end of the bed. After staring at my broken closet doors for a while, he laughed once. "I need to fix those."

"Please do."

"Travis is getting married before me. I don't know how to feel about that."

"You wish them well. They could be married forever and have ten kids, or they could get divorced next year. And that's all if Travis doesn't end up . . ."

Trenton looked down at me.

"I'm betting on the ten kids scenario."

"Me, too," he said. He leaned his head back against the headboard, and closed his eyes. "I'm going to marry you someday."

I smiled. "When pigs fly."

He shrugged. "I can put a pig on a plane. No problem."

"Okay, when you dance around in a thong to Britney Spears in front of your dad. That's when we'll get married."

He took in a long, deep breath, and then blew it out. "Challenge accepted."

CHAPTER TWENTY-FIVE

IT FELT STRANGE TO RETURN TO CAMPUS MONDAY MORNing. Trees were tied with black ribbons, and Keaton Hall was quartered off with yellow police tape. Murmuring could be heard in every hallway, elevator, and stairwell. People were discussing the fire, who died, who lived, and who was to blame. They were also gossiping about the rings on Travis and Abby, and speculation about a pregnancy began to circulate.

I just let them talk. It was nice to hear something other than theories and conspiracies surrounding the fire. The police had already been by Jim's and spoken to Trenton, so I wasn't letting on that I knew a damn thing.

After classes, I trudged through the muddy lawn to the Smurf and froze when I saw T.J. leaning against the side of the bed of the Jeep, tapping on his phone. He stood up straight when he noticed me standing twenty feet away. I continued to walk, albeit slowly.

"I wondered if you would come back," I said.

"Took the first flight out."

"Checking on everyone?"

He nodded. "Damage control."

"What can you do?"

He shook his head. "It's both of them."

"You leave Trent out of it," I snapped.

He laughed once without humor, clearly surprised at my anger. "It's not me, Camille."

"If you're not here for work, then why are you here?"

"I can't tell you the specifics, Camille, you know that. But I'm here, now, to see you."

I shook my head. "T.J., we've talked about this. Your random drop-ins are making things a lot harder than they have to be. So unless you're ready to come clean . . ."

He shook his head. "I can't do that right now."

"Then you should go."

"I just wanted to say hi."

"Hi," I said, offering him a small smile.

He leaned in to kiss my cheek, and I backed away. As much as he wanted to pretend that it was all innocent and friendly, we both knew it wasn't.

"I was just saying good-bye."

"Good-bye."

T.J. nodded, and then turned around and walked away.

I drove home to grab a snack before leaving for the shop, feeling sad. I made a couple of ham-and-cheese sandwiches, and then ate one on the way, thinking about the stuffed animals and flowers that had begun to pile up in front of Keaton.

When I pulled up to Skin Deep, the Intrepid and Hazel's Talon were already there. I walked in, but no one was at the desk or in the vestibule. I walked a few steps down the hallway, immediately seeing Trenton's yellow boots, one of his feet bouncing up and down.

"Just fucking do it, Hazel! Are you waiting for Christ to come back? Fuck!"

"No," she said sweetly, glancing at me. "I was waiting for her."

She impaled his ear, and he stifled a growl, followed by a string of expletives—some I'd never heard before.

"Beautiful!" she said.

"Really? I'm getting fucking gauges for you, and you call me beautiful? How about manly? Studly? Badass?"

"Pretty!" Hazel said, planting a kiss on his forehead.

Trenton groaned.

"I brought you a ham and cheese," I said, picking off tiny bites of ham in the remainder of mine. "It's in the bottom cubby up front."

Trenton winked at me. "Love ya, baby."

"Next!" Hazel said.

Trenton's smile vanished.

Hazel stabbed him again, and both of Trenton's feet came off the floor, but he didn't make a sound. "And that is why I waited for your girl. So you wouldn't cry. Damn, Cami takes your dick every night, and it's way bigger than a sixteen gauge."

I frowned. "Uncalled for. You need to get laid. You've been super in-apropos lately."

Hazel jutted out her lip. "Tell me about it!"

Trenton wore a wry smile. "But she's right, baby doll. I'm way bigger than a sixteen gauge."

I choked. "I'm outta here." I walked back to my desk, threw away the rest of my sandwich, and organized forms, counting to see which ones needed more copies. Then I walked back to the copy machine. I didn't have to do busywork for long, though. Our afternoon was soon filled with students getting tattoos for their deceased classmates, frat brothers, sorority sisters; and in one case, a father came in to get a tattoo in memory of his daughter.

I wondered if any of the people walking through our door knew the girl with the pretty toes. I closed my eyes tight, trying to fill my mind with something more pleasant. By close, we were all exhausted, but Trenton and Bishop wouldn't leave until everyone who came in for commemorative ink got what they came for.

When the last customer left the building, I rocked my hips from side to side as I logged off of the computer, trying to provide some relief to my sore back. The shop floor's carpet was placed over concrete, and standing on it all day was torture.

Hazel had already left for the night, and Calvin tore out of the parking lot five minutes after the final customer. Bishop and Trenton cleaned up, then came to the front to wait for me.

Bishop was glaring at me, and it didn't take long for me to notice. "What?" I asked, a little snippy. I was tired and not in the mood for his weirdness.

"I saw you today."

"Oh?"

"I *saw* you today."

I looked at him like he was crazy, and so did Trenton.

"I *heard* you," I said, disgusted.

"I saw T.J., too. That was *T.J.*, right?" He put emphasis on the letters. He knew.

Oh, God.

Trenton's face immediately jerked in my direction. "T.J.? He's in town?"

I shrugged, trying like my life depended on it to keep my face emotionless. "He came to check on family."

Trenton narrowed his eyes and clenched his teeth.

"I'll get the lights," I said, walking down the hallway and

opening the main breaker. I flipped the switches, and then returned to the vestibule. Bishop and Trenton were still standing there, except now Trenton was staring at Bishop.

"What did you see?" Trenton asked.

"I'll tell you. But promise me you'll think before you act. Promise me you'll let me explain." I knew I couldn't explain everything. I just needed to buy some time.

"Cami—"

"Promise me!"

"I promise!" he growled. "What is Bishop talking about?"

"He was at my Jeep when I got out of class. We talked for a little bit. It wasn't a big deal."

Bishop shook his head. "Definitely not what I saw."

"What the fuck is your problem?" I hissed.

He shrugged. "Just thought Trent should know."

"Know what?" I shrieked. "Nothing happened! He tried to kiss me, and I backed away! If you saw anything different than that you're a fucking liar!"

"He tried to kiss you?" Trenton said, his voice low and menacing.

"She did back away," Bishop said. "I'm gonna bounce. Later."

"Fuck off!" I yelled, throwing my entire organizer full of paper clips at him. I yanked on my coat and walked outside, but Bishop was already pulling out of the parking lot. Trenton came out, and I locked the door, turning it several times before pulling the key.

Trenton shook his head. "I'm done with this, Cami. I'm fuckin' done."

My chest tightened. "You're done."

"Yeah, I'm done. You expect me to keep putting up with this?"

Hot tears filled my eyes and ran down my cheeks in a continuous stream. "I didn't even kiss him! *Nothing* happened!"

"Why are you crying? You're crying over him? That's just fucking great, Cami!"

"No, I'm not crying over him! I don't want this to be done! I love you!"

Trenton paused, and then shook his head. "I'm not done with you, baby. I'm done with him." His voice turned low and frightening again. "He's done with you."

"Please," I said, reaching out for him. "I explained to him. He knows now. It was just closure, I think."

He nodded, furious. "You think."

I nodded back quickly, begging him with my eyes.

Trenton pulled out his car keys. "Is he still in town?"

I didn't answer.

"Where is he staying?"

I pressed my fingers together at chest level, and then touched them to my lips. "Trenton, you're exhausted. It's been a crazy few days. You're overreacting."

"Where the fuck is he staying?" he screamed. His veins popped from his neck and forehead, and he began to shake.

"I can't tell you," I said, shaking my head.

"You won't," he said, breathing hard. "You just . . . you're going to let him continue to fuck with us like this?"

I kept silent. I couldn't tell him the truth, so there was no point.

"Do you love me?" he asked.

"Yes," I cried, reaching for him.

He pulled away. "Why don't you tell him, Cami? Why don't you tell him you're with me?"

"He knows."

Trenton itched the tip of his nose with the back of his hand, and nodded. "Then it's settled. The only way he's going to stay away from you is if I beat his ass."

I knew this was going to happen. I knew it, and I did it anyway. "You promised."

"You're going to play that card? Why are you protecting him? I don't get it!"

"I'm not protecting him! I'm protecting you!" I said, shaking my head.

"I'm going to find him, Cami. I'm going to track him down, and when I find him . . ."

My cell phone buzzed in my pocket, and then buzzed again. I pulled it out to check quickly. Trenton must have noticed my expression, because he grabbed it from my hands.

"'We need to talk,'" he said, reading the message. It was from T.J.

"You promised!" I cried.

"So did you!" he screamed. His voice carried across the night, echoing through the empty lot.

He was right. I'd made promises to keep T.J.'s secret, and to love Trenton. I couldn't keep them both. I would meet with T.J. It was time to convince him to release me of that burden, but I couldn't risk Trenton following me, and I couldn't meet T.J. without making Trenton hate me. T.J. could be leaving the next day for all I knew. I had to go to him right then.

"I don't understand you, Cami. Are you just not over him? Is that it?"

I pursed my lips. The guilt was too much. "It's nothing like that."

Trenton's chest was heaving. He was getting emotional. He pitched my phone across the street, and then paced, stomping back and forth, with his hands on his hips. My phone landed in a patch of grass, just beneath the streetlamp on the other side.

"Go get it," I said, my voice even.

He shook his head.

"Go get it!" I yelled, pointing toward the streetlamp.

When Trenton stomped off to find the small, black phone in the dark, I walked quickly to my Jeep and slammed the door. The engine sputtered for a moment, and then finally started up. Trenton was outside my window.

He knocked a few times, gently, his eyes soft again. "Baby, roll down the window."

I gripped the steering wheel, and then looked over at him from under my brow, my cheeks wet.

"I'm sorry. I'll find your phone. But you can't take off in your car upset."

I stared ahead, releasing the emergency break.

Trenton put his palm flat against the glass. "Cami, if you want to take a drive, fine, but scoot over. I'll drive you anywhere you need to go."

I shook my head. "You're going to find out. And when you do, it's going to ruin everything."

Trenton frowned. "Find what out? Ruin what?"

I turned to him. "I'm going to tell you. I want to tell you. But not right now." I stomped on the clutch, and shoved the gear into reverse, backing out of the parking spot. I lowered my chin and cried for a few moments.

Trenton was still tapping my window. "Look at me, baby."

I took a deep breath, pushed the gear up into first, and then lifted my head, looking forward.

"Cami, you can't drive like this . . . Cami!" he said louder as I pulled away.

I made it to the parking lot entrance when the passenger door flew open. Trenton hopped inside, breathing hard.

"Baby, pull over."

"What the hell are you doing?"

"Pull over, and let me drive."

I pulled into the street and headed west. I had no plan to get to T.J., and now that Trenton was in the car, I really didn't know what to do. And then it hit me. I would just take him to T.J. Get it all out in the open. T.J. had brought this on himself. If he had left me alone, I wouldn't be in this position. But I needed to give Trenton time to cool off, first. I needed to drive.

"Pull over, Cami." Trenton's voice had an edge to it I'd never heard before. He was anxious and calm at the same time. It was unsettling.

I sniffed, and then wiped my eyes with my sleeve. "You're going to hate me," I said.

"I'm not going to hate you. Pull over, and I'll drive all night if you want. We can talk about it."

I shook my head. "No, you're going to hate me, and I'll lose everything."

"You won't lose me, Camille. I swear to Christ, but you're all over the goddamn road! We're on the edge of town, and will hit dirt road soon. Pull the fuck over!"

In that moment, a pair of glowing lights converged into one. I barely caught a glimpse of it from the corner of my eye, and then my head hit the window, smashing the glass into a thousand tiny pieces. Some of the shards flew outward, but most fell into my lap, or floated in the cab of the Jeep as it slid across the intersection and into a ditch on the other side. Time stood still for what seemed like several minutes, and then we were airborne as the Jeep began to roll. Once. Twice. And then I lost count, because everything went black.

+ + +

I awoke in a room with white walls and white blinds that kept the sunlight from peeking through. I blinked a few times, looking at my surroundings. A television was on overhead but was muted, playing an old *Seinfeld* rerun. Wires and tubes were strung from my arms to a pair of poles next to me, the monitors attached to them beeped softly. A small box was stuffed into a front pocket on my gown, the wires following one another to sticky circles attached to my chest. Bags of clear liquid hung from one pole, releasing a continuous drip through to my IV. The tubing ended with a few pieces of tape on the back of my hand.

Just beyond my fingertips was a head full of very short, brown hair. It was Trenton. He was facing away from me, his cheek resting against the mattress. His left arm was over my legs, the other was propped between the bed and his chair, wrapped in a thick, lime-green cast. There were already several signatures on it. Travis had signed his name under a short note that simply said, "Pussy." Another was from Hazel with a perfect impression of her bright red lipstick. Abby Abernathy signed it with "Mrs. Maddox."

"It's like a little guest book. Trent hasn't left your side, so everyone who's visited you has signed his cast."

I narrowed my eyes, barely making out T.J. sitting in a chair in a dark corner of the room. I looked back down at the cast. All of Trenton's brothers had signed, his dad Jim, my mom, and all of my brothers. Even Calvin's and Bishop's names were there.

"How long have I been here?" I whispered. My voice sounded like I'd been gargling with gravel.

"Since yesterday. You've got a pretty good gash on your head."

I lifted my hand to gently finger the bandages wrapped around my head. A concentration of gauze bulged at my left temple, and when I put the smallest bit of pressure on it, a sharp pain shot down to the base of my skull. I winced.

"What happened?" I asked.

"A drunk male ran the stop sign going about sixty. He fled the scene, but he's in custody now. Trenton carried you over a mile to the closest house."

My eyebrows pulled together as I looked at Trenton. "With a broken arm?"

"Broken in two places. I don't know how he did it. Must have been pure adrenaline. They had to put that cast on in your room in the ER. He refused to leave you. Even for a second. Even for the CAT scan. The nurses are all in love." He offered a half-smile, but it was devoid of any real happiness.

I sat up, and glittering stars formed in my eyes. I fell back against the bed, feeling nauseated.

"Easy," T.J. said, standing.

I swallowed. My throat was dry and scratchy.

T.J. walked over to a small table at the end of my bed and poured water into a cup. I took it from him and sipped. It burned all the way down, even though it was ice water.

I touched the top of Trenton's head. "Does he know?"

"Everyone knows. About you. About us. But not about me. I'd like to keep it that way. For now."

I looked down, feeling a sob well up in my throat. "Then why is he here?"

"The same reason I'm here. Because he loves you."

A tear fell down my cheek. "I didn't mean to . . ."

T.J. shook his head. "I know, honey. Don't cry. It's going to be okay."

"Is it? Now that everyone knows, how could it ever be anything but awkward, and tense, and . . ."

"Because it's us. We'll handle it."

Trenton's right fingers twitched. His cast became dislodged and his arm fell. He jerked awake, and then grabbed his shoulder, clearly in pain. When he realized my eyes were open, he immediately stood, leaned over, and touched my cheek with his left hand. The bridge of his nose was swollen, and the skin under both of his eyes bore matching purple half-moons. "You're awake!" He beamed while his eyes scanned my face.

"I'm awake," I said softly.

Trenton laughed once, leaning his head down until his forehead touched my lap. He hooked his arm around my thighs and squeezed gently, his entire body shaking as he cried.

"I'm so sorry," I said, hot tears burning down my cheeks and falling from my jaw.

Trenton looked up and shook his head. "No. This wasn't your fault. Some drunk son of a bitch ran a stop sign and T-boned us."

"But if I'd been paying attention . . ." I whimpered.

He shook his head again, begging me with his eyes to stop. "Ssh, no. No, baby. Even then, he would have plowed right into us." He put his hand on top of his head, and his eyes glossed over. He sighed. "I'm so fucking glad you're okay. Your head was gushing blood, and you wouldn't wake up." His eyes closed as the memory replayed. "I've been going out of my mind." He rested his head on my lap again, and lifted my left hand to his mouth, gently kissing around the tape.

T.J. still stood behind him, watching Trenton's display of affection with a pained smile. Trenton turned around, sensing someone was behind him.

"Hey," Trenton said. He stood. "I, uh . . . I'm sorry."

"It's okay. She doesn't belong to me anymore. I'm not sure she ever did."

"I love her," Trenton said, glancing back at me with a smile. He wiped his red eyes. "I'm not fucking around. I really love her."

"I know," T.J. said. "I've seen the way you look at her."

"So are we cool?" Trenton asked.

T.J.'s brows pulled together as he looked at me, but he spoke to Trenton. "What does she want?"

They both turned to me. I stared at T.J. while I slowly reached across the wrinkled sheets and blanket for Trenton's hand. Trenton sat down next to me, lifted my hand to his mouth, and kissed my fingers, closing his eyes.

My lip quivered. "I lied to you."

He shook his head. "For reasons that have nothing to do with me. Or us."

I let out a sigh of relief, and the tears fell again. "I love you."

Trenton gently cupped my jaw in his hands, and then he leaned in, kissing me tenderly. "Nothing else matters."

"It matters to me," I said. "I don't want to . . ."

T.J. cleared his throat, reminding us that someone else was

in the room. "If it's what you want, Cami, we'll make it work. I won't get in the way. It won't be an issue."

Trenton walked the few steps to where T.J. stood and gave him a bear hug. They held onto one another for several moments. T.J. whispered something into Trenton's ear, and he nodded. It was so surreal, watching them interact in the same room, after keeping T.J.'s secret for so long.

T.J. walked slowly over to my bedside, leaned over, and kissed an area of my forehead that wasn't bandaged. "I'm going to miss you, Camille." He kissed the same spot again, letting his lips linger on my skin for a while, and then he walked out the door.

Trenton puffed out a sigh of relief, and then squeezed my hand. "It all makes sense, now." He shook his head, and laughed once without humor. "Now that I know, I can't believe I didn't figure it out. California. You feeling wrong about being with me, even after you broke things off with him. It was all right there in front of me."

I pressed my lips together. "Not all of it."

Trenton rested his cast on the bed and intertwined the fingers that poked out the end with mine. "I don't feel an ounce of guilt. You know why?"

I shrugged my shoulders.

"Because I've been in love with you since grade school, Chamomile. And everyone knew it. *Everyone.*"

"I'm still not sure I believe that."

"You wore ponytails every day for years. They were perfect." His smile faded. "And that sad look in your eyes. All I've ever wanted to do was make you smile. And then you were mine, and I could never get it right."

"I've had a lifetime of wrong. You're the *only* thing that's right."

Trenton pulled something from his pocket, and let a small, silver key dangle from a key chain. It was a black strip of felt fabric with *C-A-M-I* spelled out in bright colors, bordered with black stitching. I pressed my lips together and then pulled my mouth to the side.

"What do you say?" he asked with hope in his eyes.

"Move in? Give up my apartment?"

"All in. You and me. Drinking to weird toasts after work, and Chicken Joe's on Monday nights with Olive. Simple, just the way you like it."

There was so much to think about, but after what we'd just been through—twice—the only thing I could focus on was what Trenton had said. There was only one thing that mattered. "I say yes."

He blinked. "Yes?"

"Yes," I said, giggling at his expression, and then winced. My entire body ached.

"Hell yes!" he yelled, and then offered a sheepish grin when I motioned for him to keep quiet. "I am so fucking in love with you, Cami."

I scooted over in my bed, clumsily and slowly, and then Trenton—carefully and with much effort—made his way in. He was just as sore as I was. He pushed a button on the side rail that leaned us back until we were lying flat, facing each other.

"I know you don't believe me, but I really have loved you since we were kids," he said quietly. "And now I get to love you 'til we're old."

My stomach fluttered. No one else had ever loved me as much as he did. "Promise?"

Trenton smiled with tired eyes. "Yes. And then I'll promise you again after I dance around in a thong to Britney Spears."

I managed to let out a small chuckle, but the pain was making it difficult to move. He adjusted and readjusted until he finally got comfortable enough to close his eyes and fall asleep. I watched him for the longest time, breathing in and out, with a small smile on his face. Everything was out in the open now, and I could breathe, too.

A nurse came in, and seemed surprised to see us lying together.

"Look at you," she whispered, her dark eyes somehow seeing clearly even in the dim light. "That boy has all the women on this floor swooning. He's been your guardian angel. Hasn't left your side."

"I've heard. I don't know how I got so lucky, but I'm glad." I leaned over, touching my temple to his forehead.

"Luck is most certainly on your side. I saw your vehicle down at the yard. It looks like a wadded-up piece of paper. It's a miracle either of you lived."

I frowned. "I'm going to miss that Jeep."

She nodded. "How are you feeling?"

"I hurt. Everywhere."

She shook a plastic cup, letting the pills inside rattle. "Think you can swallow a couple of pills?"

I nodded and tossed the pills to the back of my throat. The nurse handed me a cup of water, and I swallowed them, but not without effort.

"Are you hungry?" she asked while taking my vitals.

I shook my head.

"Okay," she said, pulling the stethoscope from her ears. "Just hit that red button with the cross if you need anything."

She walked out of the room, and I turned to the man sleeping next to me. "There's nothing else that I need," I whispered.

Trenton's cast was between us, and I ran my finger over the different names, thinking about all of the people who loved us that had come to my room. I paused when I came across T.J.'s signature, and silently said a final good-bye to the simple but sophisticated scribble.

Thomas James Maddox

Fancy something to put you
on the edge of your seat?

Read on for an extract of

RED HILL

PROLOGUE

Scarlet

The warning was short—said almost in passing. "The cadavers were herded and destroyed." The radio hosts then made a few jokes, and that was the end of it. It took me a moment to process what the newswoman had said through the speakers of my Suburban: *Finally.* A scientist in Zurich had *finally* succeeded in creating something that—until then—had only been fictional. For years, against every code of ethics known to science, Elias Klein had tried and failed to reanimate a corpse. Once a leader amid the most intelligent in the world, he was now a laughing stock. But on that day, he would have been a criminal, if he weren't already dead.

At the time, I was watching my girls arguing in the backseat through the rearview mirror, and the two words that should have changed everything barely registered. Two words, had I not been reminding Halle to give her field trip permission slip to her teacher, would have made me drive away from the curb with my foot grinding the gas pedal to the floorboard.

Cadavers. Herded.

Instead, I was focused on saying for the third time that the girls' father, Andrew, would be picking them up from school that day. They would then drive an hour away to Anderson, the town we used to call home, and listen to Governor Bellmon speak to Andrew's fellow firefighters while the local paper took pictures. Andrew thought it would be fun for the girls, and I agreed with him—maybe for the first time since we divorced.

Although most times Andrew lacked sensitivity, he was a man of duty. He took our daughters, Jenna, who was just barely thirteen and far too beautiful (but equally dorky) for her own good, and Halle, who was seven, bowling, out to dinner, and the occasional movie, but it was only because he felt he should. To Andrew, spending time with his children was part of a job, but not one he enjoyed.

As Halle grabbed my head and jerked my face around to force sweet kisses on my cheeks, I pushed up her thick, black-rimmed glasses. Not savoring the moment, not realizing that so many things happening that day would create the perfect storm for separating us. Halle half jogged, half skipped down the walkway to the school entrance, singing loudly. She was the only human I knew who could be intolerably obnoxious and endearing at the same time.

A few speckles of water spattered on the windshield, and I leaned forward to get a better look at the cloud cover overhead. I should have sent Halle with an umbrella. Her light jacket wouldn't stand up to the early spring rain.

The next stop was the middle school. Jenna was absently discussing a reading assignment while texting the most recent boy of interest. I reminded her again as we pulled into the drop-off line that her father would pick her up at the regular spot, right after he picked up Halle.

"I heard you the first ten times," Jenna said, her voice slightly deeper than average for a girl her age. She looked at me with hollow brown eyes. She was present in body, but rarely in mind. Jenna had a wild imagination that was oh-so-random in the most wonderful way, but lately I couldn't get her to pay attention to anything other than her cell phone. I brought her into this world at just twenty. We practically grew up together, and I worried about her, if I'd done everything—or anything—right; but somehow she was turning out better than anyone could have imagined anyway.

"That was only the fourth time. Since you heard me, what did I say?"

Jenna sighed, peering down at her phone, expressionless. "Dad is picking us up. Regular spot."

"And be nice to the girlfriend. He said you were rude last time."

Jenna looked up at me. "That was the old girlfriend. I haven't been rude to the new one."

I frowned. "He just told me that a couple of weeks ago."

Jenna made a face. We didn't always have to say aloud what we were thinking, and I knew she was thinking the same thing I wanted to say, but wouldn't.

Andrew was a slut.

I sighed and turned to face forward, gripping the steering wheel so tightly my knuckles turned white. It somehow helped me to keep my mouth shut. I had made a promise to my children, silently, when I signed the divorce papers two years before: I would never bad-mouth Andrew to them. Even if he deserved it . . . and he often did.

"Love you," I said, watching Jenna push open the door with her shoulder. "See you Sunday evening."

"Yep," Jenna said.

"And don't slam the . . ."

A loud bang shook the Suburban as Jenna shoved the door closed.

". . . door." I sighed, and pulled away from the curb.

I took Maine Street to the hospital where I worked, still gripping the steering wheel tight and trying not to curse Andrew with every thought. Did he have to introduce every woman he slept with more than once to our daughters? I'd asked him, begged him, yelled at him not to, but that would be inconvenient, not letting his girl-of-the-week share weekends with his children. Never mind he had Monday through Friday with whoever. The kicker was that if the woman had children to distract Jenna and Halle, Andrew would use that opportunity to "talk" with her in the bedroom.

My blood boiled. Dutiful or not, he was an asshole when I was married to him, and an even bigger asshole now.

I whipped the Suburban into the last decent parking spot in the employee parking lot, hearing sirens as an ambulance pulled into the emergency drive and parked in the ambulance bay.

The rain began to pour. A groan escaped my lips, watching coworkers run inside, their scrubs soaked from just a short dash across the street to the side entrance. I was half a block away.

TGIF.

TGIF.

TGIF.

Just before I turned off the ignition, another report came over the radio, something about an epidemic in Europe. Looking back, everyone knew then what was going on, but it had been a running joke for so long that no one wanted to believe it was really happening. With all the television shows, comics, books, and movies about the undead, it shouldn't have been a surprise that somebody was finally both smart and crazy enough to try and make it a reality.

I know the world ended on a Friday. It was the last day I saw my children.

CHAPTER ONE

Scarlet

My chest heaved as the thick metal door closed loudly behind me. I held out my arms to each side, letting water drip off my fingertips onto the white tile floor. My once royal-blue scrubs were now navy, heavily saturated with cold rainwater.

A squashing sound came from my sneakers when I took a step. *Ick.* Not much was worse than wet clothes and shoes, and it felt like I'd jumped into a swimming pool fully dressed. Even my panties were wet. We were only a few days into spring, and a cold front had come through. The rain felt like flying death spikes of ice.

Flying death spikes. *Snort.* Jenna's dramatic way of describing things was obviously rubbing off on me.

I slid my name badge through the card reader and waited until the small light at the top turned green and a high-pitched beep sounded, accompanied by the loud click of the lock release. I had to use all of my body weight to pull open the heavy door, and then I stepped into the main hallway.

Fellow coworkers flashed me understanding smiles that

helped to relieve some of my humiliation. It was obvious who all had just arrived on shift, about the time the sky opened up and pissed on us.

Two steps at a time, I climbed the stairs to the surgical floor and snuck into the women's locker room, stripping down and changing into a pair of light-blue surgery scrubs. I held my sneakers under the hand dryer, but only for a few seconds. The other X-ray techs were waiting for me downstairs. We had an upper GI/small bowel follow-through at 8:00, and this week's radiologist was more than just a little grumpy when we made him run behind.

Sneakers still squishing, I rushed down the steps and back down the main hallway to Radiology, passing the ER double doors on my way. Chase, the security guard, waved at me as I passed.

"Hey, Scarlet," he said with a small, shy smile.

I only nodded, more concerned with getting the upper GI ready on time than with chitchat.

"You should talk to him," Christy said. She nodded in Chase's direction as I breezed by her and her piles of long, yellow ringlets.

I shook my head, walking into the exam room. The familiar sound of my feet sticking to the floor began an equally familiar beat. Whatever they cleaned the floor with was supposed to sanitize the worst bacteria known to man, but it left behind a sticky residue. Maybe to remind us it was there—or that the floor needed to be mopped again. I pulled bottles of barium contrast from the upper cabinet, and filled the remaining space with water. I replaced the cap, and then shook the bottle to mix the powder and water into a disgusting, slimy paste that smelled of bananas. "Don't start. I've already told you no. He looks fifteen."

"He's twenty-seven, and don't be a shrew. He's cute, and he's dying for you to talk to him."

Her mischievous smile was infuriatingly contagious. "He's a kid," I said. "Go get the patient."

Christy smiled and left the room, and I made a mental note of everything I'd set on the table for Dr. Hayes. God, he was cranky; particularly on Mondays, and even more so during shitty weather.

I was lucky enough to be somewhat on his good side. As a student, I had cleaned houses for the radiologists. It earned me decent money, and was perfect since I was in school forty hours a week at that time. The docs were hard asses in the hospital, but they helped me out more than anyone else while I was going through the divorce, letting me bring the girls to work, and giving me a little extra at Christmas and on birthdays.

Dr. Hayes paid me well to drive to his escape from the city, Red Hill Ranch, an hour and a half away in the middle-of-nowhere Kansas to clean his old farmhouse. It was a long drive, but it served its purpose: No cell service. No Internet. No traffic. No neighbors.

Finding the place on my own took a few tries until Halle made up a song with the directions. I could hear her tiny voice in my head, singing loudly and sweetly out the window.

> *West on Highway 11*
> *On our way to heaven*
> *North on Highway 123*
> *123? 123!*
> *Cross the border*

That's an order!
Left at the white tower
So Mom can clean the doctor's shower
Left at the cemetery
Creepy . . . and scary!
First right!
That's right!
Red! Hill! Rooooooooad!

After that, we could make it there, rain or shine. I'd even mentioned a few times that it would be the perfect hideaway in case of an apocalypse. Jenna and I were sort of post-apocalyptic junkies, always watching end-of-the-world marathons and preparation television shows. We never canned chicken or built an underground tank in the woods, but it was entertaining to see the lengths other people went to.

Dr. Hayes's ranch would make the safest place to survive. The cupboards and pantry were always stocked with food, and the basement would make any gun enthusiast proud. The gentle hills kept the farmhouse somewhat inconspicuous, and wheat fields bordered three sides. The road was about fifty yards from the north side of the house, and on the other side of the red dirt was another wheat field. Other than the large maple tree in the back, visibility was excellent. Good for watching sunsets, bad for anyone trying to sneak in undetected.

Christy opened the door and waited for the patient to enter. The young woman stepped just inside the door, thin, her eyes sunken and tired. She looked at least twenty pounds underweight.

"This is Dana Marks, date of birth twelve, nine, eighty-nine. Agreed?" Christy asked, turning to Dana.

Dana nodded, the thin skin on her neck stretching over her tendons as she did so. Her skin was a sickly gray, highlighting the purple under her eyes.

Christy handed the woman loose folds of thin blue fabric. "Just take this gown behind the curtain there, and undress down to your underpants. They don't have any rhinestones or anything, do they?"

Dana shook her head, seeming slightly amused, and then slowly made her way behind the curtain.

Christy picked up a film and walked to the X-ray table in the middle of the room, sliding it into the Bucky tray between the table surface and the controls. "You should at least say hi."

"Hi."

"Not me, dummy. To Chase."

"Are we still talking about him?"

Christy rolled her eyes. "Yes. He's cute, has a good job, has never been married, no kids. Did I mention cute? All that dark hair . . . and his eyes!"

"They're brown. Go ahead. I dare you to play up brown."

"They're not just brown. They're like a golden honey brown. You better jump on that now before you miss your chance. Do you know how many single women in this hospital are salivating over that?"

"I'm not worried about it."

Christy smiled and shook her head, and then her expression changed once her pager went off. She pulled it from her waistline and glanced down. "Crap. I have to move the C-arm from OR 2 for Dr. Pollard's case. Hey, I might have to leave a little early to take Kate to the orthodontist. Do you think you could do my three o'clock surgery? It's easy peasy."

"What is it?"

"Just a port. Basically C-arm babysitting."

The C-arm, named for its shape, showed the doctors where they were in the body in real time. Because the machine emitted radiation, it was our jobs as X-ray techs to stand there, push, pull, and push the button during surgery. That, and make sure the doctor didn't over-radiate the patient. I didn't mind running it, but the damn thing was heavy. Christy would have done the same for me, though, so I nodded. "Sure. Just give me the pager before you leave."

Christy grabbed a lead apron, and then left me to go upstairs. "You're awesome. I wrote Dana's history on the requisition sheet. See you later! Get Chase's number!"

Dana walked slowly from the bathroom, and I gestured for her to sit in a chair beside the table.

"Did your doctor explain this procedure to you?"

Dana shook her head. "Not really."

A few choice words crossed my mind. How a doctor could send a patient in for a procedure without an explanation was beyond me, and how a patient couldn't ask wasn't something I understood, either.

"I'll take a few X-rays of your abdomen, and then fetch the doctor. I'll come back, make the table vertical, and you'll stand and drink that cup of barium," I said, pointing to the cup behind me on the counter, "a sip at a time, at the doctor's discretion. He'll use fluoroscopy to watch the barium travel down your esophagus and into your stomach. Fluoro is basically an X-ray, but instead of a picture, we get a video in real time. When that's done, we'll start the small bowel follow-through. You'll drink the rest of the barium, and we'll take X-rays as it flows through your small bowel."

Dana eyed the cup. "Does it taste bad? I've been vomiting a lot. I can't keep anything down."

The requisition page with Christy's scribbles was lying on the counter next to the empty cups. I picked it up, looking for the answer to my next question. Dana had only been ill for two days. I glanced up at her, noting her appearance.

"Have you been sick like this before?" She shook her head in answer. "Traveled recently?" She shook her head again. "Any history of Crohn's disease? Anorexia? Bulimia?" I asked.

She held out her arm, palm up. There was a perfect bite mark in the middle of her forearm. Each tooth had broken the skin. Deep, red perforations dotted her arm in mirrored half-moons, but the bruised skin around the bites was still intact.

I met her eyes. "Dog?"

"A drunk," she said with a weak laugh. "I was at a party Tuesday night. We had just left, and some asshole wandering around outside just grabbed my arm and took a bite. He might have pulled a whole chunk off if my boyfriend hadn't hit him. Knocked him out long enough for us to find the car and leave. I saw on the news yesterday that he'd attacked other people, too. It was the same night, and the same apartment complex. Had to be him." She let her arm fall to her side, seeming exhausted. "Joey's in the waiting room . . . scared to death I have rabies. He just got back from his last tour in Afghanistan. He's seen everything, but he can't stand to hear me throw up." She laughed quietly to herself.

I offered a comforting smile. "Sounds like a keeper. Just hop up on the table there, and lay on your back."

Dana did as I asked, but needed assistance. Her bony hands were like ice.

"How much weight did you say you've lost?" I asked while situating her on the table, sure I had read Christy's history report wrong on the requisition.

Dana winced from the cold, hard table pressing against her pelvic bone and spine.

"Blanket?" I asked, already pulling the thick, white cotton from the warmer.

"Please." Dana hummed as I draped the blanket over her. "Thank you so much. I just can't seem to get warm."

"Abdominal pain?"

"Yes. A lot."

"Pounds lost?"

"Almost twenty."

"Since Tuesday?"

Dana raised her brows. "Believe me, I know. Especially since I was thin to begin with. You . . . don't think it's rabies . . . do you?" She tried to laugh off her remark, but I could hear the worry in her voice.

I smiled. "They don't send you in for an upper GI if they think it's rabies."

Dana sighed and looked at the ceiling. "Thank God."

Once I positioned Dana, centered the X-ray tube, and set my technique, I pressed the button and then took the film to the reader. My eyes were glued to the monitor, curious if she had a bowel obstruction, or if a foreign body was present.

"Whatcha got there, buddy?" David asked, standing behind me.

"Not sure. She's lost twenty pounds in two days."

"No way."

"Way."

"Poor kid," he said, genuine sympathy in his voice.

David watched with me as the image illuminated the screen. When Dana's abdomen film filled the screen, David and I both stared at it in shock.

David touched his fingers to his mouth. *"No way."*

I nodded slowly. "Way."

David shook his head. "I've never seen that. I mean, in a text-book, yes, but . . . man. Bad deal."

The image on the monitor was hypnotizing. I'd never seen someone present with that gas pattern, either. I couldn't even remember seeing it in a textbook.

"They've been talking a lot on the radio this morning about that virus in Germany. They say it's spreading all over. It looks like war on the television. People panicking in the streets. Scary stuff."

I frowned. "I heard that when I dropped off the girls this morning."

"You don't think the patient has it, do you? They're not really saying exactly what it is, but that," he said, gesturing to the monitor, "is impossible."

"You know as well as I do that we see new stuff all the time."

David stared at the image for a few seconds more, and then nodded, snapping out of his deep thought. "Hayes is ready when you are."

I grabbed a lead apron, slid my arms through the armholes, and then fastened the tie behind my back as I walked to the reading room to fetch Dr. Hayes.

As expected, he was sitting in his chair in front of his monitor in the dark, speaking quietly into his dictation mic. I waited patiently just outside the doorway for him to finish, and then he looked up at me.

"Dana Marks, twenty-three years old, presenting with ab-dominal pain and significant weight loss since Wednesday. Some hair loss. No history of abdominal disease or heart problems, no previous abdominal surgeries, no previous abdominal exams."

Dr. Hayes pulled up the image I'd just taken, and squinted his eyes for a moment. "How significant?"

"Nineteen pounds."

He looked only slightly impressed until the image appeared on the screen. He blanched. "Oh my God."

"I know."

"Where has she been?"

"She hasn't traveled recently, if that's what you mean. She did mention being attacked by a drunk after a party Tuesday night."

"This is profound. Do you see the ring of gas here?" he asked, pointing to the screen. His eyes brightened with recognition. "Portal venous gas. Look at the biliary tree outline. Remarkable." Dr. Hayes went from animated to somber in less than a second. "You don't see this very often, Scarlet. This patient isn't going to do well."

I swallowed back my heartbreak for Dana. She either had a severe infection or something else blocking or restricting the veins in her bowel. Her insides were basically dead and wither-ing away. She might have four more days. They would probably attempt to take her to emergency surgery, but would likely just close her back up. "I know."

"Who's her doctor?"

"Vance."

"I'll call him. Cancel the UGI. She'll need a CT."

I nodded and then stood in the hall while Dr. Hayes spoke in a low voice, explaining his findings to Dr. Vance.

"All right. Let's get to it," the doctor said, standing from his chair. We both took a moment to separate ourselves from the grim future of the patient. Dr. Hayes followed me down the hall toward the exam room where Dana waited. "The girls doing okay?"

I nodded. "They're at their dad's this weekend. They're going to meet the governor."

"Oh," the doctor said, pretending to be impressed. He'd met the governor several times. "My girls are coming home this weekend, too."

I smiled, glad to hear it. Since Dr. Hayes's divorce, Miranda and Ashley didn't come home to visit nearly as much as he would have liked. They were both in college, both in serious relationships, and both mama's girls. Much to the doctor's dismay, any free time they had away from boyfriends and studying was usually spent with their mother.

He stopped, took a breath, held the exam-room door open, and then followed me inside. He hadn't given me time to set up the room before he came back, so I was glad the upper GI was cancelled.

David was shaking the bottles of barium.

"Thanks, David. We won't be needing those."

David nodded. Having seen the images before, he already knew why.

I helped Dana to a sitting position, and she stared at both of us, clearly wondering what was going on.

"Dana," Dr. Hayes began, "you say your problem began early Wednesday morning?"

"Yes," she said, her voice strained with increasing discomfort.

Dr. Hayes abruptly stopped, and then smiled at Dana, putting his hand on hers. "We're not going to do the upper GI today. Dr. Vance is going to schedule you a CT instead. We're going to have you get dressed and go back to the waiting room. They should be calling you before long. Do you have someone with you today?"

"Joey, my boyfriend."

"Good," the doctor said, patting her hand.

"Am I going to be okay?" she said, struggling to sit on her bony backside.

Dr. Hayes smiled in the way I imagined him smiling while speaking to his daughters. "We're going to take good care of you. Don't worry."

I helped Dana step to the floor. "Leave your gown on," I said, quickly grabbing another one and holding it behind her. "Slip this on behind you like a robe." She slipped her tiny arms through the holes, and then I helped her to the chair beside the cabinet. "Go ahead and put on your shoes. I'll be right back. Just try to relax."

"Yep," Dana said, trying to get comfortable.

I grabbed her requisition off the counter and followed the doctor to the workroom.

As soon as we were out of earshot, Dr. Hayes turned to me. "Try to talk to her some more. See if you can get something else out of her."

"I can try. All she mentioned out of the ordinary was the bite."

"You're sure it wasn't an animal?"

I shrugged. "She said it was some drunk guy. It looks infected."

Dr. Hayes looked at Dana's abnormal gas patterns on the monitor once more. "That's too bad. She seems like a sweet kid."

I nodded, somber. David and I traded glances, and then I took a breath, mentally preparing myself to carry such a heavy secret back into that room. Keeping her own death from her felt like a betrayal, even though we'd only just met.

My sneakers made a ripping noise as they pulled away from the floor. "Ready?" I asked with a bright smile.

CHAPTER TWO

Scarlet

By lunch, Dana had already been in and out of surgery. Christy told us they only opened her up long enough to see there was nothing they could do, before closing her back up. Now they were waiting for her to awaken so they could tell her she would never get better.

"Her boyfriend is still with her," Christy said. "Her parents are visiting relatives. They're not sure they'll get back in time."

"Oh, Jesus," I said, wincing. I couldn't imagine being away from either of my daughters in a situation like that, wondering if I would make it in time to see her alive one last time. I shook it off. Those of us in the medical field didn't have the luxury of thinking about our patients' personal lives. It became too close. Too real.

"Did you hear about that flu?" Christy said. "It's all over the news."

I shook my head. "I don't think it's a flu."

"They're saying it has to do with that scientist over in Europe. They say it's highly contagious."

"Who are *they*? *They* sound like troublemakers to me."

Christy smiled and rolled her eyes. "*They* also said it's breached our borders. California is reporting cases."

"Really?"

"That's what they say," she said. Her pager buzzed. "Damn, it's getting busy." She pushed a button and called upstairs, and then she was gone again.

Within the hour, the hospital was crowded and frantic. The ER was admitting patients at a hectic pace, keeping everyone in radiology busy. David called in another tech so he and I could cover the ER while everyone else attended to outpatients and inpatients.

Whatever it was, the whole town seemed to be going crazy. Car accidents, fights, and a fast-spreading virus had hit at the same time. On my sixth trip to the ER, I passed the radiology waiting room and saw a group of people crowded around the flat-screen television on the wall.

"David?" I said, signaling for him to join me in front of the waiting room. He looked in through the wall of glass, noting the only seated person was a man in a wheelchair.

"Yeah?"

"I have a bad feeling about this." I felt sick watching the updates on the screen. "They were talking about something like this on the radio this morning."

"Yeah. They were reporting the first cases here about half an hour ago."

I stared into his eyes. "I should leave to try to catch up to my girls. They're halfway to Anderson by now."

"As busy as we are, no way is Anita going to let you leave. Anyway, it's highly contagious, but disease control maintains that it's just a virus, Scarlet. I heard that those that got the flu shot are the ones affected."

That one sentence, even unsubstantiated, immediately set my mind at ease. I hadn't had a flu shot in three years because I always felt terrible afterward, and I'd never gotten one for the girls. Something about vaccinating for a virus that may or may not protect against whatever strain came through didn't sit well with me. We had enough shit in our bodies with hormones and chemicals in our foods and everyday pollutants. It didn't make sense to subject ourselves to more, even if the hospital encouraged it.

Just as David and I finished up our last batch of portable X-rays in the ER, Christy rounded the corner, looking worn.

"Has it been as busy down here as it's been up there?"

"Yes," David said. "Probably worse."

"Can you still do that port for me?" Christy said, her eyes begging.

I looked to David, and then back at Christy. "The way things are going, if I take that pager, I'll be stuck up there until quitting time. They really need me down here."

David looked at his watch. "Tasha comes in at three thirty. We can handle it until then."

"You sure?" I asked, slowly taking the pager from Christy.

David waved me away dismissively. "No problem. I'll take the pager from you when Tasha gets here so you can go home."

I clipped the pager to the waistband of my scrubs, and headed upstairs, waving good-bye to Christy.

She frowned, already feeling guilty. "Thank you very, very much!"

I passed Chase for the umpteenth time. As the hours passed,

he'd looked increasingly nervous. Everyone was. From the looks of things inside the ER, it seemed like all hell was breaking loose outside. I kept trying to sneak peeks at the television but once I finished one case, the pager would go off again to direct me to another.

Just as I had anticipated, once I arrived on the surgery floor, there would be no leaving until David relieved me at 3:30. Case after case, I was moving the C-arm from surgery suite to surgery suite, sometimes moving a second one in for whomever was called up for a surgery going on at the same time.

In one afternoon I saw a shattered femur, two broken arms, and a broken hip, and shared an elevator with a patient in a gurney accompanied by two nurses, all on their way to the roof. His veins were visibly dark through his skin, and he was covered in sweat. From what I could make of their nervous banter, the patient was being med-flighted out to amputate his hand.

My last case of the day was precarious at best, but I didn't want to have to call David up to relieve me. My girls were out of town with their father, and David had a pretty wife and two young sons to go home to. It didn't make sense for me to leave on time and for him to stay late, but I had already logged four hours of overtime for the week, and that was generally frowned upon by the brass.

I walked past the large woman in the gurney, looking nervous and upset. Her hand was bandaged, but a large area was saturated with blood. I remembered her from the ER, and wondered where her family was. They all had been with her downstairs.

Angie, the circulation nurse, swished by, situating her surgical cap. It was covered in rough sketches of hot-pink lipsticks and purses. As if to validate her choice of head cover, she pulled out a tube of lip gloss and swiped it across her lips. She smiled at me. "I hear Chase has been asking about you."

I looked down, instantly embarrassed. "Not you, too." Was everyone so bored that they had nothing better to do than fantasize about my non-love life? Was I that pathetic that a prospect for me was so exciting?

She winked at me as she passed. "Call him, or I'm going to steal him from you."

I smiled. "Promise?"

Angie rolled her eyes, but her expression immediately compressed. "Damn! Scarlet, I'm sorry, your mom is on line two."

"My mom?"

"They transferred her call up a couple of minutes before you came in."

I glanced at the phone, wondering what on earth she would be calling me at work about. We barely spoke at all, so it must have been important. Maybe about the girls. I nearly lunged for the phone.

"Hello?"

"Scarlet! Oh, thank God. Have you been watching the news?"

"A little. We've been slammed. From the few glimpses I've gotten, it looks bad. Did you see the reports of the panic at LAX? People were sick on some of the flights over. They think that's how it traveled here."

"I wouldn't worry too much about it. Nothing ever happens in the middle of the country."

"Why did you call, then?" I said, confused. "Are the girls okay?"

"The girls?" She made a noise with her throat. Even her breath could be condescending. "Why would I be calling about the girls? My kitchen floor is pulling up in the corner by the refrigerator, and I was hoping you could ask Andrew to come fix it."

"He has the girls this weekend, Mother. I can't really talk right now. I'm in surgery."

"Yes, I know. Your life is so important."

I glanced at Angie, seeing that she and the surgical tech were nearly finished. "I'll ask him, but like I said, he has the girls."

"He has the girls a lot. Have you been going to the bars every weekend, or what?"

"No."

"So what else is more important than raising your children?"

"I have to go."

"Sensitive subject. You've never liked to be told you're doing something wrong."

"It's his weekend, Mother, like it is every other weekend."

"Well. Why does his weekend have to be the weekend I need help?"

"I really have to go."

"Did you at least send dresses with them so their daddy can take them to church? Since he's the only one who seems to care to teach them about the Lord."

"Good-bye, Mother." I hung up the phone and sighed just as Dr. Pollard came in.

"Afternoon, all. This shouldn't take long," he said. He held his hands in front of him, fingers pointing up, waiting for Angie to put gloves on them. "But by the looks of it we're all in for a long night, so I hope none of you had plans."

"Is that true?" Ally, the scrub tech, asked from behind her mask. "About LAX?"

"It happened at Dulles, too," Angie said.

I glanced at the clock, and then pulled my cell phone from the front pocket of my scrubs. I could be written up if someone felt like ratting me out for being on it, but an extra piece of paper in my file was worth it in this case. I pecked out the words *Call Me ASAP*, and then sent them on to Jenna's phone.

After a couple of minutes with no response, I dialed Andrew. It rang four times, then his voicemail took over.

I sighed. "It's Scarlet. Please call me at the hospital. I'm in surgery, but call me anyway so we can coordinate. I'm coming there as soon as I get off work."

Nathan

Another eight-hour day that didn't mean a damn thing. When I clocked out from the office, freedom should have been at the forefront of my mind, or should have at least brought a smile to my face, but it didn't. Knowing I had just wasted another day of my life was depressing. Tragic, even. Stuck at a desk job for an electric co-op that made no difference in the world, day in and day out, and then going home to a wife who hated me made for a miserable existence.

Aubrey hadn't always been a mean bitch. When we first got married, she had a sense of humor, she couldn't wait until it was bedtime so we could lie together and kiss and touch. She would initiate a blowjob because she wanted to please me, not because it was my birthday.

Seven years ago, she changed. We had Zoe, and my role

switched from desirable, adoring husband to a source of constant disappointment. Aubrey's expectations of me were never met. If I tried to help, it was either too much, or it wasn't done the right way. If I tried to stay out of her way, I was a lazy bastard.

Aubrey quit her job to stay home with Zoe, so mine was the only source of income. Suddenly that wasn't enough, either. Because I didn't make what Aubrey felt was enough money, she expected me to give her a "baby break" the second I walked in the door. I wasn't allowed to talk to my wife. She would disappear into the den, sit at the computer, and talk to her Internet friends.

I'd entertain Zoe while emptying the dishwasher and prepping dinner. Asking for help was a sin, and interrupting the baby break just gave Aubrey one more reason to hate me, as if she didn't have enough already.

Once Zoe started kindergarten, I hoped it would get better, that Aubrey would start back to work, and she would feel like her old self again. But she just couldn't break free of her anger. She didn't seem to want to.

Zoe had just a few weeks left in second grade. I would pick her up from school, and we would both hope Aubrey would turn away from the computer just long enough to notice we were home.

On a good day, she would.

Today, though, she wouldn't. The Internet and radio had been abuzz since early morning with breaking news about an epidemic. A busy news day meant Aubrey's ass would be stationed firmly against the stained, faded blue fabric of her office chair. She would be talking about it with strangers in forums, with friends and distant family on social networks, and commenting on news websites. Theories. Debates. Somewhere along the way it had become a part of our marriage, and I had been edged out.

I waited in my eight-year-old sedan, first in a line of cars parked behind the elementary school. Zoe didn't like to be the last one picked up, so I made sure to go to her school right after work. Waiting forty minutes gave me enough time to decompress from work, and psych myself up for another busy night without help or acknowledgment from my wife.

The DJ's tone was more serious than it had been, so I turned up the volume. He was using a word I hadn't heard them use before: *pandemic*. The contagion had breached our shores. Panic had broken out in Dulles and LAX airports when passengers who'd fallen ill during their international flights began attacking the airline employees and paramedics helping them off the plane.

In the back of my head, I knew what was happening. The morning anchor had reported the arrest of a researcher somewhere in Europe, and while my thoughts kept returning to how impossible it was, I knew.

I looked into the rearview mirror, my appearance nearly unrecognizable to anyone that had known me in better days. The browns of my eyes were no longer bright and full of purpose like they once were. The skin beneath them was shaded with dark circles. Just fifteen years ago I was two hundred pounds of muscle and confidence; now I felt a little more broken down every day.

Aubrey and I met in high school. Back then she wanted to touch me and talk to me. Our story wasn't all that exciting: I was on the starting lineup of a small-town football team, and she was head cheerleader. We were both big fish in a small pond. My light-brown, shaggy hair moved when a breeze passed through the passenger side window. Aubrey used to love how long it was. Now all she did was bitch that I needed a haircut. Come to think of it, she bitched about everything when it came to me. I still went to the gym, and the women at work were at times a little forward, but Aubrey didn't see me anymore. I wasn't sure if it was being with her that sucked the life out of me, or the disappointments I'd suffered over the years. The further away I was from high school, the less making something of myself seemed possible.

An obnoxious buzzing noise on the radio caught my attention. I listened while a man's robotic voice came over the speakers of my car. "This is a red alert from the emergency broadcast system. Canton County sheriff's department reports a highly contagious virus arriving in our state has been confirmed. If at all possible, stay indoors. This is a red alert from the emergency broadcast system . . ."

Movement on the side of my rearview mirror caught my attention. A woman was sprinting from her car toward the door of the school. Another woman jumped from her minivan and, after a short pause, ran toward the school as well with her toddler in her arms.

They were mothers. Of course they wouldn't let the logical side of their brain talk them into hesitation. The world was going to hell, and they were going to get their children to safety . . . wherever that was.

I shoved the gearshift into park and opened my door. I walked quickly, but as frantic mothers ran past me, I broke into a run as well.

Inside the building, mothers were either carrying their children down the hall to the parking lot, or they were quickly pushing through the doors of their children's classrooms, not wasting time explaining to their teachers why they were leaving early.

I dodged frightened parents pulling their confused children along by the hand until I reached Zoe's classroom. The door cracked against the concrete wall as I yanked it open.

The children looked at me with wide eyes. None of them had been picked up yet.

"Mr. Oxford?" Mrs. Earl said. She was frozen in the center of her classroom, surrounded by mini desks and chairs, and mini people. They were patiently waiting for her to hand out the papers they were to take home. Papers that wouldn't matter a few hours from now.

"Sorry. I need Zoe." Zoe was staring at me, too, unaccustomed to people barging in. She looked so small, even in the miniature chair she sat in. Her light-brown hair was curled under just so, barely grazing her shoulders, just the way she liked it. The greens and browns of her irises were visible even half a classroom away. She looked so innocent and vulnerable sitting there; all the children did.

"Braden?" Melissa George burst through the door, nearly running me down. "Come on, baby," she said, holding her hand out to her son.

Braden glanced at Mrs. Earl, who nodded, and then the boy left his chair to join his mother. They left without a word.

"We have to go, too," I said, walking over to Zoe's desk.

"But my papers, Daddy."

"We'll get your papers later, honey."

Zoe leaned to the side, looking around me to her cubby. "My backpack."

I picked her up, trying to keep calm, wondering what the world would look like outside the school, or if I would reach my car and feel like a fool.

"Mr. Oxford?" Mrs. Earl said again, this time meeting me at the door. She leaned into my ear, staring into my eyes at the same time. "What's going on?"

I looked around her classroom, to the watchful eyes of her young students. Pictures drawn clumsily in thick lines of crayon and bright educational posters hung haphazardly from the walls. The floor was littered with clippings from their artwork.

Every child in the room stared at me, waiting to hear why I'd decided to intrude. They would keep waiting. None of them could fathom the nightmare that awaited them just a few hours from now—if we had that much time—and I wasn't going to cause a panic.

"You need to get these kids home, Mrs. Earl. You need to get them to their parents, and then you need to run."

I didn't wait for her reaction. Instead I bolted down the congested hallway. A traffic jam seemed to be causing a bottleneck at the main exit, so I pushed a side door to the pre-K playground open with my shoulder, and with Zoe in my arms, hopped the fence.

"Daddy! You're not supposed to climb the fence!"

"I'm sorry, honey. Daddy's in a hurry. We have to pick up Mommy and . . ."

My words trailed off as I fastened Zoe into her seatbelt. I had no idea where we would go. Where could we hide from something like this?

"Can we go to the gas station and get a slushie?"

"Not today, baby," I said, kissing her forehead before slamming the door.

I tried not to run around the front. I tried, but the panic and adrenaline pushed me forward. The door slammed shut, and I tore out of the parking lot, unable to control the fear that if I slowed down even a little bit, something terrible would happen.

One hand on the steering wheel, and the other holding my

cell phone to my ear, I drove home, ignoring traffic lights and speed limits and trying to be careful not to get nailed by other panicked drivers.

"Daddy!" Zoe yelled when I drove over a bump too fast. "What are you doing?"

"Sorry, Zoe. Daddy's in a hurry."

"Are we late?"

I wasn't sure how to answer that. "I hope not."

Zoe's expression signaled her disapproval. She always made an effort to parent Aubrey and me. Probably because Aubrey wasn't much of one, and it was clear on most days that I didn't know what the hell I was doing.

I pressed on the gas, trying to avoid the main roads home. Every time I tried to call Aubrey from my cell, I got a weird busy signal. I should have known when I got there that something was wrong. I should have immediately put the sedan in reverse and raced away, but the only thing going through my head was how I would convince Aubrey to leave her goddamned computer, what few things we would grab, and how much time I should allow to grab them. An errant thought ran through my head about how much time it would take the Internet to cease, and how ironic it was that a viral outbreak would save our marriage. There were so many *should haves* in that moment, but I ignored them all.

"Aubrey!" I yelled as I opened the door. The most logical place to look was the den. The empty blue office chair was a surprise. So much so that I froze, staring at the space as if my vision would correct itself and she would eventually appear, her back to me, hunched over the desk while she moved just enough to maneuver the mouse.

"Where's Mommy?" Zoe asked, her voice sounding even smaller than usual.

A mixture of alarm and curiosity made me pause. Aubrey's ass had flowed over and cratered in the deteriorated cushion of that office chair for years. No noise in the kitchen, and the downstairs bathroom door was open, the room dark.

"Aubrey!" I yelled from the second step of the stairs, waiting for her to round the corner above me and descend each step more dramatically than the last. At any moment, she would breathe her signature sigh of annoyance and bitch at me for something—anything—but as I waited, it became obvious that she wouldn't.

"We're going to be very late," Zoe said, looking up at me.

I squeezed her hand, and then a white envelope in the middle of the dining table caught my eye. I pulled Zoe along with me, afraid to let her out of my sight for a second, and then picked up the envelope. It read "Nathan" on the front, in Aubrey's girly yet sloppy script.

"Are you serious?" I said, ripping open the envelope.

Nathan,

By the time you get this I'll be hours away. Your probably going to think I'm the most selfish person in the world, but being afraid of you thinking bad of me isn't enough for me to stay. I'm unhappy and I've been unhappy for a long time.

I love Zoe, but I'm not a mother. You are the one that wanted to be a father. I knew you would be a good daddy, and I thought that you being a good daddy would make me a good

mother, but it didn't. I can't do this anymore.
There are so many things I want to do with my
life and being a housewife isn't one of them.

    I'm sorry if you hate me, but I've finally
decided I can live with that. I'm sorry you have
to explain this to Zoe. I'll call tomorrow when
I'm settled and try to help her understand.

Aubrey

I let the folded paper fall to the table. She could never spell *you're* correctly. That was just one of a hundred things about Aubrey that bothered me but I never mentioned.

Zoe was looking up at me, waiting for me to explain or react, but I could do neither. Aubrey had left us. I came back for her lazy, cranky, miserable ass, and she fucking left us.

A scream outside startled Zoe enough for her to grip my leg, and reality hit about the same time that bullets came crashing through the kitchen windows. I ducked, and signaled Zoe to duck with me.

There would be no calling Aubrey's friends and relatives to find out where she was so I could beg her to come back. I had to get my daughter to safety. Aubrey might have picked a horrible first day for independence, but it was what she wanted, and I had a little girl to protect.

More screams. Car horns honking. Gunfire. *Jesus. Jesus, Jesus, Jesus.* It was here.

I opened the hallway closet and grabbed my baseball bat, and then walked over to my daughter, kneeling in front of her to meet her tear-glazed eyes. "Zoe, we're going to have to get back to the car. I need you to hold my hand, and no matter what you see or hear, don't let go of my hand, do you understand?"

Zoe's eyes filled with more tears, but she nodded quickly.

"Good girl," I said, kissing her on the forehead.

**INTENSE. DANGEROUS. ADDICTIVE.
MEET YOUR NEW OBSESSION . . .**

BEAUTIFUL DISASTER

Good Girl

Abby Abernathy doesn't drink or swear and she works hard.
Believing she has buried her dark past with her new life at
college, her dreams of invisibility are quickly challenged by the
university's walking one-night stand.

Bad Boy

Travis Maddox, sexy, built, and covered in tattoos, is exactly
what Abby needs to avoid. He spends his nights winning money
in an underground fight club, and his days as the notorious
college womanizer.

Imminent Disaster

Intrigued by Abby's resistance to his charms, Travis tricks her
into his life with a simple bet. If he loses he will remain celibate
for a month, but if he wins Abby must move in to his apartment
for a whole month! Never one to miss out on a bet, Abby takes
the challenge – but can she handle the consequences?

Available in eBook and paperback

**Paperback ISBN: 978-1-47111-503-5
eBook ISBN: 978-1-47111-504-2**